MW01701549

THE KILLER CUPCAKE

DEADLY AND SWEET

THE POISON CHERRY SERIES
BOOK THREE

SIENNA MYNX

SIENNA MYNX

FOREWORD

Have I ever told you how writing saved my sanity?

Maybe I have. Over the years, I've shared so much about my writing journey—the highs, the lows, the moments when words abandoned me, and the moments when they returned like old friends. But this return to my first love has been different. It's been about me, about growth, about remembering why I fell in love with storytelling in the first place. In a world gone mad, I discovered I could create my own sanctuary, one page at a time.

That's what the Poison Cherry Series has become for me—a rebirth. A fresh canvas where I could paint with all the colors I'd forgotten I possessed. And this book, *Killer Cupcake,* is vintage Sienna Mynx. Every page pulses with the passion and mafia romance, along with heart-crushing drama that first made my heart race as a writer. You'll find echoes of my other works here—ghosts that haunt these pages in the best possible way. Through Carmelo and Kathy, through their impossible love and unbreakable bond, I'm rediscovering what makes me tick as a storyteller, what truly sticks to my soul.

Within these pages, you'll find answers to questions that have lingered since book one. You'll meet characters so layered, so beautifully complicated, that you'll question whether you should root for them—right before you realize you already are. Most importantly, you'll be prepared for the grand finale that awaits in book four: *Lethal Crumbs,* where I'll take you back to the Amalfi Coast to uncover famiglia ties that will leave you breathless.

I'm free again.

Free to tell stories in my own voice, free to take risks, free to give you the drama, passion, and heart-stopping romance you've been craving. To those of you who've stayed with me through the silence, through the waiting, through the wondering if I'd ever return to this world we love—I am so deeply grateful. You are the reason I can fly again.

We have such a thrilling journey ahead of us, my dear readers. So buckle up, pour yourself something delicious, and prepare for one hell of a bumpy ride.

With all my love and gratitude,

Sienna Mynx

P.S. - Trust and believe what you want you can achieve!

Authors Note:

There is a side story within this one. It's "The Creoles," and it's the story of Jean Baptiste and Willa. I am considering making this a weekly, free story available for my readers to read on my website. Leave a comment in your review for this story if you'd like to see me offer that story for free!

Book One

Carmelo and Kathy

CHAPTER 1

LAC TREMBLANT, QUEBEC – 1978

The promise of a day of fun in the sun did not go as planned. Carmelo had insisted on sailing despite the reports of rain.

"I want to take Nino fishing," he announced after lunch and wiggled his brows.

"Melo? Again?" she sighed.

"What? He wants to fish?" Carmelo shrugged.

"What about the phone? We're getting it installed today, remember," she reasoned. "You've taken him three times already."

"Four times is what I promised," he said with a wink.

"What about your promises to me?" she teased, not wanting to mention the phone again, but she was anxious. She needed to call her baby girl.

He stared at her in a way that warmed her all over.

"Later, I'll fulfill my promise and get my reward. You can count on it," he said.

She shook her head, believing every word. So, they went sailing. And after the rain, the boys were left to their fishing games. From the upper deck that the staff had wiped and dried, she gazed down at them.

Carmelo, with his cigar tucked in the side of his jaw and his hands gripping the large fishing reel as he struggled to pull in some catch. He was shirtless, except for his long, white linen pants and the fisherman's hat his older brother loved for him to wear, while Nino walked around in a captain's uniform and hat. Carmelo would do anything to make his brother smile.

Nino, nearly six feet four and 330 pounds, jumped up and down at Carmelo's side. He clapped with excitement. Both of them were speaking in rapid Italian as Carmelo's men cheered on their boss for his big catch.

Kathy smiled and reclined into her bliss. At forty-eight, she rarely allowed herself such moments of peace, especially not vacations that stretched beyond three or four days. But these were different times. Her husband had earned the right to peace. He'd done the hard work to amend every broken promise or betrayal. Now he needed her. With the war between her community and his escalating into arrests and federal indictments, she lived in constant fear of losing him.

Then came the news that he and Nino had been killed in a car bombing.

For two days, she teetered on the edge of madness, unable to reconcile the mere thought that he would be dead. Not after everything they'd survived in the past thirty years. How could it all end this way? But the news stations and every print magazine or paper in New York insisted he was dead. He was just… gone, ripped away from her. Game over.

Then, the call came.

An F.B.I. agent demanded a meeting.

In the dim glow of her bakery, long after closing, with Brother in the storage room stocking shelves, Debbie at the salon with Daphne tending to customers, and Junior in the streets, the agent delivered the impossible news: her lover, her secret husband, her best friend, was alive in protective custody. And he needed her.

Now.

She wanted to tell Brother, but the agent said no.

She needed to call Sandy and prepare her, but the agent said there was no time.

The only way she could see Carmelo was in complete secrecy.

She agreed.

Jersey. A plane. Him. It all happened so fast.

She didn't hesitate to celebrate his resurrection by pampering him, spoiling him, holding her tongue from voicing the questions pounding in the back of her mind. He always swore that he was a Wolf, not a Rat. He would never turn against Omertà or La Cosa Nostra. And she believed him.

She couldn't tell Debbie why she was leaving. She couldn't explain to Sandy, still in D.C., how long she'd be gone. None of that mattered. She had to reach him—to care for him, like she always had because loving the Wolf meant tending to the boy trapped inside the man—the boy whose father had tried so hard to destroy.

Now, stranded in Quebec, she hadn't spoken to her family in two weeks. How much longer could the silence last? There had been no plan. No F.B.I. operatives with secret deals to protect him, no whispered strategies to reclaim his life. Just endless, suffocating stillness—broken only by the desperate, love-starved hunger they had for each other.

Morning, noon, night—he consumed her. Sex was always on the menu, as if touch alone could erase the hurt they carried from betraying each other in the past. Between stolen passionate moments on the yacht, in his bed, in the garden, even on the kitchen floor when she escaped him to get something to eat, he crafted distractions: lazy riverside picnics, impulsive drives through the mountains, laughter-filled evenings with Nino in town watching a play reserved for children or a picture show.

And the days blurred into a sunlit purgatory.

No news. No contact. No way out. *No phone!*

The isolation coiled tighter around her, thick as the forested cliffsides outside their villa. She felt it now—the same disorientation that had once hollowed him out.

What was the plan? There had to be a plan. Right?

She needed to call home. Tell Debbie to talk to Matteo. Together, they had to find a way to save the Wolf. To save her man. It was his turn for rescue.

She closed her eyes and exhaled.

Typically, she would not sunbathe on the upper deck—she was naturally bronzed by the sun and gifted with melanin by her ancestors. She hated the heat. Hated to sweat or have her hair frizz from the salt of the sea. The fireball in the sky reminded her of a life entirely different. Those sweltering days she'd spent down in the Delta on the Jensen farm, once known as the Cloverfield Plantation. Even working in the washrooms instead of the fields picking cotton or peas, she'd suffered from heat strokes. Sometimes the labor was so hard she could barely drag herself inside Big Mama's cool house and drop into bed.

It was a long time ago. Thirty-one years since she'd first met Carmelo when she was seventeen and he was nineteen—two kids from different worlds who thought loving each other was the only challenge they faced. Boy, were they wrong.

A time lost to her now, buried beneath recent memories of pain and suffering. All the people she had loved and who loved her were gone, except for her beautiful daughter and the family she, Debbie, and Brother had made.

Were the Freemans cursed?

The thought followed her like a shadow. There had been a time—oh, how clearly, she remembered—when Carmelo had believed both their Dads were cursed, and had passed it down to them. But curses could be broken. And after decades of longing, she had finally surrendered to the truth her heart had always known.

She had been his wife from the very start.

No curse, no shadow, no force in this world could steal the future she would build with him.

As the yacht swayed gently beneath her, Nino's laughter wrapping around her like sunlight, she let sleep pull her under—dreaming, at last, of tomorrow, and the end of curses.

* * *

CARMELO ASCENDED the short staircase to the yacht's upper deck, where a plush lounge area opened onto the breathtaking panoramic view of Lac Tremblant. The vast, glacial lake spread before him, deep and impossibly blue, cradled between mountain ridges like a sapphire held by ancient hands.

This place was a haven for the world's elite—millionaires carving fresh powder on skis during Quebec's brutal winters, oligarchs basking in luxury during the fleeting summer months. As sunlight danced upon the pristine waters, Carmelo's mind drifted back to his twenty-eighth year, to the winding coastal roads between Sorrento and the Amalfi, and that fateful meeting with Don Tommasino Battaglia after he had accomplished his ultimate revenge. His father's death.

It was 1957. The Castellamare medallion had burned in his pocket then; Mama Stewart's last words were hard in his ear, her prophecy now visited upon him in her death. Its weight was heavier than the Beretta gifted to him by Lucky Luciano in Naples. His heart had pounded—not from fear, but from the heady anticipation of a prince about to seize his rightful throne. That journey had irrevocably altered his course, more profoundly than discovering his mother's suicide or firing the bullet that sent his father backward out of his chair.

He had justified it all—claimed he acted for his brothers, for the Family, for the sacred crown of la cosa nostra. But as he stood now, decades later, aboard this luxurious yacht, wealthier than his father could have dreamed, he could finally admit the raw truth: When he'd boarded that plane to Italy after his older brother was forced into joining the Vietnam War, when he'd knelt to kiss Don Tommasino's ring, he'd done it for one reason only—power. Pure, unadulterated power, to take back what was rightfully his. To one day destroy his father's throne.

Of course, he needed power for her.

By then, she'd already torn his heart out. When the truth exploded between them, she rejected his fairytale love and refused to play her part. Worse—she agreed to marry another man, reducing their love to some bastardized half-lie.

That betrayal ignited something monstrous in him. The rage forced casualties in both their lives. The desperate, clawing need to have her believe him, forgive him, give him peace ate away at his soul. The Wolf was born in that fire.

(She would tell it differently, of course. She always did.)

She had been his last tether to the man he'd hoped to become. If he couldn't be her hero, he'd transform into something far more potent—a force she couldn't look away from, couldn't pretend didn't exist, couldn't deny. And take her back as his wife without her consent.

He approached.

Kathy lay peacefully on the wide circular sofa that faced the lake's most spectacular vista—multiple bays and seven islands stretching toward the horizon, green, like scattered emeralds. She hadn't aged, not really. Silver threads of grey wove through her dark hair like moonlight, and tiny crow's feet appeared at the corners of her eyes when she laughed, but she remained as beautiful today as she had been every single day they'd spent together across the decades.

Carmelo eased closer, slowly, drinking in the sight of her relaxed form. He settled onto the plush sofa beside her, the cushions wide enough for them both yet somehow never wide enough to contain the magnitude of what pulsed between them. When he pulled her against him, feeling her curves melt into his chest, a wave of relief crashed over him so powerful it nearly undid him. He pressed his lips to her shoulder and murmured her name like a prayer.

Kathy...

His mother had taken her own life. Eight months after that trauma, he'd seen Kathy again—been able to hold her, to confess only fragments of his truth. Many nights across many years, he'd wished he could return to that reunion and bare his soul completely. He wished he hadn't told the one lie that had driven him from her heart, creating the perfect opening for another man to slip in and claim what should have been his forever. To touch her. To know her physically and spiritually. To ease into her heart in place of him was unforgivable. He hated Ely's ghost. He could never measure up to the memory of a war hero. He hated her. He hated himself most of all.

He should have run the night he put that bullet in his father. Should have fled straight to Mississippi, swept her up, and disappeared into whatever life they could have built together. A few years later, she had betrayed him, yes—and he had punished her for it. Oh, yes. But she was never a victim. She was an Elliott woman, fierce and strong, and unbreakable. She was Henry Freeman's daughter, tough and made from grit like her Big Mama. He learned that, too.

Now, in what should have been the happiest time of their lives, he'd told another unforgivable lie. Tonight, he would have to confess and risk suffering the same devastating loss he'd endured years ago when her trust had shattered like crystal in his hands.

Could he survive losing her again? *Would he?*

Should he even try to keep her, knowing what he'd faced, what he'd done?

Should he?

Or should he let the Wolf of Harlem take over? Lock her away, go after his daughter next. Steal them from their lives, family, and identity. Give them a new one. His baby girl, Sandra, would forgive him for his sins. Of that, he was sure. But his Kathy? Her memory was as long as the Nile. She'd never let him get away with it, unless he gave her no choice. So, it was decided. No matter the punishment or consequence. He'd keep them both with him, always.

Breathing in her scent, memories crashed over him. The soft weight of her pussy when she rode his dick, the molten heat of her sex when he was inside of her, and his cock stretched, reached deep into her soul.

The plunge she took with her jezebel moves as her nails cut red stripes across his chest as she fucked him good, perfect in every way. The rise and fall of her breasts, once small before childbirth, but perfectly perfect after, as she arched back in abandon, lost to everything but breath and sensation. How her nipples swelled to the size of grapes when her neck stretched and her head dipped further back, and breathing was a labored chore for them both. The way their lovemaking stripped him bare of pretense, quieted the chaos in his mind, and anchored him to something real. Something sane. Their bodies had always spoken truths their words couldn't manage. His hands began to undo the tie to her cover-up. She stirred. His palm eased down to her bikini bottom. She moaned. His middle finger slid through the hairs over her pussy to slide between the plump lips of her sex and touch the dewy love button at the hooded center. She shuddered. Eyes opening. She moved to stop him. He put a hand over her mouth to silence her and let his finger go in.

She struggled at first. Modest. Not wanting to be seen.

"Shhh... don't fight me. They are right there. They'll hear, they'll see," he whispered.

Her eyes stretched upward, and she peered at a few crew members inside, setting up what would be lunch for them. If she made a noise, they could look their way and see her half-open robe, and his hand in her bikini bottom. He pumped his finger in and out of her channel as his erection pressed hard and long against her butt. Kathy's eyes fluttered shut.

"Mmmm," he moaned. He wanted her. More of her. All of her. Just in case this was the last time.

Kathy surrendered. She opened her eyes when he began to masturbate her clitoris with the precision only he could do to make her cream. She stared at the workers, praying they would not look as she shuddered and kicked her feet, then her eyes fluttered shut again. The new wave of heat and ecstasy crashed through her vagina up into her core all at once.

"Let me in," he whispered and licked her ear.

She wanted to object, but he had her. There was no escape. If the ladies doing the cleaning looked over, she'd be mortified. She dared to open her eyes again.

They were gone.

She relaxed, and her bikini bottom was ripped off, and he was fucking her from behind. Surrender was her greatest reward.

CHAPTER 2

THE FIRST LIE | NEW ORLEANS 1950

Kathy, baby girl,

Got your letter. It made me smile wider than a cottonmouth in August. Of course, you forgive me—we Elliott girls always do forgiveness after a proper punishment. Come on down, sugar.

I know about Carmelo's fight. The Marcellos own this city. Boxing, gambling houses, and even the music breezing out of the windows of the French Quarter at midnight. Sicilians got all the keys to all the doors that matter. My Boanno does business with 'em, so yes, it's all set. But you listen to your Tante Janey. Be careful chasing that boxing boy around in the South. These Sicilians smile with their teeth and cut with their lies.

Oh. In your letter, you mentioned the Klan? Des sauvages. Carmello must have warned you. The Klan's been raising holy hell since the Marcellos started skimming their protection money. Bombed three shops on Rampart last month—made it rain rosary beads for two blocks. Now they've got some corn-

fed giant they're calling "The Cotton King" fighting your Carmelo. Word is, Nazi money's backing him. Even got some of our own people dancing to their tune for the right price. Shameful, but hunger and greed makes devils of us all.

Come to me in Tremé, ma petite. My house has got galleries sweeter than café au lait, and walls that know how to keep secrets. Nobody here asks questions unless they want the kind of answers that come with a side of my special candies. And Kathy, I'll show you things while you're here. Things that'd make your Harlem heart spin like a roulette wheel for the bayou instead.

Come before the heat makes everyone stupid and bloody.

The city's changing, chère. Prosperity of the coloreds in the Tremé done stirred up everything. White folks nervous, colored folks restless, and people like us—nous autres—we walking a tightrope stretched between heaven and hell.

Your Carmelo, he's gonna need someone who understands the music between the notes, if you catch my meaning. And you? You're gonna need someone who knows how to love a man without losing herself to the fantasy. Because until you both face the world like all Elliot women do, you are a liar, and your love affair is just a dream.

It's okay to lie, not for a man but to a man. Don't worry, I'll teach you the difference. Just come. Viens vite, before the summer heat makes me lazy.

Love you like gumbo loves rice,

Auntie Janey

P.S. - Burn this letter after you read it twice. I don't want Big Mama getting a whiff of this plan. She mad at me enough. And bring that skinny shadow of yours—Willa?—as cover. Make up something, Kathy, but don't let her or your love-sick Ely know you're coming to Auntie.

Kathy crumpled the letter in her fist. She'd disobeyed—kept it instead of burning it. Janey's words always cut deep, layered with meanings that revealed themselves only after the third or fourth reading.

She glanced over at the traveler next to her. Her name is Willa. A vibrant, beautiful girl with deep ebony brown skin and hair so thick and dense it coiled and had to be worn under a scarf. She'd been sleeping against the train window since the sun disappeared behind the Mississippi pines. Poor Willa. For her, she was escaping the subjugation of the Jensens, only to be used by Kathy as an alibi.

Willa had been orphaned as a child and given to white folks who promised care but delivered servitude to the Jensen family instead. Almost every day since arriving in Butt's, she'd declared to anyone who'd listen—white and black alike—that she was going to find her people and go home someday. The words had become her prayer, her battle cry, her reason for breathing.

They'd become friends the moment Kathy arrived, two girls lost in different ways but finding solace in each other. When Debbie visited for Christmas, Willa grew even more attached to Kathy. Together, a pregnant Debbie and Kathy braided Willa's hair into intricate patterns, dressed her in Kathy's nicest clothes, and spent long evenings talking about the heartbreak that gnawed at them—their boyfriends in New York tangled up in troubles too dark to fully understand, troubles that had deepened after Mrs. Ricci's suicide.

Through the stress-filled months that followed, Willa became Kathy's confidant and co-conspirator. Ely had given up and walked away. Willa was her only friend now. She was the person to help Kathy craft the elaborate deception.

The plan was simple but brilliant. It required Kathy to track down her Aunt Janey. An impossible task she imagined, but she wrote to Boanno and nearly fainted when Janey wrote back. It was the power of the pen.

Kathy then wrote a letter to Willa, one that Willa carried to Mrs. Lottie Jensen with trembling hands and practiced words. The letter spoke of a long-lost sister living in Texas—a sister Willa desperately wanted to visit, if only for a week. She even produced a train ticket, bought with money saved from months of kitchen scraps and mending work. Though Willa was rarely allowed beyond the Jensen property line without permission, they'd always treated her more like family than servant. Kathy suspected that Lottie Jensen genuinely loved the girl, because she did something she wouldn't have done even for Big Mama—she gave her blessing and agreed that Kathy should accompany Willa as a chaperone to ensure her safe return.

Convincing Big Mama after that had been surprisingly easy. Her beloved grandmother respected the Jensen family's judgment, and the idea of Kathy acting as protector for young Willa appealed to her sense of propriety. Even sweeter was the beautiful coincidence neither Big Mama nor Mrs. Jensen questioned: the train to Texas ran straight through New Orleans.

It was destiny. It had to be. After all this time, after all the terrible fragments Debbie had shared about what had happened to Matteo and Carmelo—secrets her sweet, protective boyfriend couldn't or wouldn't burden her with—she was finally going to be with him again.

Happiness bloomed in her chest. This was the beginning of the future the girls whispered about in dark corners and promised each other under Mississippi stars.

She was ready. Lord help her, she was more than ready.

CHAPTER 3

THE TREMÉ

The Illinois Central train released a final, exhausted sigh as it yielded to the platform beneath a suffocating blanket of magnolia-scented humidity. Kathy stepped down first, her fingers instinctively lacing through Willa's trembling hand as they emerged into a world that announced its brutality before they'd taken three steps.

"Girl, you're shaking like a leaf," Kathy murmured, pressing close.

"I know, I'm sorry. Just... ain't never seen so much of the world all at once," Willa whispered back, her Mississippi drawl thickening with awe.

Instead of the grand concourse with its marble floors and crystal chandeliers, Kathy had glimpsed through the train windows, they were herded into the "Colored Only" annex—a claustrophobic sweatbox reeking of coal tar, stale urine, and something sharper beneath: the metallic bite of humiliation. A freshly stenciled sign glared above the doorway: **"WAITING ROOM FOR NEGROES."**

To Kathy—Harlem-raised, then tempered by the long Greyhound ride into the French Quarter—this was expected. The way white porters shoved their luggage at them was like handling contaminated goods. The way "WHITE" and "COLORED" signs splintered the station like hatchet blows. But behind her, Willa stood paralyzed. Her Sunday dress, painstakingly pressed for this journey, suddenly looked drab against the riot of Black elegance surrounding them: women crowned in emerald and ruby turbans, men in razor-creased suits, all carrying themselves with a defiance that turned segregation into a runway.

*"Sweet Jesus, Kathy,"*Willa breathed as a white policeman strolled past, his billy club *thock-thocking* against his thigh like a countdown. *"Look at these folks."*

Kathy surveyed the unapologetic splendor of colored people around them and grinned. This was the South's best-kept secret—a beauty that Willa's sharecropping life had never shown her.

"You think this is something?" Kathy squeezed her hand."Just wait till you meet Aunt Janey."

As if summoned, the crowd suddenly parted like the Red Sea.

A woman materialized from the sweat-shimmered air, dressed head to toe in blinding white. Elbow-length silk gloves. A pillbox hat with French lace veiling her face, now etched in spiderweb shadows across cheekbones, sharp, lips, ruby red. She moved through the "Colored" section with the serene dominion of a queen, ignoring a peasant revolt—utterly indifferent to the glares from white travelers and the hissed, indrawn breaths from the women of color.

"Janey Boanno," Kathy chuckled to herself now that she knew her aunt really was. "Look, Willa, that's my aunt, my Ma's baby sister. The baby of the family of girls."

Janey swept forward with arms extended, and Kathy dropped Willa's hand. She rushed into her aunt's warm embrace. Janey pressed her lips to each of Kathy's cheeks in the Continental fashion of a cultured lady. Her perfume—an intoxicating blend of jasmine and vanilla—completely obliterated the station's oppressive stench.

"*Ma petite chérie*! You made it safely," Janey purred in that voice like aged wisdom, then turned her golden, cat-like gaze to Willa. "And here she is. The brave little one who helped us spread the lie?"

"Aunt Janey!" Kathy gasped.

Willa's eyes stretched, like a scared cat.

Janey let out a peal of laughter that made the heads of both black and white men turn. "Oh, I'm just kiddin' suga. *Bienvenue à la Nouvelle-Orléans*, my darling."

Willa's mouth fell open as her eyes scanned Janey's bold confidence. Kathy knew what Willa was thinking. Janey's skin was the color of milk with a touch of honey, her eyes flecked with gold were sharp with intelligence—a woman who could have easily passed for white in any Northern city if she hid from the sun, but who chose to stand here, magnificent and uncompromising, in this segregated area.

With a sharp snap of her gloved fingers, Janey summoned a tall Black chauffeur who materialized as if from thin air, efficiently loading their modest luggage onto a gleaming brass cart. "This way, *mes beautés*. Alphonse has the Caddy waiting."

* * *

THE 1949 CADILLAC SERIES 62 sat curbside like a pearl dropped from heaven—pristine white with chrome that gleamed under the Louisiana sun. A white man in a rumpled seersucker suit blocked the sidewalk as Janey ushered the girls toward the magnificent machine.

"*Dégage, connard,*" Janey muttered under her breath.

The man sneered, and Kathy could see Willa shrink next to her and lower her gaze. Kathy looped her arm around Willa's and pulled her close as they prepared to walk around him, but Janey, who led them, nearly bumped him over as she kept walking straight. And he had to step aside. The girls mimicked Kathy's aunt's confidence. And soon she felt Willa's spine straighten and her walk with confidence as well.

For Willa, the car's interior was a revelation that bordered on the sacred. She ran her fingers over the upholstery, softer than anything she'd ever imagined, struck speechless as they glided past St. Charles Avenue's towering antebellum mansions—palatial homes.

For Kathy, New Orleans revealed itself as Harlem's more elegant, yet infinitely more dangerous, cousin. Gas lamps flickered off over elaborate wrought-iron balconies as the night gave way to day;

talented Black musicians played sultry jazz for clusters of white tourists on street corners, their music floating through the humid air like liquid soul. But she couldn't ignore how eyes followed Janey's Cadillac—some filled with friendliness, others with naked hatred.

Janey lit a cigarette with a golden lighter that flashed like captured sunlight. She exhaled smoke through slightly parted lips. "Y'all can breathe now, darlings. In my car, you belong to me. Ain't no Jim Crow laws in this Caddy—just my rules, and my rules say you're royalty."

They turned into Tremé, and suddenly the world transformed into a symphony of visual and auditory delights: Creole cottages painted in sherbet colors lined tree-shaded streets, and the mouthwatering aroma of beans simmering with cayenne pepper. It filled the air.

Then Janey's house rose before them, regal and royal.

It was a three-story "shotgun mansion"—an impossibility that shouldn't exist but stood there nonetheless, painted a defiant periwinkle blue with intricate white gingerbread trim that looked like lace frozen in wood. Wrought-iron galleries on each level dripped with emerald ferns and purple bougainvillea. Through a gate adorned with gilded *fleur-de-lis*, they glimpsed a hidden courtyard where a fountain sprouted, cooling the air with its water.

Willa stopped dead on the sidewalk, her eyes wide as saucers. "This... this is a colored house? Sweet Jesus, it's bigger and prettier than anything in Butts!"

Inside, Kathy felt her breath catch and hold.

Chandeliers hung over mahogany floors that gleamed like dark mirrors. Oil portraits of Creole elite who weren't Janey's ancestors—proud men and women in satin and silk, their eyes blazing with the fire of rebellion—gazed down from gilded frames that probably cost more than most families earned in a year. Where a cotton scale might have dominated the corner of a Mississippi parlor, a magnificent grand piano stood like a shrine to culture and refinement.

Janey tossed her gloves onto a Louis XVI settee with casual elegance, the gesture speaking volumes about a life where luxury was routine rather than aspiration. "Welcome to Liberté, *mes petites*. My husband bought this from one of the wealthiest Octroons in all of

Louisiana. Her great-grand-mère bought this land in 1829—paid in gold coins. That's the story they tell."

A Black maid in a starched white apron trimmed with delicate lace appeared as if summoned by magic, offering sweet tea in cut-crystal glasses that caught the light like liquid amber. Willa approached the piano and pressed one key with a finger. The note sang pure and clear through the magnificent room, and tears glistened in her eyes. "I never knew... I never dreamed our people could live like this. Like kings and queens. No one ever told me."

"We don't just live, *ma chère*. We thrive. We take what the world says we can't have and make it ours through grit like Big Mama, through pain like my Mama, and sometimes a little bit of wickedness like me."

Kathy frowned. She had heard an earful from her mother about the wickedness in Janey. Some of it she refused to believe. But looking at her life, and the unapologetic way she moved through it, she had to think the word 'wicked' should be replaced with 'wonder'.

Kathy approached the wide picture window overlooking the courtyard's orange trees, their fruit glowing like lanterns in the gathering new day. Suddenly, Carmelo's world—violent yet lavish, dangerous yet defiant—crystallized in her understanding. She remembered visiting his house for the first time and being awestruck by the opulence.

This wasn't simply a house or even a home. This was a declaration of war won through wallpaper and chandeliers, a testament to the power of refusing to accept limitations imposed by others based on race.

Questions burned in her mind. How did Boanno find her aunt after he left Butts all those months ago? Why didn't he take her to Paris like he promised? Was she still in trouble with the law in California?

"Kathy?" Janey spoke.

"Yes'm," Kathy turned.

"Carmelo's here," Janey said.

Willa looked up from the piano bench.

Janey's sly smile was slick with mischief. "Not here in the house, but in the Quarter. He'll be arriving soon. You've traveled far, baby. Don't you want to change for the reunion?"

Kathy nodded eagerly.

Janey's gaze slipped to Willa. She was the darkest of the three of them, her beauty covered by her meager existence on the Jensen farm, never pampered, never nurtured. "You girls have to look and behave like royalty here. I have a reputation with these Creoles. Come with me, Willa."

Willa got up from the piano and walked over to Janey, who took her hand. "I'll work on you myself." She then addressed Kathy. "Your clothes are in the room to the right on the second floor. You will know it when you see it. That is yours and Carmelo's room, and Pinkie will make sure she has everything you need."

Willa looked at her with eyes stretched wide and pleading for help. Kathy smiled. "It's okay, Janey will be gentle."

Janey tossed out a playful laugh and walked away. Kathy glanced at the servant and then at the stairwell that led up to her new wardrobe. Thrilled, she hurried up each step.

CHAPTER 4

SHAMROCK ATHLETIC CLUB

The Shamrock stank of cigar smoke and bloodstained canvas—the perfume of violence that clung to every corner of the low-ceilinged gym. Carmelo rolled his shoulders, feeling the weight of the entire city pressing down on him like humid Louisiana air. New Orleans wasn't just another fight—it was the battlefield the mob had chosen to prove Sicilian dominance over the Klan's stranglehold on the South. And for Carmelo, it was his only shot at getting back to Kathy.

"You good?" Caesar's voice was gravel, his calloused hands worked the tension from Carmelo's neck with practiced precision.

Carmelo nodded, though his mind was elsewhere. "Yeah. Just wish Matteo was here."

Caesar's grip tightened—just once—before he stepped back. "Debbie's due any day. You know he ain't leavin' her."

The unspoken truth hung between them like smoke: Matteo wasn't just staying for the baby. After their mother's suicide, Matteo had spiraled into a darkness that seemed bottomless—drunk, reckless, dangerous, his fists and knives always seeking someone to destroy. It had taken Carmelo swallowing his own grief, facing the mob about shooting his own father, and then overcoming retribution with Mama

Stewart's help, and humbling himself before Debbie to pull her in to rescue his brother. Debbie and the baby she carried had become Matteo's only lifeline. Together, he and Debbie, with Mama Stewart's guidance, found him, sobered him, and helped restore his sanity.

Matteo had switched his obsession—from saving their mother and making her happy to protecting the mother of his child. Every breath Debbie took, every need she had, Matteo was hypersensitive to it all. Luckily for them all, José didn't mind. Matteo had full access to their home. Carmelo understood that kind of obsession. He'd started the same way with Kathy. Except he didn't have her warm embrace to cry into after losing madre—just stolen phone calls and carefully hidden letters to sustain him through eight torturous months. And always, the solemn death wish of his mother that he had to honor.

Now, with Debbie about to give birth, Matteo refused to repeat history. He'd stay. He'd be a father. Even if it meant Carmelo faced this fight alone. More frightening still—Carmelo knew his father suspected the truth but said nothing. What was Cosimo Ricci waiting for?

Caesar stood at Carmelo's back like a second shadow. Most people mistook him for Matteo—same dark glare, same coiled violence beneath olive skin. In a way, they were family. When promoters got greedy or rival camps got bold, Caesar stepped in. Six of Cosimo's men had come as insurance, but Caesar was the one Carmelo trusted with his life.

The announcer's bell rang, sharp and commanding.

Time for the weigh-in.

Carmelo shrugged off his silk robe, the expensive fabric pooling at his feet like liquid silver. Across the cramped room, a murmur rippled through the crowd.

The Cotton King, renamed for the fight as the Mississippi Mauler, had arrived.

The Klan's champion stood barefoot in dirt-streaked overalls, his massive frame built more for hard labor than refined fighting. No robe. No shirt. Just a sneer curling his lips as his handlers—thick-red-necked men in cheap suits—prodded him forward like a prized bull.

"Look at that," one of the Marcello men muttered. "They dug him straight out of a damn field."

Carmelo said nothing. He'd seen this before—men turned into weapons by people who didn't care if they broke in the process.

The Mauler's small, beetle-like eyes locked onto his. "Heard you Sicilians fight like girls."

Carmelo kept his face blank as marble. *Let him talk.*

The weigh-in passed in a blur of shouted numbers and aggressive posturing. Then—inevitably—the tension snapped like a taut wire.

"This ain't your city no more, Meatball!" A Klansman named Sheffield jabbed a thick finger at one of Marcello's top men.

"Fuck you and your bedsheet *putanas*," the mobster shot back, his hand moving toward his jacket.

Caesar grabbed Carmelo's arm, steering him away before fists and bullets could fly. "We're done here. Let's get you to the room."

The backroom was a sanctuary, guarded by two stone-faced Marcello triggermen with Thompson submachine guns slung casually over their shoulders. Caesar clapped Carmelo on the shoulder with genuine affection. "Giorgio's handling the politics. You just focus on staying alive."

Then he was gone, leaving Carmelo alone with his thoughts.

Until—

Carmelo entered the room. A man in an expensive fedora sat quietly by the exam table, a silver-topped cane resting between his knees. The shadow from his brim hid his eyes, but Carmelo felt the weight of his stare like a physical presence.

"You Boanno?" Carmelo asked. Kathy and Debbie had worked with Matteo to flesh out the details. She'd told him with breathless excitement about the plan: *It's all covered. My auntie's husband is with the mob. He will bring you to me, Melo.*

The man exhaled slowly, like a man carrying secrets. "Call me Carmine." He stood with deliberate care, his cane thudding against the wooden floor.

Their handshake was firm, but Carmelo's chest tightened with sudden anxiety. This was Kathy's lifeline? He looked more like one of the men who would service his father than someone devoted to a Negro woman's desires. *Could this be a setup?* Had Matteo vetted this thoroughly enough?

"Don Marcello says you're under my care," Carmine said, his voice smooth as aged bourbon. "You'll stay with me and my wife in Tremé."

"Wife?" Carmelo frowned. Kathy had been so excited about the visit and her aunt's help that she'd left out this crucial detail. Her aunt was married to a Sicilian? Legitimately? In the segregated South?

Carmine's smile was sharp as a blade. "Yes, wife. Though sometimes I have to remind her of the fact."

Carmelo's pulse jumped. "And Kathy—?"

"Already there." Carmine's eyes glittered with something unreadable. "Get dressed. She's waited long enough."

* * *

CARMINE BOANNO DROVE with deceptive ease, one hand on the wheel, the other arm resting on the edge of the open window with his elbow poking out. Carmelo kept stealing glances at him, wondering about the walking stick and the careful way he moved, which contrasted with his otherwise calm and erect physical demeanor. He didn't bother asking. Men in their world didn't appreciate being questioned about weaknesses.

Carmine's pale blue gaze slipped over to him as they navigated the crowded streets. "So you love an Elliot woman?"

"Elliot?" Carmelo frowned, confusion coloring his voice.

"Your girlfriend. Kathy is an Elliot," Carmine said as they slowed to a stop for horse-drawn traffic. He lit a thin cigarillo with practiced movements. All the windows in the Cadillac were rolled down to combat the oppressive heat of New Orleans.

"My girlfriend is a Freeman. I don't know what you—"

Carmine exhaled smoke through slightly parted lips. "Your girlfriend is an Elliot woman, and that is something you must understand right away." His tone carried a warning wrapped in silk.

Carmelo's frown deepened. "How so?"

"Her mother and my wife are sisters. To the best of my understanding, there are eight of them scattered to the wind. I don't know all of them—only met four since Janey and I got married. But they exist, born to torment men like you and me." There was dark humor in his voice, but something else too. Something that sounded like hard-earned wisdom.

"Watch your fucking mouth. Don't speak of Kathy that way!" Carmelo said coolly.

Carmine's smile was knowing, almost pitying. "It's not an insult, boy. Her grandfather was a mean son-of-a-bitch named Elliot Wynn. And her grandmother was a black servant who killed him. She birthed nothing but girls. All Elliot women birth girls. When you love an Elliot woman and she loves you back, it's like touching heaven. But when she doesn't love you..." His grip tightened on the steering wheel. "It's the worst pain you can ever imagine. Worse than bullets, worse than broken bones. They'll tear your heart out and hand it back to you still beating. Kiss you on the lips while you're dying."

The car surged forward through the humid afternoon. Carmelo wanted to ask more questions, but Carmine drove as if he'd said all he intended to say. Carmelo understood that Sicilians in New Orleans were different from those up North. He'd heard stories from his father's men before making this trip—how they ruled the criminal underworld here, even held positions of legitimate authority in the city. They bowed to no one. They married Black women and lived with them openly, defiantly. It had sounded like paradise to him and Matteo.

But there was something troubling about Carmine. He wasn't broken, exactly, but he seemed perpetually wary, as if he carried a weight that could never be fully offloaded.

Elliot women? What did that mean for Kathy, exactly?

The neighborhood was a revelation—homes painted in jewel tones, people of every shade of brown dressed with sharp elegance and an air of quiet prosperity. It was like Harlem infused with a culture he'd never experienced, more refined and alluring all at once. Once again, he was reminded of how shortsighted he'd been when he first met Kathy. They could have gone anywhere, built anything, if they'd truly understood the scope of the world beyond their narrow experience and so much time wasted on lessons they'd had to learn the hard way.

Carmine pulled the Cadillac to a smooth stop in front of a magnificent shotgun mansion painted periwinkle blue, its three stories rising like a monument to defiance. Wrought-iron galleries dripped with emerald ferns and cascades of purple bougainvillea, while orange trees heavy with fruit in the dappled shade of ancient live oaks.

"A few rules," Carmine said, his voice taking on a deadly serious tone.

Carmelo nodded and waited, suddenly alert.

"Janey is my wife and a gracious hostess, but never—and I mean *never*—accept any treats or candies from her hands. Never accept a drink she hasn't shared from first. And never, under any circumstances, cross the line with her." His pale eyes bore into Carmelo's. "These aren't suggestions."

"I wouldn't disrespect you. I'm grateful that you're hosting Kathy and me here."

Carmine's chuckle was dry as autumn leaves. "You really have no idea who they are, do you?"

Carmelo shook his head slowly. "No."

"Stick to those rules and you'll be fine. Repeat them back to me."

"No treats, no drinks unless she shares them first, be respectful," Carmelo recited.

"Good boy." Carmine got out of the car, reaching for his cane with practiced grace. "Remember—Elliot women are like beautiful storms. Magnificent to behold, but they'll destroy everything in their path if the men frighten or anger them. So be kind to your Kathy. Trust me. Janey is watching."

Carmelo grabbed his bag and followed, his mind spinning with questions. As they walked up the long, shaded walkway lined with blooming jasmine and sweet trees, the ornate front door suddenly flew open with dramatic flair.

And there she was.

Kathy appeared like a vision, framed by the doorway as if she'd stepped out of his dream. She wore a pristine white summer dress that cinched perfectly at her narrow waist, with a delicate milkmaid collar and romantic puff sleeves that made her look like something from a fairy tale. Her dark hair was pinned back from her face in elegant victory rolls that caught the filtered sunlight, and her smile—*my God, her smile*—was bright enough to illuminate the entire world.

She hurried down the steps with grace and urgency, and Carmelo dropped his bag without a second thought. They met somewhere in the middle of the walkway, between the jasmine and the fountain, between the past and the future.

Time stopped.

She was in his arms before he could draw another breath, her soft curves molding against him as if they'd been carved from the same piece of marble. Her lips found his with desperate love, and he kissed her back with eight months of longing, eight months of dreams, eight months of believing this moment might never come.

The world disappeared. There were no rules, no segregation laws, no disapproving families or dangerous enemies. There was only Kathy's warmth against him, her familiar scent of vanilla and roses, the way she fit perfectly in his arms as if she'd been made specifically for him.

"I missed you so much," Kathy whispered when their lips finally parted, her voice breaking with emotion. Tears streamed down her beautiful face as she held onto him like he might vanish. "Every day, every night, I missed you until I thought my heart would stop beating if this day didn't come soon."

"I missed you, too, Kat, so damn much," he said, his own voice thick with tears he couldn't control. No matter how hard life hit him—punches in the ring, grief and strife in his family—no pain had ever hurt enough to bring him to tears except for the loss of his beloved mother and her. "I dreamed about you every single night."

The midday afternoon light filtered through the live oak canopy above them, casting dancing shadows across their reunion while a gentle breeze carried the scent of magnolia and sweet oranges.

"Okay, lovebirds, let's take this inside before the neighbors start charging admission," Carmine drawled as he walked past them with the aid of his silver-topped cane, though there was something almost fond in his gruff tone.

They reluctantly released each other just enough for Carmelo to reach down and retrieve his bag, though neither wanted to break the spell. They had a full week ahead of them—it was Monday and the match wasn't until Saturday. No one knew or cared where he spent his personal time. He was a man, she was a lady, her own person, and here they were together. Not since those stolen moments in the attic had they enjoyed such blessed freedom.

He slipped his arm around her shoulders, marveling at how perfectly she fit against his side, and together they walked up the remaining steps into what felt like the beginning of their real life together. Not the one he kept from her, back at home.

That secret was the only stain on their perfect union. And he'd do anything to keep her from ever discovering it. Not until he had a chance to make it right.

Behind them, the fountain spewed large droplets into the glistening water in the ceramic bowl around it. The birds sang a gentle song, and the orange trees glowed like beacons in the gathering new day, all of beauty bracing for the next crisis to rise.

CHAPTER 5

JANEY'S PLACE NEW ORLEANS

"Wow," Carmelo breathed as a primly dressed older Black man—clearly the butler—took his bag with practiced efficiency and glided away with silent dignity.

"That's Elmer," Kathy explained in a low voice, "and over there is Pinkie, his daughter." She gestured toward a young woman in a crisp white apron who was arranging fresh magnolia blossoms in a crystal vase. "His wife Pearl works in the kitchen. They're the family of servants who tend to Janey's place with a few others. They live in a cottage behind the mansion in the courtyard. Really good people."

Carmelo frowned, confusion flickered across his features, but he gave Pinkie a respectful nod when she glanced their way. He'd never heard of Negroes employing Negro servants before—not even in all the books he'd devoured about different worlds and cultures. The social dynamics were more complex than anything he'd encountered.

Kathy caught his unspoken question and nodded knowingly. "I was thinking the exact same thing. It's... different here."

"There he is!" a melodious voice sang from above, floating down like honey poured over silk.

Carmelo reluctantly tore his gaze from Kathy's beautiful face and looked up toward the grand staircase. His smile faded completely, replaced by a look of stunned recognition.

At the top of the sweeping mahogany stairs stood the most breathtakingly beautiful woman he'd once before laid eyes on. The woman he met that terrible night, his mother died.

And she was looking directly at him with eyes that seemed to hold secrets darker than his.

"Not drinking, *ragazzo*?" came a soft voice like chimes. Livia materialized beside him, gardenias in her hair and a sharp almond note under her perfume. "*Che ti tormenta, campione?* What troubles you, champion?"

"Oh—no, I—" Carmelo stammered, staring at his glass. "It tastes... kind of fizzy. Like gasoline bubbles." He managed a crooked smile. She was beautiful—different from Kathy, but in a strange way, familiar.

She smiled back. "You're Carmelo, right? The prizefighter. Don Ricci's youngest son." Her gaze lifted to a banner above them, his face in boxing gloves.

"That's me," he said.

"A tough guy," she teased.

"I'm just a fighter."

She bit her nail, eyes dancing. "Seems your father doesn't like you making new friends."

He glanced across the room at the table, where his father and DeMarco both watched Livia with intent expressions. Two dangerous men were transfixed by her presence. Yet she remained cool, focused on him alone—those melting honey-brown eyes framed by dark lashes. Suddenly, they reminded him of Kathy.

"He's not staring at me," Carmelo said quietly. "He's staring at you. And that's not a good thing, sweetheart."

Livia's brow rose. "Is that so?"

"Be careful," Carmelo warned. "He's not someone to tease. And DeMarco's worse. If that's possible."

"Do you always speak so fondly of *la famiglia?*" She laughed, a clear bell that drew glances from nearby guests. Unfazed, she leaned close, her breath warm against his ear as she whispered, "Don't worry—I'm the deadliest candy in the room." Then, softer still: "Kill 'em in the ring, kid. Leave the monsters for Aunt Janey."

JANEY BEGAN her descent down the sweeping stairs, her eyes locked onto Carmelo with predatory focus. Carmine accepted a drink from Pinkie, and Carmelo could feel the man's penetrating gaze burning into him as well. What could he say? What could he do? It was her—the mysterious woman from that terrible night. And she was Kathy's aunt? An Elliot woman?

A million times he'd heard Kathy lovingly speak the name Janey, but the trauma of his mother's death had washed both her face and that whispered identity from his memory like blood down a drain. How could he have forgotten the woman who'd called herself "the deadliest candy in the room"? What did it mean that she'd been masquerading as someone named Livia, moving through DeMarco's world like she owned it?

Then the pieces slammed together with sickening clarity. DeMarco's death. How José had said he was poisoned just like King Redmond—slow, agonizing, deliberate. His heart hammered against his ribs like a caged bird desperate to escape.

"Carmelo, you okay? You look like—" Kathy squeezed his hand, concern flooding her voice.

"Like he's seen a ghost," Janey finished smoothly as she reached the bottom of the stairs. "Am I your ghost, Carmelo?"

She approached him dressed in beauty that made her look like a vision of royalty, reminding him painfully of his mother when she'd dressed up for one of Matteo's special shopping trips—elegant, untouchable, and heartbreakingly lovely.

He felt the room tilt dangerously toward his long-suppressed madness, which he kept caged inside, only to unleash in the boxing ring.

Janey walked directly to him with grace, placed her soft hands on his shoulders. She kissed his left cheek, then his right, in the Continental fashion. When she stepped back, Carmelo caught sight of Carmine, who now looked like a coiled rattlesnake ready to strike. Even this innocent greeting sparked a dangerous flare of rage or jealousy in the Capo's pale eyes.

"Hi, uh, sorry. I just wasn't expecting you to be..." Carmelo stammered.

"To look like a white woman? Or Sicilian, maybe?" Janey laughed, the sound like silver bells. She turned and eased over to Carmine with feline grace. He set his glass down but kept his hand firmly gripped on his cane's silver top. She touched his face tenderly and leaned in to kiss him. Janey closed her eyes and gave him a full, passionate kiss right in front of Carmelo and Kathy, then giggled softly and wiped the crimson lipstick from his mouth with her thumb. She whispered something naughty to him—not in Italian, but French, Carmelo was certain. Carmine's deadly gaze shifted from her to Carmelo, lingered with obvious threat, then he nodded curtly. He kissed her again, deeper this time, before he walked away without a word.

"Don't worry about him, children. He's a bit overprotective and jealous, but he's harmless enough. I'll take care of him later. If he's up to it," Her smile was sharp as broken glass. "Now come with me. Lunch is already prepared."

"Where is Willa?" Kathy asked.

"She needed a bit more work than I could accomplish here. I had my girls come for her. She'll be back this evening, transformed."

"Aunt Janey, I'm not supposed to let her out of my sight. Willa frightens easily. You should have come and told me first." Kathy's protest carried a hint of panic.

"Nonsense, darling. She's perfectly fine. We take care of our own." Janey dismissed the concern with a wave of her manicured hand and walked ahead of them.

"Why are you being so strange?" Kathy whispered urgently to Carmelo.

"We need to talk about your aunt. I met her before—the night my Ma died," he whispered back, his voice tight with barely controlled tension.

Kathy's eyes went wide as saucers. Janey cast a sly, knowing smile back at them both over her shoulder. They were certain she'd heard every word, but she didn't acknowledge it. She simply let them both stew in the uncomfortable knowledge, like a cat playing with trapped mice.

The dining room spread before them was a vision of Southern abundance. The food was something to behold—aromatic and inviting, from perfectly seasoned red beans and rice to rich, dark gumbo and exotic Creole dishes Carmelo couldn't begin to name. Then came the desserts: pralines gleaming like amber jewels, delicate beignets dusted with powdered sugar, and an array of petit fours that looked almost too beautiful to eat.

Kathy stood transfixed, unable to speak at the lavish display.

Carmelo found his voice first. "This looks incredible. I'm absolutely starving."

"It's all for you two lovebirds." Janey's smile was warm but somehow predatory. "I'm going to settle whatever's bothering my dear Carmine about your arrival Carmelo. Leave you alone to catch up properly. But I won't be far, so do behave yourselves." She winked at Carmelo.

He nodded, throat suddenly dry. They watched her aunt walk out. Pinkie gave them a meaningful warning look and quietly closed the French doors to grant them privacy.

"What do you mean you met her in Brooklyn? Why didn't you tell me!" Kathy whispered the moment they were alone.

Carmelo ran a hand through his dark hair. "She didn't say she was your aunt. She had a different name—called herself Livia. She was with DeMarco, the consigliere who caught us at Mama Stewarts."

"And?" Kathy pressed, her voice tight with dread.

"And now he's dead," Carmelo said quietly. "Poisoned, according to José. He said DeMarco died exactly like King Redmond." His dark eyes searched her face. "Kathy, what does that mean?"

Kathy turned away from him abruptly and walked to the window. She pressed one hand to her forehead and the other to her chest, which was rising and falling with rapid, shallow breaths. Carmelo watched in growing confusion and alarm.

"Talk to me," he said softly, moving closer. "Did she... could she have killed DeMarco?"

"Hush!" Kathy spun around, eyes blazing. "Don't ever say that again. And for God's sake, don't say it to her husband. Do you understand me?"

He nodded, chastened. "Then tell me—who are the Elliott women?"

"Who told you that name?" Kathy's voice was barely a whisper.

"Carmine. He said to beware of Elliott women. Told me never to eat any candies from Janey's hands, never to cross her. Kathy, what's going on? Are you in trouble? Are you in danger here?"

"No! No... no..." She rushed to him and wrapped her arms around his waist, holding tight. "We're safe. My aunt is... complicated. She lives between two worlds—white and black. Sometimes she disappears into one, then goes to the other. I think she went to New York to help me, to find you, and help bring you back to me. She didn't poison anyone. It's not true."

For the first time since he'd known her, Carmelo sensed Kathy was lying to him. The realization hit like a physical blow. Not because she wasn't entitled to secrets—God knew he had plenty of his own—but because this particular secret felt like serious, life-threatening trouble.

"Can we please not focus on that right now?" Kathy's voice broke slightly. "Let's focus on us. On being together."

He kissed her cheek tenderly and pulled out a chair for her. Instead of letting her serve him, he insisted on doing the honors, walking around the elegant table and carefully selecting delicacies he thought she'd enjoy, piling them onto fine china plates. Kathy giggled despite her worry and asked if he'd ever had pralines before, mentioning that her mama could make them too. So he added plenty to his own plate as well.

For the first ten minutes, they could barely speak, both famished from their respective journeys. They ate as if they were starving, savoring rich flavors and tender textures. It took several deep swallows before Carmelo finally came up for air.

"I can't tell you how incredible this is," he grinned, some of the earlier tension melting away.

Kathy giggled, her natural joy surfacing. "I know! Aunt Janey always did everything in grand style."

Carmelo's expression grew serious. "I really have missed you, Kat. Letters aren't enough anymore."

"Me too," she said sadly, reaching across the table. "Tell me what really happened. You barely write about it, and I don't trust Debbie's version. She always blames you and praises Matteo," she said with an eye roll. "Did you actually shoot your father?"

Carmelo froze at the question, then slowly lowered his gaze to his plate.

"Melo? Please tell me?" she pleaded, offering her hand for support across the polished table.

He managed a weak smile but refused to take her hand. He wasn't that same boy anymore. Eight months had changed him in ways that showed in the new hardness around his eyes, the careful way he held himself.

"Yes. I shot him," he finally admitted—an answer he'd refused to give in all their previous conversations.

"Why?" Her voice was barely a whisper.

"For Madre. For you. For my brothers. For me. In that exact order." His jaw tightened with remembered pain. "He just kept destroying everything and everyone I loved. But he didn't die. He won't die, unfortunately. Not unless he takes me with him," Carmelo mumbled. "He doesn't deserve to live."

"What happened after he survived?" she pressed gently.

"When he came back home…" Carmelo paused, struggling with the words. "He saved my life."

Kathy frowned in confusion.

"How could he save your life after you shot him?"

"*La Cosa Nostra* doesn't forgive patricide," Carmelo explained quietly. "Killing my father couldn't be overlooked, but wounding him and being forgiven by him... that gave me my stripes. Gained me respect among killers. And kept his men and his enemies from making an example out of me. A life for a life, as they say. Matteo was in a bad way, vulnerable. My father was at his weakest point. So I made a deal with the devil—we both agreed on a truce. Mama Stewart helped make the terms for my father, which he hated but agreed to. Boxing, Matteo, was given a rank when he was ready. Money of our own, and territory. Now we... wait."

"Wait for what?" Kathy asked, though she feared the answer.

"For our chance to be kings," he said. "It may not be our gun that ends the life of the devil, but the devil in this thing that we do, doesn't live long."

"Assassination?" she asked in horror.

"The fate of all the powerful men that have come before my father," Carmelo said bitterly. "If you are Don, your ending is already written."

"Just promise me. You can't go up against your father again. Promise me you won't ever try to replace him or be him," she pleaded, gripping his hand tightly.

"I'll make you that promise," he said slowly, "but first, tell me the truth about Janey. Did she kill DeMarco? Did she kill King Redmond? I've confessed my darkest secret to you. Now tell me yours."

Kathy sat back in her chair, shaking her head as if she couldn't—or wouldn't—answer.

"Don't you trust me, Kat?" he asked.

"I do but—" she began.

"No secrets. Remember? Not for us," he said.

She nodded. Her gaze lowered then, in a voice so quiet he had to lean forward to hear: "She didn't kill King Redmond, Carmelo. I did."

Carmelo blinked, certain he'd misheard. But Kathy's tortured expression told him everything.

In halting, painful words, she confessed the entire story. The threats against her father and mother. King Redmond's attempt to assault her mother escalated to the point that he wanted to take down her father next. The family secret of revenge was passed down through generations of Elliot Wynn's daughters. Each of the girls was renamed the Elliott women, daughters born from their parents' violent war of dominance and submission, taught to fight back with sweets and trickery.

"Daughters?" he repeated.

"Far as I know, only girls. Maybe a boy here or there, but mostly all girls were born to the sisters."

"I'm a daughter of one of the eight sisters," she mumbled, "My Gran was a woman barely out of slavery who became a forced mistress. Every daughter was from rape."

"I'm sorry, Kathy," he said.

She shrugged. "Her only act of rebellion, she taught each girl the art of herbs, those that can heal and those that can kill—how to use them to make someone fall in love, cure sickness, or to make them disappear forever. The knowledge was passed down to my mother, to Aunt Janey, and then to me."

She told him about the special recipe, mixed with cherries, the poison made King Redmond's death look like some strange blood disease. How she'd baked it into a cupcake with her own hands, delivered it with a smile, and watched justice be served when Redmond took the first bite.

"A killer cupcake took down King Redmond?" he frowned.

"I've tried to repent, to ask for forgiveness," she whispered, tears streaming down her beautiful face. "But I know in my heart I don't mean it. I'll never be able to escape what I've done. Not truly."

Where she saw shame and sin, Carmelo saw nothing but courage and fierce devotion. These women didn't cower—they fought back against monsters who thought they were untouchable. How could he ever blame her for that?

Carmelo pushed up from his chair and went to her, pulling Kathy from her seat and into his arms. She went to him, letting his strength support her.

"I guess we're not the innocent people we pretended to be," she said softly against his chest.

"We never were innocent, Kat," he murmured into her hair. "Maybe that's why we understand each other so completely."

"I can't escape what I am, what I've done," she whispered.

"Maybe someday you'll forgive yourself," he said gently, "because you're the only person in this world who's blaming you."

She looked up at him with eyes full of love and gratitude, seeing acceptance instead of judgment, protection instead of condemnation.

"Want to go upstairs?" she asked with a soft smile that held promises and healing.

His answering grin was filled with eight months of longing. "Yes."

Kathy took his hand and led him out of the parlor toward their shared future, two damaged souls who'd found perfect understanding in each other's arms. They'd both did what they could to protect the people they loved, and somehow that terrible bond made their love even stronger, more precious, and absolutely unbreakable.

CHAPTER 6

THE PRICE FOR PASSION AND PAIN

Janey froze at the bedroom doors as crystal shattered against a hard surface inside. She pressed her palm to the cool wood, feeling the vibrations of destruction. Carmine was in one of his black moods—when her sophisticated husband became the beast who'd survived her poison and trapped her in his heart and wouldn't let her go—no matter her crimes.

She drew in a steadying breath, painted on her most patient smile, and pushed open the door like a warrior woman walking into a lion's den.

Her husband prowled the expensive, imported carpet with predatory grace, despite his silver-topped cane, shards of what had once been a priceless Baccarat crystal tumbler glittering like deadly diamonds around his Italian leather shoes.

"Close the door," he commanded without looking at her, his voice carrying the quiet menace of a man who'd ordered executions with the same tone.

She obeyed, the soft click of the latch sealing them in together—predator and prey, though which was which remained dangerously unclear.

When he turned those pale blue eyes on her, Janey saw the

restrained fury of the mobster who lived beneath his cultured exterior —the monster she'd tried to kill with cherry-laced pie, the man who'd refused to die. Only in moments of severe jealousy and crushing disappointment did that lethal creature surface, emerging from behind Carmine's gentleman's mask like a wolf shedding sheep's clothing.

"Lie to me again, *bella*," he said, the endearment dripping with dangerous honey. "Tell me you didn't slip away to New York like a whore in the night. Tell me that Carmelo boy didn't see you playing your games with the Ricci family and cozying up to another man. A man like me. Lie to me. Say you didn't do it."

She lifted one elegant shoulder in a careless shrug, though her heart hammered against her ribs and fear made her cautious. There were times she did worry that his jealousy would join her in her insanity. That he'd take them both out of this world to stop her wanderlust.

"I'm not going to lie to you, *cher*, but—"

The silver-topped cane whistled through the air like a deadly serpent. Carmine swung it with the precision of a master craftsman, shattering the antique mirror behind him into a thousand gleaming fragments. She flinched as glass rained down like frozen tears, each shard catching the afternoon light as it fell.

He stood amid the destruction like an avenging angel, methodically destroying every remaining piece until nothing but an empty frame remained. Only then did he turn back to her, his pale eyes blazing with barely leashed violence.

"The Ricci's!" The word erupted from his throat like a curse. "Those maggots! The men are already whispering about DeMarco's death—how strange it was, how sudden. How he bled! It was you, wasn't it?" His voice dropped to a whisper more terrifying than any shout. "Did you fuck him?"

Janey's gaze fell to the Persian carpet, her fingers twisting in the white silk of her dress.

"*Did you?*" The roar that tore from his chest made the remaining crystal in the room tremble in sympathy.

She raised her head slowly, a sinister smile curving her crimson lips like a blade. "I killed him." The words hung in the air between them, sharp as winter wind. "I killed him nice and slow, *cher*. Crept into his hospital room at night and pretended to care so I could watch," she whispered the rest: "I watched the light fade from his eyes while he begged for mercy he'd never shown. He hurt my baby girl, Kathy, and that simply could not stand. I would have killed that Don, too, if his wife hadn't jumped from that bridge."

Carmine raked trembling fingers through his dark hair, closing his eyes as if the very sight of her pained him. She kept her distance, reading the dangerous tension in every line of his body. Though he knew better than to touch her in anger, she knew better than to push him past the point of reason.

Their marriage had been shattered by her methods before—the way she wasn't above using her body as a weapon, seducing her victims with honey before delivering poison. It had destroyed his faith in her, leaving cracks in their foundation that still ached like broken bones. But she was stronger now, no longer ruled entirely by the demons that whispered in her head for vengeance. She would not betray him. Not after the Senator. Not after everything he'd sacrificed to keep her from the electric chair.

His eyes found hers across the wreckage of their bedroom. "Did you fuck him?" The question came out broken, desperate.

"I already answered—"

"*DID YOU?*" The demand exploded from him like a gunshot, but beneath the fury, she heard something else—a plea wrapped in barbed wire, a desperate need to believe she hadn't betrayed him again. Killing men he could live with, but a man between her thighs, in her pussy, her giving away what belonged to him, that is where he drew the line.

The sound of his pain made her stomach clench with sick guilt. Even now, the poison cherry was slowly eroding away at his soul, day by day, bite by bite, he was dying. He was her heart walking around outside her body, and she hated herself for failing to take better care of something so precious. To hurt him so badly, so often.

She approached him the way one might approach a wounded tiger —slowly, carefully, ready to retreat at the first sign of actual danger. "Are you calm?"

"No." The word ground out between clenched teeth like gravel.

"Then calm yourself, Carmine. Be still for me." She stopped just within arm's reach, close enough to see the pain flickering behind his rage. "Look into my eyes when I answer you. You know me—the real me, not the monster. *I did not fuck him*. I let him taste my pussy, and touch my body, and that was all. I simply invited him to trust me, then I killed him. And I left and came home to you. Izzy told me you went to Butts. Spoke to Mama… Big Mama, you talked to a sheriff. You lied about that to me. I didn't care. I understood. I came home to you, *caro*."

Carmine's eyes drifted shut as if her words were a benediction. She reached up to touch his jaw with her fingers, feeling the tension coiled beneath his olive skin.

"I'm sorry, *cher*. I have failed you more than any wife should ever fail her husband. I am sorry for causing you so much pain. For not giving you a child." Her voice broke. "But I am your wife now, truly and completely. I kept my promise and came home. I've been a good girl, haven't I, Daddy?"

His hands shot out to grip her shoulders, shaking her with barely restrained violence. The rough handling shocked her so completely that she gasped, her carefully maintained composure cracking like ice.

"The Riccis are not the Marcellos!" he snarled, his face inches from hers. "If that boy tells anyone who you really are, what you've done, we're all dead—including that precious niece of yours. Don't you understand that?"

Something cold and deadly flickered behind Janey's honey-brown eyes. "Let. Me. Go." Each word dropped like ice into still water; her voice carried the quiet menace of a woman who'd killed men for far less. "You know better than to ever put your hands on me in anger."

Carmine released her as if she'd burst into flames, stepping back with his palms raised in surrender. He turned away, moving stiffly without the support of his cane, and she could see how the poison had weakened him even as it made him more dangerous.

"Get out," he said without looking at her.

"I will not." She crossed her arms, chin lifted in defiance.

His glare over his shoulder could have melted steel. "I said—"

"I didn't fuck him, Carmine!" The words erupted from her like a dam bursting. "That's all you really care about, isn't it? Not justice for Kathy, not protecting our family—just whether I spread my legs for another man! I didn't touch him. When I came home to you, I told you it was the last time I'd disappear into that other world. That I was home for good. Why can't you believe me?"

"Because you are the reigning queen of lies!" His voice cracked like a whip. "An innocent woman is sitting on death row in a California prison cell right now for a murder *you* committed. The things I've done to cover for you, Janey... the blood on my soul because of your crusades..."

She pressed her palms over her ears like a child, her sophisticated mask slipping to reveal something broken underneath. "Da-da-da-da-da-da..." The childish chant was her only defense against truths too sharp to bear.

The sight of her retreat cut through his anger. Carmine crossed the room to her in three quick strides without his cane, gently pulling her hands away from her ears before gathering her into his arms. She collapsed against his chest, sobbing with the raw desperation of a woman drowning.

"You know I can't help it," she wept against his shirt. "You promised you would fix me, make me whole again. But you never do! You never make it stop. You never do! It's your fault, not mine!"

"I can't fix you, *cara mia*," he whispered into her hair, his voice gentle as prayer. "I can only love you. And I'm fighting death to stay here for you."

He held her as she cried out eighteen years of accumulated pain. Carmine stroked her hair until her sobs gentled to silence, then soft humming. When he lifted her face in his hands, that familiar dazed look had returned to her eyes—the one that meant the killer had retreated, leaving only his Janey behind. The scared girl trapped in that swamp with that rat cajun bastard, who broke her spirit. The young woman he'd spend whatever remained of his life trying to protect.

"Are you angry with me?" she asked in a soft and meek voice.

"Not anymore." And it was true. When the honest Janey surfaced—vulnerable, broken, achingly beautiful—he could no more suppress his love than he could stop breathing. "I believe you, *cara mia*. My darling Jane."

She lifted her face and closed her eyes, waiting for his kiss. Carmine smiled through his tears. Though his body wasn't as virile as he wished—the poison had seen to that—it still worked well enough for a man condemned to an early grave.

He lifted her in his arms as if she weighed nothing, carrying her to their massive four-poster bed. She curled into his embrace like a cat seeking warmth, no longer the brazen killer but simply his woman, his heart, his damnation and salvation rolled into one impossible package.

He laid her down with infinite care, then undressed her the way a man might unwrap the most precious gift imaginable—slowly, reverently, memorizing every curve and hollow. The seduction wasn't entirely his, though she had a way of making him feel as if it were, a way of slipping into his mind and taming the raging beasts without him even realizing she'd done it.

As Carmine began removing his own clothes, his eyes misted with unshed tears. Someday—perhaps sooner than later—he would not be able to touch her, love her, protect her from the consequences of her choices. What would happen to her when that inevitable day arrived? If she could not control her need for vengeance against the white men who preyed on innocents, then eventually other men would find a way to hunt her down and control her through methods far less gentle than his own.

The thought seized him with paralyzing terror, part of the madness that had consumed him since the night she'd tried to kill him. His Janey wasn't safe in this world. Maybe he should end it all.

Take her with him. Maybe in the afterlife, they could have peace with just each other. If only he were sure that it was true.

"You still want to kill me, cher?" she asked.

His face flushed. "No, Janey."

"It's okay. I can see it in your eyes. If I thought death would give us peace, I'd bake a cake for both of us. But my sins will not be forgiven. I will have to pay. Heaven is what we got now. Here."

Janey stared at him. He was frozen, gazing down at her, tears glistening like gems on his dark lashes. She knew that look intimately—first came the anger and rage over perceived betrayal, then the forgiveness that made her feel whole again. But sometimes, before the sweet nectar of making love to the only living man she'd ever truly loved, came something worse: fear, pain, sorrow, grief for the life they'd built together that could end any day, any moment.

"Forgive me," she said, almost child-like.

He shed his clothes with deliberate slowness, each movement a promise and a threat. Janey didn't blink. When he joined her on the bed, his kisses whispered gentleness while his hands spoke a harsher language—one written in bruises from spankings during sex, and even his hand at her throat until she released a breathless surrender. Carmine's appetites in sex had broken lesser women, sent them fleeing from desires that bordered on sadistic cruelty. But Janey never ran from his darkness. She once told him, when he had her tied to the bed for two days, only giving her water and bathroom breaks while he explored his sexual desires and perversions on her, that all of it was just sex play. That she was the darkness. Then she poisoned him to prove it. Janey Elliot Wynn was his match, meeting his sadism with her own twisted hunger, their lovemaking a battle neither truly wanted to win.

She groaned when his dick thrust into her hard and punishingly. He caught himself from fucking her too hard and too fast. He made gentle love to her vagina and body first with his tongue instead, and then saved the punishing penetration and unbridled lust with all of his energy for her whipping. Spanking both cheeks with his belt until they were fiery red, he oiled her up and fucked her hole with pistoning thrusts, keeping her wrists bound tight to the bedpost.

She whimpered and endured. It had been months since she'd been adequately punished. And she had lied to him. She had let DeMarco fuck her. She lied, and he knew it. The only way to get close enough to the evilest of men was to give in. She enjoyed DeMarco's attention, but it turned to addiction when she refused to let him fuck her more. She tortured him with teasing promises and sweet treats she made for him. Softening him up for the cherry pie.

When the spanking became too much, she began to cry. Carmine stopped, and then Janey collapsed into laughter that dissolved into more tears—the line between pleasure and pain blurred beyond recognition. When he finally released her from their dark ritual, she lay still, wrists marked by silk bonds.

"Don't hurt me, cher," she whispered, voice raw.

He heard her plea. He studied her—still the most beautiful woman in Tremé, even broken and remade by their twisted dance. Part of him wanted to keep her bound, suspended her from the ceiling, and keep her trapped naked that way for the rest of eternity while he worshipped at her feet. At that moment, she was entirely his.

"We have company. They will not understand our games, my love. Stop the spankings and breaking of things. Let me take care of you," she purred.

She turned and winced at the sting to her buttocks when she had to position herself in a sitting pose before him. He extended his hand to her, and she stood slowly, carrying the evidence of their violence like armor. His seed leaked from between the cheeks of her red and inflamed ass.

"Are you okay?" The question felt absurd even as he asked it.

She looked back, tears cutting through her smile. "I feel better now. Thank you."

As she left to compose herself, he knew she'd return with salves and tenderness—the other half of their ritual. He closed his eyes and wondered, not for the first time: How would this end? When would it?"

CHAPTER 7

LOVE ANEW IN THE BAYOU

The guest room Janey had prepared for them was a sanctuary of understated elegance—pale yellow walls adorned with delicate watercolors of French gardens, gossamer curtains that filtered the afternoon light into something soft and golden, and a magnificent four-poster bed draped in creamy white fabric.

Kathy closed the door behind them. For eight months, they had existed in limbo, sustaining themselves on memories and wishes. Now they stood facing each other in the hushed quiet of their temporary paradise, suddenly shy as newlyweds despite everything they'd shared.

"You know we are married," Carmelo reassured her.

Kathy smiled. "I… don't think so… it's not leagal and…"

"We are. Legally. No matter what anyone says to you. We are married. Maybe not blessed by God in a church, but our paperwork is legitimate. It has the state seal. We are married," Carmelo said.

Kathy nodded to reassure him. The courthouse didn't have that paperwork he bragged about, nor did the church. To her, it wasn't sealed until they could be husband and wife properly. But she refused to state that.

"I can't believe you're really here," Kathy whispered.

Carmelo stood by the window, hands clenched at his sides, his silhouette rigid against the lace curtains. "Two hundred and forty-three days. I counted everyone."

The distance between them felt like miles and inches all at once. She stepped out of her shoes, the floor cool beneath her feet. When he began unbuttoning his shirt she moved closer without thinking.

"You look different," she said softly.

"How?" His voice was rough.

"Harder. Like the world's been at you." Her hands replaced his at the buttons, and they both stilled at the contact. His skin was warm beneath her fingertips.

"You look..." He swallowed, eyes searching her face. "Like a woman now. Not the girl I left behind."

"I was so afraid," she confessed, working the buttons slowly, needing the task to steady herself. "That time would change us. You're out there boxing, living a life we never planned. What happened to the zookeeper? The animal doctor?"

His laugh was unexpected, warm. It made her smile despite everything.

"Same thing that happened to the scientist," he teased gently.

"Now I'm teaching Science in Butt's," she winked.

He kept smiling.

She tried to speak, but her voice was caught up in emotion. "Waiting. Always waiting. And Big Mama—her sugar's getting worse."

"*Cara...*" His hand covered hers, stilling her movements.

"She's strong. We're managing." She couldn't meet his eyes, couldn't let him see her fear. "That's why I need to be there. Mama comes every two or three months to help. We're protecting her until..."

The words hung unfinished. His thumb stroked across her knuckles, and suddenly the room felt too small, the air too thick with everything unsaid."

"I'm sorry," he said.

"Don't be," she blinked away the tears and looked into his eyes. She is strong. We are strong together."

A silence fell between them.

"Mama said DeeDee got married recently," she chirped.

His brows furrowed, not understanding.

"To an Irish boy." She watched comprehension dawn on his face.

"Oh."

"I lied. I know what you said was the truth, Melo. Mama Stewart was right—that judge José loves, he really did marry us. We could take that paper to the courts, make it legitimate. But it's not legitimate unless we do that. Do you understand? We aren't married, unless we take that step."

"Kathy—"

"DeeDee didn't marry no gangster. And the law in New York don't care about gangsters and Black girls being married." Her voice cracked with heartbreak. "But our families do. They always have. That is why we are here. Hiding, pretending. Because we can't face them, they hate each other."

"They always will," he said quietly.

"Even Mama. She told me she's glad I didn't do what DeeDee did." Tears spilled over Kathy's cheeks. "We're liars, me and Debbie. Lying to everyone. Forever."

"Not forever." He cupped her face, thumbs brushing away tears. "I swear it."

"Time hurts, Carmelo. The longer we're apart, I think maybe this is all we'll ever be. Stolen moments. Secret phone calls. Letters we have to hide." Her voice dropped to a whisper. "That scares me. My life is empty in Butts. You're seeing the world. I see nothing but trees."

"Scares me too. I want to give you the world, Kathy. I do! I will show you the world. I will."

"What if you find someone else?" she asked.

"Never." The word came out fierce, certain. He captured her wrists, made her meet his eyes. "You're written on my soul, Kathy. Eight months, eight years—it makes no difference. My plan is working. It keeps shifting, but it's working."

He was close enough to see unshed tears making her eyes luminous, and the tremor in her lips portrayed her desperate need. If she knew the truth, her guarded love might shrivel and die.

His greatest sin was the burden he couldn't share—his mother's suicide note, her final plea. As a Catholic, she'd sacrificed her soul, knowing she'd be barred from heaven. Honoring her request meant betraying every vow he'd made to Kathy.

He wanted to drop to his knees, confess why he hadn't fled to Mississippi, climbed through her window, and stolen her away to the life they'd dreamed of. Maybe she'd forgive him if he explained it right.

But he was a coward. Better to trap her in this limbo than risk losing her entirely.

He pressed her hand against his racing heart. "Feel that? That's what you do to me. Always have."

Then his gaze fell to her hand, where a ring sparkled brightly. How had he missed it before? He lifted her hand to his lips, planting a tender kiss on the ring. The last barrier between them seemed to dissolve like morning mist. Whatever happened beyond these walls—the danger from their families, the complexities of Janey's world, the uncertainty of their future—none of it mattered in this sacred space they'd created together.

"Carmelo," she breathed. "Tomorrow morning, there is no hurry. And the next day, and the next. Every night you're mine."

Then words became unnecessary.

"Don't undress me," he said roughly, pulling his half-open shirt over his head. "Undress for me." His hands moved to his belt as she stepped back, and suddenly the shy veneer lifted from her features like a curtain being drawn away.

She held his gaze with newfound boldness as she reached behind her neck, her fingers working the delicate buttons at the back of her dress with deliberate slowness. The white satin whispered down her body and pooled at her feet like spilled moonlight. Next came the slip she wore beneath, the fabric sliding over her curves like a caress.

When she reached for the clasp of her bra, he was already bare below the waist. Eight months of separation and longing were written in every uncharted inch of his erection.

He saw that she noticed.

Carmelo's breath caught when his eyes lowered. Her body was unveiled as the last barrier of modesty fell away. His appreciation for her lovely breasts and shapely thighs caused his erection to throb with heat. He'd seen her body before but had been too anxious and too virginal to know what possessing someone so beautiful could mean. He understood that now.

She took a moment to breathe. It was all the permission he needed. He pulled her against him. His mouth slammed down on hers. His kiss was urgent, desperate. Months of longing poured into that single kiss. His manhood felt painful to resist because his loins remembered her touch, the sweet heat of her wet and tight vagina with aching clarity. Every fiber of his being demanded the pleasure and relief that only being inside of her could bring.

Like every other time, her kisses were a slow burn until it was a wildfire. Guiding her backward toward the four-poster bed, he cupped her rounded buttocks, her ass fully seated in his hands, while he lifted her effortlessly.

Kathy's legs instinctively wrapped around his waist, locking him close. They sank onto the mattress in one fluid motion, his weight pressing her deep into the soft sheets. He entered her with a single, powerful thrust—no teasing, no foreplay—just the raw intensity of their emotional and physical bond manifesting in a union. She felt seized, needed, and deeply fulfilled. And he could tell by the way the tension in her pussy released, and how he was granted deeper access than he ever had before. *Did she want a seduction?* The timid, clumsy sweetness of their first time. The exploration he performed on her body that awakened them both after their marital ceremony in Debbie's place. Yes. He was certain she did. But this was what he hungered for. Reality, authenticity, complete dominance, and unfiltered devotion were all needed to refill his soul after so much loss in just eight months.

His deep, smoky voice was in her ear. *"Cazzo! I missed this, you."*

The proclamation shot down her spine and arrowed through her pelvis, extending, heightening the explosion of delicious, sensational currents distressing her vagina as he pumped his dick in and out of her and pinned her thighs far apart to make sure she felt every strike.

She gasped for relief, but the pressure, the tension, the pure unfiltered rawness of it all stole her breath. She gripped the sheets and then clawed at his back, not sure what to do to survive the storm.

"Oh, oh, help me," her voice finally broke through, releasing the plea. He only went faster, harder. And without proper instruction or training, her body moved in sync. Her thighs quivered with hot intensity from muscle strain, and she was released so he could trap her hands that were scratching him along his back. He used his hands to pin her wrists down on the bed. There would be no escape. She locked around his waist, and her back arched as his rapid hip thrusts drove him deep, then deeper.

His head lifted, his eyes seductively low as he stared into hers. "Do you want me to stop?" he taunted her.

She trapped her bottom lip between her teeth with a grin and shook her head fast. She didn't know this Carmelo. Her body was learning, and so was her womanhood. He was becoming the maestro of their affair, her man, with each deliberate stroke.

But how? How had this transformation come?

Carmelo's mouth lowered to hers, and her lips parted to receive a tender kiss as his hard thrusts began to melt into something soothing, stimulating. Her distressed vagina yawned then constricted in response as a quake tickled her core, sending a heat wave of tingles that had her entire pelvis vibrating. Her dark lashes fluttered, her eyes rolled into her head as what must have been the orgasm that Debbie swore Matteo insisted he'd give her during their sex. Debbie said Carmelo owed her one. More than one. A thank you for all the suffering and enduring she had to go through, having to live in Mississippi. And all at once it began to surface.

And then he froze mid-thrust, swiftly rolling them so she was astride him. She gasped at the sudden change in position, her surprise turned to giggles as she stared down at him. She was now in a power position she hadn't conceived.

"Move for me," he breathed. "Up and down not back and forth!" he smacked her ass. His command was urgent, not wanting to lose the moment. "Move! Kathy!"

She glanced down at his heaving chest, her gaze sliding slowly up the glistening, muscular expanse to meet his eyes. His firm grip on her hips guided her, setting a bouncing rhythm she instinctively matched. She pressed her palms flat against his chest for balance as she rose and fell on his thickness in a sexual dance she'd never performed before, savoring each stroke and his hardness stretched her at a new angle, putting her inner womanhood in distress. The motion sent waves of pleasure through him as well. Her body stiffened and relaxed on its own.

And that was what their lovemaking became—a carousel of exhilarating highs and torturous lows. She moved with deliberate, tantalizing slowness, shocked by the sheer torment on his face and the foreign sensations seizing through her loins. Sex was not like this before with him. No matter how much she tried on their wedding night, she could never get over her discomfort. The tables had turned, just as Debbie had said they would. Now she held the power and pleasure. She drove her hips in natural rhythms that stimulated her more than anything else. She wasn't selfish in life. She was a dutiful daughter, a good girl for Big Mama, a hard worker for the Jensens, a patient girlfriend, but she had never tasted power before. A new kind of power. And she liked it. More than she could have ever imagined. And she was a fast learner. She learned what unraveled him most. Her hips rocked in a deliberate, sensual motion as he clenched his jaw, fighting desperately for control once he delivered upward thrusts, making the pleasure tenfold.

"This is your *figa* button. Press it," he said in his husky, breathless voice. He took her hand and guided it down to stroke her clitoris. The moment she touched herself, she understood why. Her climax rushed over her—a fierce, overwhelming torrent of ecstasy and release—so intense that he surged upright, holding her tightly as tremors overtook her body. She cried out so loudly that she feared her aunt might overhear. He buried his face into her shoulder, holding her close, as their bodies met the peak they'd never reached together before.

It was pure divinity.

Kathy lifted her head, looking at him with a mixture of confusion and wonder. "Wha-what… was figa?"

"Pussy," he wheezed.

Her eyes stretched over the vulgarity, and he corrected himself immediately. "That was love," he whispered.

"But how did you know… how did I?" she murmured, frowning slightly.

"We're made for each other, Kathy." He gently kissed her lips, then her nose, while she felt him softening slowly inside her.

Then a troubling thought occurred to her. What if? What if he'd been with another woman, learned these things elsewhere? Something felt different—something guarded in his eyes, something she couldn't fully grasp.

He cupped her cheek tenderly. "*Cara mia*? It was good, right? You liked it?"

She nodded slowly, her vision blurring as tears welled. Imagining him loving someone else, leaving their shared intimacy behind, struck her deeply. How long would he be satisfied with stolen moments, as his celebrity grew in the boxing world and his life moved forward in New York without her? How long until the letters stopped, until secret phone calls faded away? How would their story end?

Kathy began to cry softly.

Startled, he grasped her face gently, forcing her to meet his gaze. "Kathy? What is it? Tell me! Did I hurt you?"

"I'm scared, Melo," she sobbed. "I don't want to lose you. I'm so scared. You're doing it to another girl." She wrapped her arms tightly around his neck, pressing her face to his chest. She felt his heart racing, mirroring her fear.

"Never," he vowed fiercely. "I'd die before I'd ever let you go. I'd cut my dick off before I put it in someone else. I learned these things from the men. They talk sex all the time, on the road. It's all they talk about. I swear it! On my soul!"

"Promise me. Promise you won't choose anyone else. Promise you won't leave me here. I'll learn. I'll be a good wife. I'll do anything for you. Promise we'll go away together, someday, and be together openly." Her voice shook with desperation.

"I promise, Kathy. I swear it. You're my wife, my heart—my Kathy. *Sempre.*"

Slowly, her panic began to subside, allowing her to catch her breath. She reassured herself it was only insecurity talking. He was hers; they were bound to each other. Even if their marriage wasn't recognized everywhere, she knew their bond was unbreakable.

She wouldn't allow doubt to enter again.

CHAPTER 8

LAC TREMBLANT, QUEBEC – 1978

Present. After her shower, Kathy entered the lower cabin, where Carmelo had asked her to join him for dinner. Earlier, he'd sent for a boat to remove Nino. His men escorted Nino back to their villa, insisting on spending the rest of the evening alone with her at sea. Though the open sky and shimmering waters should've felt vast and liberating, the now orchestrated isolation tightened around her.

He wouldn't answer questions. He kept brooding when he thought she wasn't aware. Something between them shifted as the sun began its descent.

She'd chosen a summer dress she knew he'd appreciate: the slit daringly high, the neckline enticingly low. The color was a vibrant and happy yellow. She took a flower from the arrangements and put it in her hair. With just the two of them here, there would be none of the dangerous jealousy that often shadowed their interactions. Still, unease lingered from his constant brooding throughout the day.

When Kathy entered, Carmelo stood at the bar, pouring himself another drink—a habit she wished he'd never acquired. Between the Scotch, bourbon, and the ever-present cigars, bitterness had grown inside him, a bitterness she could smell on him. His back was to her.

He drained the glass and poured another. Then, abruptly, he slammed the bottle down, gripping the edge with white-knuckled intensity, muttering fiercely under his breath in Italian—words she couldn't understand but whose frustration she felt deeply.

She approached cautiously. Her eyes drifted to the crystal tableware laid out elegantly for their meal. On the pristine white porcelain plate sat a ring she hadn't seen in decades, tarnished but unmistakable. The ring she thought she'd tossed away the day he fought for her love, and she rejected his pleas. The night she'd truly lost him and her faith in their love.

It was the ring he'd slipped onto her finger decades ago after their time in the attic, back when they were young and desperately in love. Despite the diamonds he showered her with now, that simple ring had always been her greatest treasure. Tears welled before she could suppress them. A quiet gasp of appreciation escaped her lips.

Carmelo glanced back sharply. Kathy removed the diamond wedding band he'd given her and replaced it with the tarnished ring. Her voice trembled with awe and disbelief.

"You kept it? You found it? All these years, you never said a thing? Why?"

He didn't answer. His silence was scary. All these years, through the calmer moments and storms alike, he'd never revealed he'd had her ring.

Kathy searched his expression for a meaning. "What's going on, Carmelo? Time for the truth. Why are we still out here on this lake?"

He turned fully, meeting her eyes. His voice was heavy, almost resigned. "I've done something—something you won't like. Something I can't change. It's done, and we have to find a way forward. As husband and wife."

A chill gripped her heart. How often had she heard him say similar words? Secrets and vengeance had always been part of the Wolf's world, that ruthless side of him. Again and again, lives had been crushed beneath the weight of his magnetism, manipulation, cruelty, and relentless crusade to reclaim what he'd lost—a life with her, and with their daughter. To the Wolf, everyone was guilty, including

Kathy. But she still saw Carmelo beneath the hardened facade—the tender, passionate young man yearning simply to live freely.

Kathy steeled herself, refusing to be swayed by memories of their youthful love. If he had lied, she knew how to deal with it. She'd had practice. If he had done something criminal, it would not have fazed her. She was, after all, Henry and Brenda Freeman's daughter. What could be the crime this time to warrant this? She touched the ring for strength, swallowing back her fears.

"What have you done?" she said quietly. "Let's deal with it."

"You'll be angry," he replied.

"I'll get over it," she mumbled and crossed her arms

His brow arched. "Not this time. This time, you have the right to be angry."

"I've had the right many times before, Melo. You just refused to give me that courtesy," she sighed. "But I don't want to go back in the past. I'm done with the past. Okay? It happened. We happened. We hurt each other, but we got over it. We're over it now. This is a fresh start."

"No, it's not. The moment I disappoint you, you overreact, and this thing between us becomes war—you never forgive... just judge me!" he huffed, angry tension settling in his posture.

"Stop stalling! Just tell me," she insisted.

"I can deal with your anger. I just... I need you to try to understand my reasons," he said. "Because... I—"

"Tell me! What did you do?" she demanded.

"I had you murdered. You're dead. We're both dead."

New Orleans, 1950

Kathy woke up to a body pressed against hers. The room was hot and the air dewy. The scent of sex, sweat, and musk was heavy, just like his body. She could feel the rhythmic beat of his heart in his chest against her back. The wiry, bristling pubic hairs along his pelvis arrow up in a silky wave to his navel against her buttcheeks. The warmth and moist breath from his nostrils blew over her shoulder. He was sleeping, halfway inside of her. They'd exhausted themselves so much during sex that they both passed out in exhaustion.

She moved.

"Mmm, more," he groaned and stirred. She squeezed her eyes tight, hoping he'd go back to sleep. Her vagina ached, as did her legs, her pelvis, and even her throat from all the times he had driven her to sexual madness, forcing her to cry out his name—over and over again.

His flaccid penis was between them as she pushed back with all the strength she could summon, causing him to flip over to his back. Relief flooded her from the release. Carmelo snored—not gently as Kathy remembered from their earlier days together, but with a deep, rumbling rhythm like distant thunder following lightning. She smiled softly, reaching out to touch his face. Their lovemaking had been intense, decadent, leaving her body humming pleasantly from the passion and aching from some of his savagery. Yet Debbie's words from Christmas echoed clearly in her mind, a warning about how quickly passion could lead to pregnancy.

What would happen to them then?

Kathy leaned forward, gently kissed his cheek, and slipped quietly from the bed. She found a simple, modest blue house robe suitable enough for a quick trip down the hallway. Stepping into the silent corridor, the floorboards creaked beneath her bare feet as she made her way to the bathroom. Once inside, she took her time washing away the sticky traces of their intimacy, feeling refreshed and ready to return to him.

She opened the bathroom door—and gasped.

Aunt Janey stood there smiling knowingly.

"I heard you two," Janey teased lightly.

"What?" Kathy stammered, mortified.

Janey chuckled. "Relax, I wasn't listening long. I just wanted to make sure you were all right. After all that hollering you were doing!"

Kathy frowned, concern flickering in her eyes. Janey took her hand and gently pulled her along. "Willa's back, and she's excited to see you."

"Wait, Janey—why were you at our door in the first place?" Kathy asked as she struggled to keep pace while descending the stairs.

"My house," Janey replied breezily. "Besides, my husband worries about Carmelo. Thinks he might bring trouble."

"Why? He doesn't even know Carmine," Kathy protested softly.

"Because he's a Ricci, sweetheart. Everyone knows what that name means in New York. Why do you think they brought him down here to fight the Klan in the first place?" Janey explained, guiding her toward the brightly lit parlor. "Since he tried to be with you, they claim he's a Negro lover. Understands the savages. It's all slick and sick. Sometimes you can be so naive. Wake up, Kathy. If you're going to love a mobster, there are rules."

"He's not—"

"Don't back-talk me!" Janey snapped sharply.

Kathy fell silent. They paused before the parlor doors. Her aunt's sweet demeanor faded, replaced by a hard glint in her eyes. "This isn't that fairytale you spin about Romeo and Juliet in an attic. This is the mob. This is the South. This is real life. You've already tasted the apple from the forbidden tree. Now it's all about consequences. You hear me? If you want that man-boy, you're going to see him for what he truly is... and what he *isn't*. And you're going to do that now. I ain't risking my Carmine's life again. So grow the fuck up. Or get the hell out of New Orleans!"

The truth hit like a physical blow.

Carmelo had felt different since their reunion. The way he talked, the way he looked at her, the way they made love. All the while, she could feel the changes in him, but couldn't name them. She lowered her gaze. Things would never be the same as they were before. Too much had happened. She would have to change, too.

"I'm sorry, okay?" Janey touched Kathy's cheek gently, her voice softening. "I forget sometimes why Brenda gave you the soft life up there in Harlem instead of the one she and I endured. Sometimes it's good to be a dreamer, Kathy. Dreams are what make it bearable to be a black woman in this world. You chose a hard path. You done lied to Big Mama and your folks by coming here. *You ain't innocent.* You know what we Elliot girls are. Stop pretending you different. If you want Carmelo, dreams won't be enough anymore. Understand?"

"Did you go to Harlem? Did you kill DeMarco the consigliere, Auntie?" Kathy asked quietly.

Janey lowered her hand. "We can talk about that later. First, see Willa. See what being married to the mob can do for you and that girl you care about."

Janey turned on her heel and walked away.

When Kathy stepped into the parlor, she stopped abruptly at the sight before her. Willa stood gracefully from the velvet settee, transformed so completely that she bore only the faintest resemblance to the timid sharecropper's daughter who had arrived in the Tremé. Her rich, dark skin glowed from the pampering, polished to a magnificent ebony sheen through care and proper nourishment. Her hair, previously hidden beneath worn scarves, now framed her face in sophisticated waves that caught the afternoon light like spun black silk.

Willa wore a spring dress of soft lavender, made of satin, that complemented her complexion beautifully. The expert tailoring celebrated her natural bosom and slender waist, with the skirt redefining her feminine lower curves. Delicate pearl earrings caught the gentle sunlight filtering through the lace curtains, while cream-colored leather pumps gave her an air of refined confidence. Subtle makeup enhanced rather than masked her features, bringing out the intelligent warmth in her dark eyes and the generous curve of her smile.

This wasn't a changed Willa—this was Willa revealed, an empress finally given the center stage she'd always deserved.

"Oh my, Willa," Kathy breathed in wonder.

Willa smiled. "Look at me, Kathy. Just look at me!"

"I ain't never seen anyone more beautiful," Kathy whispered. "Ever."

Willa burst into tears, overwhelmed with joy. Kathy rushed forward, and they hugged tightly, bouncing and squealing happily.

"Your aunt is an angel, Kathy! This place is unreal. I went to a salon just for us Black women, where they sat us in chairs and pampered us. They served tiny sandwiches with no crust, and tea in fancy cups like at Ms. Lottie's house. They bathed me, rubbed oils into my skin until I smelled like flowers." She released Kathy and walked to her reflection in the window, astonished. "I'm beautiful. Truly beautiful."

"Yes, you are," Kathy agreed warmly.

"I can't ever go back, Kathy. Ever. This place was made for us—for Coloreds. We should stay. Nothin in Butts to go home to. The Tremé is the sweet life!"

Kathy blinked, her stomach tightening anxiously. This wasn't the plan. Yes, she wanted Willa to experience the joy and dignity she'd never known back home, where she was treated barely better than the mules on the farm. But she had promised the Jensens she'd bring Willa back safely and assured Big Mama no trouble would come to Willa. Though they'd offered Willa little in her life but labor and chores, the Jensens' attachment to Willa's gentle spirit ran deep, having reared her since she was six or seven.

"Willa, let's not think about that right now. We just got here. There's so much to see and do."

Willa grinned brightly, pointing to the opposite side of the room, which was filled with shopping bags and boxes. "I'm nervous to open them. Aunt Janey said to throw away my old suitcase. I ain't never had a real present before in my life."

Kathy took Willa's hand and guided her toward the pile. "Well, welcome to Christmas, then. Let's see what you got."

After several minutes of admiring pretty dresses and evening wear, the parlor door opened abruptly. Both girls quickly stood.

Carmine Boanno entered slowly, leaning on his cane. His pale blue eyes swept sharply over them, lingering in surprise on Willa's transformation before shifting to Kathy.

"This is Janey's doing, I presume," he said.

"Yes, sir," Willa replied nervously, lowering her head as though caught misbehaving.

Kathy frowned slightly.

"Where is Janey?" he asked.

"I—I dunno, sir," Willa stammered, voice trembling.

"It's alright, Willa," Kathy reassured her. "She left us here, Mr. Boanno."

Carmine paused thoughtfully. Perhaps seeing Willa's anxious expression softened his demeanor. He nodded respectfully, adding gently, "You look very beautiful, Willa. Enjoy your stay. And please call me Carmine—not sir."

"Yes, sir!" Willa blurted, covering her mouth immediately after.

Carmine nodded once, then slipped out, his cane tapping softly against the hardwood floor.

The moment the door clicked shut, the girls erupted into giggles, clutching each other like schoolgirls with a secret. Willa plucked at the delicate fabric of the dress in her hands, suddenly self-conscious. "Maybe I oughta change into somethin' less… fancy," she murmured. "Ain't like we goin' out. She got me a pair of pants and a nice shirt."

Kathy grinned, mischief lighting her eyes. "Oh, we're goin' out alright. Tonight, we're hittin' *La Reine Noire*."

Willa's eyes stretched wide. "The La *what* now?"

"Janey told me in her letter," Kathy said, lowering her voice like they might be overheard. "It's a mob-run speakeasy—one of them hidden juke joints, but fancier. Now it's where the big shots go to hear jazz and pretend they ain't crooked." She leaned in. "It's tucked under some café on Royal Street. And tonight? It's where they're throwin' Carmelo's fight party."

Willa's mouth fell open. "You mean we gon' be rubbin' elbows with *gangsters?*"

Kathy laughed. "I think we get to see him get his announcement, and then we leave. No funny business."

Willa swallowed hard. "Lord… I ain't never even *seen* a place like that. Just read about it in the books you gave me."

"Me neither," Kathy admitted. She picked up a modest yellow cotton shirtwaist dress—perfect for daytime—and handed it to her friend. It reminded her of the dresses Janey had given her upstairs.

Gathering all of Willa's new belongings, they headed toward the stairs. As they passed the hallway, they glimpsed Janey wrapped in Carmine's arms, swaying gently as he whispered softly to her. Janey lifted her face to his and kissed him tenderly. Kathy noticed the usually stern Carmine almost smiling, kissing Janey in return before leading her away, one arm around her waist, the other hand on his cane.

"They seem so in love," Willa observed. "Strange seeing it. I mean, I know your Carmelo is like him, but it is still strange to see it."

"I think they truly are," Kathy agreed softly. "They are made for each other. I can feel it."

"And your Carmelo—is he here?" Willa asked eagerly.

Kathy smiled. "Yes. We had our reunion when you were gone."

"Is he okay? I mean, it's been eight months for you and his family and all…"

Kathy shook her head. "He's a little different. He's been through a lot so that will change ya. He'll be okay though. Never mind it. Don't mention anything I've told you about his family. I'm helping him. He's with me now, so he's gone be okay. So change quickly, and you can meet him."

Willa grinned excitedly. "I can't wait."

CHAPTER 9

HARLEM NEW YORK 1978

Present. The heavy *thunk* of Debbie's purse hitting the formica countertop echoed louder than she intended in the deserted salon, *Debbie's Place*.

Janey moved past her, the scent of her perfume trailing in her wake. With deliberate calm, she walked through the shadowed rows, her heels tapping on the black-and-white checkerboard linoleum. One by one, banks of fluorescent lights flickered and hummed to life overhead. The glare reflected harshly on the chrome-plated styling chairs, the glass shelves of rattail combs and perm rods, the posters of black women with impossibly tall Afros frozen in time—the lingering smells of peroxide, setting lotion, and hairspray mixed uneasily with the tension.

"Where's Willa?" Debbie asked, her voice tight. She watched Janey move like a panther surveying its territory.

"Home," Janey replied, her tone clipped. She stopped before a plush, avocado-green styling chair and sank into it, a queen claiming her throne. She carefully removed her small, black velvet pillbox hat and the delicate net veil that had obscured the upper half of her face. Her eyes, dark and unnervingly sharp, locked onto Debbie's. "I brought Coffey with me instead. Told her to stay parked out front in the Cadillac. Figured this... *reunion*... was best kept between you and me. Woman to woman." A ghost of a cold smile touched her ruby red lips. "Cousin to cousin."

Debbie flinched at the word 'cousin'. She glanced nervously towards the street visible through the salon's large plate-glass window, then back at Janey's unnervingly composed figure. She walked stiffly down the aisle and took the chair directly opposite, its vinyl squeaking under her weight. She sat ramrod straight, hands clasped in her lap like a shield. War had been declared.

"Kathy's gone, Janey," Debbie stated, the rehearsed words tasting like ash. "And Cassandra's home. It happened... fast. Too fast. They found her car off Route 17 in Jersey. Burnt down to the frame. There was... a body inside. A woman." Debbie swallowed hard, the image seared into her own nightmares. "They couldn't... We had a closed-casket service. We buried her last Tuesday. The hurt... it's raw for everyone."

Janey's crimson lips parted. A slash of defiance against her composed, mocha-brown face–slowly curled into a contemptuous smirk. "My Kathy," she stated, each word dropping like ice, "is *not* dead. Try again, Debbie. And this time, try the truth."

Debbie drew a shaky breath. "Matteo's out of prison, Janey."

A soft, utterly humorless laugh escaped Janey. "For how long this time? A weekend pass?"

"He's *out*. Pardoned," Debbie pressed on, her voice gaining a desperate edge. "And Carmelo... Carmelo's *dead*."

The smirk vanished from Janey's face like a snuffed candle. Her eyes narrowed to slits, pinning Debbie in place. The temperature in the salon seemed to drop ten degrees. Debbie started talking fast, the words tumbling out under the pressure of that murderous gaze.

"It started with the big arrests. You must have heard, even, hell, I don't know where you live now, but the news went everywhere. The Feds swept through Harlem like locusts. Took down Nikki Barnes and his whole damn 'Black Council'. Left a power vacuum big enough to drive a truck through." Debbie stumbled through the rest. "The mob smelled blood. They're moving in. Starting fires and shaking down businesses, Kathy worked hard to keep things clean… It's a different kind of war with the Wolf gone. And Matteo is finally Don. But he has enemies everywhere, even in his own family."

"I don't care about Mafia wars. What happened to Carmelo?" Janey demanded.

"Upstate." Debbie closed her eyes briefly. "Carmelo was there visiting Nino. Someone planted a bomb in Melo's Lincoln. Tore it apart. They said… they said there wasn't enough left of the men to fill a shoebox."

Debbie opened her eyes, meeting Janey's frozen stare. "Kathy… she went wild when she heard. I mean, it really broke her. Screamed it wasn't true and fought Brother when he tried to keep her from going out to Staten Island to confront Matteo and the Riccis. Came to me several nights later, eyes like a madwoman's. Said Carmelo *couldn't* be dead. She could feel him. Told me to watch the store, the books, everything. Said she was going to 'see someone' who could tell her the truth. To find out the truth. Then… she vanished. Just gone. A week later… Jersey. The car. The fire." Debbie spread her hands helplessly. "The cops, the papers… they're saying it's not connected, that it was just an accident, case closed."

She took another breath, plunging into the deepest betrayal. "Matteo… he doesn't believe it either. Not about Carmelo. Or Kathy. He thinks… he thinks they're *alive*. That they staged it, and he thinks… he thinks the answer is in Kathy's diaries. Don't ask me why, or what is in those diaries that could fix any of this, but Matteo is stuck on it. Sandy's been holed up in Kathy's house for days now, reading through them all. Matteo thinks if she reads enough, *remembers* enough… it'll lead him to the truth."

Silence descended, thick and suffocating. Janey sat perfectly still, only the icy fury in her eyes betraying the storm within. Debbie remembered the whispers about Janey – poison was her art, but the Senator she'd shot point-blank in California was proof she wasn't afraid to get her hands bloody. And she'd walked away clean. Another woman was burned in the electric chair for her crimes. Even now,

Kathy and Debbie could never figure out how Willa survived Janey's wrath, how Coffey came to be.

"Kathy," Janey's voice was a low, dangerous rasp, cutting the silence, "would *never* fake her death and leave Sandy behind. *Never.* Not for Carmelo, not for the Pope, not for God Almighty. That means this..." Janey pointed a long, manicured finger at Debbie, "... is *his* doing. The Wolf, she spent half her life trying to tame, finally bit the hand that loves him. The fucking bastard! I should have killed him when I had the chance!"

"What do you *want* from me, Janey? I'm telling you the truth," she insisted. "You and your sisters! You vanished! Paris, Ireland, Kathy said you and Willa dragged poor little Coffey everywhere after your husband died. You were ghosts in Hawaii the last time she spoke to you! Kathy stopped talking about you years ago. *How was I supposed to find you?* I tried! I called down to Butt's, asked the Browns about Izzy. They said they hadn't seen hide nor hair of her or you in two years! How *was* I supposed to tell you?"

Janey dismissed the plea with a flick of her wrist. "Spare me the theatrics. *Where* would they run? If they *did* run? Where would the Wolf take my girl to ground?"

"Are you even listening?" Debbie snapped, desperation turning to anger. "I *told* you, Matteo doesn't know! He thinks Kathy's diaries hold the key! That's why Sandy's reading them!"

"That child's head is empty," Janey hissed, standing, "full of as many holes as this cockamamie story you're spinning! Fake deaths? Mafia and FBI takedowns? Matteo *pardoned*? Burnt cars in Jersey?" She took a step towards Debbie, the soft life Carmine and the Marcellos' money provided, and the strange, ageless aura that always clung to her, making her seem impervious to time.

"It's *bullshit*. But I'm here now. I'm going to peel back every layer of this lie until I find the truth. Coffey and I will stay with Sandy."

"Wait, *no*!" Debbie surged to her feet, panic flaring. "You can't! Leave Cassandra out of this! She doesn't know about the Poison Cherry."

"Liar! She's reading her mother's diaries. What the hell do you think is in them?" Janey spat.

"Leave her out of it, Janey," Debbie pleaded. "Whatever you're planning. Leave her be."

Janey's sculpted eyebrows arched high. "*Leave her out*? You just sat there and confessed that *you* and Matteo are neck-deep in dragging her into it and making her pour over her mama's private thoughts like some... some *treasure map*! Diaries full of things that child *doesn't understand*! Like who her daddy is, and what her Mama did to keep that secret!" Janey's voice dropped to a venomous whisper. "I'd bet my last dime she's gonna find out, reading those 'stupid books' Kathy put her soul into and it's gonna snap what little sense she does have."

Debbie deflated, sinking back onto the edge of the chair. "I... I have a *plan*, Janey. A way to handle this. I check on Sandy every day. We *need* her to remember, naturally. The good *and* the bad. The past. We *need* those memories back. But you can't force them! It doesn't work like that! That's not what the doctors told Kathy after... after the accident, the seizures, the surgeries, the medication. This... the diaries, familiar things... It's *supposed* to be the way. Gentle. Natural. Kathy always told me that if something happened to her, to give Sandy those diaries. I swore to her I would."

Janey moved like lightning. Before Debbie could react, Janey's hand shot out, fingers like steel vices gripped Debbie's chin, forced her head up. Debbie gasped at the strength and the sudden intimacy of the assault. Janey's face was inches from hers, eyes burning with decades-old resentment, her irises golden like flames.

"I told Kathy," Janey said each word slow, her voice trembling with suppressed rage, "that *you* were the real poison in this family. Not me. Not Willa. Not Izzy. Not Mae. *You*. I never forgot, Debbie. Never forgot how you covered for that Wolf when he married that *puttana* Maria Romero. Smiling and encouraging Kathy to believe in her fantasy love while he slunk down to New Orleans, playing the dutiful boyfriend, filling her head with lies until her belly swelled with a baby like yours, except you got your prince and my Kathy only got shame!" Janey's grip tightened. "*I* had to show her the truth *you* knew about all along. You were a lying bitch then, Debbie. And you're a lying bitch now."

Debbie wrenched her chin free with a sob, dropping back into the chair. Hot tears welled, threatening to ruin her carefully applied mascara. "Get out!" Debbie choked, pointing a trembling finger towards the door. "Get out of my salon!"

Janey didn't hurry. She smoothed the front of her elegant black silk suit, walked back to her styling chair, and picked up her hat and purse with deliberate calm. She placed the hat precisely back on her head, the veil casting a slight shadow over her fierce eyes. She paused at the door, turning back for a final shot.

"I'll be staying with Sandy," she announced again, her voice regaining its chilling composure. "Whatever secrets you and Matteo think are buried in my sweet sugar-baby's broken mind, *I'm* going to find them first. And when I do," she unlocked the deadbolt with a decisive click, "I'll bring Kathy home myself."

The bell above the door jingled with obscene cheerfulness as Janey stepped out into the Harlem morning sun, sashaying towards the waiting Cadillac like a queen returning from battle. Debbie stood frozen for a second, then the dam broke. Sobs wracked her body as she crumpled inside. Janey's words were knives, twisting the oldest, deepest wound. Kathy *had* forgiven her for that sin, for the betrayal over Carmelo's marriage. But Debbie had never forgiven herself. Every kind word, every shared struggle in the hard years since, felt like ashes now after Janey's lashing.

The sudden, shrill ringing of the salon phone shattered her tears. It rang and rang, insistent, demanding. Wiping furiously at her smearing mascara with the back of her hand, Debbie walked towards the cluttered reception desk near the front. She snatched up the receiver.

"Why the hell aren't you answering? My guys called – said some woman showed up at the salon! I already have Junior bringing Sandy to my penthouse...."

"What? You have Sandy?" she said with relief.

"Of course! We're getting married. You forget? You were just supposed to grab your damn appointment book and come straight back!" Matteo's voice was a furious rasp on the line.

Of course, he had men watching, Debbie thought with a fresh wave of exhaustion. *Always watching her.* The tears came harder, uncontrollable gasps escaping her.

Matteo's tirade stopped abruptly. He heard the raw distress. "Debbie? Debbie! What happened? Who was there?"

She couldn't form words; only harsh, shuddering breaths crackled down the line.

A beat of silence, then Matteo's voice, lower, harder: "Stay there. Don't move. Don't talk to anyone. I'm on my way." The line went dead.

Debbie slowly replaced the receiver. The silence of the overlit salon pressed in again, now charged with a different kind of dread. She turned, her gaze sweeping over the empty chairs, the gleaming mirrors reflecting her own shattered reflection, the lingering scent of Janey's gardenias mixed with the acrid smell of her own fear. Mechanically, she walked past the silent hairdryers, through the archway leading to her small back office. She didn't turn on the light. She dropped onto the worn velvet sofa in the dark, pulled her knees to her chest, and waited for the next storm to arrive. The mysteries of Kathy and Carmelo's disappearance now had two ruthless, opposing forces digging – and Sandy, fragile and unaware, was caught squarely in the middle.

CHAPTER 10

LA REINE NOIRE - 1950

The humid breeze off the Mississippi clung to Kathy's skin and dampened her carefully styled hair as Carmelo guided her down moss-covered stone stairs through a crumbling courtyard off Bourbon Street. Somewhere above, the clip-clop of a mule cart and the distant wail of a trumpet spoke of the segregated city that existed in daylight. But here, behind an unmarked iron door, jazz pulsated like a living heartbeat. This was where another South breathed—underground, alive, and unapologetically free.

Aunt Janey swept in first, a regal silhouette in emerald silk that made the massive Sicilian bouncer snap to attention like a soldier before his general. "Evenin', Miss Janey," he murmured, his eyes darting nervously to her companion, Capo Carmine Boanno, whose diamond cufflinks caught the amber light. The bouncer didn't speak to Carmelo, who gently pushed Kathy and Willa forward to enter before him, but gave the young fighter a nod of unmistakable respect.

Then came the assault on the senses—the heat, the noise, the intoxicating aliveness of it all.

The speakeasy was a cathedral of sin and smoke, where morality came to die and be reborn as something more honest. Ceiling lighting dripped golden luminance onto a swirling dance floor, where Black musicians tore into a hypnotic mix of Zydeco, South Louisiana Creole-infused rhythm and blues, and swing music that had evolved from jazz. Their horns wept and soared with the passion of the truly free. Creole women in bias-cut gowns that cost more than most people's yearly wages laughed intimately with their men, who all looked to be of wealth and prominence. Sicilian men had several of their ladies on their arms. These men in sharply tailored suits, gold crucifixes glinting against black and curly chest hair, gazed at you no matter where you stepped. At the bar, a stunning light-skinned beauty passed aged whiskey to a mob captain with a scar carved through his left eyebrow like a badge of honor.

There were no "White Only" signs here. No segregated corners or apologetic glances. Just the mob's iron law, more absolute than any government decree: Money outranks color, always.

Kathy felt Carmelo's hand tighten possessively at her hip, his touch burning through the silk of her dress. "This is my world now," he bragged, his voice low and intense. "I want you to see it. All of it."

She glanced back over her shoulder at him, and without warning, he boldly brushed his lips across hers in a kiss that tasted of defiance. Kathy's eyes fluttered in shock—it was the first kiss he'd ever dared give her in public, around his people. She would rather die than kiss him in front of her father, yet here he was, claiming her openly.

The acceptance rendered her speechless, her heart hammering against her ribs as her gaze swept over the mobsters around the room, his tongue delving deeper. A few gave her sly smiles and appreciative looks, their eyes holding nothing but interest. None seemed angered or disgusted by their obvious affection.

Carmelo's smile was triumphant, almost boyish in its pride when their lips parted.

Then a gasp next to them made her snap out of it.

"Willa!" she called out urgently. "Carmelo!"

Two men had descended on Willa like sharks scenting blood—one to her right, another to her left, both easily twice her age and speaking at her simultaneously in rapid-fire French, English, and Italian. Willa looked terrified, overwhelmed by the aggressive attention. A man touched her chin.

Carmelo immediately stepped toward the predators, his entire demeanor shifting from lover to enforcer in the space of a heartbeat. He said a few quiet words that made both men step back with raised hands and apologetic smiles, then pulled Willa protectively closer to their group.

"Stay close to us," he commanded gently but firmly.

"Sorry," Willa mumbled, her voice small with embarrassment. Gone was any trace of the timid sharecropper's daughter from Mississippi. In her place stood a vision in champagne lace—Janey's borrowed pearls glowed like captured moonlight against Willa's slender throat, her dark eyes wide as saucers as she took in the velvet banquettes, the musical clink of champagne coupes, the sheer audacity of this hidden world. Willa touched her hair, newly styled into sleek finger waves, as if checking that this Cinderella transformation was fundamental and not some elaborate dream.

Carmelo moved through the crowd like a young prince, greeting other men with embraces and handshakes that spoke of genuine affection and hard-earned respect. The girls instinctively found each other's hands, seeking comfort in the familiar touch.

"You okay?" Kathy whispered.

"It's like... like walkin' inside a diamond!" Willa breathed, wonder replacing her earlier fear.

"You've never seen a diamond before," Kathy teased.

"I read about them in your books. And Debbie has that pretty bracelet with diamonds and sapphires. Remember?" she asked.

"Oh, yeah, you right," Kathy nodded.

Suddenly, Carmine Boanno's voice cut through the music. He stood in the center of the room with a crystal glass raised high, Janey at his side, grinning with feline satisfaction.

"*Salute al campione!*" he roared.

The response was instantaneous and thunderous. Mobsters, both Black and Sicilian, beautiful women, and Creole gamblers turned as one organism, glasses raised toward Carmelo in a toast that felt almost religious in its fervor. Saturday's fight wasn't just a boxing match—it was war declared. This would be a testament to power and territory that would echo through both the legitimate and criminal worlds.

A young man approached through the crowd, moving with the confidence of someone born to wealth and privilege. His gaze bypassed Kathy entirely, fixing on Willa with the focused intensity of a hunter spotting new prey. He was breathtakingly handsome—skin like warm caramel, wavy hair the color of copper slicked back to perfection, and clear green eyes that seemed to glow with their own inner light. He was so polished, so flawlessly groomed, that he didn't quite look real.

He murmured something in liquid French that neither Willa nor Kathy understood, the words flowing like music. Before either could respond, he lifted Willa's hand to his lips and kissed it with old-world gallantry, his eyes never leaving her face.

Kathy felt her own pulse quicken at the electric connection crackling between them. "Kathy? What's happening?" Willa whispered, her voice filled with confused wonder.

"I think he likes you," Kathy murmured back, unable to suppress her smile.

"I... what? What do I do?" Willa asked desperately.

The mysterious suitor extended his hand with a bow worthy of European royalty, then led her toward the dance floor with the confidence of a man who'd never been refused. Willa looked back over her shoulder, seeking rescue, but Kathy made the decision to let her go. This was Willa's moment—her chance to feel special, desired, beautiful in a way she'd never been allowed to experience. When the stranger swept her into his arms and she began to sway against him to the hypnotic rhythm, Kathy saw the instant connection that was worth savoring, worth the risk.

"Looks like Willa's found her match," Carmelo said, his arm slid around Kathy's waist to pull her back against the solid warmth of his chest. She relaxed into him, feeling safe and claimed as they swayed near the table where the Ricci crew held court.

"We shouldn't be so open," Kathy said, though her protest lacked conviction. "We could get in trouble. That kiss was enough. People were watching."

"We're fine here. My father's men don't care about this. My father doesn't care. Not really. Not about this," Carmelo murmured against her ear, his breath sending shivers down her spine.

"What?" Kathy twisted in his arms to face him, confusion clouding her features. "What does that mean—he doesn't care? Not really? Of course he does, Melo. He has a hit out on me. I can't return to Harlem. My father's life is hanging by a thread because of us!"

Carmelo's eyes widened slightly, and she caught something—a flicker of deceit, of knowledge he wasn't sharing. "Yes. Right. He wants us separated, but they... uhm, they don't know who you are here. They don't care about—"

"Stop." Kathy stepped back, her intuition screaming warnings in her head. "You're lying to me. I can see it in your eyes." Her voice grew stronger, more certain. "Don't treat me like I'm stupid, Carmelo Ricci."

"Kat... come on, don't be angry," he pleaded, reaching for her, but she evaded his grasp.

"Let me go!" She shoved him away with both hands, the force of her anger surprising them both. "You're lying to me about something important, and I won't stand for it! I felt it earlier, and I feel it now. Tell me. Tell me."

He opened his mouth. The truth was there, on his tongue. But one look into her lovely face and his heart raced so fast he could barely breathe, let alone speak. He closed his mouth and lost his nerve.

"Kat!" Carmelo called desperately as she stormed away from him.

Kathy headed straight for her aunt's table, her silk dress swishing with each determined step. Carmelo stood frozen in the middle of the dance floor, caught between truth and deception, unsure what words could possibly repair the damage.

A heavy hand dropped onto his shoulder like a lead weight. He glanced back to see Caesar's grim face. "It's time."

"In a minute. I need to talk to Kathy—she's upset," Carmelo said, starting to move toward his retreating girlfriend.

Caesar's grip tightened, stopping him cold. "It's Don Marcello. He wants to see you now. You can't say no to this."

Carmelo looked back toward the table, where Janey sat, watching him with those penetrating cat-like eyes, while Kathy settled beside her aunt, clearly venting her frustrations about his strange behavior. He could see Janey absorbing every word, filing away information with the calculating mind of a woman who collected secrets like other people collected jewelry.

He cursed under his breath, torn between duty and love, and reluctantly turned away from the woman who held his heart, toward whatever fate awaited him in the shadows of the criminal world he'd chosen to embrace.

* * *

"WILLA HAS FOUND a new love in the Quarter," Janey said.

Still fuming over Carmelo's sudden disappearance and his complete dismissal of her feelings, Kathy wasn't really listening. She glanced toward the dance floor and paused over the scene. Willa was wrapped in her gentleman's arms, but now they were kissing. Passionately! Lost in each other as if the rest of the world had ceased to exist.

“Whoa, we need to bring her back to the table," Kathy said, starting to stand.

Janey's manicured hand pressed firmly against her wrist. "Sit," she commanded softly.

"She doesn't know him," Kathy protested, concern evident in her voice.

“She's getting to it,” Janey smirked, clearly enjoying the romantic drama unfolding before them.

But Kathy had seen enough. She stood decisively and hurried onto the dance floor, weaving between other couples until she reached Willa. Without ceremony, she grabbed her friend by the arm and pulled her out of the stranger's embrace.

"Kathy!" Willa gasped, dazed and clearly intoxicated by more than just the kiss.

The suitor's expression hardened as his gaze shifted from Willa to Kathy, his mesmerizing eyes flashing with annoyance. He took a threatening step toward them, then suddenly froze. Kathy followed his line of sight and realized he was looking beyond them to the table where Janey sat watching the entire scene with an unwavering stare. A dare? Something more? The man's demeanor changed instantly—he gave Janey a respectful nod that seemed almost apologetic, winked at Willa, and then turned and melted back into the crowd without another word.

"Why did you do that?" Willa shouted, her face flushed with embarrassment and anger.

"You don't know him," Kathy said firmly, still watching the spot where the mysterious man had disappeared.

"So what, Kathy! I was having fun for once in my life!" Willa's voice cracked with disappointment.

"Did he give you something to drink?" Kathy said, and moved in closer to smell her breath.

"Leave me be!" Willa said as she stormed back toward their table.

Janey sat there smirking at Kathy as if the entire event was set for her entertainment. Between Carmelo's games and Willa's sudden attitude, and her aunt's trickery, Kathy had reached her breaking point. She threw her hands up in defeat and headed in the opposite direction. Maybe she should have something to drink. Initially, she walked toward the bar, but then spotted a lighted corridor that obviously led toward the restrooms.

She needed air. She needed space. She needed to be free.

CHAPTER 11

LA REINE NOIRE II - 1950

The cigar smoke hung thick as swamp mist, catching the dim glow of candlelight. Carmelo accepted the hand-rolled cigar, his smile a razor's edge in the gloom. "*Grazie,* Don Marcello, for your hospitality," he murmured, drawing deeply—smoke plumed from his lips—a dragon's breath, a silent vow. Carmine Boanno stood near the heavy velvet drapes, his stern gaze a physical weight. *Distrust radiated off him like heat.* But the Marcello men? They watched Carmelo with the cold appraisal of butchers sizing up a prize bull.

Don Stefano Marcello was a relic propped against crimson velvet. Seventy or older, if Carmelo had to guess. Skin like crumpled parchment stretched over brittle bones. He had no sons. Caesar's briefing echoed in Carmelo's mind: *Twelve daughters. Husbands stripped of their birth names, reborn as Marcellos. Blood diluted, loyalty enforced.*

Six of these adopted "sons" flanked the old Don now, crammed into the circular booth that dominated the speakeasy's left wing. Their eyes, flat and reptilian, tracked Carmelo's every flicker of expression.

"*Prego.*" The Don's voice was a dry rattle, the Sicilian dialect thick as tar. It wasn't a question. It was a test.

Carmelo's gaze slid to Carmine, then back to the ring of faces. He exhaled a slow stream of smoke through his nostrils again. Once upon a time, these men, natural-born killers like his father, would have frozen his blood with fear. Before his mother's suicide. Before the gunshot that tore through his father's shoulder. Before his big brother's mental collapse. Back when he was the baby of the family, he was protected and shielded from the harsh realities of the criminal world.

All of his innocence came and was taken before he understood that the snake-eyed evil festering beneath their tailored suits wasn't a perversion of tradition—*it was tradition's beating, rotten heart.*

Necessary evils?

No.

These men were the architects of destiny. A destiny he could not escape. The balance in this country is to provide for the darkness in men like them and him.

The Don leaned sideways, lips brushing the ear of the man on his right—Lenny Marcello, the eldest son-in-law, face shriveled with meanness. Lenny nodded once. His eyes, the color of dirty ice, locked onto Carmelo.

"Saturday," Lenny's voice scraped the air. "There will be no losses."

The silence that followed was absolute. Even the distant wail of a trumpet from the main floor seemed to choke itself off. The other Marcello sons-in-law didn't blink. The Don stared through hooded lids, a vulture perched on a tombstone. The unspoken threat hung heavier than the humidity: *Lose, and you lose everything. Your name. Your future. Maybe your breath.*

Carmelo carefully set his cigar on the crystal ashtray. The ember glowed like a malevolent eye. He leaned forward, elbows on the table, invading the Marcello circle's sacred space—a challenge.

"The Mississippi Mauler, Cotton King, whatever he calls himself, he bleeds like any man," Carmelo stated, his voice low, devoid of bravado. Pure, chilling fact. "He fights with his height and muscle, not skill. If this were a wrestling match, I would be concerned. *It is not.* There will be no footwork from him. No finesse to dodge, no skill to counter or escape. I will use that to my advantage. I fight for the blood in my veins. For the name *Ricci.*" Carmelo paused, letting the weight of his father's shadow fill the booth."And for the men who understand that territory isn't won with a ballot box... but with shattered bones. I fight and win for these agreements, such as, *La Cosa Nostra* would give the Sicilians unchecked power in the French Quarter."

Lenny's jaw tightened. One of the younger sons-in-law shifted with a smile of acceptance. The Don's papery hand twitched on the tablecloth.

"The Klan's fighter isn't just strong, he's a butcher, kid," Lenny countered. A crack appeared in his steel composure. "He trains for these matches with pure hate. Hates the white men who put him in that ring to face you, and he takes it out on every white face he fights. The only negro I ever seen kill three white men in the ring and get a goddamn bonus for it. They ain't sending him to box you. They're sending him to bury you. You grasp that?"

Carmelo's smile returned, arctic and sharp. "Rage is a wildfire. Burns hot, burns fast, burns blind. Read that once." He lifted the cigar, its ember pulsing like a tiny, furious heart in the gloom. "I'm a scalpel, Signore Marcello. Precise. Trained not just to win, but to slay any beast, white, Sicilian, or black. Even the Devil bleeds. Find me where the Mauller does. What is his weakness? Where is it? *Give me the cut.*"

Lenny sat back, a flicker of genuine surprise cutting through his disdain. Even Carmine Boanno, a statue in the corner, shifted his weight, his stern gaze sharpened. Carmelo saw it. The doubt etched on their faces. *Too young. Too pretty. Too arrogant to understand the meat-grinder waiting for him in that ring.*

They didn't know.

He'd survived Cosimo Ricci's hammer. Lessons disguised as beatings that cracked his jaw and his soul. He'd lost Kathy once, a wound that still seeped, making every moment with her feel stolen. Pain wasn't his enemy; it was his life. He was learning the language, syllable by agonizing syllable.

"Let the Mauler choke on his rage. Let the Klan hide in their sheets. When that bell rings," Carmelo's voice dropped, cold and absolute, "they'll learn the difference between anger... and annihilation. Get me this boxer's weakness. I'll give you New Orleans."

One of the younger sons-in-law shot a questioning look at Lenny, the clear favorite of the Don. A curt nod went between the men. The young man excused himself, disappeared into the smoky shadows to retrieve Carmelo's demanded intelligence. Carmelo held Lenny's gaze, letting the predatory calculation in his own eyes reflect back – the cold fury of the Wolf taking shape.

Carmine Boanno dipped his chin. A fraction of an inch.

The Don stirred. A skeletal hand, liver-spotted and trembling slightly, lifted from his tailored sleeve, knuckles presented.

Carmelo stood. He leaned *into* the Marcello circle's power, grasped the Don's frail hand, and pressed his lips to the heavy gold ring – a gesture of respect that felt like a claim. Only one thought crossed Carmelo's mind. The same thought that surfaced when his father returned home after Mama's Stewarts' mending and was handicapped to his bed.

Your time is ending old man. Mine is coming.

Caesar materialized beside him as they stepped away from the booth. "*Sangue freddo, Melo,*" he murmured, a rare note of admiration in his voice. "Like ice."

Before Carmelo could respond as he turned away from the men, movement caught his eye – Kathy, weaving past the crowded bar, heading towards the other side of the room. The tension in her shoulders was visible even across the room. He needed to reach her, to anchor himself in something real before the uncertainty settled in.

"I need to talk to Kathy," he started after her.

Carmine's cane tapped the floor, and he swiftly blocked his path. The older man studied him, his expression unreadable.

"Impressive," he rasped.

Carmelo offered a tight smile. "You expected less?"

"Expected a boy facing lions," Carmine countered, a dry chuckle rattling in his chest. "Saw a man. You move like him, you know. Your father. Knew Cosimo back in the old country."

Carmelo's smile vanished. "I am *nothing* like him."

Carmine's bushy eyebrows lifted. "Oh? Not a fan of Papa? I see. Cosimo wasn't a hero. But fear? That wasn't in Cosimo's blood. It isn't in yours either. That bravery you carry?" He tapped his own temple with a finger. "It's your inheritance, boy. Hard-earned. Use it on Saturday. Or it'll bury you alongside the Mauler. Because if the Klan kills you, we kill him in your honor. Don Marcello has ordered it."

Carmelo's eyes stretched.

Carmine gave him a sly nod and moved away. Carmelo looked over to Caesar to see if he heard the message within the message.

"Am I in trouble here? You and Matteo have prepped me, but he's a giant. He's a killer." Carmelo said, his bravado now wavering.

Caesar gave him the best smile he could. "You need to be careful and always alert in the ring. Not cocky. It's not bravery that makes you a winner, Melo. It's your heart. It's made of something tough."

Carmelo smiled. "That's Caesar."

"No problem. I have my orders. Before they can get to you, they have to go through me," said Caesar.

* * *

JAZZ BLED THROUGH THE WALLS, a frantic counterpoint to the sudden silence between Kathy and the man leaning against the peeling wallpaper. He was a slab of muscle in a cheap suit, fedora pulled low, shadowing eyes that tracked her like a predator sizing prey.

"Excuse me," Kathy said, her voice steady despite the ice sliding down her spine. She moved forward, aiming for the faint outline of a door at the hall's end—the promised exit to the courtyard bathrooms.

He didn't move aside. Instead, he unfolded himself from the wall, planting his bulk squarely in her path. The dim light caught the sneer twisting his lips.

"You lost, sugar?" The drawl was thick, laced with a malice that had nothing to do with directions.

"No." Kathy kept her chin level, meeting his gaze. Harlem had taught her that much. "Just need to pass." She took another step.

He moved faster than his size suggested. One moment blocking the way, the next lunging. Shock froze Kathy for a critical heartbeat. Then instinct screamed: *RUN!*

She whirled, dress whipping around her legs. A choked cry

escaped her lips. Too slow. An arm like an iron bar locked around her waist, yanking her off her feet. A sweaty, calloused palm clamped over her mouth, crushing her lips against her teeth, the taste of stale tobacco and grime flooding her senses. She kicked wildly, heels scraping his shins, connecting with nothing solid. Her hands flew up, nails raking desperately for his eyes, clawing at the shadowed flesh beneath the fedora's brim. She felt skin tear, heard a guttural curse spat in a language she didn't know – Italian? Sicilian dialect? – sharp and vicious. He grunted, tightening his grip, hauling her backwards towards that ominous door. Panic, cold and absolute, seized her. *Outside. If he gets me outside...* Images flashed – dark alley, rough brick, silence swallowing her screams. She redoubled her efforts, bucking, twisting, a wild animal caught in a snare. But he was stronger, fueled by a cruel purpose, his breath hot and rank on her neck, his tongue flicking at her skin as he chuckled at her terror. He was winning. The door handle loomed, inches from his reaching hand.

Carmelo.

He'd seen her slip away, seen the unease on her face, and heard the stifled sound that wasn't just the saxophone's wail. What he saw now was a tableau ripped from his deepest nightmares: Kathy, small and fierce, engulfed by a brute, being dragged towards darkness. The fragile control Carmelo had worn like armor in the Marcello meeting shattered.

He charged them like a bull. A force of nature unleashed. No shout, no warning, it was just a blur of motion. He didn't *attack* the man; he *erased* the space between them.

One fist, driven with the piston force of a boxer's knockout blow, slammed into the side of the attacker's head. The sickening *crunch* of bone meeting bone was audible even over the distant band. The man's grip on Kathy vanished instantly. She dropped, stumbling, gasping, crawling backwards on her hands as her assailant reeled, stunned.

Carmelo didn't pause. Rage, cold and incinerating, consumed him. His fists became pistons, hammering into the man's face, throat, chest – a brutal, rhythmic tattoo of violence. Left hook to the jaw, snapping his head back. A right cross splits his lip wide open. Uppercut driving into the solar plexus, forcing a wheezing gasp.

The man crumpled against the wall, sliding down, trying feebly to raise his arms. Carmelo followed him down, kneeling, driving his knuckles into the already ruined face–thud, thud, thud. The blood sprayed in dark arcs onto the grimy wallpaper, onto Carmelo's white shirt, onto Kathy's shoes. The man's pleas were gurgling, incoherent bubbles in the mess of his mouth. The relentless jazz from the main room drowned out the sounds of breaking bones, a grotesque soundtrack.

Kathy stood frozen, not in horror at the violence itself. She'd seen her father gunned down in the bakery, witnessed the casual cruelties of the South. It was Carmelo and the violence from him that stopped her heart. This wasn't the charming boy who promised life could be sweeter. This was a primal fury brought to life. A terrifying avatar of retribution wearing Carmelo's face. The sheer, focused brutality of it stole her breath.

As the man lay groaning, a broken, bloody heap who spat crimson onto the floorboards, Carmelo surged to his feet. His chest heaved, his knuckles raw and slick in blood. His eyes, when they found Kathy, weren't human.

He didn't comfort her. He *grabbed* her upper arm, fingers digging in, and shoved her roughly towards the moaning figure on the floor.

"Kick him!" The command was a guttural snarl, ripped from a place beyond reason.

Kathy flinched, stumbling. "What?!" Disbelief warred with the adrenaline screaming through her veins.

"KICK HIM!" Carmelo roared, the sound raw and terrifying in the confined space. He pointed a bloody finger at the man. "NOW!"

Kathy's gaze snapped down to the attacker. The fedora was gone, revealing a face pulped and swelling. One eye was already sealed shut with blood and swelling flesh. But it was the *intent* she saw beneath the damage, the predatory malice that had been in his eyes moments before. The reality slammed into her: *He was going to rape me. He would have done worse. He's done it before to girls like me.*

A coldness, different from fear, settled in her gut. A resolve forged in terror and fury.

She lifted her foot. Not a tentative nudge, but a deliberate, powerful stomp, driving the heel of her shoe straight into the man's ribs.

A wet, cracking sound. A strangled scream that was more a desperate wheeze.

"AGAIN!" Carmelo's voice was iron.

Kathy kicked. Harder. Aiming for the same spot. She felt something give beneath the point of her shoe. Another agonized gasp. Then, with a surge of pure, furious energy, she drew her leg back and kicked him square in the face. Her heel connected with his nose with a sickening *crunch*. His head snapped back, hitting the floor with a dull thud. He convulsed once, then lay still except for shallow, ragged breaths.

Carmelo didn't wait. He seized Kathy's hand–not gently, but with a fierce, possessive grip–and hauled her towards the back door. He kicked it open, revealing the stinking, garbage-strewn alley behind the speakeasy. The sudden rush of cooler, foul air hit Kathy like a physical blow. She stumbled, doubling over, sobbing, gasping for breath that wouldn't come, her body trembling violently.

Before she could straighten, Carmelo was on her. He grabbed her shoulders, spinning her around to face him. He put her up against the wall. The moment he did, the sky exploded, and rain soaked them both. His eyes, still blazing with residual fury, scanned her face, her body, searching for injury.

"Did he hurt you?!" The question was a demand, laced with a terrifying promise of more violence if the answer was yes.

"Yes!" Kathy gasped, the word torn from her, encompassing the violation of the grip, the terror, the taste of his hand. She saw the madness flare again in Carmelo's eyes – the boxer ready to return to the ring – and instantly she corrected her statement, her voice stronger, "No! I mean… not like that. He didn't… he didn't get the chance."

The tension in Carmelo's frame eased a fraction, but the intensity didn't fade. He shook her, not gently. "NEVER, Kathy! Never let a man put his hands on you like that! You fight! You hear me?! SCRATCH, BITE, KICK, GOUGE! YOU FIGHT LIKE HELL!" His voice cracked, raw with a fear deeper than anger.

"I tried, Melo!" she shouted at him in the rain.

"Try harder, damn it! I won't always be here! You fight, goddamn it! YOU FIGHT! You kill anyone who tries to hurt you! YOU ARE HENRY FREEMAN'S DAUGHTER! You're my fucking girl! You're no ones victim! Please Kathy! Promise me! You'll fight!" he broke before her. Tears consumed him, the rain washing them down his face. "I can't lose you. Ever! I can't ever let anybody take you from me. I won't survive it again. I won't!"

Tears streamed down Kathy's face, hot and cleansing. She nodded, a sharp, jerky movement. "I promise, Melo. I'll fight harder. I'll always fight back. Always," she whispered and kissed his face.

"I'm okay. I'm okay," she said and held his face.

The ferocity drained from Carmelo's face, replaced by a sudden, overwhelming vulnerability. The Wolf inside of him receded, leaving just a man trembling with adrenaline and terror. He returned her kiss with more passion than she offered. Pinning her to the wall. The rain meant nothing. The exposure meant nothing. It was only the deep, unyielding love he felt that held them together. Her legs went up around his waist. He ripped down his zipper, his tongue delving in and out of her mouth as he forced his cock up into her. One thrust after another, and he went deeper and deeper. She clung to him. And let their love explode. As the passion dimmed, so did the rain to a drizzle, and everything centered on their slowed breathing. She didn't even remember why they fought. She just wanted to stay with him forever.

She pressed her face against his neck, inhaling the scent of sweat, cigar smoke, and the metallic tang of violence. In that filthy alley, amidst the reek of garbage and the fading echoes of terror, they clung to each other not just as lovers, but as soldiers binding wounds after a skirmish in an endless, brutal war.

CHAPTER 12

SEVEN MONTH'S EARLIER - NEW YORK

Carmelo lay still in the predawn gloom, Kathy curled against his chest like a secret he'd stolen from the world. Her breath warmed his skin, a gentle contrast to the harsh memory of the night's violence.

After the fight, the Marcello crew had dragged the offending soldier—one of their own—into the alley's deeper shadows. Don Marcello's command had been swift, delivered with the casual finality of his authority: *Silenzio permanente.* An insult to a Ricci demanded a blood payment. The man's strangled cry had disappeared into the darkness soon after the gunshot. It was just another lost sound in a city built on secrets.

But Carmelo had buried that grim punctuation beneath borrowed moments of normalcy—Kathy's fingers intertwined with his own, cheap red wine softening his senses, Willa's wide-eyed laughter as Janey spun enchanting tales of Creole balls. They'd laughed louder than necessary, drank enough to blur reality's sharp edges, and stumbled back to the Boanno home in a joyous tangle. Too weary for passion, they'd shed their clothes and collapse into cool sheets, clinging to each other until sleep took hold. Kathy had drifted off immediately, her body fitting against his with effortless trust, anchoring him until exhaustion finally claimed him too.

Now, in the gentle stillness before dawn, Kathy slept on. Pale light traced softly along her cheek, the sweep of her eyelashes, her lips slightly parted in peaceful repose. She seemed untouchable—an angel.

Carmelo stared at the ceiling, the heaviness in his chest surpassing any blow from any opponent he'd faced. Three days. That was all that remained left, separating this delicate dream from the violent storm awaiting him in the ring.

His gaze returned to her sleeping form. Her hair fanned darkly across the pillow, lips softly parted, impossibly delicate in slumber. She was his compass, his sanctuary, his entire trembling world. The terror of losing her was not merely a thought; it was an abyss opening beneath him, colder and darker than any grave. More than death itself, he feared the moment her eyes would dim upon finally seeing the truth unmasked.

Brooklyn, New York (Months Earlier)

"Melo... Mama?"

Carmelo jolted awake. Nino loomed over his bed, a mountain of a man clutching a threadbare teddy bear—the one Mama had scrubbed stains from a hundred times. Moonlight bled through the curtains, painting Nino's face in streaks of silver and shadow. His eyes were swollen, raw from crying.

"Melo... Mama?" he whimpered again, his voice breaking like a child's.

Carmelo sat up, his heart aching like his brothers for their mother. *"Go back to bed, Nino,"* he whispered.

But Nino's breath hitched. His fists clenched. Then—

"Mama! Mama! Mama! Mama!" he screamed. The desperate cry was a hammer blow to Carmelo's heart. Nino began hitting himself in the temple, hard, the way he did when the world became too much. Carmelo got out of bed and grabbed his brother's wrists. The teddy bear tumbled to the floor.

"Shhh..." Carmelo picked it up and pressed the bear back into Nino's massive hands, his own voice cracking. *"Mama's coming. She's coming."*

The lie tasted like ash.

Nino crumpled, his sobs muffled. Carmelo guided him back to his bed, tucking the covers around him like armor. He smoothed Nino's sweat-damp hair—just as Mama used to—and hummed the old Sicilian hymn she'd sung at the stove, her voice warm with saffron and garlic. The sound scraped his throat raw.

It took forever for Nino's breathing to even out. When sleep finally claimed him, Carmelo slid to the floor, his back against the bedframe. The house was too quiet. Too empty.

He reached under his bed, fingers brushing dust before closing around the shoebox. Inside, the iron hammer gleamed dully in the moonlight—the same one his father had swung into his ribs, his spine, his skull. Beneath it lay Kathy's letters, their edges soft from being handled too much.

And then, the one thing he couldn't bear to touch but couldn't bear to burn:

Mama's letter.

The paper whispered as he unfolded it. The scent of her rosewater perfume clung to the fibers, faint but unmistakable. Carmelo wiped his eyes with the heel of his hand. Then, in the suffocating dark, he read her words again.

Each sentence.

Each word.

My Dearest Carmelo,

If you are reading this, the waters of the East River have taken me. Forgive me, figlio mio, for the sin I commit this day. Forgive me for leaving you, and for the burden this letter places upon your soul. Know that I stand before God now, guilty of self-murder, my eternal soul condemned to toil in fire.

I accept this torment willingly. It is the price I pay for your future and the survival of our blood.

I have watched. I have judged. I have loved my three sons with a mother's heart. I have tried. The future of the famiglia rests on the shoulders that must bear the impossible. It cannot be Nino. My sweet firstborn, his mind forever trapped in innocence... the world would devour him whole. He needs protection. It cannot be Matteo. My second son burns with pride like his father, but his fire is brittle. When he learns of my death – how I died – that brittle pride will shatter. He will need healing, Carmelo. He will need you, just as Nino will. He does not have the spine to lead. He does everything from his heart. Do not let Matteo's toughness fool you.

It must be you, Carmelo. My youngest. My fiercest. My sacrifice.

I watched your father's hammer break your bones. I saw your eyes, figlio. There was nothing but defiance. You spat blood and threats instead of begging for mercy. You shielded me even as the blows fell, refusing to apologize or submit.

You have your father's strength, cunning, and ruthlessness—everything that makes him a Ricci. But unlike him, you still have a heart that fights for something, not just against. You fight for us.

But your heart, my brave son... it is also your vulnerability. I know about the girl. Kathy. I see how she pulls you towards a life beyond what I had dreamed for you. That life is a dream, Carmelo. A beautiful, deadly dream. Cosimo knows. He will use her to break you, to destroy you before you can stop it. The order is already whispered: the black death on her, on her family.

My death is the only message I could send to you and your father to stop this war between you. To force you to see the truth. You need each other. You will be the head of the family, the heir he wanted. You will take your father's place because it is the only way to protect those you love, including Kathy. But to gain his trust, you will have to make a sacrifice. You will marry Maria Romero. Hear me, Carmelo. This is my only request in death.

This marriage is your defense. It restores your father's pride from the shame of your running away with a colored girl. Use his pride. Negotiate with your father. Tell him you will marry Maria, you will step into your birthright as he always demanded... but only if the hit on Kathy and her family is lifted. Permanently. He will agree. A son, finally, for him to mold would be his greatest temptation. He will secure a powerful alliance, which is worth the life of one black girl to him. It is the only way to save her life, Carmelo. The only shield you can raise between her and Cosimo's vengeance.

I know what I ask will break your heart. It will break hers. This I know. Sometimes, figlio, the deepest love demands the cruelest sacrifice. To protect her, you have to let her go.

Do not let my soul burn in vain. Unite our broken family. And one day, when you are strong enough, finish what your father started with that hammer. Break him.

I loved you. I love you.

Mama

CARMELO WEPT until his chest ached and throat burned raw—silent, racking sobs of a man whose childhood had died with his mother. Tears fell onto the worn floorboards as grief consumed him completely.w

When no more tears would come, he wiped his face and made the sign of the cross. He pressed his lips to his mother's letter, tasting salt and sorrow on the paper, then folded it carefully and placed it with Kathy's love letters—artifacts from another lifetime. As he slid the box back under his bed, his fingers closed around the cold steel of the hammer.

The weight of it felt heavier than before, as if it had absorbed some essential piece of his soul.

He drew in a deep, shuddering breath, held it until his lungs burned, then exhaled slowly through parted lips. Each movement felt deliberate, ritualistic—a condemned man's final preparations. The journey to his parents' bedroom felt both endless and too brief. He hadn't crossed that threshold since the terrible morning when he'd collected his mother's burial clothes for the ceremony held at a funeral home instead of the Catholic church. Now he paused before the heavy oak door, his hand hovering over the brass handle for a long moment before pushing it open into suffocating darkness.

The room reeked of stale cigarettes, unwashed sheets, and the bitter medicinal smell of a man slowly dying from his wounds. Heavy curtains blocked every trace of natural light, creating a tomb-like atmosphere that seemed fitting for what was about to unfold.

His father lay sprawled across the massive four-poster bed like a broken king on his deathbed, his once-powerful frame diminished by pain and grief. The moment Carmelo's footsteps whispered across the carpet, Cosimo's eyes snapped open. Without hesitation, he raised a chrome-plated pistol with his good arm—the left one, since Carmelo's bullet had rendered his right shoulder completely useless—and aimed it directly at his son's heart.

Carmelo stood perfectly still, the hammer hanging loose at his side like an executioner's tool. He felt no fear, only a strange sense of relief. Death would be infinitely preferable to fulfilling his mother's last request.

"Go ahead," Carmelo said quietly, his voice steady as stone. "It would be a mercy."

Father and son stared at each other across the chasm of mutual destruction they'd created—two Ricci men who'd lost everything that mattered, including each other. After what felt like hours, Cosimo slowly lowered the weapon, his eyes studying his youngest son with an expression that bordered on recognition.

"I will take care of Nino," Carmelo began, his voice carrying the hollow tone of a man reciting his own death sentence. "I will find Matteo and bring him home." He paused, the next words sticking in his throat like broken glass. "And I will marry Maria Romero."

Cosimo's eyebrows drew together in confusion. Despite everything—the shooting, the months of recovery, the poisonous hatred between them—this was not what he was sure his father expected to hear.

"You will marry Maria Romero?" he asked, his voice hoarse from disuse. "Who asked you to marry her?"

"Madre. She asked. I will marry her, Padre, under one condition." Carmelo's grip tightened on the hammer until his knuckles went white. "You lift the black death order on the Freeman family. You inform Bumpy Johnson that a permanent truce has been established between our families. You do that, and I will fulfill Madre's dying wish and whatever you demand of me."

Cosimo struggled to push himself up to a sitting position, his damaged arm hanging useless at his side. He set the pistol aside on the nightstand with deliberate care, never taking his eyes off his son's face.

"Why?" The word came out as barely more than a whisper. "Why have you decided this now?"

Carmelo's laugh was bitter. "Mama is gone. Dead. You might as well have pulled the trigger yourself," Carmelo said.

"You've already killed the boy in me. I don't care what happens to me as your son anymore. Mama's gone. Her death has to mean something. So. You win. Because what she wanted was for you to win. To give you a daughter. To give you a family. To be the perfect wife. And you never allowed it. Now she wants me to do the same."

Cosimo's gaze fell to the hammer in his son's hand—that terrible reminder of the night he'd lost control, the night he'd beaten his own child with the same tool.

And then, for the first time since Lucia's funeral with only two sons at his side, the great Don Cosimo Ricci broke completely.

"I loved Lucia. I loved her and I will burn in hell next to her for making her do what she did," he said.

Don Cosimo wept with the raw anguish of a man who'd destroyed everything he'd ever loved. For his wife, whose gentle spirit he'd crushed beneath his brutality. For his sons, whom he'd made into weapons instead of men. For the family legacy he'd poisoned with his own hands. Every night in that tomb-like bedroom, he prayed to a God who'd stopped listening, begging for the impossible return of the woman who'd been his conscience, his redemption, his only humanity.

Carmelo watched his father's breakdown with empty eyes, feeling only distant satisfaction that justice had finally come. Without a word, he turned and walked out, leaving Cosimo to drown in his choices.

He returned the hammer beneath his bed with the reverence of laying flowers on a grave, then slipped under the covers beside Nino. His brother slept on, innocent and unaware that his world had just shifted on its axis.

Only then, in the darkness beside the one pure soul left in the Ricci family, did Carmelo cry—not for what he'd lost, but for what he'd just agreed to become. A liar. He wept for Kathy.

CHAPTER 13

THE TREMÉ

Kathy felt wonderfully renewed when she woke. Carmelo, of course, slept like the dead beside her. She tried twice to rouse him gently, but it was the third attempt that finally stirred him—and his response was to pull her closer and make love to her with sleepy passion. Not that she minded in the least.

Intimacy with him had transformed into something addictive and deliciously wicked. He had guided her to lie on her stomach, his body covering hers as he loved her from behind with slow, deliberate intensity. Twice she buried her face in the pillow when the sensations became overstimulating, her body responding to his surging cock with an urgency that surprised her. The weight of him above her, the steady rhythm of his movements that seemed to reach deeper into her very soul—it was all breathtakingly wonderful. Soon she was on her knees with her head down on the pillow while he was behind her delivering hip thrusts and his surging dick until she cried out for mercy.

When he finally found his release, she discovered her own, their bodies moving together in perfect, synchronized bliss as they collapsed flat to the bed.

Now, after a refreshing bath, she had changed into a cheerful floral summer dress and pinned her hair into a neat ponytail to avoid dealing with the tangles from yesterday's rain. As she descended the stairs, she heard her Aunt Janey's melodious voice mingling with Willa's bright laughter and the sound of an unfamiliar man speaking. Not with the hard Sicilian accent of Boanno—this man possessed the smooth, languid drawl of a true New Orleanian.

She stepped off the last stair and made her way to the sun-drenched garden room, where she found Janey and Willa enjoying breakfast with their visitor. The man turned at her approach, and her breath caught—it was the Creole gentleman from the speakeasy.

He was even more striking in the morning light than he had been in the smoky amber glow of the underground club. He stood gracefully from his chair, revealing a tall, lean frame draped in an impeccably tailored tan linen suit that spoke of both wealth and refined taste. His crisp white shirt was left casually open at the collar, suggesting a man comfortable with his own sophistication.

His skin was the warm color of café au lait, smooth and unmarked except for the faint lines around his eyes that appeared when he smiled. Those eyes—a mesmerizing shade of golden honey—seemed to hold secrets and promises. But it was his hair that truly set him apart: thick waves, the rich color of ground cinnamon, expertly slicked back from his aristocratic features to reveal a broad forehead and sharp cheekbones that could have been carved by a master sculptor. His full lips curved into a smile that was both charming and slightly dangerous, the kind that had undoubtedly broken hearts across New Orleans.

Everything about him radiated the confidence of money and privilege—from his perfect posture to the way he held his coffee cup with elegant fingers that had never known manual labor. He was polished perfection, a man who belonged in drawing rooms and private clubs, yet there was something in his gaze that suggested hidden depths beneath the refined surface.

"*Bonjour*, mademoiselle," he said, his voice carrying the musical cadence of refinement.

"Good morning?" Kathy locked eyes with Janey in surprise, clearly wondering why this man was there.

"I don't believe we were properly introduced last evening. I am Jean-Baptiste, but everyone calls me JB." He took her hand and brushed his lips across her knuckles. She glanced toward Willa, who was positively glowing like a lustrous pearl in her crisp white summer dress, a delicate magnolia blossom tucked behind her ear. Janey's ruby red lipstick on her lips.

"Nice to meet you. I'm Kathy."

"*Oui, ma chère,* I have been told many lovely things about you," he said smoothly, pulling out a chair with fluid grace. "*S'il vous plaît,* join us for *petit déjeuner*."

Kathy sat and studied him carefully. He was undeniably handsome, carried himself with impeccable manners, and wore an expensive cologne that spoke of European sophistication. Yet something about him set her teeth on edge. She hadn't forgotten the sharp look he'd given her when she'd interrupted his pursuit of Willa the night before—a flash of cold displeasure that had revealed something calculating beneath his charming exterior. There was an air of entitled arrogance about Jean-Baptiste that made her instinctively distrust him, no matter how perfectly he played the role of gentleman suitor.

"JB arrived this morning to ask permission to take Willa to Café du Monde," Janey explained with a knowing smile.

JB gave Kathy a polite but measured nod. "*Bien sûr,* it is segregated, but certain established families have... *arrangements*. I could ensure she and I enjoy some *beignets* and café au lait without difficulty. Then perhaps a stroll through Congo Square—even during the week, there is music and street entertainment."

"I told him you were her guardian and the decision was yours," Janey said smoothly.

"Please, Kathy! I really want to go," Willa pleaded, her eyes bright with excitement.

Kathy studied JB, who leveled his evergreen-colored eyes on her with unwavering confidence. Her mind flashed back to her attacker, to the promise Carmelo had made her swear—never let a man hurt her unpunished. Then she looked at sweet Willa, so naive and hungry for attention. There was something smugly entitled about the man before her, and she trusted her instincts completely.

"I'll speak to Carmelo. Willa will not go anywhere without both of us accompanying you to chaperone."

"Kathy!" Willa protested indignantly.

"I'm sure he'll agree. Come back in two hours and we'll be ready for our *adventure*," Kathy said firmly.

The confident smile on Jean-Baptiste's face dimmed noticeably. He gave Kathy a curt nod and sipped his freshly squeezed orange juice with deliberate calm. Kathy glanced up at Pinkie, who stood quietly in the corner—there was clear approval in the young woman's expression. No matter how much Willa pouted, she knew she'd made the right choice.

"*Très bien*, I shall return in a few hours," he said, pushing back his chair and glancing toward Janey. "*Madame* Janey, *c'est toujours un plaisir*."

"Nice to see you again, Jean-Baptiste," Janey replied warmly.

"*Ma belle* Willa, I cannot wait to show you the real Tremé," he said with renewed charm. Elmer appeared to escort him to the door while Pinkie began clearing his place setting.

"Kathy! Why? I don't need a chaperone!" Willa insisted, crossing her arms.

"You do! And I need an explanation, Auntie. Why let that man in here? Who is he really?" Kathy demanded.

Janey's smile turned calculating. "He's a Thibodaux, *chère*. His great-grandfather owned one of the largest sugar plantations before the Civil War. The family transitioned to sugar refining and distribution after reconstruction. They're among the ten wealthiest Black families in the world."

"Really? A plantation?" Willa frowned. "They owned slaves?"

Janey nodded slowly. "Louisiana is different, *ma petite*, and so are the Blacks and Creoles here. JB is one of the most sought-after young men in this city. And he has developed quite a taste for pretty girls like you."

Willa's smile brightened, but Kathy's expression darkened. "Well, he won't get a taste that's for sure."

Janey gave a light chuckle. "*Il sait mieux*—he knows better than to hurt my family."

"Did you tell him Willa was your family?" Kathy snapped, growing angrier by the minute.

"*Mais non*, she's a guest," Janey said dismissively. "You are my family."

"That's what I thought." Kathy turned her stern gaze to Willa. "You want to go?"

"Yes! Yes, I do! He's so handsome and charming. I like him," Willa said dreamily.

"Then here are the rules. We go with Carmelo, and you can let him hold your hand—but that is all. No kissing, no inappropriate touches. And you will not slip away with him no matter what sweet words he whispers. You stay with me at all times, Willa. If you don't, I'll have Carmelo do to him what he did to that man behind the speakeasy—the one I told you about last night."

Janey chuckled knowingly. "Carmine was quite upset about that incident."

"Do you hear me, Willa?"

"Yes, Kathy," Willa said softly, lowering her gaze in submission.

"Can I speak to you, Auntie? Alone!" Kathy pushed back from the table and marched out. Janey dabbed delicately at the corner of her mouth with her linen napkin and rose from her chair with deliberate grace to follow.

Kathy swept into the music room with its magnificent grand piano and began pacing. Janey entered and closed the French doors behind her with a soft click, sealing them in for privacy.

"Why did you let that man near her after what you witnessed last night? Why is everything a source of amusement to you? You act like we're here for your personal entertainment!" Kathy exploded.

Janey's pleasant smile evaporated. "Careful, niece."

"No!" Kathy's voice cracked like a whip. "She is young and sweet and trusting. And he is a predator—you know it! You know it! You act like you're some defender of women, but you're ready to hand her off to any man who knocks on your door with the right pedigree."

Janey took a threatening step toward Kathy, her honey-colored eyes flashing dangerously, but Kathy held her ground with Elliott defiance. "Did I hand her off? Did I? I gave you the decision. You could have sent him away ceremoniously, and the matter would have been settled. Looks to me like you're the one feeding poor Willa to the jackal."

"Why is this all a game to you?" Kathy shouted, her voice echoing off the high ceilings.

"Because life is!" Janey's mask finally slipped, revealing the steel beneath the silk. "You're an Elliott, and I'm raising you to be one. The reason you agreed to this charade is because we Elliott girls don't run from danger—we walk straight into it. We don't cower, we stand up for ourselves, and we make damn sure anyone who hurts the people we love pays dearly for it." Her voice dropped to a deadly whisper. "Last night, Carmelo beat that man nearly to death, as he should have, niece. But you? You should have cut his throat while he still drew breath. If Willa is under your protection, then protect her. It's not my fucking job—it's yours!"

Kathy stood in stunned silence, processing the brutal truth in her aunt's words.

Janey's predatory smile returned. "Creole men, *ma chère,* are every bit as deadly as the Sicilians in this town when it comes to young dark-skinned girls who catch their fancy. You keep your eyes on him."

With that pronouncement, she turned and walked from the room, leaving Kathy alone with her racing thoughts.

Kathy sighed deeply and rubbed her temples as unwanted memories surfaced—flashes of her attacker's leering face, the primal rage she'd witnessed in Carmelo's eyes, the way he'd turned that violence on her and demanded she participate in the retribution. And now

Janey with her twisted games and brutal lessons. She didn't want a life steeped in violence, but she was born from it. She was Henry Freeman's daughter, and despite her best intentions, she had developed a taste for it.

"*Madame*," came a soft voice.

Kathy spun around, surprised to find Pinkie standing quietly just inside the doorway. "Yes?"

"Should I have breakfast taken upstairs to Monsieur Carmelo?" Pinkie asked in her gentle accent.

"Yes, please," Kathy said automatically. As Pinkie turned to leave, Kathy called out impulsively. "Pinkie! Can I ask you something?"

"*Oui, madame*," Pinkie said, turning back with patient attention.

"I saw the look on your face when that man was here. You know him?" Kathy asked directly.

"*Non, madame,* not personally," Pinkie replied carefully.

"But you know of him?" Kathy pressed.

Pinkie nodded slowly, her expression growing troubled.

Kathy studied the young woman more closely. She was plainly dressed in her servant's attire but possessed a natural beauty that reminded her achingly of Willa—the same quiet grace that could attract the wrong kind of attention. "Can he be trusted with Willa?"

"*Non, madame,* he cannot," Pinkie said with quiet conviction. "You must keep your eyes on Mademoiselle Willa here in the Tremé, especially around the men who are in the world of the Boanno's. Most especially around a Thibodaux."

Kathy exhaled slowly, her worst fears confirmed. "Thank you, Pinkie. I appreciate your honesty."

"*De rien, madame*," Pinkie said with the hint of a conspirative smile before slipping away as silently as she'd appeared.

Alone again, Kathy stared out at the courtyard where orange trees cast dancing shadows in the morning light. She was learning that in this world of beautiful surfaces and hidden dangers, the servants often saw the truth more clearly than their employers. And the truth was that protecting Willa would require more than good intentions—it would demand the very Elliott steel that Janey was so determined to forge within her.

* * *

"So why are we going?" Carmelo asked as he nibbled thoughtfully on his buttered toast.

"You have to start training tomorrow. This is your last free day before the fight. I figure we can get out and see the city together," Kathy reasoned, settling beside him on the bed.

"We don't have to go with him, you know. I can call Caesar and have him show Willa around. Then you and I can stay in bed all day." Carmelo's smirk was wicked.

Kathy rolled her eyes with fond exasperation. "My privates are sore from your attention. No more lovemaking for now. Besides, Willa really wants to go and see the city."

Carmelo sighed heavily. "She wants to go with a man she shouldn't trust, and you want to let her go with a man she shouldn't trust. That makes no sense, *cara mia*."

"I want her to feel adored for once in her life. I want her to experience being appreciated and desired. And he's a skilled actor—he'll make her feel special." Kathy's expression grew more serious. "Besides, I know what forbidden fruit does to a girl. It only makes us crave it more desperately. I try to stop her and she wants him more. Men like Jean-Baptiste come in all shades and from all backgrounds. Janey is right. Willa needs to see the danger with her own eyes, not be sheltered from it. That's what my auntie is trying to teach me. That's what you were trying to teach me."

Carmelo stopped chewing, his dark eyes clouding with regret. "I'm sorry for making you participate in that situation last night, Kat. I just lost control—"

"Hey," she reached over and touched his hand gently, her fingers tracing the fresh scars across his knuckles from the brutal punches he'd delivered to her attacker's face. "No one makes me do anything, remember? I'm my own person. Your other half."

"My wife. My true wife," he said softly, bringing her hand to his lips.

"Right. Your *only* wife," she corrected him with quiet emphasis.

Carmelo's smile was weak but genuine. She pushed up from the bed and moved toward the washbasin. "Hurry up and finish eating so I can help you bathe. We need to be ready for our grand adventure."

CHAPTER 14

WOLF IN SHEEPS CLOTHING

A pristine 1950 Cadillac Series 62 convertible, gleaming pearl-white with luxurious tan leather interior, glided to a stop before the Boanno mansion like a chariot fit for royalty. Both girls' mouths fell open at the magnificent sight—the chrome bumpers and spoke wheels caught the Louisiana sunlight, which shone brighter than diamonds, while the soft top was folded back to reveal an interior that spoke of wealth beyond their wildest dreams.

Carmelo's eyes narrowed as he studied the driver with the calculating gaze of a man assessing potential threats. Jean-Baptiste tooted the horn melodiously, gesturing with confident charm for them to join him.

Willa squealed with unrestrained excitement, bouncing on her toes like a child on Christmas morning. Kathy caught her hand firmly and gave her a meaningful look.

"Remember what we talked about," she whispered.

Willa nodded obediently, though her eyes never left the gorgeous automobile or the man behind the wheel.

Carmelo slipped on his dark sunglasses with deliberate slowness and walked ahead to open the wrought-iron gate, every movement radiating the controlled power of a fighter preparing for combat.

Jean-Baptiste hopped effortlessly out of the convertible without bothering to open the door—a show of athletic grace—then walked around with fluid steps to open the passenger door for the ladies.

"*Mesdames,* your chariot awaits," he said with a sweeping bow.

The front seat was pulled forward, and the girls settled into the plush rear seats, sinking into leather that felt like butter beneath their summer dresses. Carmelo stood motionless for a long moment, his jaw working as if deciding whether this adventure would proceed at all.

"We haven't been properly introduced," Jean-Baptiste said smoothly, extending a manicured hand. "They call me JB. I'm a friend of the Boanno family, and you must be the champion everyone's talking about."

Carmelo stepped forward, his handshake firm enough to make a point. "I expect you to be a perfect gentleman with Willa. We clear on that?"

JB smiled. "*Plus clair que le cristal*—clearer than crystal, *mon ami.*"

Carmelo held his gaze for another beat, then nodded curtly and walked around to slide into the front passenger seat. JB smoothed his silk tie with manicured fingers and shook his head with amused respect before returning to the driver's seat—but not before sending Willa a theatrical wink that made her smile.

The drive through New Orleans was nothing short of magical. The summer heat was oppressive, but the breeze created by their movement provided sweet relief, carrying the intoxicating scents of jasmine, café au lait, and the mysterious spices that seemed to perfume every corner of the city.

Kathy found herself mesmerized by the people they passed. Fashion and prim dressing had been important in Harlem, but this was something else entirely—as if looking beautiful were a municipal law rather than a personal choice.

The quads' first stop was the legendary Café du Monde, where crowds of well-dressed patrons fanned themselves with ornate paper fans while waiting for tables. JB had spoken truthfully about his family's "arrangements". With a discreet word to the maître d' and a folded bill that changed hands like a magician's trick, they were escorted past the waiting white customers and seated at a prime table overlooking the bustling French Quarter.

The famous beignets arrived dusted with powdered sugar, like sweet snow, accompanied by café au lait so rich and perfect that it seemed almost criminal. Before long, Kathy found herself laughing freely, blooming under the pampered attention like a flower finally given proper sunlight. Even Carmelo's temperament softened enough for genuine smiles to break through his protective mask.

Jean-Baptiste proved to be more than just a pretty face—he was a natural storyteller and historian who could seamlessly transition from discussing baseball statistics to explaining the complex political divisions between the Sicilians, Irish, and Germans, who all vied for power in New Orleans, leaving the Cajuns and Blacks out of options. He positioned the Black Creoles and the broader African American population as a people who lived by their own sophisticated rules, creating their own society within the larger, segregated world that suited them fine.

And everywhere they went, they witnessed this truth in action.

Congo Square had been transformed into an impromptu street festival, a celebration of culture that made the air throb with rhythm and blues so infectious it seemed to enter through the skin. Twice, JB stopped their leisurely stroll to sweep Willa into spontaneous dances beneath the shade of ancient magnolia trees, their movements drawing appreciative murmurs from passersby who recognized the natural chemistry between the two.

Kathy lost herself completely in the rapture of absolute freedom. Here, in this magical pocket of New Orleans, she could eat jambalaya from street vendors and feed it to Carmelo without sideways glances, could be pushed high on a rope swing suspended from a massive oak tree with Carmelo's strong hands steadying her, and no one cared. She could laugh without restraint as the warm wind whipped through her hair, and his kisses and fondling didn't draw a sideways glance.

It was Carmelo who kept them all tethered to reality. Like a hawk protecting his nest, he watched everything and everyone with unwavering vigilance. If not for his constant attention, Willa would have slipped from their sight at least twice—once when a jazz band drew her into their impromptu parade, and again when a flower vendor's son tried to lead her away to see "the prettiest courtyard in the Quarter."

Each time, Carmelo's gentle yet firm intervention brought her back to their group, his protective instincts as sharp as those of any bodyguard. He seemed to understand intuitively that in this world of beautiful surfaces, there were hidden dangers.

For one perfect afternoon, they existed in a parallel universe where love conquered prejudice, where money trumped color, and where four young people could simply be happy together under the Louisiana sun. It was a glimpse of what the world could be—if only the rest of America could learn the lessons that New Orleans had already mastered in its own complicated, imperfect way.

* * *

"KATHY, PLEASE!" Willa pleaded, her voice breaking with desperation.

"My answer is still no," Kathy said firmly, though her heart ached at the pain in her friend's eyes.

Willa's face crumpled like paper in flames. She fled from the parlor, her sobs echoing through the grand hallways. Kathy sighed deeply, watching her disappear up the mahogany staircase. She glanced over at Pinkie, who stood quietly in the corner and gave her another subtle nod of approval.

"Keep an eye on her, make sure she doesn't leave her room," said Kathy.

"You think she'll defy you, mam?" Pinkie asked.

"I would," Kathy shrugged.

Pinkie nodded. "Yes, ma'am."

Despite the guilt gnawing at her conscience, she knew she was doing the right thing. Instead of following to comfort Willa, Kathy went to join the men, pushing the screen door open and stepping out to the long wraparound porch where Jean-Baptiste shared a pitcher of sweet tea with Carmelo. The men were deep in conversation about the upcoming boxing match, and she caught a glimpse of genuine concern in Carmelo's dark eyes. But their discussion ceased abruptly when they noticed her approach.

"JB, I want to thank you for the wonderful day you gave Willa. She's never had so much fun in her entire life," Kathy said graciously.

Jean-Baptiste gave her a curt nod, his green-colored eyes unreadable.

"Unfortunately, my answer remains no. Willa is only seventeen—we think. We don't even know her real age for certain. She's young and inexperienced. I am her guardian, and it wouldn't be appropriate for her to keep company with gentlemen callers." Kathy's voice grew stronger with conviction. "I know she's upset with me, and I'd like to invite you to join us for dinner before we leave New Orleans, but this must be goodbye." She extended her hand with finality.

For one brief, unmistakable moment, she caught a flash of raw anger in JB's golden eyes—something cold and predatory that made her blood run chill. But it dissolved as quickly as mercury, replaced by the practiced smile that rose to his lips like a curtain falling over a stage.

He stood, he stepped forward, and shook her hand with perfect composure. "I thank you for allowing her to spend the day with me. She is truly a special young lady, and I appreciate you considering my request." His voice was honey-smooth. "Would it be acceptable if I went inside to say goodbye?"

Kathy glanced toward Carmelo, who gave her a slight turn of his head in disapproval. "Time for you to leave," Carmelo said.

"*Bien sûr, chérie*," JB replied with that charming smile, then turned and went down the steps. Kathy walked to the edge of the deck and watched as he got into his shiny ride and drove away.

Kathy released a long, weary sigh and sank into the wicker chair beside Carmelo.

"You're going to make a wonderful mother someday," Carmelo said softly, admiration evident in his voice.

"You think so?" Kathy smiled.

"I know so. I'll trust our daughters to your wisdom," he said, taking her hand, he pulled her from her chair to come over and join him in his. She gently plopped down onto his lap. She wrapped her arms around his neck, breathing in his familiar scent.

"I feel terrible. I know how desperately she wants to be loved and free—I understand that feeling better than anyone. But something's wrong with him. And the way Aunt Janey just let him slither into our lives... It's like she's instigating this," Kathy shook her head. "I don't trust his interest in Willa."

Carmelo nodded in agreement. "Men are exactly what you think they are, *cara mia*. In a world full of wolves, it makes sense to protect the lamb."

Kathy lifted her head and stared down at him with sudden inspiration. "That's it!"

"What is?" Carmelo asked, confused.

"You said you were looking for a fight name—something that would stick. You should be called the Brooklyn Wolf or the Wolf of Brooklyn. Yes!"

Carmelo laughed, the sound rich and warm. "That's ridiculous."

"No! It's perfect! Think about it—the Wolf of Brooklyn! He'll rip you apart limb by limb!" She threw playful jabs at the air, her fists cutting through the humid evening with surprising skill.

"You've got killer instincts, Kathy," he chuckled, catching her hands.

"Please! For me! Be the Wolf! I want the Wolf! Ooooowwwwwoooo!!" Kathy howled with theatrical drama.

Carmelo growled playfully and pretended to bite her arm. They wrestled and kissed and held each other with such joy and tenderness that time seemed to slip away like sand through their fingers. The world beyond the porch ceased to exist—there was only them, only love, only this perfect moment stolen from an imperfect world.

CHAPTER 15

THE LIE AND THE LIGHT OF TRUTH

Willa took a shaky breath, her heart hammering against her ribs like a caged bird desperate for freedom. She gathered her worn leather satchel, carefully stuffing it with as many of the beautiful things Aunt Janey had given her that could fit—the lavender dress, the pearl earrings, the cream pumps that made her feel like a lady. Each item was a treasure she'd never dreamed of owning, and now they were hers to take into her new life.

She crept to the bedroom door and pressed her ear against the cool wood, listening intently. The hallway beyond was shrouded in silence, empty of the soft footsteps that usually echoed through the grand mansion. She had waited exactly as Jean-Baptiste instructed—until the moon climbed high enough in the velvet black sky to cast silver shadows through the lace curtains. He was so clever, so worldly. The thought of him and that devastating smile made her own lips curve upward despite her nervousness.

Carefully turning the brass handle, she slipped into the darkened corridor and began creeping toward the mahogany staircase, her bare feet silent on the Persian runner were muted. Her shoes in her hand.

Willa knew she hadn't had much in her short life—certainly nothing like the luxury she'd tasted these past two magical days. But now, with Jean-Baptiste's promises ringing in her ears, she felt like he held the entire world in his hands and could give it to her. He was someone straight out of the fairy tales Big Mama used to tell—rich beyond imagination, popular in all the right circles, devastatingly handsome, and most miraculous of all, in love with her.

He'd told her so himself. Tonight, they would begin their real life together, far from guardians and rules and people who didn't understand that love conquered everything.

* * *

THE HOUSE SLEPT. Alone in the silence, Willa moved toward freedom.

There's a whole world, chérie, JB had said. *Let me give it to you.*

Willa was ready to leap.

"Où vas-tu à cette heure, petite?"

The voice, cool as tombstone marble, froze her mid-step. When she didn't respond, Janey asked her question in English. "Where are you going, little one?"

Willa closed her eyes. Shoes dangling from one hand, satchel slung over her shoulder, she turned.

Aunt Janey materialized from the shadows. Her black satin robe drank the moonlight—a stark contrast to the daytime whites she wore like armor. At night, Janey embraced the darkness.

"Je... I'm leaving, ma'am," Willa confessed, chin lifted. She was old enough. Grown. Kathy meant well, but Kathy didn't understand the fire JB had lit in her belly—the promise of his townhouse in the Marigny, servants wanting to do her bidding. He'd get her a job typing in some air-cooled office. Anything beats Mississippi's sun-baked fields, the copper stench of her own blood blooming beneath torn nails. She'd pay whatever price JB asked for that taste of freedom.

"Come." Janey gestured toward the parlor, already gliding away. "One last sherry. *Pour l'adieu—before the parting."*

Willa hesitated, gaze darting to the door where JB's convertible idled to whisk her away like a chariot. Defiance warred with instinct.

She set down her satchel, slid her feet into pumps, picked it up, and followed.

Pinkie waited in the parlor.

Not the starch-collared maid, but a woman transformed: hair a cascade of obsidian waves framing high cheekbones, a silk robe the color of crushed violets draping her lush curves. She held out a crystal glass of amber sherry.

She was no longer a servant or shadow in the home, she was Janey's equal in every way.

"He's waiting—" Willa stammered. "I really need to go."

"He'll wait," Janey smirked.

"But—" Willa protested.

"Il attendra." Janey settled into her wingback throne, swirling her drink. "Sit, Willa. Regarde. Look at Pinkie. Really look at her."

Willa looked—*really* looked. Pinkie's skin was as deep as mahogany as her own, luminous. Her hair, free of its habitual kerchief, fell in thick, defiant waves—a silent rebellion against the creamy ringlets prized in the Quarter's *gens de couleur libre*. She was... magnificent—a queen in exile. Yes, Janey was beautiful, but the earthy realness of Pinkie's beauty made Janey's dim in the moonlight.

Janey's gaze, sharp as a stiletto, drifted between them. "When I married Carmine ten years ago," she began, tracing the rim of her sherry glass, "I brought Pinkie and the family into this house. Put them on payroll, gave them rooms with silk curtains. But the truth?" Her voice dropped, warm as bourbon. "They walked into my life long before I ever wore Carmine's ring. Found me when I was nothing but rags and rage. Saved me when the world wanted me dead."

Janey's gaze lifted. She held Pinkie's stare. "They're not servants. They're my blood, stronger than any tie I have to the sisters. Always will be."

Willa lowered her satchel. The leather strap slipped from her shoulder like a surrender. She took the sherry glass Pinkie offered, the crystal cool and heavy in her palm, and sank into the velvet armchair. The scent of beeswax and gardenias hung thick in the air.

"I ran here like you," Janey continued, staring into the middle distance of her thoughts where Mississippi's ghosts lingered. "fourteen years old, with nothing but a stolen knife and the devil on my heels. Followed the river south until my shoes fell apart. Ended up in the swamps—half-dead, all desperation with my mother's recipes in my pocket."

Pinkie stepped forward, her shadow stretched long in the lamplight. "I was eight," Pinkie said, her voice softer than Willa had ever heard it. "Gram sent me to fetch herbs near the froglands at dusk. That's where I saw her." She nodded at Janey. "Looked like something the swamp coughed up. Skinny as a shad, clothes ripped to ribbons. Face so bruised and swollen... scratching the mosquito bites, I guess." Pinkie's breath hitched with emotion. "...you couldn't tell if she was pretty or plain. Just... broken. She'd collapsed under Gran's favorite chinaberry tree. I couldn't drag her no further. When I brought Grann and Ma, we found flies buzzing 'round her open sores."

Pinkie knelt beside Willa's chair, the memory pulling her close. "Mama carried her inside. We bathed her in Gran's big tin tub—water turned rusty with blood and dirt. Fed her spoonfuls of broth 'til she stopped shivering. Tended her for weeks. Gran sang old hymns while changing her bandages. Mama rubbed salve on the whip marks and spider bites. She had old and new ones." Pinkie touched her own cheek, remembering. "We called her 'Little Ghost' 'cause she never spoke. She was older than we thought she was because she was skinny and frail. Just stared at the wall with those big, hollow cat eyes of hers... 'til one morning, she finally smiled and said it was the Poison Cherry."

"Poison Cherry?" Willa asked.

"Offered to pay us with it," Pinkie chuckled. "We thought she was mad. We done helped her and she wants to give us poisoned cherries. We had no clue." Pinkie stood and walked back over to her chair and sat.

Janey reached out, her fingers brushing Pinkie's hand—a rare, tender gesture. "They pieced me back together," Janey continued, the words rough with gratitude. "Gave me a name when I'd lost mine. Fed me hope with their cornbread and red beans, and kindness. Something even my sisters didn't give when Brenda left me behind." Her gaze drifted to the window, where moonlight silvered the magnolias. "Made me believe I could be human again." A pause. The shadows deepened in the lines around her mouth. "...For a while."

Willa leaned forward, the sherry glass trembling in her hand.

"Why tell me this?" she whispered, the words raw and urgent. "Why show me... all this?"

Janey set her glass down with a click. Her eyes locked onto Willa's, sharp enough to cut. "Because on that platform at the train station," she said, her voice low, "when I saw your face—those wide, shining eyes drinking in the city like it was holy water—I saw Pinkie, and then I saw myself." She leaned closer, the lamplight carving shadows under her cheekbones. "You all young, finally free, stumbling off that train from Mississippi. Convinced you'd reached paradise. Believing you'd left the pain buried at the Jensens. 'Here,' I thought..." Janey's smile was a bitter twist. "She thinks this is where negro girls come to prosper. That we ain't just surviving."

"Don't you? Look at this place. You know what's in Butt's Janey. You know where I came from? This is paradise." Willa said. She stared at the women with hope. Blank stares were all they gave her in return.

Willa's spine straightened. The memory surged—the primal thunder of drums in Congo Square, the whirl of indigo and crimson silk as dancers spun under live oaks, the throaty laughter spilling from Storyville's glowing doorways. This place was a dream, and she couldn't be convinced otherwise.

A silent exchange passed between Janey and Pinkie—a language forged in shared suffering.

"Alive, oui," Janey conceded, her smile bittersweet. *"But paradise? Non, chérie. No Eden for women like us—not handed down. We claw it from the rot. Brick by bloody brick."*

Pinkie spoke: "You think that Thibodeaux boy's heart flutters for you? Maybe it does... today. But men like Jean-Baptiste?" She spat the name. "They collect girls like us. Pretty dark birds to cage. He'll whisper love, fill you with champagne dreams… use your body and convince you that you like it, then install you in some back-alley room. You'll scrub his wife's floors by day, warm his bed by night until you're used up. Or until his sister finds you."

"JB wouldn't—"

"Crois-moi." Pinkie's command cut like glass. With deliberate slowness, she rolled up her sleeve.

The scar wasn't just skin. It was a landscape of torment—thick, ropy keloids snaking up her forearm, flesh melted and remade by agony. "Claire Thibodeaux. JB's dear sister. Boiling water. Because her husband… he liked the way I looked serving coffee. I was only ten, *Willa. Dix ans.* My skin slid off thick and bubbling."

Janey's knuckles whitened on her chair. Fury, cold and absolute, radiated from her.

"What happened? Did you… did he get punished?"

"We screamed for justice. But justice?" Janey's voice dropped to a venomous hiss. "That door stayed locked. I hammered on it—begged Don Marcello who owned the cops, even confronted his appointed sheriff, Carmine Boanno, himself, to help us. Of course, all Carmine Boanno wanted from me was sex. And do you know what he said to me after I gave it to him? Let him abuse and use my body in some of the most wicked ways?" She leaned in, eyes blazing. "A burned colored girl? *Who gives a shit?* No one can tell with skin like that anyway."

Janey took a deep breath, feeling her anger even more. Pinkie reached over and rubbed Janey's arm to soothe her. Janey closed her eyes and spoke with them closed. "Claire's husband cried his pretty crocodile tears for the judges. Made a whole show of his wounded honor. And walked away clean. Not a damn stain on his shiny reputation in Creole society."

Pinkie's voice was flat, resigned. "Papa tried. Went to the *gens de couleur* council. The next night, men dragged him to the levee. Left him broken. Walks crooked now. My word against Claire's? Against a Thibodeaux?" Pinkie gave a bitter laugh, hollow. *"Janey… she fixed things her way."*

"I went to the Thibodeaux myself, apologised, and entered their world. They had no problem welcoming a Elliot into their society, one of my sisters had passed through their doors and married well. She lives as a white woman in Oregon now. It wasn't hard to make myself worthy." A shadow crossed Janey's face—something feral, satisfied. "Six months later, Madame Geneviève Thibodeaux took ill. *Tragique*. Bleeding from places a lady shouldn't. Screaming like a banshee. Then Claire… ah, poor Claire. Such a mysterious wasting sickness claimed her, too. Three other Creole elite's that were on the council fell ill and died. Doctors whispered of 'cursed blood.' Andrew, that saintly husband? Vanished. Poof." Janey snapped her fingers, the sound sharp in the heavy air. "And Carmine? *Mon mari*? He fell ill, too. Nearly died. A problem, that one. Sicilian blood is supposed to curdle like créole cream, but it was made of something stronger. At least his blood is."

"That's enough, Janey," Pinkie whispered. "Stay calm. Carmine loves you. Remember? You forgave him."

"I won't be silenced in my home, Pinkie," Janey turned on her. Pinkie only smiled and rubbed Janey's hand like a parent would do for a spoiled child.

"Are you saying that you made them sick? Dead?" Willa gasped. Neither of the women spoke. "And your husband? Carmine? But you nursed him back," Willa breathed, understanding dawning—terrible and bright.

"Kathy's mother came and helped fix Carmine. She prayed with me. We decided he was mine. It's our way as Elliot women. If they save our lives, like Henry saved Brenda, then we are theirs, faithful and strong. But if we decide to save theirs, then they are damned and belong to us, our pets, our slaves. My life for his life and his life for mine. He made the ultimate sacrifice by surviving my cherry. Just like All men must pay a price to be worthy. That is the key, Willa. Men must be worthy; if not, they should be judged."

"Janey and I don't agree on her methods," Pinkie interjected. "Janey isn't a killer. She's simply saying that men should earn your love, not take it as a trophy."

Janey waved off the correction and sipped her drink.

"That's why you married him. Carmine? Because you love him?" Willa asked.

"I suppose. And it's why Pinkie's family stays," Janey said softly. "Not servants. Gardiens. My shadows. My blades in the dark."

Willa stared at these women—one forged in fire, one wrapped in silk and secrets both lethal and committed to one another. "Why'd you run? From Butts to Jackson and then here. To the Tremé ? What was chasing you? Kathy would never tell me."

Janey's amusement vanished. Her eyes, usually dancing with mockery, turned flat and hard as river stones. "That story stays buried deeper than Madame Thibodeaux. Now." She stood. *"Va. You heard the truth. Make your decision. Will you go to your Jean-Baptiste? Taste his promised world. Be the lamb instead of the prize?"*

Willa stood. She glanced at Pinkie, who held a plea in her eyes for Willa to make the right choice. She then looked into Janey's eyes, which were wild with mockery and delight over the dilemma. Wanting something to happen.

Willa's grip tightened around her satchel strap. "JB wants something from me—I know that. I can see it when he looks at me. The way he licks his bottom lip when he talks to me." Her voice was low, stripped of illusions. "And I know what men see when they look at all of us, especially me and Pinkie. Easy prey." She met Janey's gaze without flinching. "But I'm not you, Aunt Janey. I don't have your… advantages or beauty."

Pinkie shot up and stepped forward, her robe rustling like a sigh. "Honey, that 'advantage' ain't armor. When they see us—light, dark, in-between—they see the same thing: a body to use. Janey's skin might've opened doors, but behind those doors, nothing was better for her. Not even now with Carmine. It's rare to find a lover, a friend, all wrapped in a man who doesn't punish and call it love. And it won't be better for you."

Willa's composure frayed. "You think I don't know that? But if you'd ever felt this… hollowness?" She pressed a fist to her chest. "Like Butts scooped out everything good inside me—hope, family, dreams—left nothing but dust? You'd understand. Anywhere is better than back there. One day Kathy gone leave, her prince gone take her to her own palace. Like what Janey got. And I'll still be there, washing Ms Lottie's drawers and mopping floors. Eating scraps from her table. Anyone is better than that emptiness."

Silence hung thick between the women.

Janey's eyes—amber and unreadable—switched to Pinkie. A lifetime of understanding passed between them: *She's already gone.*

"Tell Kathy..." Willa swallowed, the ghost of Butts cotton fields choking her. "Tell her it was my choice. And that I'm... I'm sorry."

"What happens next stains your soul, not Kathy's. You walk with eyes open now, petite. And if the shine fades... if the cage door clangs shut and you want an escape... You find me. *Toujours,*" Janey said and kissed her on the left and right cheek. A benediction. A warning.

Pinkie remained silent, her expression carved from sorrow. *"Don't do this, child,"* she said softly. "Even if JB is different from the others, his sisters and brothers won't be. This is another dead end."

"Hush now," Janey said to Pinkie. "Her choice is made. We all get to make our own choices! And we all have our scars to bear. It's time she got hers. It'll make her strong."

Pinkie shook her head.

"JB knows not to go too far," Janey shrugged. "He knows who I am and what I am, even if he is too scared to say it aloud."

Willa walked over and hugged Pinkie. She hugged her tightly. "I'ma be okay, Pinkie, this is what I want," she whispered, the truth raw and stark. "Even poison tastes sweet when you're starving."

She let her go and hurried away.

Outside, Jean-Baptiste leaned against his sleek convertible, haloed by streetlight. His smile, when he saw her, was a masterpiece of boyish charm. Janey watched from the doorway, a specter in black. Pinkie stood beside her, a silent statue.

JB opened the passenger door with a flourish. Willa slid in, the leather cool against her legs. As the engine purred to life, JB turned. His eyes met Janey's across the manicured lawn.

He tipped his hat. "Madame Boanno, *merci.*"

Janey didn't blink. Her returning nod wasn't acknowledgment—it was a promise. A line drawn in blood that only they could see. The car pulled away, carrying Willa toward the glittering, gilded dark.

Pinkie shut the heavy door. The click of the lock echoed like a tomb sealing.

"You set that poor girl up, Janey. You and I both know that a Thibodeux wouldn't dare touch anyone near you without permission. Why did you give her to him? You need another cause? Another righteous reason to kill a man again? That poor girl has no hope with those demons."

Janey went to the window and stared into the night where the taillights had vanished. "*Non.* But she might survive becoming. And that… *ma chère…* is the only paradise we get—learning to survive. I hate the innocent living unaware of the darkness. Scars don't have to heal. They can make a woman stronger. My mama taught me that."

Janey looked at Pinkie. "Now you stay out of it, Pinkie. I'll deal with Kathy. I gave you a chance to make Willa stay. She made her choice! You live with it. You hear!"

Pinkie looked at Janey, heartbroken. She watched her waltz back up the stairs and return to Carmine's arms. Defeated, Pinkie turned away in tears.

CHAPTER 16

DEBBIE'S PLACE - HARLEM 1978

Present. Matteo's Lincoln Continental screeched to the curb. He was out before it fully stopped. His soldiers held every corner that mattered in Harlem now, watching everything. A crew maintained round-the-clock surveillance on the Freeman brownstone—Janey hadn't arrived, Sandra had already been taken by Junior.

Matteo's heart hammered against his ribs like a machine gun as he reached Debbie's salon and found the steel security gate pulled down, the "CLOSED" sign mocking him through the bulletproof glass.

He'd told her to lock herself inside and wait for him. A wise woman, who finally started to listen.

Fumbling for his keys with hands that trembled slightly—not from fear, but from barely controlled rage—he thought about Caesar breaking that locksmith's jaw just three days after his return from prison. Debbie had refused to see him. He had a remedy for that. Whether Debbie liked it or not, she could never keep him from her again. Never keep him from protecting what was his. So the locksmith got him keys to every door to every place she owned or lived.

The lock turned with a satisfying click, unlocking the door. He stepped into the familiar sanctuary of her world—the scent of hair relaxer and expensive perfume, the gleaming chrome chairs, the mirrors that had witnessed a thousand secrets. She rushed toward him immediately, her usually flawless makeup streaked with tears, mascara painted dark rivers down her cheeks.

"Matteo!" She threw herself into his arms before he could fully close the door behind him. He locked it quickly, then wrapped her tightly against his chest, feeling her whole body shake with suppressed hysteria.

"What happened? What did that crazy bitch say to you?" His voice was deadly calm, but his mind was already calculating how many different ways he could make Janey Boanno disappear.

"She's completely unhinged! She's always been unhinged, but this —" Debbie's words tumbled out in a rush. "She says she's going to stay with Sandy and tell her everything. She says it's my fault Kathy's dead, that I should have called the family. She says she hates me for keeping secrets—secrets you made me keep!"

"Stop. Stop." He cupped her beautiful face in his hands and kissed her forehead with infinite tenderness. "Breathe, *Debbie*. Just breathe."

Debbie nodded and closed her eyes, drawing in shaky gulps of air. Matteo felt his own pulse begin to slow. When he'd heard the terror in her voice over the phone, a hundred nightmare scenarios had flashed through his mind—the Feds kicking down her door, rival families making their move, politicians playing their power games. He'd driven through Harlem like a man possessed, running red lights and leaving his security detail scrambling to keep up.

"Now. Tell me exactly what she said," he commanded gently, guiding her to one of the salon chairs and pressing her down into the buttery leather.

"She was waiting outside when I arrived this morning," Debbie said, her voice steadier now.

"Was Willa with her?"

"No. She had Coffey waiting in the car. Said Willa was back home in New Orleans, didn't want to make the trip. That has to be a lie," Debbie sighed deeply. "Willa would never let her come back to

Harlem without her after Carmelo told Janey not to return. I think she just snatched Coffey and came."

Debbie paced and kept talking. "She said one of Izzy's sons contacted her, told her that Kathy was dead. Said the Elliott sisters were furious that no one called them, that we had a funeral without the family blessing. I told you I should have contacted them!"

"She's not dead," Matteo said firmly, though doubt gnawed at his gut like acid.

"How do you know that, Matteo? How can you be so certain?" Debbie's voice cracked. "What if she is dead? What if they both are? What if I've been lying to myself all this time? Thinking I could make up for all the fucking mistakes I made with this family. With you! Damn it, I never should have listened to you! We can't change the past!"

She started to stand from the chair, but he moved faster, blocking her path with his body. "Please, please. Stop. Sit. Stay calm."

"You didn't see her, Matteo. You know how Janey gets when she's on one of her crusades—and Willa isn't here to keep her grounded. Carmine's dead. Pinkie's dead. Aunt Brenda's dead. Kathy's gone. No one can stop Janey. She'll do anything, say anything. She'll destroy everything Kathy and I have built!"

"I can handle Janey," he said with the quiet confidence of a man who'd ordered the deaths of stronger opponents. "Let me worry about her. But this does change our timeline. Fuck." He ran a hand through his dark hair. "Those diaries won't mean shit now if Janey starts filling Sandy's head with her version of history. She's a distraction I can't afford. I'm running out of time."

"What do you mean, running out of time? What's happening now?" Fear flickered in Debbie's eyes—the kind of fear that came from loving a man whose world operated by its own deadly rules.

Matteo realized he'd said too much. The last thing she needed to know about was the federal task force breathing down his neck, or Jersey and Philly making moves on his business deals, or the mayor's promises to clean up organized crime before the next election cycle.

"The press is circling like vultures. All these arrests have the mayor boasting about chasing out the mob, cracking down on our legitimate businesses across all the families. I'm handling it. Don't worry about any of that."

"I do worry. I worry constantly," Debbie whispered, reaching up to touch the faded scar on his jaw—a souvenir from Vietnam that reminded them both how fragile life could be.

"I know you do, *amore*. I understand." He caught her hand and pressed it flat against his chest, where his heart still beat too fast. "But I need you to love me. It's my fire. It gives me strength."

"I do. Tell me what to do, Matteo."

"Marry me. Now. Let's get that done first. Then we go to war."

Debbie blinked her tears. "You got a one-track mind."

He smirked. "Or we can get on that sofa in your office, and I'll make you feel better before we go."

"No!" she pushed him away. "You always think about sex. I'll get my purse. Let's get married."

"Okay, then the honeymoon, right?" Matteo joked as she walked back to her office. When she disappeared, his smile dimmed. Janey's arrival was not in the plan. He let go of a deep breath. Time was up.

Lac Tremblant, Quebec

"You overreact, and then—you never forgive, you just punish!" Carmelo's voice cracked with desperation.

"Just tell me! Please stop trying to get in my head and twist everything around. Be honest with me," she demanded, her voice steady despite the hurricane of emotion building in her chest.

"I can deal with your anger. I just... I need you to try to understand my reasons," he said, his dark eyes pleading.

"Tell me! What did you do?" she asked.

A bitter smirk touched his lips as he finally revealed the unthinkable: "I had you murdered. You're dead. We're both dead."

Kathy blinked twice, her mind struggling to process words that made no sense. She had envisioned murder and mayhem, but this didn't register in any reality she could comprehend. "Dead?"

Carmelo's stare turned cold as steel, his voice stripped of all emotion. "That federal agent who told you I was in witness protection —the one who met you in Jersey at our safe house and helped get you here to Quebec? He was a paid actor. It was all a lie to get you out of New York so I could blow up your car with a dead woman's body inside. Someone we dug up fresh from a grave in Queens. To make the police think it was you."

Kathy's mouth fell open, and the world stopped spinning. She took an involuntary step backward, her hand falling away from the ring she'd been unconsciously twisting for strength.

"I did it for me and Nino. They all think we're dead now. That's why there's no phone here. That's why you've been isolated with me for over two weeks," he finished, each word driving another nail into the coffin of her trust.

"You wouldn't do that. Not to us. Not to Sandy." But even as she said it, she knew from the set of his jaw that he absolutely would.

He nodded with the terrible certainty of a man who'd crossed every line. "Matteo and Debbie have Sandy. In two weeks, Marco goes for our girl, after everything settles around your 'death,' Sandy will get a similar message. She'll tell everyone she's going back to D.C., then she'll let my men take her to us. And it will be done—my *famiglia*—you, me, Nino, and Sandy. We'll disappear together. For good."

"Are you fucking insane! You are! You're completely insane!" The words tore from her throat like a primal scream.

"I waited, Kathy. I waited for forgiveness, for acceptance, for my chance to be your husband, to have my family…"

"...I'm married to you…" Kathy protested.

"All because of me! Because of what I had to do to make you love me!" he shouted.

"No… no, that's not true…"

"I waited for any chance to have what's been stolen from me over and over again. I begged you for years to walk away, to run away with me."

"Stop talking! Shut up!" She pressed her hands to her temples as if she could physically stop the horror from penetrating her skull. "I need to think. Oh God, my baby thinks I'm dead. My family thinks I'm dead. Oh God!"

Carmelo walked over, and she stepped back. He kept advancing, refusing her space or time to deal with her emotions. He was close enough to touch her, and if he did, she would scream. She felt cornered and terrified. "We *are* family. You and me! Not them! It's just us!"

The slap cracked across his face like a gunshot, jerking his head back with savage force. She'd only struck him once before in her life—when he'd kidnapped their daughter after discovering she'd lied about Sandy's paternity. She'd never regretted that slap, and she didn't regret this one. She struck him this time for everything he'd done since then to own her, to possess her, to fight against every attempt she'd made to be free of their toxic past. Everything he'd done until she finally understood the terrible truth—that without him, there was no her. He was her soul, her damnation, her salvation, just like Debbie could never escape Matteo. Just like Willa could never escape Jean-Baptiste. Just like Janey and Carmine Boanno.

She stepped back from him in absolute horror. "You can't do this, Melo. Not again."

"I've done it!" His voice exploded with finality. "And I'm not sorry!"

Overwhelmed by the magnitude of his betrayal, she pulled off the ring he'd just noticed her wearing. With deliberate precision, she placed it on the table beside the wedding ring he'd given her when they'd officially renewed their vows, and she agreed to convert to catholicism. He stared at the abandoned jewelry, then at her, his face crumpling with hurt.

"You never understood," she said, her voice breaking like glass. "You never had to make me love you. You just had to let me love you."

"Kathy…you won't go. Not this time. I'm not going to let you." He reached for her desperately.

She threw up her hand to stop his approach, then turned and fled up the stairs to the yacht's upper deck. She ran from him and from the truth, seeking escape in the night air. The fresh lake breeze filled her lungs, the scent of pine and cold water sharp in her nostrils. All of it sobered her even as the tears refused to stop falling.

She felt trapped—not just by his suffocating love, but by her own inability to stop the Wolf from consuming the man she'd wanted back so desperately. Every chance they'd had at happiness, this anger, this pain always returned, always brought out the worst in him, the most destructive impulses. He'd killed for her. He'd done even worse and said it was all for her. She never wanted any of it.

Her blood sang with rage and the ancient knowledge of what was to come if she didn't join him. If the Wolf didn't get his way.

She kicked off her heels, the expensive shoes clattering across the polished deck, and went barefoot to the yacht's railing. The dark water below looked like liquid obsidian, promising oblivion.

"Kathy!" His voice behind her carried pure panic.

She ignored him completely.

Without hesitation, she vaulted over the railing and plunged into the night-black water. The lake was shockingly cold, stealing her breath as she sank beneath the surface. She closed her eyes and let herself drift deeper into the abyss, weightless and free for the first time in weeks. The silence was absolute, peaceful, a temporary escape from the chaos.

Of course, he was there within seconds, his powerful arms wrapping around her waist as he hauled her back toward the surface. The yacht's floodlights blazed to life, turning the dark water into a stage as he swam them both back to safety, cursing himself in rapid-fire Italian for hurting her, for making her hurt herself.

It wasn't suicide. She could swim. It was just her desperate need to be free.

Strong hands pulled her from the water, her soaked dress clinging to her body like a second skin. The crew tried not to stare at her exposed curves as Carmelo hauled himself aboard, water streaming from his hair, his eyes wild with fear and rage. She fled from him again, racing to their cabin and slamming the door behind her, turning the lock and securing it.

She pressed her back against the door as he pounded on it. The

Wolf threatened to break it down. His threats were raw with desperation as he begged to fight with her, to reason with her, to make her understand his twisted logic. But gradually his voice faded, and all the memories crashed over her like a tsunami.

Ely and that damn war he insisted on joining, which took him from her, Carmelo's fault. Her father's death, his father's death, the bloody cycle of vengeance that defined their world, their shared fault. That car hit Sandy in the street, and the way Carmelo had screamed in anguished tears when he'd picked up their broken daughter from the asphalt, saying it was his fault. The madness that had consumed him that day gave the Wolf complete control. The boy she loved died when his daughter's skull was cracked and she bled in his arms. The poor driver of that car was tortured for weeks before the Wolf finally showed mercy and killed him with a hammer. And his and Maria's kids were cast from his heart. Nicolas never recovered from losing his father's love. He treated him in the same way Cosimo treated Matteo. It drove her and Maria into a friendship as they tried to protect the children from the Wolf. Their life was never the same after that moment. *He* was never the same. No matter how hard she loved or forgave him.

She stripped off the clinging dress and wrapped herself in a silk robe, then sat on the edge of the bed and let the memories slam into her consciousness. She got up and turned on the transistor radio, pulling up the antenna to get the news broadcast from New York. From the lake, she heard him listening to the baseball game at Yankee Stadium. She let it play, and God granted her wish after several news bites; the truth was laid bare. The broadcaster announced her death and the investigation. It was real. It was true. She was dead.

The Wolf started again, kicking at the door. Eventually, he forced the cabin door open—Aunt Janey had taught her that locks only worked if men allowed them to. But the door held. She could see him in her mind. He paced the small space like a caged predator, giving her an endless list of justifications for what he'd done, switching frantically between Italian and English as his control fractured completely

—threatening the world if she refused to forgive and accept their condemned fate.

She watched him fall apart and said nothing, her mind working with the cold calculation that was her birthright. She had to pull this back from the brink. She remembered what Aunt Janey had taught her about managing dangerous men. She remembered her mother's marriage to her father and the calm in Brenda that often tamed the beast in Daddy. Carmelo wasn't in control, though he desperately believed he was. She was his strength and his weakness, his anchor and his destruction.

And she would have to fix this catastrophe to save them both. Or go down in flames with him, but save their child.

Though it killed something vital inside her to suppress the volcanic rage burning in her chest, she did it anyway. She stood and opened the door. He turned around with madness in his eyes. She opened her arms to the Wolf, knowing precisely what he needed to hear, what he needed to feel.

He was on her in an instant, holding her too tight, his robust frame shaking as he kissed her face and whispered false promises of change, of better days, of a future that didn't exist.

"Shhh..." she whispered against his ear, her voice soft as silk. "Stop talking. Just let me hold you."

Carmelo did as she commanded, and wept with relief to be forgiven. She held him close, stroking his hair as if he were a child, a mother comforting him. And she held back her fury, banking it like coals that would burn hotter for being contained.

For now.

But the Elliott women never forgot. And they never, ever gave in.

CHAPTER 17

THE WOLF, THE MAN, HER PLAN

Kathy turned over, her slight movement waking Carmelo immediately. She felt his touch, his hand sliding beneath the sheet, gently tracing from her hip toward her pelvis. She shut her eyes tightly, determined to ignore him. Twice already since their argument, he'd tried to seduce her or initiate intimacy, and each time she'd firmly told him no. She'd warned him that if he persisted, he'd have to leave her bed.

Yet, here he was, reaching for her pussy again.

"Stop, Melo," she whispered, and shifted away. He moved with her, pressing his lips softly against her shoulder. His hand eased downward again, but she kept her thighs firmly closed. Rebuffed, his hand slid upward over her belly with a slow caress.

"I'm sorry," he murmured.

"Just go to sleep," Kathy responded firmly, her voice carrying the exhaustion of someone who'd fought too many battles in one night.

His hand found her breast beneath the silk robe, making her roll her eyes behind closed lids—irritated yet helplessly conflicted. He always wielded their physical connection as his most devastating weapon, knowing exactly how it could shatter her carefully constructed defenses. Tonight, though, she was determined not to let him win so easily.

He had hurt their family, Sandy, and he wasn't sorry. Not sorry enough.

She turned abruptly to confront him, but the moment her face aligned with his, his mouth captured hers. He moved with swiftness to put her beneath him before she could protest. Kathy's hand shot to his throat, applying just enough pressure to break the kiss and freeze him in place. Her nails pierced his jugular, and her gaze blazed with defiance.

He paused, breathing hard against her lips, though his powerful thighs had already pushed between hers, forcing her legs to part. She could feel the head of his erection, hard and insistent, positioned at her entrance—so close that the slightest movement of her hips would grant him access to what he craved most.

She held perfectly still.

His dark eyes met hers in a silent communication that was part plea, part command—that familiar combination of vulnerability and dominance that had always been her undoing.

They remained frozen in their intimate standoff, locked in a battle of wills that neither wanted to lose. The air between them crackled with tension, with unspoken words, with the weight of everything that had shattered between them tonight.

Finally, inevitably, her resolve cracked. Carmelo felt the exact moment of her surrender when her lower body responded, and she moved to give him access. He released a low groan and surged forward. She took him inch by inch, his cock slipping deep, her body welcomed him with reluctant acceptance. He filled her completely, each inch a claim, a promise, a punishment.

His mouth found the sensitive curve of her neck and collarbone as he pinned her wrists above her head, his movements becoming more urgent, more desperate. Each thrust spoke of his fear of losing her, his need to possess her so completely that she could never leave him again—even as she lay beneath him plotting exactly that.

A wave of overwhelming despair crashed over her—for her daughter, for her family who believed she was dead, for the impossible situation Carmelo had trapped them both in. Without warning, Kathy burst into tears that seemed to come from the depths of her soul.

Carmelo froze, alarmed. He looked down at her, crumbling emotionally beneath him, and something in him broke.

"I'm sorry, Kathy," he whispered, his voice rough with self-loathing. "I don't know why—I mean, I know why I need you so much—but I don't understand why I can't stop myself from destroying everything I touch."

She turned her face away, tears streaming silently down her cheeks as the full weight of their situation crashed down on her. He moved off her carefully, watching helplessly as she curled inward like a wounded person.

All Kathy could think about was Sandy—her brilliant, fragile daughter who believed her mother was dead. Sandy, who had always been so carefully protected, sheltered in the safe bubble of independence she'd meticulously crafted in Washington. For every hole in her memory, she filled it with the make-believe life she wanted to give her. Now her baby was completely vulnerable, beyond her reach, probably devastated with grief and open for trauma to return.

What kind of mother was she to have allowed this to happen?

"Kathy?" Carmelo reached out again, his touch gentle this time, but she sat up abruptly and pulled her silk robe around herself like armor.

"I'll sleep on the sofa. Just stay away from me, please, please, stay away from me!" she said without a look back at him. She didn't need the inevitable excuses or justifications.

As the cabin door closed behind her, Carmelo collapsed back against the pillows with a deep, shuddering sigh. He pressed the heels of his hands against his eyes, knowing he'd expected this outcome from the moment he'd conceived his elaborate deception. Every action in his life had come with brutal consequences—he'd learned to accept both the punishments he inflicted and those he endured. Like watching Kathy walk out of his life, marry another man, and keep his daughter hidden from him for years. He had survived it all through sheer force of will.

But this felt different. This felt like the beginning of the end.

He lowered his hands. He stared at the empty space beside him in the bed where her warmth and perfume still lingered, then slowly reached out to run his palm over the indentation her body had left in the sheets. The gesture was achingly tender for a man who'd just orchestrated the cruelest betrayal imaginable.

Closing his eyes, he listened to the gentle lapping of waves against the yacht's hull and accepted the truth he'd been avoiding: all he could do now was wait to see if the woman he loved more than life itself would ever be able to forgive him for loving her this much.

Three hours later.

Kathy stirred with a soft moan, her body stiff from sleeping curled on the narrow sofa. Through the haze of exhaustion, she felt herself being lifted with infinite care. Her eyes fluttered open to find Carmelo's face above her, his expression tender and filled with quiet regret as he carried her back to their bed. This was the man she knew, the boy she loved. She could see him now.

Without conscious thought, she wrapped her arms around his neck, seeking the familiar comfort of his strength despite everything that lay broken between them. When he lowered her gently onto the mattress in their cabin, she immediately curled against his warmth, too emotionally drained to maintain the walls she'd tried to build.

He simply held her—no words, no attempts at justification, no desperate pleas for forgiveness. Just his arms creating a sanctuary around her exhausted form, the steady rhythm of his breathing against her forehead, and the soft press of his lips against her brow.

He pulled the covers over them both with careful movements, cocooning them in shared warmth as the yacht rocked gently on the dark water. For the first time in hours, Kathy felt something approaching peace settle over her weary soul.

Sleep came mercifully this time, soft and healing.

. . .

Morning

Kathy woke to golden sunlight streaming through the cabin windows, warming her face and painting everything in honeyed light. The yacht rocked gently around her, and for a blissful moment, she almost forgot the devastation of the night before. It had only been a dream. When she realized the space beside her was empty, she shot upright and scanned the cabin with sudden alertness.

Carmelo was there, seated in the corner chair, watching her with stillness. He had already showered and dressed in crisp off-white linen—a long-sleeved shirt and matching pants that made him look like some dangerous angel. The designer sunglasses were back in place, hiding his eyes, his expression carefully controlled.

The Wolf was back in command.

He leaned forward slightly, his gaze fixed on her with unnerving intensity even behind the dark lenses.

Kathy wasn't afraid—she'd weathered too many of his storms to be intimidated now. But she was acutely aware of the shift in him, the way he'd rebuilt his defenses while she slept. If she had woken just an hour earlier, she might have caught him while his guard was still down, when he was still the broken man who'd held her so tenderly. She could have reached him then, turned him toward her vision of a life where they stood together and faced their enemies instead of running from shadows he'd created.

But it was painfully evident in his cold, controlled presence that the window of vulnerability had slammed shut.

"I understand you're disappointed in me, Kat." His voice was carefully modulated, businesslike. "I knew this would happen. What I wanted to say last night is that taking your life was the only way I could save it. My enemies within the other families and inside the government had me backed into a corner with no other options." He stood with fluid grace, already moving toward the door. "I'll take you back to the villa and give you some space to process this. We can figure out the rest later. But understand this, there is no going back."

"Carmelo, I—" she began, reaching toward him.

But he was already walking out, his retreat as calculated as everything else he did. The cabin door closed behind him with quiet finality, leaving her alone with the morning light and her racing thoughts.

She dropped back against the pillows and rolled her eyes at the ceiling, frustration bubbling up in her chest. She bit her bottom lip, her mind already working, already planning.

"You're not escaping that easily," she murmured to the empty room.

She dressed with deliberate care, taking her time to style her hair in the soft waves he preferred and applying her makeup with the precision of a woman preparing for battle. She chose a strapless summer dress in bright yellow—something she was certain would capture and hold his attention. She massaged his favorite jasmine oil into her skin until she was as fragrant as a garden in bloom, each detail calculated to remind him of what he stood to lose.

When she emerged, he was seated at the yacht's stern, deep in conversation with the captain. She could feel his awareness of her, even if he didn't look back to see her.

"Mrs. Ricci, would you like us to prepare breakfast before we return to shore?" one of the crew members asked politely from behind her. She turned to address the crew with a lowered voice.

"Certainly. Is there television reception out here?"

The crew member smiled apologetically. "No, ma'am, there's no signal unless we're docked. The antenna is too weak at sea."

"I see. Well then, prepare breakfast for my husband and have it served on deck. I'll eat inside—I have some reading to catch up on."

"Right away, ma'am."

She heard Carmelo's low chuckle with the Captain as they joked about fishing and chose to ignore it completely. She selected a seat in the main cabin where he could glimpse her if he looked sideways, then deliberated between her leather-bound journal and the novel she'd been neglecting.

If she journaled, he'd assume she was processing their conflict, that he remained the center of her emotional universe. For Carmelo, that would be enough to satisfy his need for control. But if she chose the book, it would signal her determination to mentally escape from him, to prefer the separation he was imposing over reconciliation.

That was something the Wolf absolutely could not tolerate.

She chose the book.

When breakfast arrived for him, Carmelo glanced back toward the cabin with evident confusion. He watched her accept her own meal while appearing completely absorbed in her novel, her posture relaxed and content. His stare lingered for a long moment before he looked down at his untouched plate with visible agitation.

Within minutes, he'd gathered his breakfast and stalked into the cabin, choosing a seat directly across from her. A challenge.

Kathy felt his gaze burning into her, but continued reading with serene focus. She nibbled her toast and turned pages with unhurried ease. Carmelo cleared his throat meaningfully—she didn't even glance up. He began eating with exaggerated noise, clattering his silverware against the porcelain.

She simply turned another page.

Finally, his patience snapped. He activated the intercom with sharp aggression. "Captain, take us in. I have business to attend to." His voice was gruff and abrupt, barely controlled.

She sipped her coffee and kept reading.

After ten excruciating minutes of being ignored, he exploded from his chair and switched on the sound system, cranking Bruce Springsteen to an ear-splitting volume.

He'd won. Kathy looked up and glared at him with withering disdain. Carmelo stared back with grim satisfaction.

"What are you, two years old? Turn the music down," she said coolly, and knew he could read her lips.

"No," he replied, crossing his arms like a petulant child.

"Fine. I'll go read on deck." She stood with dignified grace.

He jumped up to block her path, and she paused with patience. "What exactly do you want, Carmelo? I'm not playing these ridiculous games with you."

He rolled his eyes and slumped back into his chair in defeat. She climbed to the upper deck with a secret smile, leaving him to sulk in his manufactured chaos.

When they docked, she accepted assistance only from the crew, pointedly refusing his offered hand in front of his men. They rode to the villa in glacial silence, the tension thick enough to cut.

Nino met them at the estate's grand entrance, sweeping Kathy into an enthusiastic bear hug that nearly lifted her off her feet. She embraced him warmly, genuinely happy to see his innocent joy. When he finally released her and led her inside, she glanced back to see Carmelo walking away in the opposite direction, his shoulders rigid with frustration.

The first round was hers.

The rest of the day passed without any sign of him, which completely undermined her strategy. It was impossible to punish someone who refused to be present for the punishment. She took a leisurely stroll through the villa's manicured gardens with Nino, then positioned herself strategically in the solarium where Carmelo typically enjoyed his evening cigars. She lingered there longer than necessary, pretending to read while actually listening for his footsteps.

He never appeared.

After an afternoon of playing games with Nino and sharing a quiet dinner where Carmelo's empty chair seemed to mock her efforts, she climbed the marble staircase to their bedroom with barely concealed hope. Perhaps he was waiting for her there, ready to engage in the emotional chess match she'd so carefully orchestrated.

The room was empty, his side of the bed still perfectly made from that morning.

Her heart plummeted like a stone dropping into dark water.

Her elaborate plan to ignore, tease, and slowly torture him with calculated indifference had backfired spectacularly. Worse, he'd turned her own weapon against her—now she was the one being ignored, the one left wondering and wanting.

She showered. Her confidence from that morning was crumbling like sand. When she slipped between the cool sheets alone, the vast bed felt like an ocean of loneliness. Every sound in the villa made her hope he was finally coming to her, but the hours crawled by in silence.

When she woke sometime after midnight and found his side still cold and empty, the tears came without warning. She pressed her face into his pillow, breathing in the faint scent of his cologne, and cried herself back to sleep—not because she missed him, she told herself, but because she'd underestimated her opponent.

The Wolf was playing a much longer game than she'd realized.

Morning.

Kathy woke with a flutter of hope, expecting to find him watching her sleep as he had the previous morning. The bedroom was empty, sunlight streaming through the windows onto cold, untouched sheets. She sat alone in the vast bed as fear began to crawl up her spine like ice water. This wasn't Carmelo pouting like a wounded lover. The Wolf wasn't toying with her emotions for sport.

Something fundamental had shifted, and she could feel it in the very air of the villa.

She slipped from bed and wrapped herself in a silk kimono that felt breezy against her skin, then began a systematic search of their floor. Nothing. She moved through the lower rooms with growing urgency, her bare feet silent on the marble floors. She could hear Nino's cheerful chatter from the breakfast room and assumed Carmelo was with him.

He wasn't.

Where the hell was he?

"Marco," she approached the only member of their security detail she truly trusted—a young, imposingly handsome man who'd been with the Ricci family for the past three years. Everyone else was new blood, hired guns with no loyalty beyond their paychecks.

"Where is he?" she asked, trying to keep the desperation from her voice.

"He asked to be left alone, Kathy. If you need him, he said—"

"Where is he?" The demand came out sharper than intended.

Marco's eyes flicked toward the left, toward the under-construction poolhouse nestled among the trees, then he turned and walked away without another word. Relief flooded through her so powerfully her knees nearly buckled. At least he hadn't abandoned her and Nino completely, hadn't escaped to some unreachable fortress while leaving them trapped here under his control.

But now she faced a more complex problem. How she approached him would determine everything. She had to push aside her mother's careful coaching about managing husbands, ignore Aunt Janey's lessons in emotional manipulation, and forget Debbie's retaliatory tactics with Matteo.

She had to reach him as simply Kathy.

But who was Kathy anymore? After years of survival and strategy, she wasn't sure she remembered that woman.

She walked toward the poolhouse, Bruce Springsteen's gravelly voice drifting through the air at near-deafening volume. Instead of approaching the door directly, she slipped around to peer through the window, some instinct warning her to observe before announcing herself.

He was there, shirtless in the wrinkled linen pants from yesterday, his dark but greying hair disheveled as if he'd been running his hands through it. A massive satellite phone was pressed to his ear while he paced, his free hand gesturing violently as he spoke in rapid, furious Italian to whomever was on the other end. In it, glinting in the morning light, was the hammer.

She froze at the sight of it, her blood turning to ice in her veins. He'd brought that cursed thing with them—the instrument of so much violence and pain in his past? She stepped back instinctively, nearly knocking over a terracotta planter. The thunderous music and his shouted conversation covered any noise she might have made.

Her heart hammering against her ribs, she turned and walked back toward the villa.

* * *

"KATHY? WHERE'S MELO?" Nino asked, looking around the dining room with a confused expression.

Kathy gently rubbed his massive hand. "Finish your dinner, sweetheart. He'll be back soon."

Nino returned to his meal, while Kathy pushed the pasta around on her plate, her appetite completely gone. Her mind kept circling back to that satellite phone in the poolhouse. She could slip out there and call Debbie, but then what? Even if Debbie told Matteo everything, what could that possibly change? Carmelo had committed federal crimes—faking his death while under investigation, reneging on his deal to turn against the other families in exchange for Matteo's pardon, robbing a grave, and using a dead woman's corpse to be her. He'd systematically torched his entire life, making sure there was no path back to their old existence.

The finality of it all hit her like a physical blow, and her eyes filled with tears just as she heard his footsteps approaching.

"Melo!" Nino bellowed joyfully, slamming his hand down on the table hard enough to rattle the crystal.

She looked up to see Carmelo freshly shaved and dressed in clean clothes, looking almost normal except for the haunted shadows beneath his eyes.

He walked directly to Nino and allowed his brother to engulf him in an enthusiastic bear hug. He patted Nino's cheek affectionately and promised to take him horseback riding the next morning. When that successfully calmed his brother's agitation, Carmelo's dark gaze found hers across the table.

She met his stare for a moment, then deliberately looked away.

He moved to her side and leaned down to brush his lips against her cheek, the gesture tender despite everything between them. With careful precision, he placed the wedding rings she'd left behind on the table beside her plate.

"I missed you," he whispered against her ear, his breath warm on her skin.

"Missed you too," she mumbled, the admission pulled from somewhere deep and honest. She put on her wedding ring first, then the other tarnished band.

Satisfied, the Wolf took his seat across from her as the staff brought his dinner. She found herself studying his face as he settled in. "Marco told me you were looking for me?" he asked.

"Yes. He wouldn't tell me where you were."

Carmelo continued to hold her gaze steadily. "I figured you wanted me to stay away. Give you the space you asked for."

"That's not what I want," she said quietly.

"What do you want, then?" His voice carried a dangerous edge. "To bake me a cupcake?"

Her eyes widened at the loaded reference. She glanced toward Nino, who was giggling delightedly. "Kathy bakes good cakes! Bake us cupcakes, Kathy! I want a pink one!"

She managed a smile for him. "Maybe later, Nino."

Turning back to Carmelo, she asked the question that mattered most: "Will you come to bed tonight?"

His eyebrow arched with sardonic amusement. "I haven't been invited."

"You want to fight with me? Keep me angry so you can stay angry?" Her voice grew stronger. "What is it with Ricci men constantly punishing the women they claim to love? Do you get off on me breaking like your father?"

Carmelo's fist slammed down on the table with enough force to make the silverware jump and ring like bells. Kathy allowed herself a small, satisfied smirk. That cupcake remark pissed her off.

"I've lost my appetite. I'm going to bed now," she sighed.

"Wait," Carmelo said sharply as she started to rise. "Please."

She settled back into her chair, waiting.

"I'm sorry. I'm not handling this right." His voice was rough with exhaustion and something that might have been defeat.

She studied his face, searching for the man beneath the Wolf's mask.

"Can I come to bed?" he asked, the question almost vulnerable.

Kathy stood and moved to Nino first, pressing a gentle kiss to his forehead. "Goodnight, sweetheart." Then she walked around the table to where Carmelo sat watching her every movement. She placed her hand on his shoulder, letting it drift down to rest over his heart, her diamond wedding ring gleaming in the warm light.

He captured her hand and brought it to his lips, pressing a reverent kiss to her palm.

She leaned close enough that only he could hear. "Play with your brother. Then come to bed. I'll listen to everything you need to tell me. I promise."

"Can I touch you tonight?" he asked, his hand on hers.

"As much as you want," she said.

She watched the tight coil of anger in his shoulders finally begin to unwind, then stepped back and left the brothers at the table. As she climbed the stairs, she understood exactly what his return to their bed would mean—and this time, she would handle things differently.

This time, she would meet him as simply Kathy, not as a wife armed for war, but as the woman who'd loved him long before she'd learned to weaponize that love. And she would make him face some hard truths, so they can finally unite and save their family.

CHAPTER 18

TREMÉ NEW ORLEANS 1950

Debbie,

By the time you get this letter, we will have already talked. But all of the things happening right now are so crazy, so wild, I have to write them down to make sure it's real. Need to tuck these thoughts away with someone safe, and that has always been you.

New Orleans felt like a fever dream at first. Aunt Janey welcomed us into a world that Willa and I could never have foreseen: Big houses dipped in ice cream colors, fancy-dressed Negro servants attending to Sicilian mobsters and their mulatto wives, jazz music spilling from every doorway. Women like Janey move through it all like empresses—café-au-lait skin, French rolling off their tongues, bowing to no earthly authority. I mistook that beauty for genuine freedom.

Lord, how I wish I'd heeded Mama's warnings about Janey. Wish I'd never let her sink those perfectly manicured claws into my heart. There's something rotten at Janey's core,

Debbie—a bitterness that spreads through everything she touches like poison in a well. It's the poison and the curse.

Janey played us. Worst of all, she played Willa. She planned Willa's destruction with the precision of a master chess player.

From the moment we stepped off that train, Janey transformed our sweet girl: draped her in expensive silks, arranged her hair in sophisticated styles, whispered seductive lies about "privilege" and "claiming your rightful place." Last Wednesday morning, I woke to find Willa's bed cold and empty. She'd vanished in the night—run off with Jean-Baptiste Thibodeaux, a Creole snake wrapped in old plantation money and European manners.

These people aren't like us, Debbie. They own a world between Black and white: French passed down through generations, skin ranging from warm honey to pale cream, eyes like golden amber or Spanish moss. Some pass for white when it suits them; all of them wield their mixed bloodline like a weapon against those they consider beneath them. They worst than the white people, because they are supposed to be us.

I knew he was trouble the moment he first set eyes on Willa—like a hunter studying prey, calculating exactly how to spring his trap. I tried everything, begged her to see past his charm. But Janey? She might as well have delivered Willa to his doorstep with a ribbon around her neck. She handed our innocent Willa to a man who collects dark-skinned beauties like other men collect hunting trophies.

Four days now. Not a whisper of news, not a trace of where he's taken her. Carmelo and Caesar attempted to storm the Thibodeaux plantation yesterday, even without Marcello's blessing, because I've been so upset. They were met by armed guards and turned away at the gates like common trespassers.

Their "family compound" sprawls across so much land it's bigger than the Wynns and Jensens' combined.

When I confronted Janey, she merely sipped her imported sherry with those eyes glittering like something was amusing her. My pain made her smile. And if it wasn't my pain, it was her own. Because that's what I think is wrong with Aunt Janey. Whatever happened to her when Mama left her behind has stolen her soul. And she spends all night thinking of ways to steal the souls of others.

I begged her to tell me why she did it. She said: "Innocence is such a burden, chère. Survival is what transforms girls into women who truly matter." What kind of monster speaks such words about an innocent girl? What manner of woman destroys a child to prove some twisted philosophical point?

I've left that cursed mansion and taken refuge in a boarding house room in the Quarter, where the drunkards and prostitutes can be heard outside my window all night. Of course, Carmelo is with me. I even go to watch him practice for his fight in the ring. The Sicilians don't care when I'm around. Like I said. It's different here.

Tomorrow brings Carmelo's fight—the entire city buzzes with anticipation—but every prayer I whisper is for Willa alone. Praying, she draws breath. Praying she remembers the way back to people who genuinely love her in Butts. Praying that whatever happened to her doesn't turn her into Janey. Praying she survives.

Protect that precious baby. Tell him his Aunt Kat loves him.

I miss you,
Kat

. . .

Kathy folded the letter with deliberate precision. She sealed the envelope with a lick and then addressed it to Debbie in her most careful penmanship. *Mail it. Coffee. Find news of Willa.* A mechanical checklist in her mind to keep her anchored in sanity.

She turned from the scarred wooden desk, her gaze inevitably drawn to the rumpled bed that dominated the tiny room.

Her stomach clenched with a mix of memory and shame.

Carmelo's sexual appetite had increased to a level she could not have originally conceived. Last night, his mouth had mapped territories on her she hadn't known existed—his tongue relentless, demanding surrender until she'd sobbed his name, while forcing her to sit on his face until her body convulsed. He worshipped her body like a sacrament, leaving her trembling and reborn. Then showed her things he wanted her to do to herself while he watched. Every night, Carmelo came up with something new and tantalizing. There was just nothing left unexplored but one. He wanted her to put his penis in her mouth, and she refused. Nothing in her life prepared her for the incandescent ruin of her virginal thoughts of intimacy.

And he left a message that he would come home early because he wanted more.

The problem? Sex made babies. Babies without marriage destroyed girls like her. Hell, it destroyed girls everywhere.

Kathy toiled over her growing concerns as she stripped the sheets with sharp, angry movements, the scent of sweat and sin rising like an accusation from the tangled linen. Bundling the evidence under her arm, she pressed Debbie's letter against her ribs and headed out.

How come sex was all he wanted when they were alone? What about reading books and telling stories to each other, or playing cards like in the attic? What about just lying together and being one person as they talked about Africa and safaris?

This. This was why mothers preached marriage before passion, why the Church built walls around desire. What she and Carmelo shared wasn't mere pleasure—it was playing with lightning over and over. Her prayers this morning had been desperate whispers that dissolved into shaky sobs of relief when her period arrived on time that morning.

Downstairs, the boarding house hallway reeked of mildew and yesterday's cooking grease, the narrow space cramped with the dreams of people who couldn't afford better.

"Mr. Chen?" Her voice sounded thin and brittle in the quiet. "I need to arrange washing for my linens."

The elderly Chinese proprietor glanced up from his meticulous ledger, spectacles catching the dim gaslight. "Afternoon tubs available. All empty now." He accepted the bundle with a nod and handed her a numbered slip. Kathy fumbled twenty cents across the scarred counter, the coins cold against her palm. "I'll return soon," she promised, already turning toward escape.

She pushed through the heavy door—and froze.

The Quarter's morning mist hung thick and heavy over the street, softening the edges of slick cobblestones and the muddy swell of the Mississippi it floated in off of. Parked directly across the narrow street was Carmine Boanno's gleaming sedan, its chrome bumpers catching what little light penetrated the fog.

He leaned against the front fender with deceptive casualness, his silver-topped cane planted firmly, its tip disappearing into the thick waves of fog on the uneven stones. Even at this distance, she could feel the weight of his pale gaze studying her like a specimen under glass.

Kathy spun on her heel, heart hammering against Debbie's letter.

"Janey misses you terribly, Kathy." Carmine's voice cut through the damp morning air with the precision of a blade, calm but carrying easily across the empty street. "She sends her sincere apologies."

Kathy quickened her pace, her heels clicking against the wet stones. She dashed inside the postman's store and caught her breath. She then went to the counter and mailed her letter to Debbie. When she came out of the door, Carmine had driven the car further down the street to greet her.

"Don't make an old cripple chase you through these streets!" he called after her, and she caught the thread of genuine strain beneath his commanding tone. "These damaged legs won't cooperate with such athletics."

She stopped despite every instinct screaming for flight. The raw wound of Janey's calculated betrayal throbbed like an infected tooth, demanding something she couldn't name. Answers? Justice? Some acknowledgment of the devastation that betrayal brought?

Carmine opened the passenger door without another word—an invitation.

Kathy crossed the treacherous cobblestones to the car. She slid onto the cold leather seat.

The door closed. Carmine eased himself behind the wheel, intimately acquainted with pain, his cane clattering into the foot well. The powerful engine purred to life beneath them.

"I'm only here," Kathy said without looking at him, her gaze fixed on the fog-shrouded street ahead as the sedan pulled smoothly into the sparse morning traffic, "because you know something about Willa. I can feel it."

Carmine guided the car through the winding streets with practiced ease, his reflection in the rearview mirror as grim as a funeral director's. "I know everything, *ma chère*. That's precisely why I came." He adjusted the mirror with one leather-gloved hand. "Let's discuss it properly—over a cup of coffee and biscuits."

"Fine. As long as Janey doesn't join us," she mumbled.

Carmine chuckled. "You have no idea how much my Janey loves you. But no, she won't be present. Just a talk, and I'll deliver you to the gym."

CHAPTER 19

THE COFFE DISAPPOINTS. THE TRUTH IS BETTER THAN A LIE

Carmine tapped his silver spoon against the delicate porcelain saucer, the sound sharp as a funeral bell in the café's intimate atmosphere.

"The coffee disappoints?" He nodded toward her untouched cup, steam curling up.

Kathy's lip pressed into a thin line.

"Why are you stalling, Carmine? Every time I ask about Willa, you pivot and weave like one of the street hustlers." Her voice carried the cutting edge of barely controlled desperation. "You promised me answers over this 'mysterious coffee' you kept insisting on. So either tell me how to get my Willa back from those vultures—or admit this is just another one of Janey's twisted mind games."

Carmine's slender, dark eyebrow arched with what appeared to be genuine surprise.

"You truly hold anger for Janey? After everything she's done for you?" he asked.

Kathy's laugh scraped raw against her throat.

"That shocks you? Because we share Elliott Wynn's blood? Think all the women in our family are cursed with just his blood. Janey's mother, my grandmother, was made from iron and steel and taught us being sweet wasn't a weakness but our greatest protection." She leaned forward across the small table, the café's genteel chatter fading to meaningless static around them. "Janey is—"

"Say it," Carmine commanded quietly, his ice-pale eyes narrowing to predatory slits. The gentleman's mask slipped for just an instant, and Kathy glimpsed the killer Carmelo had warned her lived beneath the cultured surface.

"Evil." The word tore from her throat. "But not me, and not my Mama. Janey is a devil."

Carmine didn't flinch, didn't blink. Only the subtle tightening of his jaw betrayed the cold fury coiling like a serpent in his chest. This was not what Carmelo would become, Kathy realized with chilling clarity—a man who loved a woman's darkness so completely he became its willing guardian. She and Carmelo may not be perfect, but they weren't Janey and Carmine.

A shadow fell across their table like a cloud passing over the sun.

Kathy turned to find Pinkie standing there, wringing her gloved hands with barely contained anxiety, her usually bright eyes red-rimmed and haunted.

"This was a setup from the beginning," Kathy seethed. She surged upward to flee.

But Pinkie caught her wrist, not restraining, but anchoring her with gentleness.

"Please, Kathy." Tears gathered and threatened to spill. "Just five minutes. Woman to woman, heart to heart. *I'm* begging you."

The raw vulnerability in that plea undid something fundamental in Kathy's anger. She slumped back into her chair as Carmine stood with fluid grace, adjusting his fedora. He pressed a protective kiss to Pinkie's temple—the gesture both tender and submissive—then walked away with the aid of his cane.

"I'm not staying unless you tell me how Willa is. Where is Willa?" Kathy demanded the moment they were alone. "Is she even still breathing?"

Pinkie dabbed at her streaming tears with a delicate lace handkerchief, her composure fracturing like fine crystal.

"My cousin works in the Thibodeaux kitchens, has for years. She's been watching over Willa as best she can."

"You've actually seen Willa?" Kathy gasped.

"Can't get anywhere near her, *chère*. Thibodeaux land is a fortress disguised as a sanctuary—high walls, armed men who work for the family, secrets buried deeper than any roots." Pinkie's voice grew softer, more troubled. "But my cousin sees her sometimes... walking the gardens on Jean-Baptiste's arm. Smiling at something, he whispered. Letting him hold her hand like they're courting properly. He doesn't bring her in around the family. She is kept there in one of the cottages for him."

Kathy's palm cracked against the table with enough force to rattle the delicate coffee cups and silence nearby conversations.

"Kept or a prisoner? That man is taking advantage of her, tricking her. I told you she came to Butts as a little kid, traumatized; she didn't even talk. We don't know her real age or birthday. He's hurting her!"

Pinkie's gaze held steady.

"We warned her, Kathy. That night, Janey and I told her everything, how wealthy men of privilege like J.B. collect beautiful dark-skinned girls like exotic dolls for their amusement, how the Thibodeaux fortune was built on sugar and suffering, on the broken backs of enslaved people who looked exactly like us, how that same family hurt me. And when they inevitably tire of their playthings and discard them when the fun fades."

Kathy went completely still. This wasn't the story Janey had told her at all.

"And Willa? What she say?" Kathy asked.

Pinkie was slow to respond.

"Did she believe you? Understand?" Kathy asked.

"She said she'd rather swallow sweet poison in New Orleans than starve slowly on empty hope in Mississippi, that she was tired of being invisible, of not mattering to anyone. She wanted to be seen—truly seen—even if it was all a lie."

The truth hit Kathy hard, stealing the breath from her lungs.

Her own tears came then, hot and bitter. *Invisible.* Willa had named the wound they all carried.

"Why didn't you wake me that night?" Kathy asked. "Why didn't you give me a chance to talk her out of it?"

Pinkie reached across the chipped tabletop, her touch surprised Kathy at how comforting it felt.

"Would it have mattered, *ma douce*? Janey told me about your history and her trip to New York. When you ran to Carmelo despite every warning, every obstacle—did any voice of reason stop you?" Her smile was sad. "Some hungers drown out everything else, even good sense."

Kathy's heart broke then—for Willa's naive courage, for her own mirrored recklessness, for all the women who'd chosen dangerous love over safe emptiness.

"Will he hurt her?" Kathy asked.

Pinkie's answer was carefully measured, brutally honest.

"Carmine made certain arrangements before she left. Her body will remain safe—Jean-Baptiste knows the consequences of damaging what's under protection. Her heart? Her mind? Her spirit?" Pinkie gave a helpless shrug. "When he inevitably tires of her, she'll come home to us. Changed, raw with shame perhaps, but alive. That's been my experience."

"But he could love her, right? Like, Carmelo loves me? Is it possible?" Kathy pleaded. "They could actually be in love."

Pinkie shook his head slowly. "I've known of Jean Baptiste since we were kids. Never seen him love anybody but himself. She will survive him."

"And that's supposed to be enough? Surviving?" Kathy choked out.

"Survival is the first victory for girls like us, *chère*. Everything else is luxury we can't always afford."

A weighted silence stretched between them, heavy with unspoken truths about their world's cruel mathematics. Then Pinkie leaned closer."I hate to do this. To ask this. When you are so upset, but I have no choice."

"Ask what?" asked Kathy.

"Janey's having one of her spells."

"Spells?" Kathy repeated.

"Unraveling—worse than I've witnessed since she came back from California, and Carmine was upset with her. She had left us for two years before she returned, then ran off to you in Butts. It nearly drove him mad."

"I know, she told me she was in California," Kathy said. "What do these spells do to her? What causes them?"

"Losing her favorite niece's love and respect, I suppose. You never know what triggers Janey. Her mind cracks at times, and the spells come and go. Some of them are worse than others. This one looks bad."

"I don't care what happens to that woman—"

"She's your blood!" Pinkie insisted. "Love doesn't quit when someone disappoints—it fights harder to pull us back from the edge. And Janey? She's standing on a very high cliff right now, Kathy. We can't reach her. But you might. She was so excited about you and Willa coming. She planned everything for you girls. In her twisted way, she thought giving Willa to the Thibodeauxs was a good thing. She really did."

Kathy stared toward the café entrance where Carmine waited like a well-dressed soldier; his mission was clear. Guard and protect Janey at all costs.

"Fine," Kathy breathed, the word turning to ash in her mouth. "I'll come. But I'm not promising forgiveness or understanding."

Pinkie's "thank you" was barely audible, a tremor of desperate relief as she guided Kathy toward the door.

CHAPTER 20

JANEY'S ATONES

The house didn't just welcome them—it swallowed them whole.

Kathy stepped across the threshold into a silence so thick it pressed against her eardrums. No creak of floorboards. No distant clatter from the kitchen. Only the frantic drumming of her own heart.

Carmine walked stiffly through the gloom, his cane *humping* dully as he veered left toward his study—and the bourbon that waited there. In the span of the drive, he'd aged. Streaks of silver threaded his temples, Kathy hadn't noticed before; his shoulders sagged under an invisible weight. Every step seemed labored, pain radiating from him in waves.

"It drains him," Pinkie whispered, watching him disappear. She set her purse on the hall table with deliberate calm, then peeled off her gloves, finger by trembling finger. "When Janey shatters... he shatters too. When she disappears, he becomes a ghost in life. It's just torture. Getting her well is the only way to mend him."

She turned to Kathy, eyes dark with exhaustion. "Here's how this visit goes. Mama gave Janey laudanum in her tea. Pa..." Pinkie's voice hitched. "Pa tied her wrists to the bedposts. They're too old to wrestle her demons anymore. I made them do it for their safety when we decided to come for you."

Kathy was shocked. "You tied her up? Like some—"

"Like someone who tried to claw her own eyes out last night!" Pinkie's composure snapped. She turned on Kathy. "She was screaming about spiders under her skin. About blood in the walls. Would you rather we let her break her hands on the window trying to fly?"

There was a beat of horrified silence.

"We go in, united," Pinkie whispered. "When the laudanum fades… she'll need us. *Both* of us."

Kathy's gaze slowly moved to the staircase looming like a dark spine in the hall. "Will she… try to hurt us?" The question felt small, childish. "Has she ever hurt *you*?"

"Never meaning to. Even at her worst, the harm's never aimed outward." Pinkie paused, the memory tightening her voice. "And I never tell her when it happens that she does hurt one of us. Truth would shatter what's left of her. You don't know how fragile she is beneath all that fire."

She turned, facing Kathy fully.

"I had just turned eleven when I found them. Carmine on their bedroom floor, drowning in his own blood—vomiting it, choking on it. Janey was naked, fresh bruises from their sex games, kneeling beside him, covered in his blood, rocking back and forth like a child asking him to please and hurry and die. She'd baked him a pie days ago, and nothing. She then slipped poison little candies into his whiskey and convinced him to drink. All to avenge me."

"I didn't run for a doctor. I ran to the train station, sent a telegram to your mother: 'JANEY DYING COME NOW.' Your mama came on the first train south. She walked into that nightmare… and pulled them both back from the edge. Stopped the bleeding. Flushed the poison. Sat with Janey for three days straight, singing hymns while Janey raved about devils in the wallpaper and the Tinsel man."

A tear traced Pinkie's cheek.

"Wait? Mama has a cure? Knows a cure?" Kathy asked.

"She knows a lot about the poison. I think their mother spent the most time with your mother, teaching her how to use and care for the person. I seen it with my own eyes. Carmine is alive because of your Mama."

"I don't know my family at all," Kathy said.

"Your mother is a good woman. But she doesn't have any faith in Janey. She didn't see the broken girl who poisoned the man she loved because she thought love was the sickness that needed to be cured. She didn't understand—Janey's pain doesn't lash out. It turns inward." Pinkie pressed a fist to her own chest, mirroring the old wound.

"Why is she like *this*?" Kathy asked.

Pinkie extended her hand. "Help me bring her back. Just this once."

Kathy took her hand in solidarity. They ascended the stairs, hands clenched like lifelines.

"Untie her," Pinkie said.

Elmer limped to the bedside. With practiced care, he and his wife loosened the restraints binding Janey. Elmer pressed a kiss to Janey's feverish brow—a gesture of such patient devotion that Kathy's throat tightened.

Mama needs to see this, she thought. *How they love her.* Kathy thought.

As the elderly couple retreated, Pinkie stripped away the heavy blankets Janey's other mother had insisted on.

Pinkie tossed aside the cold cloth. "Mama's stuck in the old ways," she murmured, smoothing Janey's sweat-soaked nightgown. "Thinks she's possessed. That we need an exorcism." Her eyes met Kathy's, weary. "It's not that simple."

"Nothing about Janey is simple," Kathy murmured.

Pinkie nodded. "Complicated doesn't begin to cover it."

"Will she wake up soon?"

"Should fade soon—we've been gone two hours." Pinkie gestured to the window seat. "Sit. She'll talk when she's ready."

"You mean wake up?" Kathy slid into the chair, leaning toward the breeze.

"No. *Talk*. You'll see." Pinkie picked up her magazine. "We wait."

Another hour bled past.

Janey's eyes opened—lucid, and fixed solely on Kathy.

Kathy glanced at Pinkie, still absorbed in her reading, then back at her aunt. Frozen, wordless. Janey lay perfectly still, her gaze unbroken, dark hair stark against the pillow, and partially in her face.

"She's awake," Kathy said softly.

Pinkie's head snapped up at the sound. She blinked rapidly, then nodded with sudden understanding. Closing her magazine with deliberate care, no fast actions. She stood. Kathy started to follow suit, uncertain of the protocol, but Pinkie gestured gently for her to remain seated.

Kathy heard Pixie speak to Janey in French, and immediately, Janey's eyes fluttered closed. Tears began streaming down her face like a dam had finally burst. Only then did Pinkie approach the bed with careful steps.

Janey reached for Pinkie with the urgency of a lost child seeking her mother's embrace. Pinkie gathered her close without hesitation, cradling Janey's trembling form against her breasts. Janey wept openly now, her words tumbling out in broken French while Pinkie murmured soothing responses and stroked her hair with tenderness.

Kathy sat frozen in her chair, wishing that she could understand the words that caused such profound anguish. Part of her longed to cross the room and offer comfort, but something held her back—uncertainty, old hurt, or perhaps the recognition that this moment belonged to Pinkie and Janey alone. So she remained still and silent, bearing witness to her aunt's breakdown while her own heart ached with conflicted emotions.

Soon, Janey's tears subsided, and she calmed down. Pinkie leaned closer, speaking gently to her. Janey opened her eyes, meeting Kathy's gaze, and gave a slow, hesitant nod.

Pinkie carefully helped Janey sit up.

"You came here to apologize to me?" Janey asked Kathy.

Kathy blinked in surprise, glancing briefly at Pinkie, who was smoothing the tangles out of Janey's hair. Pinkie gave her a reassuring wink.

"Yes, I came to say sorry," Kathy replied softly.

Janey sniffled slightly, nodding again. "Okay, okay. We can talk. But we need to hurry—Pinkie says Carmine has a surprise for me."

"Yes, he does," Pinkie affirmed gently. "You talk with Kathy, hear her out, and then explain your side of things. Everyone is fine. I'll tell Carmine you'll be ready soon. Ma is upset you missed her breakfast. You know how she loves to feed you."

"Alright, stop fussing," Janey said, gently pushing Pinkie's hands away with a slight smile.

Pinkie chuckled softly. "I'll be back soon, ladies." She stood and walked to the door and then closed it quietly behind her.

Kathy swallowed nervously; her heart lodged in her throat as Janey slowly eased herself out of bed.

"You said some awful things to me, Kathy," Janey said, moving to her vanity and beginning to pin up her hair.

"I know, Auntie. I was upset. Willa left, and it seemed like you didn't care."

"That's not my fault!" Janey spun around sharply, eyes blazing. "I always get blamed for everything! Mama died, and all the sisters blamed me. If Elliot Wynn hadn't kicked me, Mama wouldn't have poisoned him and gotten herself hanged. I took all the blame. Only Brenda believed me, and she left me with Mae."

"Mae? Who's Mae?" Kathy asked cautiously.

"Mae! The oldest sister!" Janey exclaimed, turning back to the mirror. Kathy stood up. She stared at her aunt's reflection in the mirror, and Janey noticed the fear on Kathy's face. She steadied herself, calming slightly. "Mae is the oldest. Then came Izzy, Pearl, Lizzie, Everlene, Betsie, Brenda—and then me. We're sisters. Mae was in charge. Mae told us what to do, who to go with, and who to marry. Mae told Brenda to leave me behind. Brenda obeyed, and Mae took me with Izzy back to Jackson."

Kathy nodded gently. "What happened in Jackson, Auntie?"

Janey took a shaky breath. "The Tinsel Man. Cajun. Swamp rat. He came. He said he needed a worker to collect all the tin cans for the recycling. Mae and Izzy fought about it, but Mae insisted I had to earn my keep, so Izzy couldn't stop him. He took me. He kept me. Mae and Izzy came looking when days go bye and I didn't return, but he told them I was dead. Said the gators took me on the river. It was a lie—I heard him say it. Izzy didn't believe him and came searching for me twice, but Mae never did. He kept me there and did terrible things to me," Janey started to scrub her face with the rag and bin of warm water on her vanity, her voice trembling. "He hurt me so badly I can't have children, and I can barely do anything with sex without the pain between my legs. But one night, I gave him pain. Real pain. I got away into the swamps and went back home. I told Mae and Izzy everything, but Mae didn't believe me. Because I killed the Tinsel Man, she said I had to leave. That if the law didn't hang me, then the Cajuns would feed me to the gators. Izzy packed me a bag and sent me to Big Mama. I was there, and Big Mama tried to help, but Mae came for me. Say I hers. I her sister. Take me again to give me away to another man. Izzy help me run when she heard Mae make another deal. Gave me Mama's recipe book, and told me to follow the Mississippi—that she'd find me someday. So I left."

"The Tinsel Man? He dead?" Kathy approached.

"I didn't mean to hurt Willa," Janey whispered. "I wanted to help her. She needs to be strong, not a silly dreamer girl. Do you know what Mae does to silly dreamer girls? Willa has to face the pain, like we all did. Then I can help her just like I helped you when I went to New York and dealt with the consigliere. Like I've helped Pinkie and the others."

Janey dropped the rag in the water with a sloshing splash. She went to her vanity, opening a drawer filled with various hair bows and clips. Kathy noticed one—a favorite she'd lost in Butts, when Janey came to stay. Janey had taken it. She also saw Willa's hair scarf, among many other women's trinkets—tokens from lives Janey had encountered.

"I keep them safe," Janey explained softly. "I protect everyone from the Tinsel Man. From the spiders in the box. The knives he uses on you. I tried telling Brenda, but she called me evil when I explained and told me to repent. None of the sisters wants me around except Izzy.

Only Izzy loves me. And my new family. And my Carmine. He likes to hurt me, too, but he takes care of me, too. And now I got you. Soon I'll have Willa. She'll be mine when Pinkie leaves."

Kathy reached out and pulled Janey into a comforting embrace. Janey wept softly on her shoulder while Kathy soothed her gently, doing her best to understand despite the confusing revelations. After Janey calmed down, Kathy helped her get ready for Carmine.

She carefully washed her off, applied soothing oils, and gently groomed and styled her hair. While Kathy tended to her, Janey recounted her wedding to Carmine, describing how all of Creole society attended and called her the most beautiful bride they'd ever seen. Said that the painting is hanging in her special room and she will show it to her.

Before long, Janey was smiling again, and Kathy found herself smiling too. She selected a black lace dress for Janey instead of the white one, and Janey agreed happily. Once they finished, they stepped out of the room and encountered Pinkie waiting in the hall.

Pinkie glanced over Janey, raising an eyebrow playfully. "I thought we wore black at night?"

"Kathy suggested it," Janey replied.

"She needs more colors than just white, green, and black," Kathy explained. "We should go shopping and get her every color of the rainbow, but I think she looks the prettiest in this."

Pinkie nodded approvingly. "I agree."

"Is Carmine ready for me?" Janey asked eagerly.

"Yes, he's hungry. He said to hurry," Pinkie answered with a grin.

Janey smiled brightly and marched ahead of them. "He's always so impatient, I swear."

* * *

BEFORE KATHY LEFT to return to the Quarter, she paused in the courtyard, quietly observing Carmine and Janey. Pinkie joined her, and together they watched as Carmine set aside his cane and guided

Janey gracefully into a slow, circular dance as the jazz record played. Janey's face lit up with pure joy.

"He truly loves her, doesn't he?" Kathy murmured.

"More than you know," Pinkie said softly.

"Then why does she run from him, from this place that gives her safety?" Kathy asked.

"She goes to find others who need her help—those who need her deadly candies," Pinkie explained sadly. "She thinks it's her purpose, the reason she can't have children, why the Tinsel Man still haunts her dreams along with the spiders that ate away at her every night in his cabin when he locked her in a box. Carmine has learned to accept the bargain because she owns his soul."

"She says he hurts her during sex," Kathy asked.

"She told you that?" Pinkie eyes stretched.

Kathy nodded.

"They are strange. Trust me, we protect her, and there is nothing anyone can do to separate those two." Pinkie hesitated, then continued quietly, "Can I tell you something? Just between us?"

Kathy nodded. "Of course."

"I'm leaving soon. I want an education, to marry, to build a life. Carmine's health is failing—he could live another day or another decade. I believe Janey took your Willa and let Jean Baptiste hurt her, not to punish or teach her, but because Janey will need someone once Carmine is gone, once I'm gone. She needs someone vulnerable she can care for, heal, and love. Someone who will be loyal and love her back. She sees that in Willa. That's what I think."

Kathy stared out at Janey, now swaying gently in Carmine's arms, his hand tenderly stroking her back as he whispered loving words only a husband would share.

"I don't understand why there's so much pain in the world," Kathy said softly. "Why can't we just love freely and openly?"

"Don't ask why, Kathy," Pinkie said gently. "Just live—live each day like it's your last."

Kathy smiled faintly and nodded. "I'll try."

CHAPTER 21

THE WOLF OF NEW ORLEANS - 1950

The night blazed like hell's furnace. Even the air seared her lungs when she breathed as Kathy pushed through the sweat-slicked French Quarter crowd, grateful for Carmine Boanno's armed escort and the reconciliation that had made her and Janey family again.

She needed her own support tonight. For three days, she'd watched Carmelo transform in the ring—her gentle lover becoming someone feral and dangerous. She'd tended his bruises, loved his pain away, whispered encouragement against his battered skin. But what girl wanted to watch the man she adored summon rage like a weapon? What woman could bear seeing her heart walk willingly into slaughter?

The whispers followed her: *The last man who fought the Klan's boy face was crushed and his neck snapped.*

"You okay, *chère?*" Janey squeezed her trembling hand.

"I think so," Kathy whispered.

Above Bourbon Street's garish neon, the Shamrock Arena's marquee blazed:

SOLDATO "THE WOLF" RICCI vs. "MISSISSIPPI MAULER" Sicilian Steel vs. Southern Savagery

"They changed his name," Janey observed.

Kathy stared at the electric letters spelling out her lover's new identity. "I see."

"*Dai, andiamo!*" A Sicilian capo cleared their path through the mob, delivering them ringside past the Marcello family and New Orleans' Black elite. Men's eyes devoured them both—desire and fear in equal measure. She kept her eyes averted, feeling undressed by their intense stares.

"Ignore them, *chérie*," Janey winked. "They can look but never touch."

Inside, the arena reeked of cigar smoke, cheap gin, and blood-hunger. Kathy's gut twisted as she studied the ring—a squared circle of stained canvas under merciless lights. The Mauler paced like a chained gladiator, a beast of a man, while his Klan handlers smirked from their corner in pristine white suits.

Then—*him*.

Carmelo emerged from the shadows like a angel of war. Caesar draped emerald silk edged in gold across his shoulders, but beneath the Marcello colors, his body gleamed with sweat and liniment. Every scar told a story of survival: the hammer-blow ridge along his ribs, fresh bruises from brutal training, the faint pink stain on his lips from her ruby kiss—the one he'd refused to wipe away after she made love to him in a tight closet before leaving him to his fate and getting dress for the event.

His eyes, black as midnight water, found hers across the screaming crowd.

He winked.

I'm here, her heart hammered. *I love you.*

The bell clanged like a funeral chime.

Round 1:

The bell barely finished ringing when the Mauler exploded forward—*330 pounds of muscle and malice*. His first punch wasn't a strike but a wrecking ball, whistling past Carmelo's temple so close it stirred his hair. *Whiff*. Carmelo pivoted on slick soles—*Brooklyn foot-*

work threaded with Sicilian grace—letting momentum carry the brute past him.

The crowd roared as the Mauler's second swing cratered the air where Carmelo's ribs had been. But the third? A sledgehammer left hook *cracked* into Carmelo's shoulder.

THUD.

Kathy's teeth rattled in her skull as if *she'd* been hit. Carmelo staggered, the impact vibrating through his spine—but as the Mauler wound up for the decapitating right haymaker, Carmelo *dropped*. Not away. *Down and through.*

The Mauler's fist swung over his ducked head, hitting empty air with enough force but nowhere to land.

Carmelo rose, smiling through split lips.

First blood drawn: the giant's balance tested. Now for the rest.

Round 3:

Blood trickled from Carmelo's nose; each breath he took sent fire through ribs that felt like cracked glass. The plan was working—barely. *Wear down the giant, then unleash hell.* That is what Matteo said to him on the phone before the fight. It's what Caesar coached him from the corner of the ring. But Christ, every blow from those sledgehammer fists felt like it was crushing his bones to powder.

The Mauler's breathing had turned ragged, his massive frame finally showing cracks in its armor. Sweat poured down his face like a river, but his grin remained vicious as he taunted in a drawl thick from his swollen jaw: *"That all you got, little meatball? My mammy hits harder than you."*

Carmelo's left eye was swelling shut, his shoulder screaming from absorbing punishment that would have flattened lesser men. But he'd felt the giant's punches losing their snap, seen the hesitation creeping into those wild swings.

Now.

Carmelo answered with his finesse. He feinted left and caught the Mauler leaning. It was then his right cross-hook *cracked* against the giant's jaw like a rifle shot. The big man's eyes rolled white for a heartbeat, his knees buckling.

The crowd gasped as over 300 pounds of fury swayed like a falling tree, barely holding firm.

"Your mammy's a bitch!" Carmelo spat, and the bell rang, and he walked away.

Round 5:

Pure savagery. The Mauler drove Carmelo into the ropes like a battering ram, his massive fists hammering kidneys with sickening thuds that echoed through the arena. Each blow sounded like meat hitting concrete.

Kathy sobbed openly now, mascara streaming down her cheeks. This wasn't boxing—it was execution. The giant was trying to kill him, and the referee was letting him.

Even Janey, who'd been languidly fanning herself with bored sophistication, sat frozen in her seat, her usual mask of indifference cracking to reveal raw terror.

The Mauler unleashed everything—two decades of rage, oppression, subjugation at the hands of the Klan on Carmelo. Every ounce of his 300-pound frame behind punches that would have shattered ribs. Carmelo's body folded like a broken doll.

He went *down*.

The referee leaped over him, counting. Carmelo's chest heaved against the stained canvas, blood pooling beneath his face. *Get up. GET UP!* Kathy screamed silently, her nails drawing blood from her palms.

At seven, he pushed himself up on trembling arms. At nine, he stood—swaying, glassy-eyed, but upright. The ref grabbed his face, checking his pupils, searching for signs of a man too broken to continue.

The fight resumed.

Then Carmelo *exploded*.

Like a switch had been thrown, like a survivor of Cosimo's hammer, he became a whirlwind of calculated violence—elbows carving through the giant's guard, pivots that turned defense into attack. He drove the stunned Mauler backward step by bloody step until the ropes trapped the beast, who moments before had seemed unstoppable.

The bell rang. Salvation.

Round 8:

Carmelo's left eye had swollen completely shut, a purple grotesquery that turned half his world black. The Mauler's nose was pulverized meat, blood streaming down his chest like war paint. They circled each other like wounded predators in a gladiator's ring, breathing fire through shattered mouths.

In the VIP seats, Don Marcello's sons exchanged cold, calculating nods. Money was about to change hands. Klansmen spat tobacco-stained curses into the smoky air. The end crackled through the arena like electricity—everyone felt it pressing down like a storm about to break.

Carmelo felt it too, and he charged straight toward destiny.

The Mauler lunged with desperate fury, telegraphing a wild haymaker meant to decapitate. But Carmelo dropped—*not falling, flowing*—into a perfect crouch, every hour of training crystallizing into this single moment. As the giant's fist sailed harmlessly overhead, Carmelo drove upward like a compressed spring releasing, his right fist connecting with surgical precision against the Mauler's exposed throat. The weak spot the Marcellos told him to aim for.

A sickening *crunch* echoed through sudden silence—a shattered larynx.

The giant's eyes bulged, his gloves clawing at his crushed windpipe. He staggered backward like a drunk man, then crashed to the canvas with the sound of a felled redwood—a thunderous impact that somehow seemed louder than the crowd's roar.

Absolute silence.

Nearly a thousand people held their breath as one. The Mauler lay motionless, a broken mountain of flesh. The referee stepped over cautiously and began his count, each number falling like a hammer blow into the hush.

"Seven... eight... nine... ten!"

Then—explosion.

"WOLF! WOLF! WOLF!"

The arena erupted as the referee seized Carmelo's blood-slicked glove and thrust it skyward. Kathy screamed until her throat was raw, and she and Janey collapsed into each other's arms—laughing, sobbing, delirious with relief and disbelief.

He had done the impossible. The Wolf had conquered the South.

* * *

THERE WAS a press shoving cameras in his face. There were the mafia bosses demanding their pot of gold. There were doctors barking orders. There were girls who'd slipped through the back doors, desperate to throw their undergarments at the champion. But through the chaos, with his one functioning eye, Carmelo searched for the only face that mattered.

The doctors won their battle, shoving everyone aside with medical authority. He wasn't doing well—not well at all. They rolled him onto his side as blood bubbled up from somewhere deep inside, his body rebelling against the punishment it had endured. Don Marcello's money had bought the best physicians in New Orleans, but even they looked worried as they worked over his battered frame.

But he had won. He had Kathy.

Then he felt it—the familiar warmth of her fingers threading through his bruised knuckles. She squeezed gently, anchoring him to consciousness. He turned his head with enormous effort, his good eye finding her through the swirling chaos.

She leaned over him like a guardian angel, her tear-streaked face the most beautiful vision he'd ever seen. The carnival of noise and bodies faded to nothing. The world contracted to just this: her eyes, her touch, her presence.

"I LOVE YOU," she mouthed silently, her lips forming each word with perfect clarity.

Then the darkness claimed him, pulling him down into merciful oblivion where nothing hurt, and love was the last thing he remembered.

A Week Later

"Any word on Willa?" Kathy asked.

They sat outside a charming café just off Bourbon Street, the afternoon sun filtering through the wrought-iron balconies above. Kathy had stayed an extra week to tend to Carmelo's injuries, which had landed him in the hospital for two days. She'd called home and told everyone who mattered that Willa had run away, which was the truth, after all.

A distressed Mrs. Lottie Jensen had offered to send Ely along with other men to Texas to help search, but Kathy declined. Even if she didn't agree with Willa's choices, the fact that Lottie insisted Willa couldn't make any decisions without her approval bothered Kathy. Instead, she'd informed Mrs. Jensen that she was staying with Willa's "sister" and her family, and would spend a week searching everywhere for her.

It had broken her heart to hear Big Mama sound so weak and frightened on the phone when she learned Willa was missing. It hurt even more to lie to the matriarch she loved so dearly. But her life had turned her into a liar long ago.

"No news," Janey set down her delicate porcelain cup, her golden eyes finding Kathy's. "And that's actually a good sign."

"How do you figure that?" asked Kathy.

"She's still with him. Pinkie says they're holed up in his cottage on the plantation grounds, and Willa's been seen smiling and content on the porch and at the window, staring out. He hasn't mistreated her or cast her aside yet. I expected her to be back by now, honestly—expected this infatuation to have burned itself out."

Kathy rolled her eyes. "It's only been a week. It will end."

"Don't be so certain, *chère*. New Orleans is different. *We're* different here. If a Thibodeaux man didn't truly want Willa, she'd be gone already, discarded like yesterday's newspaper. Something unusual is happening over there, and I intend to get to the bottom of it while you're gone." Janey smiled.

Kathy sighed wistfully. "I can't believe I have to leave tomorrow."

"Then stay," Janey said simply. "You're old enough to tell your family goodbye, to be your own woman and make your own choices."

"I can't. Melo has to return to New York for his next fight, and Big Mama needs me. Besides, Mama's coming next month to stay with us for a few weeks." Kathy's voice grew softer. "My life isn't here, Auntie."

Janey nodded with understanding, then reached across the small table with her hand extended. Kathy placed her palm in her aunt's warm grasp.

"I'm genuinely proud of you," Janey said with quiet intensity. "I see how strong you've become, and I truly admire the woman you're turning into."

"I come from good stock," Kathy smiled.

"Do you love me?" Janey asked suddenly, vulnerability flickering in her eyes.

Kathy nodded without hesitation.

"I love you too, *ma petite*. I'm deeply sorry for hurting you and betraying your trust. I never meant to cause you such pain. I wish I could be better in that regard."

"Don't apologize, Auntie. I understand the world a little better now, thanks to you and this visit. I don't judge you for what you've done. I never will," said Kathy.

Janey blinked away threatening tears and nodded, releasing Kathy's hand. "How is your Melo healing?"

"His ribs are a mess, but everything else is mending quickly. He's constantly complaining that he wants to make love when we both know he's in no condition for any of that." Kathy shook her head with fond exasperation. "He always wants to make love."

Janey laughed knowingly. "Put his cock in your mouth."

"What!" Kathy gasped, nearly choking on her café au lait. She sounded like Carmelo when he asked her to do it.

Janey shrugged with nonchalance.

"Why on earth would I do such a thing?" Kathy's face burned with embarrassment.

"Because there are many ways to please a man, *chère*. It's a woman's duty to know how to give her man pleasure as well as punishment.

Sometimes I do this for Carmine when his body lacks the strength for traditional lovemaking. Trust me—do it properly and he'll sleep like a baby afterward."

"I could never!" Kathy protested. "Semen comes out of it."

"Yet you allow him to pleasure you with his mouth where you bleed and piss from?" Janey raised an elegant eyebrow. "Is that not the same thing?"

"What are we even discussing?" Kathy's nose wrinkled in mortification. "She refused to talk dirty with her aunt, especially about her sex secrets."

"We're discussing you being a true lady—not like them," Janey glanced meaningfully at two prim white women passing by with their parasols, "but like the kind of woman who can satisfy her man completely within her own bedroom, so he doesn't need to seek pleasure elsewhere. This city has gone wild over his victory. He's in every newspaper. Soon his celebrity will have women throwing themselves at his feet while you're stuck in Butt's, all prim and proper, waiting for his return."

Janey leaned closer, her voice dropping to a whisper. "He's a man, Kathy. And men do what men do when they're lonely. Trust me on this."

Kathy absorbed this worldly advice with growing understanding, just as a car horn sounded nearby. Janey looked up the street to see Carmine driving slowly toward them in his gleaming sedan.

"There's my prince," she said, rising gracefully. "We'll be here to take you to the train station in the morning."

Kathy stood and embraced her aunt warmly. "Thank you, Auntie. For everything—the good and the difficult."

"You call me the moment you arrive home safely. And I'll keep watch over Willa—I have my ways of gathering information." Janey's smile was mysterious.

"I trust that you do," Kathy replied.

Janey walked toward the car where Carmine had stopped traffic on the narrow cobblestone street to get out and limp around to hold her door open like the gentleman he could be. She patted his cheek affectionately before settling into the passenger seat. Carmine tipped his fedora respectfully at Kathy, who nodded in return.

As they drove away, Janey waved and blew a kiss from the window. Kathy smiled and waved back, wishing desperately that she could stop time and extend these precious moments in this magical, dangerous city that had changed her forever.

CHAPTER 22

THE LAST BATH

"Get back in bed this instant," Kathy said.

Carmelo stood swaying in the hallway of their suite, one hand pressed against the damask wallpaper for support. Without even a crutch to steady his battered frame, he looked like a wounded gladiator refusing to yield. The afternoon light through the tall windows revealed the full extent of his injuries—purple bruises blooming across his ribs like dark flowers, his left eye still swollen despite a week of healing.

If she'd been delayed any longer with Janey, she feared he would have attempted the stairs alone.

"I mean it, Melo!" She pointed at him with fierce authority.

"I'm fine, dammit. I smell like shit, and it's hot as Hades in that room," he huffed, though perspiration beaded his forehead from the simple effort of standing. "Where were you? You've been gone for over an hour."

She hurried to slip her arm around his waist, feeling him lean gratefully into her warmth as she guided him back toward their sanctuary. Their upgraded accommodations were a world apart from their previous lodgings since leaving Aunt Janey's house. This place had high ceilings adorned with ornate plasterwork, burgundy velvet drapes framing tall French doors that opened onto a wrought-iron balcony, and elegant chaise lounges upholstered in cream silk. The pièce de résistance was the adjoining bathing chamber with its magnificent clawfoot tub—a luxury that proclaimed him New Orleans' newest champion.

Carmelo was a hero for defeating the Klan.

She helped him settle on the edge of their four-poster bed, the fine linen sheets still rumpled from his restless sleep. "I can prepare the tub and bathe you properly," she said, kneeling gracefully to remove his worn leather shoes. "I'd already planned to do so."

"Where were you?" he insisted, his voice carrying an unfamiliar edge.

She looked up from unlacing his boots, noting the tension in his jaw. "I told you—I had to see Janey. She's agreed to escort me to the train station tomorrow morning."

"And I told you Caesar and I would take you!" The words erupted with startling vehemence, causing her to freeze.

She studied his face properly for the first time since returning, seeing past the physical pain to something far deeper. Raw anguish swam in his dark eyes, and tears threatened to spill over his bruised cheeks. Understanding dawned like sunrise breaking through storm clouds.

"What is it, *Melo*? What's truly the problem?"

Carmelo wiped roughly at a tear sliding down his battered face, turning toward the window where golden afternoon light painted squares on the room. "I'm not angry with you—I'm furious with myself. I hate myself. Hate myself!"

Kathy stood to settle beside him on the bed, placing a gentle hand on his muscled thigh. "No, you don't. No! Stop saying that."

"I nearly died. For what? For their entertainment? For money that goes to my father, not us? I can't share anything with you." His voice fractured like breaking glass. "What about what I want? What about what I need? I need *you*, Kathy. We are here and we are husband and wife, then... I go... and... I'm not... I'm sorry."

She put her hand over his and dropped her head on his shoulder.

"We have our plan, remember? We discussed this. In a few more years, when—"

"Fuck the plan!" The words tore from his throat with devastating finality. "Fuck all of it! I made the money now. Let's take it. I know where the men are keeping the money bags. Let's take it and run, Kat. Tonight. Let's disappear and never stop. Just go!!" His hands clenched into fists. "I can't keep riding this carousel—happiness, then loneliness, then despair, then hope, then none. This endless waiting is destroying us and me. They are killing me!"

Kathy stood and gathered his head against her stomach, feeling his powerful arms circle her hips as he buried his face in the soft fabric of her dress. She stroked his dark hair, still damp with anguish.

Everyone told her to run—Janey, Debbie, and now Carmelo. What truly held her back? She closed her eyes, searching her soul, and the answer crystallized with painful clarity. She loved him beyond reason, but she could never abandon her parents. Her future with Carmelo had to include them, or there could be no future at all.

The truth formed on her lips, but she swallowed it. Some confessions were too cruel to voice.

"Can I please take care of you?" she asked instead, lifting his face in her palms until his wounded eyes met hers. "Let me love you the way you deserve. Okay. Let's not waste this time."

"But—the money..."

She pressed a gentle kiss to his lips to silence him.

"That money will come at a price. They won't let us get far with it. They'll kill us, Melo."

He nodded, the gesture heavy with surrender and trust. She kissed his forehead tenderly, then moved toward the bathing chamber. Their suite boasted modern amenities—hot and cold running water. As she turned the brass taps, she could hear the familiar sounds from the cobblestone street below: children calling up to their window, "Champ! Hey, Champ!"

Carmelo would shuffle to the balcony despite his injuries, tossing coins to his young admirers. The gesture never failed to make her heart swell with pride, but ache with longing to share this life with him longer.

She filled the magnificent tub with water cool enough to soothe his battered muscles, adding drops of salts and oil she'd purchased from a French healer on Royal Street.

When she returned, he sat exactly where she'd left him, staring at his hands. "Come," she said softly, helping him stand. "Let me wash away the pain."

She guided him slowly to the clawfoot tub, where late afternoon light filtered through frosted glass, casting everything in a dreamy, golden haze. With infinite care, she helped him out of his remaining clothes, her fingers gentle over his wounded skin.

The hot water embraced him like a lover's caress as she eased him into the tub; his groan of relief was an echo off the tiled walls. She knelt beside the porcelain edge, rolling up the sleeves of her cotton dress, and began the tender ritual.

Using a soft sea sponge, she traced the contours of his body with patience, washing away dried perspiration, soothing inflamed bruises, loving every inch of him back to wholeness. Her touch was both maternal and sensual, healing and arousing, as she worked the lavender-scented soap into rich lather across his shoulders and chest.

"Does this hurt?" she whispered, her fingers trailing along a particularly angry bruise spanning his ribs.

"Nothing hurts when you touch me," he murmured, his eyes drifting closed in blissful surrender.

She washed his hair with infinite care, her nails gently massaging his scalp, then poured warm water from her pitcher that cascaded over his head. He leaned into her touch like a man dying.

The silence between them was sacred, broken only by the gentle splash of water and his contented sighs. She traced the strong line of his jaw, now softened by healing, and pressed tender kisses to his temple, his cheek, the corner of his mouth.

"I love you," she whispered against his ear, the words carrying all the promises she couldn't make, all the futures she couldn't guarantee. "Nothing and no one can ever change it."

His hand found hers beneath the warm water, their fingers interlacing. "*Ti amo anch'io,*" he replied, his voice thick with emotion. *I love you too.*

As she rinsed the soap from his skin, watching the water carry away the physical evidence of his ordeal, Kathy memorized every detail: the way candlelight flickered across the water's surface, the sound of his breathing deepening into a peaceful rhythm, and the feel of his skin, warm and alive, beneath her palms.

This was their last night for months, perhaps longer. Tomorrow would bring farewells and separate trains carrying them to different worlds. But tonight, in this perfumed sanctuary, they had this—love distilled to its purest essence, expressed through the simple act of one soul caring for another.

She would carry this moment through all the lonely nights ahead: this perfect communion between two hearts that refused to break, no matter how far apart the world forced them to be.

When the water began to grow cooler, she helped him stand, wrapping him in thick towels warmed by the window. She dried him with the same care she'd used to bathe him, pressing kisses to newly revealed skin, whispering endearments that had no English translation.

Later, as they lay entwined in their bed, the sounds of Bourbon Street filtering through the French doors, she listened to his breathing settle into the deep rhythm of peaceful sleep. His arms held her close, as if he could keep her with him through sheer will.

Sleep came.

Later

Was it a dream? Carmelo hadn't known sleep without pain since the fight. His eyes opened slowly, drawn awake by gentle kisses brushing softly against his face. Kathy's eyes were glistening with tears; she'd clearly been awake and crying. He recognized those tears —the same tears she'd shed the last time they parted. Now it was Kathy who felt the agony of impending separation.

Desire surged through him urgently, his body responding so powerfully that it hardly surprised him. He wanted her desperately, craving the comfort and intimacy that only she could offer. Attempting to rise and move over her, Kathy's hand gently pressed against his chest, stopping him.

"No," she whispered gently. "You can't. The doctor said no."

"Please," he begged softly, "I need you."

"I need you too," she replied tenderly, pushing him back down. "But lie still."

He persisted briefly, placing hurried kisses along her neck and trying again to shift above her, but she pressed firmly against his chest once more.

"Behave," Kathy said with gentle authority. "Let's find a safe way."

Intrigued, he went still.

Kathy's hand traveled slowly down his chest, her fingers scraped across, and then combed through his pubic hair. Each digit reached for his upturned dick. Uncertain but instinctively knowing what might soothe him, she began with gentle, slow strokes. He visibly relaxed, clearly enjoying her tender touch. It wasn't easy. Without lubricant, she feared that her handling of his penis felt rough and abrasive. Curious and emboldened, she moved the covers aside to see her actions fully.

Quietly repositioning herself, she leaned down, gently taking him into her mouth. Carmelo's eyes snapped open in surprise, a soft gasp escaping his lips. As she deepened her swallowing, Carmelo sat upright abruptly, but Kathy pressed her palm firmly against his bruised abdomen, guiding him back down.

He collapsed back with a deep, guttural moan. Quickly learning his responses, she continued suctioning her jaws, swallowing him halfway, and bobbing her head up and down to keep up the motion. She did so with growing confidence, feeling his fingers gently gripping her hair, guiding and pacing her movements.

"Stop! Stop," he suddenly pleaded, overwhelmed by sensation and pain.

Seeing the intense torture etched across his features, Kathy slowly released him and repositioned herself atop him. She guided him gently inside, easing down carefully. Carmelo shuddered beneath her as she began to move rhythmically, drawing on the lessons he'd lovingly taught her. Her body gripped him tightly, her eyelids fluttering closed as she reached back to steady herself against his knees, matching his movements with a slow, powerful rhythm.

The inner muscles of her vagina tightened and quivered around his shaft, drawing an involuntary jerk from Carmelo as he fought the impulse to seize control again. Kathy sensed his struggle and gently leaned forward, pinning his wrists against the pillows to prevent him from overexerting himself. She showered his bruised chest with soft, soothing kisses, maintaining a slow, rhythmic pace as she moved atop him.

Carmelo's whimpers soon deepened into full-bodied groans, his expression a mix of pleasure and agony. Kathy leaned in to capture his lips in a gentle kiss, whispering against his mouth, "Let go, for me..."

At her words, he surrendered completely. Their climax overtook them simultaneously, and Kathy mustered all her strength to hold him firmly, increasing her rhythm to intensify his pleasure. Even after the peak passed, their kisses lingered, affectionate and playful. Carmelo's soft laughter filled the space between them as Kathy's exhausted body finally gave way, allowing him to roll them over gently. Though he slipped from her, he continued lavishing her neck with tender kisses and murmuring affectionate words she couldn't fully decipher.

Love enveloped them both, deep and comforting, until at last they collapsed into each other's arms, wrapped securely in their shared warmth.

Rising Sun...

"What time does the train leave?" he murmured against her hair, his voice thick with approaching dawn and dread.

Awake now beside him, she stared at the window where the first gray light of morning crept through the lace curtains like an unwelcome visitor. "Ten o'clock," she whispered, the words tasting like ashes.

"They haven't decided on my next fight yet. Could be anywhere—Chicago, Philadelphia, even back to New York," he said, his voice heavy with resignation.

"Maybe it will be in the South," she offered, threading hope through her words like a lifeline. "If it is, I'll be there, Melo. Right at your side, no matter what."

"It's not fair." His arm tightened around her as if he could hold back time itself. "The things I've been forced to do, just to love you. None of it's fair."

"You keep saying that, but I remember when you genuinely loved boxing," she said gently, studying the tension in his jaw. "You used to talk about it like it was poetry."

His dark eyes—windows to his soul—met hers with an intensity that made her breath catch. Once again, she sensed he was carrying secrets too heavy for one man to bear alone. The weight of unspoken truths lived in his tortured gaze like shadows in deep water.

She touched his cheek, feeling the rough stubble beneath her palm. "What is it, *Melo*? What's truly being forced on you that you can't tell me?"

He was quiet for so long she thought he might not answer. When he finally spoke, his voice was barely above a whisper, as if saying the words aloud might make them more real.

"The mob, their traditions, the whole damn system—it's changing me, Kathy. Turning me into something I swore I'd never become. Moving me further away from the man you fell in love with." His eyes glistened with unshed tears. "I'm afraid of what I'm becoming. Afraid that one day you'll look at me and see him instead of me."

She understood without him having to name the specter that haunted them both—his father's shadow, the legacy of violence and corruption that seemed to claim every Ricci man in the end.

"Me too," she whispered, the admission torn from somewhere deep in her chest. "I'm afraid, too."

But even as she spoke the words, she pulled him closer, pressing her lips to his forehead in a promise she would love him through whatever darkness was coming because some loves were worth the fear, worth the risk, worth everything—even when you could see the storm clouds gathering on the horizon.

CHAPTER 23

TRAINS TO NOWHERE

The segregated train station felt gloomy and claustrophobic now that she was about to leave. The "COLORED ONLY" signs seemed to loom larger, more menacing, as if the very walls knew she was about to cross back into a world that would never accept her love. Carmine had paid the Negro porter handsomely to handle her luggage and ensure she received respectful treatment during the long journey ahead.

Here, Carmelo couldn't touch her, couldn't even stand too close. They weren't in Tremé among the Creoles who made their own rules, or in the Quarter under Sicilian protection. This was the Deep South, pure and unforgiving.

So he stood rigid beside Caesar, his hands clenched at his sides, dark eyes drinking in every detail of her face as if trying to memorize her for the lonely months ahead.

"Let me look at you one last time, *ma chère*," Janey said, fussing over Kathy's appearance with maternal precision. She smoothed imaginary wrinkles from her traveling dress and tucked a wayward curl behind her ear. "Now you call me the moment you're home safe. We'll talk once a week—call collect, I can afford it. You hear me?"

Kathy's gaze drifted to Carmelo, her eyes already brimming with unshed tears. "I hear you, Auntie. And please watch over Willa. I'm terrified for her."

"I will, *chère*. Trust me. Might even bring her to Butt's myself for a visit," Janey said with forced lightness.

They both knew it was a beautiful lie. Willa was lost to them now, claimed by forces beyond their control. Just as fate had claimed Kathy's heart and given it to a man she could only love in stolen moments.

Desperation seized her—she started to move toward Carmelo, ready to defy the entire segregated South and throw her arms around his neck. But Janey must have recognized the rebellion building in her niece because she stepped swiftly between them, blocking her path.

"Get on that train right now, Kathy," Janey commanded, her voice carrying the steel of a woman who'd survived worse separations. "You don't want this kind of trouble. You had your time with him. You'll have it again. I'll make sure of it."

The tears came then, hot and bitter. When she dared look at Carmelo, she saw Caesar's restraining hand on his arm, holding him back with the strength of brotherhood and hard wisdom. Both stood on the knife's edge of breaking, their love and frustration radiating across the platform like heat waves.

She accepted her small traveling bag from Janey with trembling fingers and walked toward the rear of the train where the "COLORED" car waited. As she stepped up onto the metal block and climbed the narrow steps, she turned one final time to see her champion.

Carmelo stood there with tears of repressed rage and lost love gleaming in his dark eyes, his powerful frame still bearing the evidence of his recent battle. Despite his injuries, despite everything keeping them apart, he gave her a slight nod—a promise wrapped in sorrow.

In one act of defiance against the world that would tear them apart, she pressed her fingertips to her lips and blew him the kiss she couldn't give in person before disappearing into the segregated car.

She found the only window seat where she could still see them on the platform. Carmelo walked along the length of the train until he spotted her face in the glass, and despite his chipped ribs and battered body, he stood tall through sheer force of will and love. His smile was brilliant and heartbreaking.

She smiled back through her tears and pressed her palm flat against the warm window as the locomotive's horn bellowed its mournful song. The great wheels began their slow, steady churn, and she watched helplessly as Carmelo, Caesar, Janey, and Carmine grew smaller and smaller until they were nothing but memories disappearing into the Louisiana heat.

The train carried her away from everything that mattered, back toward a life that suddenly felt like a beautiful prison she'd built around herself. But his smile lingered in the glass, and his love traveled with her.

* * *

"NEED ANYTHING, CHAMP?" Caesar asked, settling into the plush velvet seat beside Carmelo, who had claimed the window seat overlooking the platform where they'd just left everything that mattered.

In the whites-only luxury car, they were grudgingly accepted despite their thick Brooklyn-Italian accents—Carmelo's newfound celebrity opened doors that would have remained sealed to two Italian boys from Queens just weeks before.

"How long is the ride back?" Carmelo asked, not really caring about the answer. The men who'd accompanied them to New Orleans had departed immediately after the fight, but Carmelo's hospitalization and slow recovery had delayed their own departure.

"Day and a half, maybe less. No transfers—straight shot home," Caesar said, adjusting his position in the comfortable seat. He pulled his fedora down to cover half his face, preparing for sleep.

"You talk to Matteo while I was laid up?" Carmelo asked. Bedridden for days, he'd been unable to speak with his brother directly, though he'd been informed that Debbie had given birth the very night of his victory. Another Ricci soldier had entered the family.

"Nah. He's hovering over Debbie like she might disappear if he blinks," Caesar mumbled from beneath his hat.

"Hovering... or loving?" Carmelo's voice carried a note of understanding.

Caesar lifted the brim of his hat, studying his friend's profile. "Melo. Can I say something you probably won't want to hear?"

Carmelo didn't respond, which Caesar took as reluctant permission.

"Forgive me if I'm stepping out of line here. I know what you and Kathy have—I've seen it with my own eyes. It's real, it's powerful. But you took sacred vows, *compare*. Maria is a good girl, a decent woman. She adores you, tries to be the wife you promised to cherish. Why not give her a real chance? Why not give yourself permission to find happiness in the life you actually have instead of the one you can't?"

Carmelo's gaze shifted slowly from the window to Caesar, his dark eyes carrying a warning that could freeze blood. "Never speak to me about Kathy and Maria in the same breath again. Ever."

Caesar raised both hands in surrender and gave a respectful nod. "Understood, *fratello*. My apologies." He repositioned his hat over his face and settled back into silence.

Carmelo forced himself to breathe, to coil the sudden rage back inside where it belonged. But the damage was done—Caesar's words had slammed him back into the cold reality waiting in New York. Maria. His wife. The woman who shared his name and his bed and deserved so much better than the shell of a man who returned to her and slept on the floor each night. Carrying another woman's love in his heart like a sacred wound.

He closed his eyes and leaned his forehead against the cool window glass, watching the Louisiana countryside blur past in a green smear of everything he was leaving behind. The weight of his choices pressed in, and for the first time since the train pulled away from the station, he allowed himself to truly hate what he'd done for dear *Madre*.

. . .

SEVEN MONTHS Earlier

Carmelo:

[Kneeling in shadow, voice graveled with exhaustion]

"Forgive me, Padre... I have sinned. Two weeks since my last confession."

PADRE VICENTE:

[Behind the confessional screen, weary but alert]

"The Lord awaits your contrition, *figlio mio*. Speak."

CARMELO:

"I... I married a woman. Her name is Maria. Ah, Maria Romero. Last month at St. Michael's. Full Nuptial Mass, white dress, my father's soldiers stood as witnesses."

PADRE VICENTE:

[Sharp intake of breath]

"*Matrimonio*? But your last confession spoke of Kathy—the girl in Harlem, who you lost for love—"

CARMELO:

[Fist striking softly against the wooden partition]

"My mother. You know what happened to her. It was her final letter, her dying wish. Made me swear on her very soul, Padre. Said marry Maria or watch Kathy die. Said it was the only way to lift the black death order my father put on her family."

PADRE VICENTE:

"*Dio misericordioso.* You bound yourself sacramentally to save another's life?"

. . .

Carmelo:

"I bound myself to a lie. Maria sleeps in our marriage bed while I take the floor like a dog. I wait until her breathing grows deep and steady, then slip in beside her—but I never touch her. *Can't* touch her. Kathy owns my heart, every beat of it. Maria? She's a deal between my father and me. A sacrilege born from my mother's death."

Padre Vicente:

[Voice tightening with concern]

"The Church recognizes no half-marriages, Carmelo. You stood before God's altar and exchanged sacred vows. The Sacrament binds you completely—"

Carmelo:

[Cutting in desperately]

"I've been married before! To Kathy! We exchanged vows!"

Padre Vicente:

[Voice gentling]

"Not before God's Church, *figlio*."

Carmelo:

[Voice breaking]

"We prayed together! We meant every word! A judge signed our certificate—it's legal!"

Padre Vicente:

[Steady, pastoral tone]

"A man of questionable character signed papers. God and His Church were nowhere present in that ceremony."

Carmelo:

[Raw with emotion]

"Do vows count when your heart is buried six feet under with your mother? Huh! When you say '*I do*' but mean '*I must do* it'? Kathy doesn't even know about Maria. If she learns the truth, she'd think I betrayed everything we promised each other. And maybe I did—*Dio santo*, maybe I did—but I had no choice."

Padre Vicente: *[*

Long pause, rosary beads clicking softly]

"You seek… annulment?"

Carmelo:

"Can you annul a gun held to your head? My mother's soul, my father's blood on my hands? I want out, Padre. But what does God see? A married man honoring his vows? Or a sinner who damned one woman to save another?"

Padre Vicente:

[Exhaling slowly]

"God sees a son drowning in his mother's grief. A young man who traded pieces of his soul to atone for his mother's sin." *[Leaning closer]* "You cannot undo the Sacrament—it is written in Heaven's book. But this arrangement? Sleeping at her feet like a servant? *That* compounds the sin. You mock both the sacred vow and the innocent woman who bears your name."

. . .

CARMELO:

[Whisper raw as an open wound]

"So I should lie with Maria? *Consummate* this farce? Destroy what Kathy and I built forever?"

PADRE VICENTE:

"No, *figlio*. You must choose: live with the choice you've made, as painful as it is... or confess the truth to both women. Face the consequences like the man God calls you to be. Let Him sort the ashes of whatever remains."

CARMELO: *[Long silence, then a choked sob]*

"Kathy will hate me. She'll never forgive this betrayal. I'll lose her completely. And if I lose her, I lose everything—I die."

PADRE VICENTE:

"Perhaps you will lose her. But right now, she loves a man who doesn't exist—one who can promise her things you cannot deliver. And lies, *mio caro,* lies are the truest condemnation of all."

A WEEK LATER -

"Maria?"

Maria stood at the kitchen sink with Caesar beside her, both laughing at something Caesar had just said. They looked up when Carmelo entered, their easy camaraderie a stark contrast to the tension he carried like a cloak on his shoulders. Caesar was supposed to drive him to the gym to meet Matteo and his new sparring partner —another step toward the championship fight that would eventually bring him back to the South, back to Kathy.

He had to break this lie. He had to tell the truth, no matter the cost.

"Can you wait in the car?" he asked Caesar quietly.

His brother's best friend read the gravity in his expression and nodded without question. "Sure thing, Melo." He squeezed Maria's shoulder affectionately. "Thanks for the coffee, *bella*."

After Caesar left, Maria returned to stirring her sauce, the wooden spoon moving in careful circles. "You hungry? I can pack something for you and Caesar to take to the gym."

"Can you... stop for a minute? Can we talk?"

"About what?" she asked, though her voice carried a note of resignation, as if she already knew what was coming.

"About us. About what's not happening between us. I think we need to—"

"You know what?" Maria interrupted, setting down her spoon and turning to face him with forced brightness. "We could go to Coney Island this weekend. Just the two of us. Ride the Cyclone, eat corn on the cob, walk on the beach." Her smile was heartbreaking in its hopefulness. "Like a real husband and wife."

He stared at her, this sweet young woman who deserved so much better than the shell of a marriage he'd given her. Since their union, his father had grown even bolder in his manipulations. Not only had he dragged Maria into their cursed life, but her mother was now living with his father, and there was talk of yet another marriage.

He sighed heavily. "Never mind, Maria. Forget I said anything."

He turned to leave, but her small hand caught his wrist, stopping him cold.

"I already know, Carmelo."

He looked back at her, his heart sinking. "Know what?"

"About her. About you and the girl you really love." Maria's voice was steady, but her dark eyes glistened with unshed tears. "Melo, everyone knows. I knew when you proposed that it was because of family obligations, not love. I'm not stupid." Her grip on his wrist tightened. "But you won't talk to me. You won't even look at me most days. You won't give me a chance to be your friend."

He stared down at her delicate hand, then up into eyes that held more wisdom and pain than any young woman should carry. "I ruined your life, Maria. I'm no better than my father—using people, destroying them for my own purposes."

"What?" Maria stepped back as if he'd slapped her, hurt flashing across her features. "How can you say that?"

The truth hung heavy between them. The house they lived in—his father's money. The car he drove—his father's gift. The clothes she wore, the food she cooked, the life they pretended to share—all of it bought and paid for by Don Cosimo Ricci. She was as trapped in this beautiful lie as he was.

"I'm sorry, Maria," he said, the words inadequate for the weight of his guilt. "I'm so damn sorry."

He started toward the door, but her voice stopped him cold.

"Melo!" The desperation in her cry made him freeze. "Please. Come back tonight. Don't leave me alone in this house again. Please." Her voice broke slightly. "Even if you sleep on the floor like always. Just... don't abandon me completely."

Carmelo closed his eyes, the weight of her loneliness crushing down on him. She wasn't asking for love—she was begging for basic human companionship from the man whose name she bore.

"I'll be back tonight," he promised quietly.

"Thank you," she whispered, her gratitude for such a small mercy breaking his heart all over again.

He hurried toward the door and the car waiting outside, carrying the guilt of two women's pain—one who loved him despite everything, and one whose love he could never return.

CHAPTER 24

MEMPHIS TENNESSE - 1952

Two Years Later. The Greyhound station was loud with the thrum of idling diesel engines. Fluorescent lights buzzed overhead, casting a sickly pallor over the cracked linoleum and vinyl seats. Janey perched beside Carmine, absently flipping the pages of a dog-eared *McCall's*. He slept beside her, head tilted back against the hard plastic, mouth slightly open, exhaustion etching deep lines around his eyes. Two years of relentless road trips – ferrying Kathy to clandestine meetings with Carmelo – had taken their toll.

Janey checked her wristwatch for the third time in ten minutes. Its gold face winked accusingly in the harsh light.

"Carmine," she murmured, nudging his shoulder. His breathing hitched, but he didn't stir. "What time did the ticket man say? She should've been here."

Only the distant *hiss* of air brakes answered her. Memphis at midnight felt worlds away from the electric buzz of Carmelo's fight camp. She studied Carmine's profile – the familiar stubborn set of his jaw even in sleep, the new threads of silver at his temples. Her fingers brushed a stray lock of hair from his forehead, the gesture tender, almost unconscious.

These past years *had* changed them in a good way. She had become the wife he needed as his illness took hold of him. And for a reward, he did everything in his power to make her happy. Whisking Kathy across state lines, outmaneuvering Big Mama and the watchful Brenda, had become their strange, shared purpose. North Carolina's pines, Texas dust, Chicago's biting wind... they'd traced Carmelo's rise in boxing together with Kathy in tow. Now Memphis. Next, whispers said, California – a state that still sent an old, cold shiver down Janey's spine since the execution of Marianne Temple for her crimes.

Carmine had returned from New York two weeks ago, tight-lipped and shadowed. The upcoming Memphis bout wasn't just another fight; it was history. The Wolf of Brooklyn is defending his belt, mob factions from Jersey to New Orleans circling like sharks, and even Sinatra is lending his Rat Pack glamour to the pre-fight gala. Solidarity, they called it. To Janey, it smelled like pressure for Carmine.

She'd tried to pierce Carmine's gloom. "He wins this," she'd said brightly just yesterday, packing Kathy's gift in her suitcase, "nothing stops them from marrying this year. Vegas. That's a good place for us all to go to, you said. A place for my baby niece can be happy and make me babies."

His response had been a grunt, averted eyes, and a sudden intense focus on polishing his cane's silver head. Sulking. Muttering under his breath like a man carrying a stone in his shoe. It wasn't fatigue. Janey knew the rhythm of her husband's moods – the rare volcanic temper, the icy calculation, the sun-warmed affection he showered her with after returning from one of his trips. This... this was different. This was the silence of a secret kept.

The roar of a big engine announced another bus's arrival, its headlights cutting through the station's gloom like twin blades. Janey's gaze snapped to the disembarking passengers, heart thumping a frantic rhythm against her rib cage.

Where are you, Kathy?

The Birmingham bus groaned to a halt, air brakes hissing like a tired serpent. "She's here!" She jabbed Carmine's ribs with her elbow.

He jolted awake with a gravelly curse, blinking against the station's harsh fluorescents. In the backseat, Deion—Carmine's sixteen-year-old apprentice, his dark skin nearly swallowed by the shadows—was already unfolding his lanky frame from the car and out of it. The teen headed to Kathy. Deion, who looked five years older than his age, was their shield against Jim Crow's jagged edges: the one who booked "colored" motels, handled gas station attendants, and smoothed their path to help them avoid hostile territory.

"Carmelo should be waiting at the Prichards', right?" Janey's voice rang with excitement. She thrived on these clandestine Southern movements, feeding on chaos disguised as calm. When silence met her question, she studied Carmine's profile in the dashboard's glow.

His jaw tightened, knuckles white on the wheel. "What's eating you? Spit it out."

"The plan's shot." He turned to face her, expression grim. "The Prichard farmhouse burned down. I told Deion to get Kathy checked into the colored hotel."

"You're telling me this now?" Janey's shock quickly turned to fury. She pointed at Deion and Kathy embracing beside the pumps, exposed under the harsh lights. "The Prichard place was supposed to keep them safe. Now what?"

Carmine exploded. "I ain't their fucking guardian angel, Janey! I got *real* business! How long did you think this circus could roll on?" He slammed his palm against the horn, drawing attention to them.

* * *

DEION MET Kathy at the bus steps and took her worn suitcase. Despite her exhaustion, she smiled, relief brightening her face.

"We're heading to the Prichards', right? Is Carmelo already there?"

"Change of plans, Miss Kathy." Deion kept his voice low. "The farmhouse burned down. Klan got word about white men and black women meeting there. The Prichards made it out safe to Carolina, but there's no sanctuary now." He shifted her bag. "I got you a room at the Douglass Hotel. Our driver Snake will take us."

A horn blast cut through the night. Kathy spun to see Carmine's car already speeding away, Aunt Janey's silhouette visible through the rear window: no wave goodbye, no acknowledgment.

Something was wrong

* * *

THEY HAD PARKED. And Janey worked on calming her temper. Outside, cigarillo smoke coiled around Carmine's head like a phantom crown. He'd gotten out of the car to escape her wrath.

He's hiding something.

And this time, she'd tear the truth from him with her bare hands. She got out of the car. Carmine glanced her way, and she shot him a threatening glare. Husband and wife stared at each other. Whoever crossed the line first would probably be the victor, because neither truly wanted to hurt the other. After a long pause, Janey heard a car arrive. She turned and looked to see Kathy exit the car last, with Deion following her with her bag, walking her to the front of the hotel.

"Go be with her, deal with me later," Carmine said with no fear, just exhaustion and exhaled smoke through his nostrils. He dropped the cigarillo and stomped it out with his shoe, then went back in the car to wait.

Janey softened a bit. She rolled her eyes and walked on toward the motel.

Two Months Earlier. New York City

Carmine Boanno crossed the room, offering the customary embrace. A careful, one-armed affair. Don Cosimo Ricci, *Capo di tutti capi* since Luciano's exile, returned it stiffly. The bullet Carmelo put in his shoulder two years prior had left its mark: the limb hung useless, hand arthritic, nerves deadened. A constant, painful reminder of betrayal beneath the fine silk threads of his suit.

"Don Ricci. Too long," Carmine said, the familiar cadence of Sicily warming his voice despite the tension. He kissed both cheeks, noting the Don's pallor beneath the tan. "You look... solid."

Cosimo grunted, easing himself behind the vast mahogany desk like a king reclaiming his throne. "Still breathing. Can't say my sons deserve credit. A humorless flicker in his dark eyes. Boanno's men remained outside the heavy oak door—a command of respect to the Ricci position among the families.

Carmine took the offered seat."I hear Matteo handles more territory. Making a name for himself. Harlem remains your jewel?"

"Harlem will be mine," Cosimo corrected, the words a soft rasp that carried steel. "Bumpy Johnson's time in the sun ends soon. The pig-pen awaits him. It's all arranged. Luciano's pet Negro falls, the dominoes tumble… exactly as I placed them." He steepled his good hand against the bad one, the gesture predatory.

"And your sons? Matteo… Carmelo? Are they positioned for this… transition?" Carmine kept his tone neutral, probing the rumors of fractures within the Ricci family.

Cosimo's gaze sharpened, becoming flinty. "I hear whispers, Carmine. Marcello's winding up? Carmelo wears our name in the boxing ring, the world champion, but he is Ricci, not Marcello. I think our little arrangement is set to expire. I can manage my sons' career going forward without the old Don's support." Cosimo leaned forward slightly to drive home his decision.

"Don Marcello is ill. Very. He may not make it to the New Year. He sends only respect, Cosimo," Carmine demurred smoothly, the lie practiced. The old man was too honery to die, but Carmine knew these families waited like vultures to sweep in to New Orleans.

He expertly changed the subject. "I knew DeMarco, back when the earth was younger, even before we met. His passing left questions. Forgive Don Marcello's concern for you and your sons. We understand that this is a family matter that has been well taken care of. In two years, your boys have risen to the top. That credit goes to you."

Cosimo acknowledged the half-apology with a curt, dangerous nod.

"As for my Don," Carmine continued, shifting gears, "he admires the champion's shine along with the profits you split. But his sights are set beyond the ring. The desert calls. Bugsy Siegel's Flamingo is spitting gold coins all over the streets of Vegas. Meyer Lansky has been seeking investors since Bugsy's unexpected demise. He courts the Battaglias... in the Almalfi, Mancini is Sicily." Carmine let the implication hang—Italians and Sicilians encroaching from across the water would never sit well with Cosimo. That would only raise Luciano's power in Italy.

"I'm listening," said Cosimo.

"Don Marcello believes this desert fruit should be harvested by our hands. He proposes a new alliance. You and him."

"Battaglia?" Cosimo's lip curled, a flash of old pride, the resentment of being an outsider when Tomosino moved in and claimed the Cammora.

"My interests," Cosimo stated flatly after a weighted silence, "are here. New York. Chicago. Detroit. Tell Marcello those jewels are greater than sand to me."

"A small stake, Cosimo," Carmine pressed gently, playing the diplomat. "A foothold. Lanskey owns Vegas, but eventually it will be in our hands. The dice will roll in our favor..."

A soft knock cut him off. The door opened.

A stunning young woman with dark hair entered, radiant in a summer floral dress. In her arms, a baby boy swaddled in pale blue. Behind her, an equally striking older woman, evidently the girl's mother, clearly held a baby girl wrapped in soft pink. *Twins.*

"*Scusi, Papa,*" the young woman murmured, her voice melodic. "We leave now. We wanted your bambini to say goodbye to Nonno."

Carmine rose automatically, a polite smile fixed in place. His eyes, however, snapped to the infants, then to Cosimo.

Don Cosimo's formidable presence dissolved. The ruthless *leader* vanished, replaced by a besotted grandfather. He pushed his chair back, his good arm opening. The baby boy was carefully placed in the crook of his inner elbow. Cosimo bent his head, pressing a tender kiss to the downy forehead. The baby girl was then transferred to his lap, receiving the same gentle affection.

"Carmine," Cosimo announced, pride swelling his voice, "my

daughter-in-law, Maria Ricci. And her mother, my wife, Rebecca. Behold the future of the Ricci family! A king and a queen!"

Carmine tipped his head, the polite mask firmly on. "My congratulations! I hadn't heard that Matteo had taken a wife. Beautiful children."

Cosimo's head lifted sharply, the warmth freezing into icy disdain. "Matteo? These are Carmelo's bambini. My son has been wed to Maria for two years."

The words hit Carmine like a physical blow. His carefully constructed smile faltered, then died. He stared at the babies – Carmelo's twins – the blood draining from his face. He forced his expression blank, a monumental effort.

"So nice to finally meet you, Signore Boanno," Maria offered sweetly, oblivious to the earthquake she'd triggered. "Carmelo speaks of you and New Orleans often. He loves it there. We hope to visit someday soon. Once he becomes the World Champion."

"Ah... does he?" Carmine managed, his voice slightly strangled. "Yes... a man of... many talents, a true champion." He touched the brim of his hat, a desperate gesture of retreat. "Cosimo, forgive me. I have other families to see, Marcello's messages to deliver. If your thoughts on the desert... evolve... You know how to reach us."

Don Cosimo barely glanced up, already cooing softly in Italian to his grandchildren.

Carmine practically fled the room, the image of those innocent twins seared into his mind, a secret now burning a hole through his loyalty to Janey and shattering everything Kathy believed.

CHAPTER 25

MEMPHIS, TENNESSEE - MAY 1952

Kathy stepped into the thick, mosquito-heavy Memphis night, and the Douglass Hotel's stuttering neon sign cast a sickly green halo over the weathered awning.

"Kathy! Baby!" Janey sang out as she fast walked out of the darkness toward her like a vision in silk and pearls. She rushed into her aunt's eager arms, their embrace fierce and warm. Janey kissed both of Kathy's cheeks before holding her at arm's length.

"Why are you here? Where is Carmine? You aren't supposed to be here, remember? This is a colored hotel," Kathy stuttered through the hug. Janey's beauty and melanin-deficient skin was alarming to anyone who would see her in the late hour at the hotel.

"Let me look at you properly, *ma chère*." Janey said.

Kathy grinned, feeling the familiar comfort of her aunt's undivided attention.

"I know it's only been two months since I saw you, but I swear it's like having Brenda standing before me every time you visit. Put on a little weight, eh? Never mind it—you look exactly like your mother when she was your age. Same eyes, same stubborn chin."

Kathy blushed at the comparison and the fact that Janey noticed her weight change. "Mama had to go back home earlier than planned to see about Daddy. She'd been with me, taking care of Big Mama. But Aunt Claire called and said there's trouble brewing with Bumpy and his men. Not sure what exactly, but Mama's never far from Daddy's side when danger comes."

"Ain't that the gospel," Janey said with a knowing roll of her eyes. "Go in and get settled. Need to work out something with Deion. Think I got us a plan."

"A plan?" Kathy asked.

"Go," she said and shooed her away.

Kathy did as she was told. Inside, she was greeted by an old man and a young girl who settled her into the process and gave her a quick tour of the hotel—an old-fashioned house turned into a boarding place. All the families were asleep, and within thirty minutes she was settled in her room. She looked out the window to see Deion speaking with some men, then getting in a car and driving off with them. There was no sign of Janey.

She waited another twenty minutes for her aunt to appear, then realized Janey probably wouldn't risk stepping into the hotel and revealing her identity. So she sat alone on the narrow bed, thinking of how she and Carmelo would connect with this new obstacle between them.

Nearly an hour later, Janey sent for her. Already in bed and half asleep, Kathy had to dress hurriedly to run downstairs into the night to meet her. And Janey was right where she left her.

Janey grinned and met her half the distance with a joyful hug. Listen, my husband is... *misbehaving* again. He's parked in the back of the hotel, waiting and pouting. But don't you worry none. I've arranged a place for you and your Melo to be together. Dieon's gonna take you to see him tonight, and we'll figure out the rest as we go."

"Wait, what do you mean—?"

Janey gently turned Kathy to face the hearse waiting like a patient shadow. She leaned close and whispered conspiratorially in her ear, her breath warm against Kathy's skin: "Auntie always delivers, *ma petite*."

Dieon leaned against an idling black 1948 Cadillac Superior hearse from *Percy & Sons Funeral Home.*

"Mr. Percy's doin' a midnight embalmin'," Dieon murmured, opening the rear door with practiced discretion. "Said you could use the old building and stay in the 'arrangements parlor' 'til the coast clears. I'll take ya."

Kathy grinned. She gave Janey another hug. "I don't know what I would do without you, Auntie. For helping us, for being there for me. I love you so much."

Janey's eyes teared as she hugged her tightly. "I love you more."

Kathy slid onto cool velvet seats originally designed for mourners, the cloying scent of funeral lilies and formaldehyde thick in the air. *A funeral home hearse.* Of course. In Memphis, the dead were sometimes granted more dignity than the living. Funeral homes were among the few businesses that crossed color lines out of necessity. Still, this felt more macabre than romantic. She and Carmelo had devised countless creative ways to meet over the past two years, but nothing quite as unsettling as romance among the tools of death and grief.

The hearse glided silently through backstreets lined with shotgun shacks and porches, past Beale Street's shuttered blues clubs where B.B. King and Muddy Waters had played just hours before. It finally came to a stop behind a red-brick building with drawn blinds and the discreet respectability that only funeral homes possess. A single bulb cast harsh shadows above a door marked "PRIVATE - BEREAVEMENT SERVICES."

Dieon tapped the horn twice as the agreed signal.

The door opened immediately. Silhouetted against the amber light stood Matteo Ricci. He jerked his head sharply—*inside, fast, before anyone sees.*

Who would see? The ghosts? There was nothing but graves and trees around them.

Kathy hurried from the hearse, but despite the urgency, she couldn't help throwing her arms around Matteo's neck in a fierce embrace. "Did you bring pictures of Junior? How big is he now?" she asked, squeezing him tight.

"Inside first! Later! I'll show you everything later, I promise," he said with a grin that reminded her so much of Debbie's happiness the last time he saw her cousin and the baby, her heart ached. She nodded and followed him into the shadows, no longer able to contain her joy at seeing family again after so many careful months apart.

* * *

THIS PART of the funeral home had been closed for two years. Every room was emptied or repurposed for storage by the Percys. Still, Kathy could guess their original purpose, especially when she descended into the basement. White tiles. Steel embalming tables. The sour-sweet stench of preservatives hung in the air like a chemical shroud. Kathy hugged herself, shivering despite the claustrophobic Memphis heat now trapped inside. When she turned around, she was alone. Somehow, Matteo hadn't followed her down.

"Matteo?" she called to the shadows. "Matteo!"

"Boo!"

Kathy screamed and whirled with a wild swing. Her fist connected hard with the side of Carmelo's head, knocking him backward. He stumbled, more startled than hurt, while she gasped and covered her mouth in horror.

Carmelo laughed, rubbing his head. "Damn, Kat! You pack a punch!"

"You scared the living daylights out of me!" She rushed into his arms, squealing with joy despite her embarrassment. Carmelo's kiss consumed her completely, desperate and hungry. The times between their meetings were shorter now—just a few months instead of the agonizing year-long separations—but it still left them both starved for each other's touch.

"Slow down, slow... down," she pushed him back gently, breathing hard. "Let me catch my breath."

Carmelo licked his lips as if they tasted like salvation itself. She blushed at the raw desire in his dark eyes. "I missed you too, *amore*."

"Why are we meeting in a morgue?" he asked, shaking his head with incredulous laughter.

"It's weird as heck, isn't it?" she giggled.

"Come here," he pulled her into a proper embrace—one that soothed instead of consumed. The world stopped spinning when she listened to his heartbeat. She wondered if it matched the rhythm of the baby growing inside her. When should she tell him? How? What would happen? Her father was in the midst of a consuming drug war with Italian families. This baby could either blow their world apart or bring it together. They had to decide their future soon.

"I have a surprise—a good one. A final one," he whispered against her ear.

"Final?" She looked up, alarmed.

He nodded solemnly.

"Tell me! Tell me right now!" she demanded.

He cupped her face in his calloused hands and looked into her eyes. "Vegas."

She frowned in confusion. "What's a Vegas?"

"A city in Nevada, out in the desert. Where we can be together as man and wife, live our lives freely. It's where I can box professionally and run a legitimate business. Where I can set us up properly." His voice grew excited. "Carmine's got connections there, great opportunities. Matteo's making moves—something I can't tell you about yet, but if his plans work, he'll be head of the family soon. He'll run everything. And he wants to take Debbie and the baby with him. We'll go too. All four of us, finally together."

Her eyes widened until they watered. "Are you absolutely sure? Is it really possible?"

He nodded slowly, his expression serious. "It's for real, Kat. This is our way out."

She released the deepest sigh of her life and hugged him so tightly she thought she might break his ribs, weeping tears of pure joy. She almost confessed her secret then, but something held her back. She'd save that news for after he won his fight, set it up perfectly. There was no way she'd tell him about their baby in a funeral home basement.

"I wish we could stay the night together. I really miss touching you," he sighed, his forehead pressed against hers.

"I miss you too, desperately. But absolutely not—I don't care if this place has been closed for business, I am not sleeping in a funeral home next to a graveyard," she chuckled, despite the heat in her cheeks.

He nodded with understanding. "How's Big Mama doing?"

Kathy's smile dimmed like a candle in the wind. "Not good at all. She's taken to bed permanently. Her feet... the doctors say they may need to amputate one or both. And she's so heartbroken she can't get around anymore." Her voice caught. "I've left the classroom to take care of her. Mama came down like I wrote you, and some church ladies are with her this week while I'm here. But I don't know... this isn't going to get better."

He nodded gravely. "She's strong, though. She has to be—she made you and Debbie."

The comment brought fresh tears to her eyes, but these were tears of happiness. It was true. Although Kathy knew her lineage traced back to the formidable Elliott women, it was Big Mama who was the source of her true grit. Big Mama had given her the backbone to survive her exile from Harlem these past two years. The mere thought of losing her always sent Kathy spiraling into grief—a fear she never mentioned to Debbie, knowing her cousin would dissolve into inconsolable fits. Everyone just prayed and planned for the best recovery.

"Hey," Carmelo lifted her chin with gentle fingers. "Look at me."

She did.

"You've done so much for me, Kathy, for us. You've been patient. You've given up family, given up everything for me." His voice grew thick with emotion. "You're my girl, but what you've sacrificed goes deeper than anything I can replace with my love. I'm sorry. I stay up at night, every night, thinking about how I can ever make it all up to you. Wishing I had power, I don't. You're my family. Other than Nino, Matteo, and Debbie, you're the only family I have left. I can't move forward or backward without you."

"You've done just as much for me. Surviving that hammer, boxing, risking your life to get us free. I see it, Carmelo. You're my hero—honest, kind, fundamentally good, and I—"

"I'm no saint," he mumbled, pulling away slightly.

She caught his hand, stopping his retreat. "You're still my hero. The bravest man I know besides Daddy. I'll wait forever for us. And even longer than that, if I have to. I will never love anyone but you." Her smile was radiant with certainty.

They embraced again, then walked through the abandoned funeral home, talking about the Mafia and Vegas. He shared how his father despised the idea of expansion with the Marcellos and secretly envied how wealthy Marcello had become in the segregated South. But Carmelo had done his research. He'd learned from Matteo that Meyer Lansky, a Jewish gangster, lived by his own rules in Nevada, and the Mafia were destined to be kings in that desert kingdom.

"Have you seen Carmine?" Carmelo asked.

"I saw him in the car when he dropped me at the bus station, but we didn't speak," she shrugged.

"That's strange. He came to New York, and we were supposed to have dinner. But he never showed. The next day, he met briefly with Matteo, then left without explanation. I've tried calling him several times, but he hasn't returned my calls. Janey called me back. Said she'd tell him my message. Nothing. Is he upset with me about something?"

"That is odd. Janey mentioned he was in a foul mood. Must be all the business pressure he's dealing with," she suggested.

"Must be. I'll see him at the hotel, try to catch up. We might need to leave Memphis for one of the smaller towns to spend time together safely. I'll work it out," he assured her.

She grinned with anticipation. "I suppose I should go."

He groaned in protest. "The weigh-in tomorrow is open to both white and colored spectators. Will you be there?"

"Yes! I promise," she smiled brightly. "I'll be there cheering you on."

He hugged her tighter, and they parted with that sacred promise hanging between them—a bridge across the darkness that would carry them to whatever came next.

CHAPTER 26

SHATTERING THE MISSING PIECES

The clink of glasses, the roar of masculine laughter, and thick clouds of cigar smoke overran the lobby of the Chamblee Hotel—a hotel that had been upgraded to high-end service for those who dwelled in society's underbelly. Men like him and his brother.

Matteo lit his third cigarillo and exhaled slowly, his sharp eyes sweeping the faces of men they knew and those they didn't. Among them all, he didn't see Carmine Boanno.

"He's not here?" Carmelo asked, tension crept into his voice.

"Doesn't look like it. Maybe he took Kathy's aunt to the Memphis Belle," Matteo suggested.

"No coloreds allowed there. That would be too risky, even for the Marcellos. He has to be here somewhere—maybe in the rooms upstairs. Gambling rooms to the back? We need to find him."

Matteo threw out his arm, stopping Carmelo's advancement. "Wait. Slow down. You're acting jumpy as a cat."

"I've got this feeling," Carmelo mumbled, running a hand through his dark hair. "Something's wrong. A fucking funeral home? No safe house for me and Kat? He isn't sloppy like this. Why does this feel… I dunno, neglectful?"

"You're pouting cause you had to leave her behind," Matteo rolled his eyes.

"No. It's in my gut. I need to talk to him tonight," Carmelo insisted.

Matteo frowned, studying his brother's agitated state. "Let me ask around."

Reluctant but without options, Carmelo stepped back toward the bar.

"Get a drink. Cool your heels. I'll be back in a few," Matteo said, slipping through the crowd like smoke.

Carmelo accepted a whiskey from the bartender, his thoughts racing. He hadn't been concerned when he'd arrived—he'd had a whole agenda planned for his visit to Tennessee. Hell, he'd even jumped the gun by mentioning Vegas to Kathy. And the truth he shared was far more complicated than desert dreams.

Matteo wanted to finish what Carmelo couldn't bring himself to do. Had sworn on their mother's grave he would kill their father. To accomplish such a lofty goal would require careful arrangement through anyone but Sicilians or Italians. Meyer Lansky and Lucky Luciano's alliance presented the perfect opportunity. Bugsy Siegel and Lansky were both Jewish, and their internal conflict had put Vegas on the map, bringing the Mafia in for a slice of the pie. Carmine and Marcello could help them get to the table and arrange the hit on Don Cosimo that would free them all.

Something in Carmelo's gut said everything was now at risk, and he had to ensure nothing stood in the way of the life he'd promised Kathy.

"Drinking alone?"

He turned to find Janey standing behind him, elegant as always in a burgundy dress that hugged her curves. There weren't many women in the company of these gangsters, but Janey wasn't like any woman he'd ever known.

"No, let me get you something. What would you like?" he asked with a forced smile.

"Answers," Janey said, stepping closer until he could smell her expensive perfume. "What is upsetting my husband?"

Carmelo's brows lowered. "What do you mean—"

"He's been in a foul mood since New York, and now that we're here, he's even worse. I know Carmine better than anyone. Something's gnawing at him, and my guess is it's you."

"Me? I didn't even see him in New York, Janey. I was looking for him. We need to discuss the match arrangements."

"Found him!" Matteo announced, walking ahead of Carmine Boanno through the smoky crowd.

Carmelo looked into Carmine's pale eyes and knew instantly. It hit him in the gut harder than his father's hammer ever had. Maria. The twins. Carmine knew everything.

"There he is!" Janey moved toward her husband, attempting to kiss his cheek, but Carmine was in no mood and pushed her aside with barely contained annoyance.

"You looking for me, kid?" Carmine asked, his voice carrying the quiet menace of a man who'd discovered betrayal.

Confused, Janey's gaze swiveled from her husband to Carmelo, sensing the dangerous undercurrents she couldn't quite understand.

Carmelo had to neutralize the situation fast. "Yes, can we meet privately? Got some things my father wanted me to discuss with you."

Without waiting for an answer, he walked quickly away from the bar, not looking back. He feared meeting Carmine's eyes again. If this was going to explode, it would have to be now, away from witnesses and innocent bystanders.

The time for reckoning had come.

* * *

THE BEST HE could find was a poker room where players were engrossed in their high-stakes game. He walked to the furthest corner and spotted a door marked "STORAGE." Beyond it lay a small room filled with crates of liquor and linens—private enough for what was coming.

Carmelo went straight inside, leaving the door open for Carmine, then began pacing as panic rose inside him like molten lava.

Carmine entered at his leisure, his silver-topped cane clicking against the wooden floor. The door closed behind him with ominous finality.

"It's not what you think!" Carmelo shouted, pacing frantically. "I would never betray Kathy. Ever!"

"Yet you are married to another woman."

"It was Mama! It was all because of Mama!" Carmelo spun around, his face flushed with desperation. He was losing his breath, crumbling under Carmine's lethal scrutiny. "My mother died—her suicide, her final letter—she said there was a hit on Kathy's father. That I had to make peace. I had no choice! Matteo was missing. Debbie pregnant. Kathy trapped in Mississippi, and I had just broken the sacrament for shooting my father. I had to." His words tumbled out in hyperventilated bursts. "I only did it because it's not real." Carmelo laughed as madness took control over him. "It's all a lie. It's all fake. A lie! I'm already married—I married Kathy first! Before a real judge! So this wedding to Maria isn't real in God's eyes!"

Carmine remained stone silent, his pale gaze bore into Carmelo's soul.

Carmelo closed his eyes, his voice dropped to a whisper. "The twins... they were... a mistake. An accident. I don't even know how they... how it happened."

"You don't know how babies are made?" Carmine asked with deadly calm.

"So much pressure at home. So much anger and pressure, and then the boxing, I carry it all. I was drinking heavily, drowning in booze after I lost my fight in Chicago. Maria said I came home stinking of liquor, and I forced her. I would never... but she said it happened, and I... I don't remember what happened that night," Carmelo said, his voice cracking.

"You're a liar and half a man," Carmine seethed, his controlled facade finally cracking. "If you were a real man, you would never call your children a mistake!"

Carmelo's tears came hot and fast now. "You don't understand! It was a mistake—a fucking mistake! I was drowning in liquor, missing

Kathy so bad I couldn't breathe, and Maria... she says I did it, says I forced her, but that's not me. I'd never—Christ, I don't even remember! Maybe I got confused, maybe I thought—" His voice cracked. "One night! One goddamn night I can't even remember, and I swear on my mother's grave—on her soul—I don't know what happened!"

Carmine turned for the door, disgust rolling off him in waves.

"Wait!" Carmelo lurched forward, desperate. "How? How the fuck did you find out? Was it my father?"

Carmine's eyes went cold as winter. "Met your bambini myself. Your pretty little wife brought them right into your father's office. Along with your new mother-in-law."

Carmelo's mind reeled. "She brought my children to a sit-down? To a closed meeting with made men?"

"What's it matter?" Carmine shrugged. "Your father's married to her mother now."

"That calculating bitch set me up!" The words exploded from Carmelo. "That fucking puttana played me!"

"Watch your mouth, boy." Carmine's voice turned dangerous. "That's your wife you're cursing. The mother of your children. She says you promised to bring her to New Orleans, introduce her to Kathy."

"Lies! All fucking lies!" Carmelo was spiraling now. "She knows everything—knows about Kathy, knows I won't touch her, knows I'm dying inside every day I'm not with Kathy. And she parades those kids in front of you—"

"Your kids," Carmine cut him like a blade.

"—because she knew! She knew you'd run straight to Kathy. Calculated every goddamn move!"

"Only thing calculated here is your stupidity!" Carmine roared back. "You made this bed, now you're crying because you gotta lie in it? Be a man! Own your shit!"

"Please." Carmelo's rage crumbled into desperation. "Let me tell Kathy myself. Let me explain—I got a plan. Vegas, right? You and Matteo been talking Vegas? I'll fight whoever, whatever—just let me tell her first. We go to Vegas, start clean—"

"With what? Your wife and babies in tow? You gonna juggle families like some two-bit player?"

"I don't want them!" The words tore from Carmelo's throat. "Never wanted them! Never asked for this!"

They faced off, two bulls ready to charge. Carmelo's whole body vibrated with fury, fists white-knuckled at his sides. Carmine just shook his head slowly, turned for the door again.

"You breathe one word—one fucking word to her—and I swear to God I'll kill you." Carmelo's voice dropped to a deadly quiet. "I'll burn this whole thing down. The fight, the deal, everything—"

Carmine's hand stilled on the doorknob. "Warned you about Elliott women, didn't I? Told you their hearts don't forgive. You had the honey, boy. Now all that's left is the sting."

"I'll fucking kill you," Carmelo whispered.

"Nah." Carmine didn't even turn around. "You already dead, Carmelo. Been digging your own grave since the day you betrayed her. Now you get to lie in it—alone. Just like every other fool who crossed an Elliott woman."

The door closed soft as a coffin lid, leaving Carmelo drowning in the wreckage of his choices.

JANEY PEELED herself away from the door and hurried out of the poker room just as the argument between Carmine and Carmelo ended. She'd caught every word through the thin wood—every confession, every desperate plea, every damning detail.

The hot blood spreading through her veins now wasn't anger. Anger was too small, too simple for what moved inside her. This was older, darker—the kind of feeling that made men bleed for their sins against women. And keep bleeding until they were dead.

* * *

MATTEO WATCHED JANEY rush out of the poker room and head straight for the stairs to take her upstairs, where the rooms were. He leaned against the bar, observing as Carmine emerged moments later with his cane, walking slowly in the same direction with a deadly purpose.

His brows lowered with concern when his brother was the last to appear. He pushed off from the bar. Carmelo wiped away tears, his face and neck were both red as a beet. He headed for the hotel's front door. Matteo followed.

He found Carmelo outside by a large oak tree, retching violently into the bushes. He ran over as Carmelo pressed both hands flat against the bark and wept openly, his shoulders shaking with grief.

"*Che cazzo è successo?*" Matteo demanded in Italian. *What the fuck happened?*

Carmelo was so distraught that he didn't even notice his brother's presence.

"Melo? *Che cazzo?*" He grabbed Carmelo's arm to bring him out of it. Carmelo swung wildly, missing Matteo's head by centimeters as he stumbled backward, lost in his anguish.

"What is it? What happened in there? Tell me!"

Carmelo shook his head and walked toward the darkness beyond the hotel's lights. Matteo had been lost before—distraught, on the verge of complete self-destruction—and it was Carmelo and Debbie who had saved his life during those months. He'd never seen Carmelo reach that low, except once before. And that was during the long recovery after losing Kathy the first time—the endless months of silence, the obsessive drawing of her face, the hollow emptiness where his brother used to be.

He'd seen that darkness and vowed when he'd made his way out of it that neither his baby brother nor anyone else he loved would ever know that kind of pain again.

He went after Carmelo, but the darkness and the wooded area beyond the hotel had swallowed him completely. He had vanished into the night like a ghost.

And for the rest of those long hours, Matteo searched desperately for him, finding nothing but shadows and the echo of his own voice calling his brother's name.

* * *

Quebec, Canada - 1978

Carmelo's eyes snapped open. He shot upright in bed, his heart hammering against his ribs with the savage rhythm of a war drum. The dream had been so vivid, so ruthless and real. It felt as if some malevolent force had transported him back through time to witness the exact moment his soul began its descent into hell.

He felt Kathy stir beside him, her warmth a stark contrast to the ice water flowing through his veins.

He looked down at her in the darkness, and tears welled in his eyes like blood from a fresh wound. She lay on her side, her dark hair now threaded with silver and tucked behind one of the silk scarves she'd taken to sleeping in—a small vanity that broke his heart with its fragile humanity. Even in sleep, she carried the weight of their shared trauma in the lines around her eyes, the slight furrow between her brows that never quite disappeared anymore.

Carmelo touched her hip with a trembling hand, needing to confirm she was alive, real, still there with him despite everything he'd done. The warmth of her skin beneath the thin nightgown was like medicine, and only then did he find the ability to breathe again. He tossed aside the covers with careful precision, desperate not to wake her and face the questions he couldn't answer.

"Melo?" Kathy moaned softly, her hand reached back through the darkness for him like a drowning woman grasping for shore.

"Be right back, *amore*," he whispered, his chest constricted with the crushing weight of his own unworthiness. Before she could fully surface from sleep, he turned and fled like the coward he'd always been when it came to causing her pain.

Did she return to his bed out of pity? When he made love to her, was she only tolerating his possessive needs to plan her escape?

He moved through the darkness like something born to it, finding his way by memory and old pain to the one room where he could stop pretending, where he'd spent these past weeks plotting fresh lies for her, then scrambling for ways to claw her heart back—that sick dance they'd been doing for decades now. Destruction and redemption, over and over, like they were both addicted to the hurt.

Every scar, every scream, every tear that ever rolled down her face —his fault. All of it. Every goddamn drop.

The door opened to his private hell. Neither Kathy nor Nino had ever stepped foot in there. The walls were covered in his drawings, taped up like evidence at a crime scene. His mother's face, frozen young and disappointed forever. Kathy at seventeen, before he'd taught her what betrayal tasted like. His father's cruel mouth. Men he'd beaten to death—some in the ring after he'd lost her, others later when he'd become the Wolf and his hammer sang its own kind of justice.

All those faces. All those ghosts. Feeding on him.

He shut his eyes and let out a breath that had been trapped for years. Here in the dark, the armor came off. Here he could finally break—could weep like the boy he'd been, could shake with the fear he never showed, could admit what he'd become.

How much was too much? When did he cross the line he couldn't come back from? What happened when the Battaglias told him to fuck off with his begging? When Kathy finally wised up and ran—took their daughter and disappeared like she'd tried before? When his lies unraveled and every enemy he'd made came to collect?

The questions circled, picking at him like buzzards. But slowly, the panic loosened its grip. He dropped onto the stool—hard, unforgiving, built for penance—and grabbed the pencil with hands that wouldn't stop shaking.

Kathy's face looked back at him from the half-finished drawing. Not the woman sleeping down the hall, but the girl who'd walked into that barn years ago in Butts and told him to his face she had cut him off clean. The day she'd finally seen what Ricci men really were. The day she'd looked at him like he was nothing and said it: "I will never forgive you."

The day he'd died inside, the Wolf was born.

His pencil scratched across paper, chasing something he'd killed—that last moment when he'd been a man she could love, before he'd become the thing she feared.

CHAPTER 27

MEMPHIS TENNESSEE, 1952

"Wake up, Sleeping Beauty."

Kathy smiled before her eyes opened, turning toward the familiar voice. Janey's lips brushed her cheek, fingers gentle as they swept hair from her brow. But when Kathy's eyes focused on her aunt's face, the smile died.

"What time is it?" She inched back against the headboard, something wild in Janey's stare making her careful.

"Early. Been here since before dawn." Janey's voice sounded wrong —hollow, like she was speaking from the bottom of a well. "Had to wait for Carmine to pass out. Walked here. In the dark."

"What?" Kathy blinked, taking in the burgundy dress from last night, now wrinkled and twisted. This wasn't the Janey she knew—the one who never had a hair out of place. This woman's makeup ran in dark rivers down her cheeks, her perfect curls hung limp, and her eyes... God, her eyes looked like she'd been crying for hours. Or planning something.

Kathy's gaze caught that her aunt had taken a chair and pulled it close to the bed. Too close. Like someone had been sitting and watching her.

"You've been in my room? Watching me sleep?" Kathy asked.

"Had to come. Had to protect you," Janey whispered. "It's your time."

"For what? From what?" she asked.

Janey leaned close, her breath hot and sour against Kathy's ear. "The big bad Wolf. He's coming for my little red riding hood."

She slipped from the bed, and Kathy saw her aunt's bare feet—caked with mud, bleeding at the edges. She'd walked here barefoot from wherever Carmine kept her. Miles in the dark. Something terrible had happened—or was about to. Something bad enough to send Janey over the edge she'd been dancing on for years.

Janey paced to the window, movements sharp and strange. "You don't ask about Willa anymore."

Kathy's eyes found the door. Another chair wedged under the knob—to keep them in or the world out, she couldn't tell.

"I write to Willa. We keep in touch," Kathy said, keeping her voice steady.

"He did it, you know. She won't tell you the truth, but he did." Janey's voice carried a sing-song quality that made Kathy's skin crawl. "Jean-Baptiste. The family cast her out like garbage seven months later. Willa was so distraught. Jean-Baptiste was a coward or complicit. Willa lived on the streets for days before someone told Carmine and brought her back to me for healing." Janey looked over at Kathy with eyes that glittered. "I had warned him, Kathy. I told him not to disrespect her or hurt her. Not to make me do what I had to do. I warned those Thibodeaux bastards."

Kathy frowned in confusion. "That's not true. Willa was pregnant. She and Jean-Baptiste have left his family. They have a small place in the Quarter. They are happy—that's what her letters said. She even sent a picture of them both together."

Janey's smile was chilling in its serenity. "Willa lost the baby. And that is when the family came for JB. That was it. The spell was broken. Willa was damaged goods, and JB had to face it. Those letters you write go to the post office, not to the cottage in the quarter.

JB had to choose between a broken Willa who had just given birth to his dead child and being poor or his freedom to be a spoiled bitch-boy Thibodeaux again. Guess what choice he made? Guess who threw her out of that little fantasy they had run off to in the Tremé and dumped her on the street."

Janey didn't pause for a breath. She kept going.

"I took care of her, made her strong again. And against Carmine's wishes, I made the Thibodeaux family pay." Her voice dropped to a whisper. "Baked a cake for his cousin's wedding and had it served by one of my girls at the reception. Took out six of them in one night, but not that bastard JB. He got away."

"No. Auntie. You didn't do that. You wouldn't?"

Janey stood frozen, a dark smile on her face.

"Auntie?" Kathy pleaded.

Janey didn't respond.

"What? What are you saying?" Kathy's voice cracked with horror.

Janey's smile widened, satisfied as a cat licking blood from its whiskers. "Everyone cried about food poisoning at the reception. But the Thibodeauxs? They knew. Oh, they knew exactly what killed six of their blood." She studied her hands like they belonged to someone else. "The whole Quarter went into mourning. That beautiful cake—it took innocents along with the guilty. A cousin's new bride. An uncle who'd only ever been kind. I'd meant to punish the ones who hurt Willa, but poison doesn't choose. It just takes."

Her voice dropped to something raw. "Carmine had to sell pieces of his soul to Don Marcello to keep me from my mama's fate—swinging from a tree while the crowd cheers. Everything we had, every favor owed, every bit of power... gone. Our house. Gone. We're owned by the Marcellos now, forever in their pocket. We've got to leave New Orleans for Vegas soon. Not to come back. Because of what I did. Because I couldn't stop myself, I've lost my family except you. You love me still."

She laughed, but it sounded like a release of sorrow. "And Willa? When she learned what I'd done for her, she ran from me like I was the devil himself. Marcellos found her later because she, too, is part of the bargain. Found her months later in one of the wash houses, hands bleeding from lye. Brought her back to me like a lost dog."

Janey's eyes found Kathy's, and they were empty as graves. "Tell me, chère—did Jean-Baptiste destroy Willa, or did I? I used to be powerful, you know. Could make men dance, make them beg, make them mine. Now?" She spread her trembling hands. "Now I'm just deadly. Like the candies my sisters taught me to make. Nothing left in me but poison."

Kathy threw back the covers and rushed to her aunt, her heart breaking through her fear. Janey trembled at the window, her eyes wild and unfocused, seeing things that weren't there. Kathy wrapped her arms around her, holding tight.

"Willa loves you. She writes about you constantly—how grateful she is, how much she loves you. This story can't be true. You're confused, Auntie. Willa's pregnant again, just wrote me about it last month."

"I am NOT confused!" Janey shoved her away with shocking violence, sending Kathy stumbling. Her voice climbed to a shriek that could wake the dead. "I don't want to kill Carmelo, Kathy. God help me, I don't. If I kill him then they will kill my Carmine. I've done so much, he can't keep protecting me. But I can't stop what's already started. He hurt you! He LIED to you! He BETRAYED you! HE HAS TO PAY!"

"What?" Kathy backed away.

"He's just like the rest of them. Never special, never different. You thought he was, but men can't be special, chère. They're heart-breakers, trust-killers, soul-destroyers. That's all they know how to be!" She spat the words like venom. "They're nothing but meat for the cutting!"

"Janey, please, you're scaring me." Kathy kept backing toward the door, her hands searching blindly for the chair blocking it. "Why are you angry at Carmelo? What has he done?"

Janey began to twitch violently. She paced in tight circles, hitting herself on the side of the head and muttering incoherently about being a bad girl and being put in the box where the spiders ate her. Kathy knew something was desperately wrong, but she couldn't remember all the things Pinkie had taught her to do when Janey's episodes turned dangerous.

A sharp knock cracked against the door like a gunshot. Kathy spun toward it, but Janey was already moving—predator-quick, clamping an arm around Kathy's chest and a hand over her mouth with shocking strength.

"Shhh..." Hot breath against her ear.

"Janey? Kathy? Open up." Carmine's voice was tight with controlled panic. "Let me in."

Kathy trembled in her aunt's grip. She could fight—maybe even win—but something told her that would send Janey somewhere they couldn't come back from.

"Janey!" The door rattled in its frame. "I know you're in there. Woke up and you were gone. You've had your time. We need to go."

That's when Janey began to whisper. Each word was a knife sliding between Kathy's ribs. Carmelo was married. Had been for two years. An Italian girl named Maria. Twin babies—boy and girl. A whole house, a whole life in New York. Matteo and Debbie coming for Sunday dinners like one big happy family. Everyone knew. Her parents knew. They'd all known while she rotted in Butts, waiting for a man who only visited when he needed what his wife couldn't give. The big bad Wolf, playing house while she played the little piggie. The fool.

The scream that tore from Kathy when Janey released her didn't sound human. She collapsed near the bed, her body trying to turn itself inside out from the pain.

Janey watched with savage satisfaction. "Now you see. Now you understand what they are. WE kill him together."

"JANEY!" The door shook violently under Carmine's assault.

Kathy couldn't stop the sounds coming from her—raw wails that felt like they were ripping her soul out through her throat.

Janey knelt beside her, stroking her hair with a mother's false tenderness. "Did you hear me? We can kill him together, *ma petite*. Or break him like I broke Carmine—make him our puppet, our slave. We're Elliott women. We don't feel pain, *chère*. We give it."

"Get away from me!" Kathy screamed. "GET AWAY!"

The door exploded inward. Carmine and Deion charged through, hotel staff crowding behind. Janey launched herself at her husband like something feral, all nails and teeth and rage. It took three men to pin her down.

Kathy stayed curled on the floor where she'd fallen, barely aware of the chaos. Janey's screams echoed down the hall as they dragged her away. Gentle hands tried to lift Kathy, women's voices murmuring comfort she couldn't hear.

She turned her face to the wall and let herself fall into that dark, quiet place she'd found the day they shot her father in front of her.

The void. Where nothing could touch her. Where nothing could hurt.

Where wolves couldn't reach.

* * *

THE SPARRING PARTNER'S punch connected with the force of a sledgehammer. Carmelo dropped hard, the canvas rushing up to meet him with a sick thud that echoed through the empty gym.

"Shit!" Matteo vaulted through the ropes, dropping to his knees beside his brother's motionless form. "Melo! Get up!"

Nothing. Carmelo lay there like a corpse, blood trickling from his split lip.

Matteo hauled him up, propping his brother against his shoulder. Carmelo's head lolled sideways, eyes unfocused. The stink of last night's bourbon seeped from his pores.

"You have to get it together. Do you hear me?" Matteo shook him hard.

Six hours ago, he'd found Carmelo face-down in a Beale Street speakeasy, mumbling about Kathy, about betrayal, about how she'd know soon and hate him forever. Matteo had carried him out on his back, dumped him in a cold shower, and forced black coffee down his throat until he could stand. Barely.

Now this. The fight was in two days. Every wise guy from here to Chicago had money riding on the Wolf delivering the South. If Carmelo didn't show, or worse, if he showed and lost...

Matteo's hand went instinctively to his neck. He could already feel the bullet.

"Get him up," he barked at his men. "Take him to the room. Ice bath, more coffee. Whatever it takes."

They lifted Carmelo between them like a broken doll. Matteo watched them go, his jaw tight. Caesar would've known what to do. Caesar always knew. But Caesar was back in New York, and Matteo was here with a brother who'd rather die than fight.

He stalked across the street to the phone booth, feeding coins into the slot with shaking hands. The operator connected him, and he waited, counting the rings.

"Hello?"

"Debs?" Matteo said.

"Hey? How are things going?" she asked.

He could hear Junior crying in the background. "What's wrong with my son?"

"He wants José's food instead of his own. Stubborn like his father," she chuckled.

"Oh? He misses me," Matteo relaxed.

"Yes, he cries when he misses you, when he's hungry, when he's wet, or just when he feels like it, Matteo. I told you it's what kids do. So stop stressing," Debbie sighed.

"You are right. I am always worried," he confessed.

"How's Kathy? Is she there? I want you to tell her to call," she said.

"Debs, things aren't good," Matteo cut in.

"What?" Debbie asked.

"Somehow, Boanno found out about Maria and the babies. Can't get the whole story out of Carmelo, but that aunt you told me about? Janey? I think she knows. Which means—"

"Kathy." Debbie's voice went faint. "You promised this wouldn't happen. You swore we'd get to Vegas, that Carmelo would explain everything before—Matteo, please God tell me she doesn't know!"

"What the fuck could I do? I don't know how Carmine found out! I did everything—"

"You made me lie to her!" Debbie's voice cracked. "She'll never forgive me. Never! I should have told her!"

"I'm sorry. Christ, I'm so sorry. But Carmelo's falling apart. If he doesn't get in that ring, he's dead. These fuckers have serious money on him. We don't deliver; they hand us over to the Klan. He has to fight. Then I swear I'll fix this."

"Fix it? How? Why are you calling me? I can't—" Debbie was crying now.

"I'm gonna find Kathy. Try to get her to talk to you. Please, Debs. She can hate him, punish him, whatever. But she has to forgive him long enough for me to get him out of Tennessee."

"She'll never forgive any of us." Debbie's voice was hollow. "I told you when they made him marry that girl. You said it was like me and José—all for show. Then the babies came, and you said they were an accident, that he didn't remember. I knew you were lying. I knew, but I was too scared to tell her. Now I've lost my cousin forever. I told you this day would come."

"Debs, please—"

The line went dead.

CHAPTER 28

QUEBEC, CANADA - 1978

Present. After thirty years, Kathy's body knew Carmelo's absence before her mind caught up. The sheets beside her had surrendered their warmth.

"Melo?" She sat up, pressed her palms hard against her eyes. "What is it now?"

The real problem wasn't what drove him from their bed—it was that they'd never learned the art of true forgiveness. They only knew how to bind themselves together with beautiful lies, pretending at healing while their old wounds festered. She remembered that first betrayal of trust, how she'd faked forgiveness to get him through the Memphis fight, only to gut him afterward with the truth: they were done. That innocence they'd shared in their love was ash, just like her heart.

Three decades later, the dance continued. Still pretending, still bleeding, still blaming. Even sex had become just another performance, another way to avoid looking at what they'd become.

She slipped from the bed, removed her nightie, and found his linen shirt, and pulled it on over her nakedness. Knowing he preferred to see her wearing it. She buttoned it, removed the scarf from her hair as she moved through the villa's darkness. Strange how this Quebec sanctuary mimicked their old Italian dreams, echoing every safe house he'd ever built for them. Different addresses, same gilded cage.

The house listened to her breathing. She aimed for the stairs—he'd be at the poolhouse, drowning in vino and regret. But then: a sliver of light bleeding from beneath a door she'd never noticed.

These upper rooms had held no interest before tonight. Now something pulled her forward. Jazz leaked through the wood—Coltrane, maybe, mournful and raw. Better than Springsteen. She pressed against the door, first her ear, then her whole body, as if it were Carmelo himself—all that beautiful defiance keeping her.

Her mother's last words surfaced, and suddenly she understood what Brenda and Henry had found before the end. Peace. Real peace. Not this endless war they called love.

She turned the handle.

What waited inside stole her breath.

1952 - Memphis, Tennessee

"Here, sweetie, drink this."

The voice pulled Kathy from the void. For a heartbeat, she saw Big Mama's face—all that worn kindness and strength. But her vision cleared, and it was someone else—another woman who knew how to gather broken girls.

Kathy sat up trembling, her mind in pieces. The cup shook in her hands as she sipped something bittersweet with honey that burned away the taste of betrayal.

"What's your name, baby?"

"Kathy, ma'am."

"Well, Kathy, I don't know what all that was about, but you're safe now. Nobody comes through that door unless Kathy says so. They call me Mabel."

"I need—" Kathy's voice cracked. "I need a ticket home."

"Where's home?"

A knock rattled the door. Kathy flinched hard, pressing back against the headboard.

"Ma, some men here asking after Kathy," came a young voice.

"Please don't let them in. Please!" Kathy. pleaded.

"Shh, now." Mabel's hands were steady on her shoulders. "Who are these men? Tell me true, child. Can't protect what I don't understand."

"They're—they want—" Kathy couldn't form the words. "They're bad people. I just need to get on the next bus home. Just a ticket. Please."

"Don't you worry, sugar." Mabel pulled her close, solid as a fortress. "Mabel's got you. We'll get you back to your people."

* * *

"What's taking them so long?" Matteo grunted and paced.

Carmine leaned against his car. He watched the young Ricci vibrate with barely contained violence. His own body ached from wrestling Janey into submission. He'd left strangers watching his wife —that couldn't hold. He needed to get back before she hurt someone or herself. But the Marcellos owned him now. Whatever independence he'd had, Janey's poison had dissolved it. Carmelo had to fight, which meant Kathy had to come with them.

"Go in and get her," Matteo demanded. "The fuck are we standing out here holding our dicks for!"

Carmine's gaze slid to Matteo and his boys. A bunch of Sicilians causing trouble outside a Negro hotel—they might as well paint targets on their backs.

"Shut your mouth, boy," Carmine said, voice like gravel.

Matteo's eyes narrowed, but he held his tongue.

Carmine pushed off the car, holding the younger man's stare until Matteo looked away. Then the hotel door opened. A silver-haired woman built like a battleship emerged, shotgun cradled like a baby, her men flanking her.

"You got ten seconds to get your narrow asses away from the Douglass or I'm putting holes in you and feeding what's left to my hogs."

"Ma'am, we only want to talk—"

She swung the gun toward Matteo. Carmine rolled his eyes. The fool would get his head blown off and all of them strung up if someone didn't intervene.

"Point that rifle at me." Carmine leaned heavily on his cane. "I'm in charge here."

Mabel pivoted, leveling the shotgun at his chest. One twitch and he'd be done. Part of him would welcome it. "Well, that ain't, so mister. You're on the wrong side of the tracks. This is Mabel's territory."

"Name's Carmine Boanno. The woman we carried out is my wife, Janey. She's half Negro, Kathy's aunt. That's what brought trouble to your door. And I'm here to collect her and pay for any damages. With apologies from Don Marcello."

"You one of them Sicilians? Don? From where?"

"New Orleans." Carmine removed his hat.

"Ah, so that's how you marry a mulatto. Not my business." Mabel's grip stayed steady. "Kathy told me she don't want to see you. She's under my protection now. So like I said—six seconds to get gone."

"I understand. Her and her aunt had words. Bad ones. She's got every right to her anger." Carmine kept his voice even. "I'd like to speak with her with your permission before we go. I'm asking you to relay my request—just me, nobody else. You can supervise. Then we leave."

"The hell we will!" Matteo snapped.

"He's young and stupid, Mabel. Kill him so that we can speak business," Carmine said without looking back.

Mabel's shotgun swung toward Matteo, and she lifted it high to aim. "Wait! No! Don't shoot!" Matteo gasped, hands up. He stumbled backward. She cut Carmine a knowing look. They had now understood each other. Matteo was still a weakling, especially in the dirty South. He had no clue about the politics here. Mabel was sure that Boanno was the one in charge.

She lowered the gun, murmured something to the man beside her, and handed it off. Smart woman—killing Sicilians would bring more heat than one scared colored girl was worth.

"Fine. But your time's short. One of them twitches wrong, my boys start shooting."

Carmine glanced at Matteo. "You heard her, tadpole. Keep your fucking mouth shut and your men in the cars. Let me handle this."

"You caused this!" Matteo's control cracked. "You told your wife, she told Kathy, and now we're all dead if Carmelo doesn't fight!"

"Death's coming regardless," Carmine sighed. He settled his hat and climbed the steps, cane clicking against wood.

Matteo ordered his men back to the cars. Watching Carmine disappear inside, he prayed to any saint listening that Kathy would see reason for all their sakes.

* * *

KATHY HAD LITTLE TO PACK. She stood still in the middle of the room. She held the lilac dress she'd sewn to wear on the night of his big fight. Even cut the fabric to look more beautiful for him. Tears fell freely. Last night, he'd painted pretty lies about Vegas, about their perfect life in the desert. All while his wife and babies waited at home.

What about the baby she'd carried? The shame of being cast out with a child? The endless months toiling in Butts, separated from everyone she loved? All for his fairytale. All lies.

She'd never thought herself capable of hating anyone more than King Redmond. But this betrayal cut to the bone.

She shoved the dress into her bag and pulled on her shoes. The door opened. Mabel entered first, but Carmine Boanno followed, making Kathy take several steps back.

“It’s okay, sweetie. He said he is married to your aunt and wants to speak, and then he is gone. It’s still your choice. My thinking is that speaking with him may settle the matter and prevent whatever brought you here from following you home. So you can have that conversation while I stay close. What do you say?”

Kathy’s gaze volleyed between Mabel and Carmine. She was so wound tight with emotion that she could barely summon her voice, so she nodded her agreement, her vision permanently blurred through tears.

"Janey left our bed in the middle of the night. I fell asleep in a chair watching over her after our fight. I need to clear some things up with you, Kathy. Last night, Janey heard me and Carmelo fight. I confronted him about what I saw on my trip to New York."

Kathy sank onto the bed. She fought the urge to cover her ears and block it out. She was barely holding herself together. To dissect the many levels of Carmelo's lies and deception may send her straight back into madness.

Carmine spoke with the weariness of a man confessing sins that weren't his own. Mabel leaned forward, her curiosity sharpening with every word.

"I went to New York to meet with his father about business." His cane tapped once against the floor. "Wasn't long before his wife and his twins walked in." He watched the words land like blows. "I was as blindsided as you are now, Kathy. Standing there, knowing what this would do to my Janey, to you. But this fight and Carmelo winning it was already written in my blood with the Marcellos. So I came here with the secret. Something I figured he would share with you after we discussed it."

Kathy closed her eyes and practiced breathing through the trauma.

"Carmelo lives in a fantasy world. Said you two were already married, and the marriage to that young girl is a lie. A suicide wish from his mother that he fulfilled to lift the black death from your father and you. That the babies came after one drunken night, and he doesn't remember. He had many reasons and excuses. It's not my place to tell you to forgive or even discuss it with him. I'm here for another reason."

"For Janey?" she managed.

"No. There is no cure for Janey. Her rage is the other half of her soul. I know how to deal with my wife. I'm here to plead with you to save all of our lives," Carmine looked over to Mabel, who was now staring at them both with a wide-eyed expression. He looked back at Kathy. "If Carmelo doesn't get in that ring and fight and *win*, none of us will leave Tennessee. My bosses have lost all patience with me. There is no room for error since the battle of the Thibodeauxs. I must see this through. And he will not fight for anything, including his own brother's life, if you break his heart."

"His heart?" Kathy exploded. "What about mine?"

Carmine raised a hand. "Say everything you need to say to him, not us. But do it after the fight. Come with me now. Dry your tears. See him, comfort him, pretend his crimes with you can be forgiven, pretend you don't know about the marriage if you have to. After he wins, I'll personally get you wherever you want to go. Back to Butts if that's what you need or straight to Harlem."

"This isn't on me!" Kathy said, and her hand went protectively to her tummy. Carmine didn't notice, but Mabel did. And when her eyes connected with Mabel's, the old woman shook her head with pity. Kathy looked away.

"Unfortunately, it is. You're all he cares about," Carmine said. "He's already fucking things up, thinking that someone has told you the truth."

Kathy looked to Mabel for help, who uncrossed her arms. "All I can tell you is Memphis is no place for you child. If there is a debt here to be paid, pay it so you keep the people you love alive."

Kathy wiped her face. "Okay. Take me to him."

Carmine exhaled in relief. Kathy hugged Mabel goodbye and followed Carmine outside. Matteo waited by the cars. He turned at the sight of her. She frowned and looked to Carmine. "Can I ride with you?" she asked. "I can't talk to him."

Matteo's face crumbled. Kathy ignored his silent plea, carrying equal resentment for him and Debbie now. Carmine extended his arm to escort her to his car. Inside, she broke completely. He sat silently until her tears ran dry.

"Done?" he asked.

She nodded.

He handed her one of Janey's perfumed handkerchiefs from the glove compartment. "Clean your face."

As she wiped her eyes, he said, "You're a woman now, Kathy. Carmelo says your father's a Harlem gangster?"

"Yes, sir."

"So you come from tough stock. Elliott Wynn is your grandfather, and then there's your father—hard men, right?" Carmine emphasized the point.

"Yes, sir."

"Then you fell for a man cut from the same cloth, didn't you?"

She nodded, unable to trust her voice.

"So you know the rules." Carmine's eyes stayed on the road, but his words cut straight through her. "You've watched the women in your family—your mother, your grandmother. They don't break when men like us disappoint them. They get harder. Stronger. That's how they love us."

"Yes, sir." The words came out cracked.

"No more tears, Kathy. Not where Carmelo can see them. You want to cry? You do it later, alone. But in front of him?" He shook his head. "Steel spine. That's the only way through this."

She pressed the handkerchief to her eyes one last time. "I understand."

"Good." The engine rumbled to life.

They'd barely left the curb when she found her voice. "Can I ask you something?"

He tilted his head—permission enough.

"Janey told me things. Terrible things. Said Thibodeaux's are dead, that she poisoned the family for what they did to Willa. Said Willa lost the baby and—" Her voice broke. "Is any of it true? Is everyone lying to me?"

Carmine's jaw tightened. "JB is dead."

"What? No. She said he survived," Kathy asked.

"She doesn't want you to hate her. He's dead. And their child is. Poor thing was born dead."

The confirmation hit like ice water. "But Willa's letters—"

"Willa's letters are to protect the truth. To protect Janey," he said in a dry monotone voice.

"From what?" Kathy asked.

"Willa is pregnant again." He glanced at her, measuring her reaction. "Living under my protection. Carrying my child."

The confession didn't make sense. She opened her mouth to say it, but nothing came out.

"After the fight. After you see it through, Carmelo wins. We play by your rules, Kathy—only your rules. And I'll explain everything. Deal?"

"Your baby?" The horror in her voice made him grip the wheel tighter. "What kind of monster are you?!"

"Do we have a deal?" His voice had gone cold, all business now.

She stared at him, this man who was Janey's husband, Willa's... what? The car suddenly felt too small, the air too thick. Another betrayal. Another secret. Another man taking what he wanted. Another reason to run and scream against the world she found herself trapped in. But why? How? What choice did she have?

"Do we have a deal?" he asked.

"Deal," she replied.

CHAPTER 29

THE CHAMP AND HIS LADY

Carmelo sat frozen in the back room, robe hanging loose on his shoulders, gloves laced, boots on. He should've been warming up, should've been in the ring twenty minutes ago. But his body had shut down, suspended between dread and hope. *Did she know? How much? Was he already dead and just waiting for the bullet?*

"Matteo's back." A voice cut through his paralysis from one of his watchers. "Got people with him."

Carmelo's head lifted like a man on the gallows spotting the governor. Matteo entered first, then Carmine, and behind them—

Kathy.

She wasn't looking at him yet, her attention caught by something in the hallway. When her eyes finally found his, he watched her face transform—soft recognition, then something harder, sharper, before a smile bloomed that didn't quite reach her eyes.

"Hey," she said, and the simple word undid him.

He launched from the chair, sweeping her into his arms and spinning her around before his mind could warn him to be careful. She hugged him back, her body fitting against his the way it always had, but when her eyes opened over his shoulder, they locked on Matteo with something fierce and unforgiving.

When he finally released her, she softened again, that practiced smile returning. "They said I could watch you warm up. You ready, champ?"

He kissed her desperately, tasting her as if it were for the first time. She went rigid for just a heartbeat before melting into him, kissing back with enough heat to fool anyone watching. When they broke apart, he kissed her again, drowning in relief.

"Carmelo, stop," she laughed, and it almost sounded real.

He pulled back, searching her face. "You... came? You okay? We okay?"

"Of course. Why wouldn't I be?" Her eyes were wide, innocent. Perfect.

Carmelo glanced at Matteo and Carmine, who both nodded—whatever had been broken was fixed. He exhaled years of tension. Kathy's hands found his face, her touch gentle. "You ready, you focused, huh?"

"I am now," he sighed.

"Then show me what you do best." She kissed him once more, her fingers stroking his jaw with such tenderness that even the men watching were convinced. Carmelo grinned like a fool, shoved in his mouthguard, and bounced out toward the ring.

The moment he was gone, Kathy's mask slipped. She stood perfectly still, as if movement might shatter her facade.

"Thank you, Kathy," Matteo started.

She turned on him with a heated glare. "Don't speak to me. And you tell Debbie—we're not family anymore. No letters. No calls. Ever. I don't ever want to see or talk to her again. After Tennessee, I hope I never see you either."

Matteo flinched as if slapped. Kathy walked out, her spine straight as a blade.

Carmine shook his head at the younger man. "There's no turning back now."

The next two days were a masterclass in torture. Kathy played her part flawlessly—at the gym, cheering from ringside; at dinners, laughing at the right moments; at the parties where Negroes were allowed, dancing just close enough to keep Carmelo happy but never alone. She had a dozen excuses to avoid his bed, each more creative than the last. A few times, he got aggressive, even reached under the table and under her skirt to touch her between her thighs. She tolerated his unrelenting desires, but kept him from gaining the prize he sought. That particular performance, she refused to give.

Meanwhile, Carmine had Janey sedated at the colored hospital, then sent home to Willa under guard. Kathy never said goodbye. How could she face her aunt now, knowing what madness and poison had wrought?

The constant pretending carved her hollow. By the second day, she felt nothing—not love, not hate, not even anger for the man she'd once built her world around. Just emptiness. And that terrified her more than anything. Because somewhere in that void, his child was growing, and she had no idea what to do about that either.

No choices left—just the performance.

"You ready?" Mabel's knock pulled her from the mirror.

The Douglass had become her sanctuary—Carmelo couldn't follow her into Mabel's domain. Kathy finished with her earrings and turned. "Yes, ma'am."

"Lord have mercy, you're something else. Every young man in this hotel's got his heart in his throat over you. Prettiest thing we've seen in ages."

Kathy studied her reflection. The lilac dress fit perfectly, sewn with her own hands for this night. Her hair was pinned just so. But it was all mechanical now—a doll dressing itself.

"You sure you want this, Carmine, taking you to the bus station so late at night? My boys would be happy to—."

"No, ma'am. Carmine and I have an understanding." She collected her bag, the smile automatic now. "It's time I went home."

Mabel studied her with those knowing eyes. "You're something remarkable. Know that?"

Kathy waited.

"When you first came here, I thought you were just another broken girl. Then I heard the whole story—how that boy lied, how you lost everything. Except..." Her gaze dropped meaningfully to Kathy's middle. "You're carrying his child, aren't you?"

Kathy stood perfectly still. If she acknowledged it, if she said the words aloud, the careful everything she'd built around herself would crumble.

"No judgment here, sweetie. Just admiring your strength. Not many could handle all this with such grace."

"One day at a time." Kathy's voice came from somewhere far away. "I've been on my own since Daddy sent me from Harlem. Guess me and this baby will figure it out together."

Mabel's smile was soft with understanding. She took Kathy's bag, and together they headed for whatever came next.

* * *

"ALRIGHT. You got this. We got this!" Matteo's hands worked Carmelo's shoulders, kneading the muscle like their mother used to when they were boys—before everything went to hell. Carmelo bounced on his toes, shadowboxing the air.

"You ready, Champ?" Matteo asked.

"Yeah, tell them I'm ready," he said. Matteo patted him on the back and started for the door.

"Wait—one thing," said Carmelo.

Matteo's hand was already on the door when Carmelo's voice pulled him back. Something in his brother's tone—too bright, too eager—made his stomach twist.

"What is it?" Matteo asked.

"After the fight, you bring Kathy straight to me." Carmelo's eyes shone with the kind of desperate hope Matteo hadn't seen since they were kids planning to run away from Pa. "I told her last night at the party—we're leaving. *Subito.* Right after the bell."

"Melo—?"

"Going west, *fratello*. Not telling anyone where, but when you make it to Vegas, I'll know. Kathy and I will find you and Debbie. Just like we planned." He threw a quick combination of air punches, dancing around, and grinning. "Like starting over, you know? Clean slate. New life."

"Listen, brother—" Matteo started.

"No, no, *ascolta*—listen to me." Carmelo grabbed Matteo's shoulders now, reversing their positions. "I almost lost her. You understand? If she'd heard about Maria from someone else, if she'd found out about—" His voice cracked. "I can't risk it again. Can't lose her. Ever."

Matteo's chest tightened. Kathy already knew. Had known for two days. Every smile she'd given Carmelo, every kiss—all performance. And here was his little brother, planning their escape like she hadn't already bought her bus ticket home.

"What about Maria? The bambini?" The words came out strangled.

"Pa's problem." Carmelo turned back to the mirror, adjusting his robe. "He wanted those kids and that marriage; he can deal with it."

"Melo, *cazzo*! They're yours! Your blood!"

Carmelo spun, and for a second, Matteo saw rage in his brother's eyes. The kind of eyes his father had. Then it vanished, replaced by that terrible, innocent hope.

"I have one wife, Matteo. *Una sola*. One family. Kathy. That's it. Those kids—Maria—they're nothing. *Niente.* You understand? They don't exist!"

Matteo felt his stomach churn. Had Carmelo's sanity snapped? The sweet kid brother he knew would never blame innocent babies or their mother for existing. He did his best to avoid betraying the vow to maintain the deception. But the man in him wanted to knock some fucking sense into his brother.

Matteo forced his features into something like brotherly understanding, even as his heart broke. "Okay. *Va bene,* I get it. You win tonight, *campione*, and tomorrow you're gone. The world is yours."

"*Fanculo il mondo*." Carmelo's voice went reverent as he made the sign of the cross in front of him and then kissed his fingers, like in prayer. "I don't want the world. Just her. Just Kathy."

Matteo nodded, not trusting his voice. He escaped into the hallway before Carmelo could see the truth written on his face. Behind the door, he could hear his brother humming—some Sinatra tune about flying to the moon—throwing punches at shadows.

Dancing like a man set free.

Matteo pressed his palms against his eyes until he saw stars. In two hours, Carmelo would win his fight. In three, he'd be waiting for a woman who was already gone. And Matteo would have to watch his little brother's face when he finally understood that some lies cut too deep to heal.

Inside the dressing room, Carmelo kept dancing, kept humming, kept believing.

Outside, Matteo stood guard over his brother's last happy moment, knowing he'd helped orchestrate its end.

* * *

"GET UP, MALONE! GET UP!"

The crowd roared as Irish Tommy Malone struggled to find his feet, blood streaming from his split eyebrow. Nine rounds in, and the Memphis boy was finally showing cracks.

From the colored section high in the rafters, Kathy gripped the railing, her knuckles tight. "Come on, Carmelo! Finish it!"

Below, Carmelo circled like a wolf, his body glistening under the harsh lights. His left eye was swelling shut, his ribs screamed with each breath, but he could taste it now—victory, redemption, everything.

Malone staggered upright at eight, raising his gloves just as the referee stepped back. The Irish fighter had fifty pounds on Carmelo and a reach like a telephone pole, but he was hurt. Bad.

"BOX!"

Malone charged, desperate, throwing wild haymakers. Carmelo slipped left, the punch whistling past his ear. Then right, another miss. The crowd was on its feet.

"Now, baby! Now!" Kathy screamed, her voice lost in the thunder of two thousand voices.

Carmelo saw it—the opening he'd been setting up all night.

Malone's right hand dropped just an inch after each wild swing, leaving his jaw exposed for half a heartbeat.

Time slowed...

Carmelo planted his back foot, torqued his hips, and threw the cleanest left hook of his life. It connected with Malone's jaw with a crack that silenced the arena. The big Irishman's eyes rolled white. His legs went rubbery. He toppled backward like a felled oak, crashing to the canvas with a thud that shook the ring.

The referee didn't even count. Malone was done.

"WINNER BY KNOCKOUT—CARMELO 'THE WOLF of BROOKLYN' RICCI!"

The arena exploded. White folks in their pressed suits, Negroes in their Sunday best up in the rafters—everyone screaming, money changing hands, history being made.

But Carmelo heard none of it. His eyes searched the colored section frantically until—there.

Kathy was on her feet, laughing and crying at the same time, waving both arms above her head. Her lilac dress swirled as she jumped up and down, her face bright with what looked like genuine joy. For this moment, in the lights and noise and glory, she was his Kathy again. Not the hollow girl who'd been going through the motions for two days, but the woman who'd believed in him.

He raised his glove toward her section, and she blew him a kiss. The gesture hit him harder than any punch Malone had landed.

He'd won. Against all odds, against the whiskey and despair and the weight of his lies—he'd won. The Marcellos would get their money. His father would get his reputation. Matteo would get them out of Memphis alive. And Kathy would get in a car and drive away with him to their future. Forever his.

Carmelo closed his eyes and let the victory wash over him, memorizing the sound of her laughter floating down from the rafters. It would have to last him a lifetime.

CHAPTER 30

WHAT DEATH OF LOVE LOOKS LIKE

"Thank you for everything." Kathy accepted the bus ticket from Carmine's weathered hand. He gave her a nod that held more weariness than respect.

"You should be fine. Matteo will stall until your bus is well on the road before he gives Carmelo your letter."

She tucked the ticket into her purse, avoiding his eyes.

"I suppose I owe you an explanation." His voice carried the weight of confessions he'd rather not make. "About Willa. Why is she with us, carrying my child?"

"I don't think I want to know." Kathy's voice was hollow. "These past two years have shown me enough darkness, enough deception. I don't expect truth from anyone anymore."

Carmine sighed, leaning heavier on his cane. "Janey didn't take Pinkie leaving well after Elmer died two months later. She started coming apart. Then Willa's tragedy. The girl had done the impossible and turned a Thibodeaux against a Thibodeaux. The two of them had moved into their own place and gotten married. She was pregnant, and JB was different. Then she lost the baby. That's when all things in their love started to crumble. He left her to go back home like a coward, and she was out there in the wind, surviving on scraps. While he came in and out of her life and she believed that she could win him back." He paused, choosing his words like a man navigating broken glass. "I thought Janey was trying to help the girl. Should've seen the poison coming. Should've stopped it before the Thibodeauxs tasted her sweet candies. But I'm old, Kathy. Tired. Can't catch Janey every time she falls anymore."

Despite herself, Kathy listened.

"Willa was broken after JB died. That's her story to tell, not mine. All I can say is—I came home one night, found them in the parlor together. Janey invited me to dinner, sat me down like it was any other evening. Turns out JB was trying to get into the family to access the money to run with Willa. And Willa was once again pregnant. That's when they told me what they'd decided." His laugh was bitter. "Janey believes a child will save her, keep her from losing what's left of her mind. And Willa... she can't let the Thibodeauxs know she is carrying JB's child. Janey decided that Willa join the family, and we let everyone know it was my baby. Just needed my compliance for the lie."

"And you agreed?" The judgment in her voice surprised them both.

"My time's running out." He straightened slightly, dignified even in his confession. "I'm taking them to Vegas. Away from the Thibodeauxs' vengeance, to protect the child, and away from the Marcellos' grasp. Away from all this blood and lies. Then I'll close my eyes for good, and maybe—maybe—this baby is my son or daughter, and my heir. That agreement means this child can heal what I couldn't in my Janey," He touched his hat brim. "So yes, I agreed. And this is goodbye."

Before he could turn away, Kathy stepped forward and embraced him. His body went rigid with surprise before he carefully returned the gesture, his arms uncertain around her.

"I don't understand Aunt Janey or Willa," she whispered against his shoulder. "May never understand them. But thank you for saving their lives all these times. For protecting them both."

She stepped back, composing herself. "Goodbye, Mr. Bonanno."

His smile was ghost-thin. "Safe travels, Kathy. Find yourself some peace."

She gathered her bag and climbed aboard the bus, choosing a window seat near the back. Through the smudged glass, she watched Carmine make his slow way to his car, each step measured against his cane. A man returning to his beautiful hell. Another man living a lie.

Kathy closed her eyes and let her head fall back against the seat. The engine rumbled to life beneath her, carrying her away from Memphis, from Carmelo, from all of them. She tried to empty her mind, to forget their faces, their lies, their twisted love.

But some poisons, she was learning, had no antidote.

* * *

Two hours. Two fucking hours of handshakes and flashbulbs while she waited.

He'd posed with every politician and wise guy who'd traveled in for the fight, his split lip screaming with each forced smile. Signed contracts with hands still swollen from the gloves and endured some newspaper hack who kept circling back to his mother's suicide until Matteo finally snapped and threw the bastard out by his collar.

Through it all, Carmelo's eyes stayed locked on the door. Kathy couldn't enter the white press rooms—Memphis rules—but he kept expecting her face to appear somehow, that smile that said she was proud of him.

When the last photographer finally packed up, Carmelo was already moving. He shoved past the lingering reporters and ignored the promoter calling his name. His ribs screamed with each step, but he didn't care. She was waiting. In twenty minutes, they'd be on the road. By dawn, they'd be halfway to nowhere, just him and Kathy and the future they'd always dreamed of.

"Melo, wait up!" Matteo's voice was behind him.

"Can't. Kathy's waiting." He walked faster, his body singing with adrenaline despite the beating he'd taken.

He burst through the dressing room door, already grinning, already reaching for her—

Empty.

The room yawned back at him, silent except for the drip of a leaky pipe. The champagne Carmine had sent sat unopened in its bucket, ice long melted.

"Where is she?" He spun as Matteo appeared in the doorway, breathing hard. "She go back to the hotel? She said she'd wait here. Said she'd—"

"Here." Matteo held out an envelope, his face carved from stone. "She left you this."

Carmelo stared at the letter like it might bite him. "What the fuck is that?"

"Read it." Matteo turned and walked out, closing the door with terrible finality.

Alone now, Carmelo opened the envelope—her handwriting, careful and precise. The paper smelled faintly of her perfume.

His legs gave out before he'd finished the first paragraph.

Carmelo,

By the time Matteo gives you this, I'll be gone. And I'm sure in this moment you know why.

I know about Maria. I know about your beautiful children. Twins? How nice. I know about the house in Queens where you play family while I rotted in Mississippi, counting days. I know it all.

You kissed me when I was seventeen years old in my family's bakery, and I thought God himself had touched me. You wrote me letters that I memorized like scripture. You married me in Debbie's place with your brother as witness, and I believed—God help me, I believed—that meant something sacred.

Do you remember what you promised me that night? That

we'd have our own bakery, our own babies, our own life. That my father would never have to bow to another man again. That your mother would love me like her own daughter. All lies, weren't they? Or maybe you believed them, too. Maybe that's your gift—believing your own fairytales long enough to make others dream them with you.

I lost everything the day they put me on that bus alone to Butts, crying for a man who would someday build a family with someone else. Now I'm on a bus right now as you read this letter, and I realize I lost it all for nothing. I gave up my home, my parents, my future. Three years, Carmelo. Three years of my life spent loving a lie.

I don't hate you. Hate would mean you still matter. I pity you—to be so empty inside that you need multiple lives, multiple women, multiple lies to feel whole. To be so careless with hearts that you don't even remember breaking them.

You were the wolf, and I was the fool who thought I could name and tame you. But wolves don't change, do they? They just learn new ways to hunt.

Don't write. Don't call. Don't send Matteo or Debbie with your apologies. Let me go, Carmelo. It's the only kindness you have left to give me.

I'm going to live the rest of my life as if you never existed. I'm going to forget the taste of pecan pie and your promises. I'm going to pretend that the seventeen-year-old girl never met a beautiful boy who taught her that love could kill you slowly.

Maybe someday you'll understand what you've done. Maybe when your daughter is seventeen and some boy looks at her the way you looked at me in your backyard, you'll finally feel the terror my father felt when he found what we left in that *attic. Maybe then you'll know why he tried so hard to save me from you.*

Maybe not. Wolves don't learn regret.

The girl you loved is dead. You killed her yourself, one lie at a time.

K.

CARMELO'S KNEES hit the concrete floor with a crack that echoed in the empty room. The letter trembled in his hands as he read it again. Then again. Each word cutting deeper, her handwriting blurring through what couldn't be tears or was he losing his sight?

The girl you loved is dead. You killed her yourself, one lie at a time.

The silence stretched until Matteo couldn't stand it anymore. He stepped back inside, found his brother kneeling like a penitent, the letter crumpled in his fist.

When Carmelo looked up, his face was that of a drowning man who still believed in rescue. "She's confused." His voice cracked like a boy's. "She thinks I lied to her. Thinks I don't love her. How could she think that?"

"Melo, Janey told her everything."

"No." He shook his head violently, struggling to his feet. "That's not what the letter says. It says our love is a lie. She's just confused—you know how Kathy gets. Too much happening, she can't process it all." He stood, though his knees were bruised. He started pacing, the words tumbling faster. "I need to explain. When I tell her about Mama, about the suicide note, about why I had to—she'll understand. She always understands."

He moved toward his clothes, hands already reaching. "Let me get dressed. Where'd she go? The Douglass?"

"Melo—"

"It's fine, Matteo. I'm fine." His movements were frantic now, yanking on his shirt. "I know my Kathy. In twenty minutes, I'll have this sorted. Then we leave. California, maybe, or—"

"She's gone, Melo."

The words stopped him cold. He turned slowly, and Matteo saw the exact moment his brother's mental began to fracture.

"What did you say?"

Matteo's throat felt drier than a desert. "She's known for two days. Since the night Carmine confronted you. We talked to her. Asked her to pretend, to support you so you could—"

"So I could what?" Carmelo's voice had gone terrifyingly quiet.

"Get in the ring. Win the fight."

For a heartbeat, nothing. Then Carmelo moved with the speed that had made him champion, launching himself at his brother with inhuman fury. His fist connected with Matteo's jaw, snapping his head back. Then another. Another.

"You knew!" Each word punctuated by bone meeting flesh. "You fucking knew!"

Matteo tried to defend himself, but grief had made Carmelo into something beyond human. He straddled his brother, fists pounding with mechanical precision, blood spattering the walls, the floor, his championship robe.

"She smiled at me!" Carmelo screamed, his voice raw. "She kissed me! And you knew it was fake!"

Matteo's nose exploded. His eye socket nearly cracked. Still the blows came.

"My brother! My blood!"

The door burst open. Men rushed in first, wrapping arms around Carmelo's chest. Two more men piled on, but grief had given him the strength of madness. He threw one against the wall, kept swinging at the others.

"Get off me! I'll kill him! I'll kill all of you motherfuckers!"

Someone brought a blackjack down hard against the back of Carmelo's skull. He swayed, still fighting, blood and spit flying from his mouth. It took two more blows before he finally dropped.

In the sudden silence, a flashbulb popped. Then another. The press had heard the commotion and pushed their way in. Tomorrow's headlines were already writing themselves: RICCI BROTHERS IN

BLOODY BRAWL. CHAMPION ATTACKS CORNER MAN. THE WOLF SNAPS.

Matteo lay unconscious, his face unrecognizable. Carmelo sprawled beside him, blood pooling beneath both brothers. The letter lay forgotten in the corner, spotted with red.

Don Marcello's man looked at the photographers, then at the disaster on the floor. "Get them out," he ordered his men. "And find a doctor who keeps his mouth shut."

But the damage was done. In every way that mattered, both Ricci brothers had died in that dressing room. What would wake up in their place would be something else entirely.

The Wolf had finally swallowed their future whole.

CHAPTER 31

QUEBEC, CANADA - 1978

P**resent.** The room stole her heart. Her face—everywhere. Hundreds of versions covered every surface, overlapping like memories that refused to die. Kathy stood paralyzed as her eyes adjusted to thirty years of obsession rendered in pencil and charcoal.

Carmelo hunched over at his drafting table, shirtless, his back to her. Coltrane's saxophone wailed through the speakers. The sound masked her entrance. His shoulders rolled with each violent stroke, muscles shifting beneath scarred skin.

She eased the door shut and ventured deeper into his privacy. Though her face dominated the walls, she recognized others—men she'd never met, his mother's eternal disappointment, Nino's gentle smile. And Sandy. Their daughter at every age, from toddler to woman. Each drawing a stolen year, a moment he'd invented to fill the void from the constant wars they waged against each other.

One sketch stopped her cold.

Sandy, small and still in a hospital bed. Him, a shadow behind glass, barred from entering. That day rushed back to her with the force of a tsunami—their daughter hit by a car, Kathy wild with grief, screaming blame at him and then herself. *Your fault. Always your fault.*

She'd wielded her own internal guilt like a weapon, never letting him forget the mistakes they made.

Had she created her monster? Was his madness her?

The realization struck—they'd both been archivists of ruin. Her journals downstairs, his drawings up here. Thirty years of parallel obsession, documenting what they'd destroyed. Preserving the truth while living the lie.

She approached on silent feet, hand hovering over his bare spine. On the paper, her face surfaced with each savage stroke—captured perfectly, loved terribly.

She touched him.

Carmelo froze mid-stroke.

"Don't be angry, I'm here." Her voice was soft and calming. "Please. I just needed to find you."

He remained still. Not breathing. Afraid to turn and see her vanish.

"I love you." The confession tore from her throat. "I've always loved you. And I see what that love has cost you. God, Melo, I'm sorry."

He spun and took hold of her, crushed her against him, face buried in her stomach. She cradled his head as his shoulders heaved—this broken boy who'd spent decades drawing ghosts.

"Don't leave me." Carmelo's voice was muffled against her. Raw with old terror. "Not again."

"Never." She held him tighter. She kissed the top of his head. "I'll never leave you again."

But even as the words left her lips, they both knew—some promises came too late to resurrect the dead.

Butts, Mississippi, 1952

Two weeks after Memphis, and still his memory clung to her. Kathy locked the schoolhouse, her students long gone into the fading afternoon. She would have to run errands before reaching home. It was three miles to town for Big Mama's medicine—a walk she'd once never needed to make when Ely was her protector before she'd torn his heart out in 1950, telling him plain that Carmelo owned her soul. Now Ely had found his own love, and she couldn't even meet his eyes at church.

Her hand drifted to the slight swell beneath her dress. Time was running out. Soon everyone would know—another disappointment for her parents, another scandal for the gossips. She pushed the thought away. Especially the one of the church that funded the school. They would fire her and cast out Big Mama for her being a harlot.

The long walk started uneventfully. With the sun lowering in an hour or so, she dreaded the walk back in the dark and silently prayed to see someone who could give her a ride home.

The engine's roar shattered her peace.

She looked up to see the car barreling down the dirt road toward her. Too fast for these parts. Dust clouds billowed, and she stepped off the road as it zoomed by, then slammed on the brakes. Her body knew before her mind—danger. She darted toward the tree line, but doors flew open and two white men poured out, running hard.

Italian voices shouted her name.

Kathy dropped everything and ran faster. The forest could hide her—she knew every root, every hollow. But they were determined, faster. Hands grabbed her arms, her waist. She fought wild, remembering too late the life inside her. They took her blows without hitting back, just holding, restraining, and dragging her to the car.

They shoved her into the back seat. One collected her scattered belongings while another slid in beside her, speaking rapid Italian to the driver. She pressed herself into the corner, as far from them as the seat allowed.

The abandoned barn materialized like a bad dream. And there was Matteo, walking toward them—Jesus Christ, his face. One eye swollen shut, bandaged. His handsome face twisted by the violence heaped upon him.

"Hi, Kathy."

She said nothing.

"He wants to talk to you."

"Take me home, Matteo." Her voice was steel. "You swore he'd leave me alone if I helped in Memphis. I did my part."

He climbed into the car and sat beside her. Up close, the damage was worse—lumps distorting his features, bruises mapping violence across his skin.

"What happened to you?" she asked.

"It was all in the papers. You should have heard about what happened after the fight?" he asked, curious.

"I don't read the papers anymore. He's in the them. And I don't want to know anything about him."

"Well, you're right. He's in them. It was Melo who attacked me." His tone was flat. "This is what happened when I tried to keep him from going after you."

Her stomach dropped. She looked away, then back over at him, stunned that Melo would hurt the brother he worshipped. "He did this?"

"You have to help me here. He's in a bad state, Kathy. Worse than before. Can't control him. And he won't go back to New York. Hell, my father approved this visit to calm him down. That's how far gone he is." Matteo's good eye found hers. "He says he wants closure, but... we both know he's lying. He wants you. And I'm trying to protect you both from each other. He's different now that you ended it."

"I don't want to see him. You can't make me go through this over and over because of his wants. What about what I want!!"

"I'm sorry." He grabbed her arm. "But you don't have a choice."

She fought, but Matteo hauled her out of the car and half walked, half dragged her to the barn door despite her struggles. He released her there, lighting a cigarette with shaking hands.

"I won't let him hurt you," Matteo said, lowering his gaze. I swear it on Junior's life. "But I have to help my brother. He's all I've got left in the world. He's only hurting himself. He loves you. You're safe."

"This isn't love! Can't you see that? It never was!" she protested.

Matteo took a long drag and exhaled slowly. "I only got one good eye, so I can't see much."

"When will this stop? What do I have to do to make him go away for good?"

"Don't know. If Debbie ran from me with my kids... I wouldn't stop." He shrugged. "Maybe you can end it properly. Make him understand. Or lie to him, and give us more time to get him some help. We'll take him to the priests in Italy if we have to."

Her hand ghosted over her belly, dropping before he noticed. She pushed through the barn door.

And there he was.

The sight of him hit like a physical blow. Love and terror tangled in her chest, stealing her breath. He looked beautiful. If a man could be considered that. He was dressed in a tailored suit as if he had groomed himself for his return. Suddenly, she was overwhelmed with the same adrenaline attraction she had felt for him when they parted. Every fiber in her body wanted to launch herself at him for him to catch her. Have him kiss her and hold her. To feel his strong arms around her, keeping her protected as his girl. Kathy closed the barn door slowly behind her.

He rushed toward her. She stumbled back as the euphoria lifted. Her hands went up in defense. "Don't touch me!"

He froze. Tears shimmered in his eyes to see her afraid of him.

"Let me explain, *cara mia*—"

"I don't want to hear it!"

"Please, Kat. Please." He dropped to his knees, prostrating himself. "I can't live without you. I'll die without you!"

"You're a liar! Just leave me be!"

"It was Mama's suicide, then the marriage—I can explain Maria." He remained on his knees in his nice tailored suit. "I slept on the floor, Kat. I was with you, not her. She says I got drunk, but I know it's a lie. I don't remember, but she had babies and I didn't know what to do—"

She stared down at him, horrified by his complete dissolution.

"I'm begging you." His face lifted, ravaged by grief and sorrow. "Forgive me. Just this once. Forgive me! I'll never lie to you again. Never! Can't I get one more chance?"

"It's too late, Carmelo. You had your chance. You had three years of chances. You left me to rot while you had another life, a wife, and kids. I had nothing. Not even my family."

He sobbed.

"I was good to you, Melo. I gave you everything. I suffered for you. And you just took and took and took, leaving me behind," she said.

"Nooo, no, no," he wept.

"Do what you always do—leave me here to while you're their champion. Get out of my life!"

He struggled to his feet, destroyed. "Take it back!"

"No!"

"Take it back!" He shouted at her, enraged. "Take it all back. You know I love you. I survived for you. I will die for you! Take it back!"

"No!"

Hyperventilating and horrified, he stumbled back from her. "Bonano's right. You're poison, Kathy. You're killing me for making one mistake! Just forgive me. I'm dying inside. Please!"

"The boy I loved is already dead. Or never existed." She forced the words past her tears. "So yes, I'm your poison. Now leave me alone!"

She turned to go. He rushed her, spinning her hard against the barn wall. Her head swam as he trapped her there, his forehead pressed hard to hers. His lips so close she feared he'd kiss her. She froze, terrified of provoking worse. What if she told him her truth? What if he knew about the baby in that moment? What would he do?

His eyes burned into hers with the first sign of rage directed at her that she truly feared for his mental state and her life. "I'll never let you go, Kathy Freeman. Hear me? Never. So bake me one of your killer cupcakes, because that's the only way you escape this."

She found her grandmother, Bessie, in her spine, just like Carmine had warned her to do.

"Come near me again," she said, voice deadly soft, "and I'll feed you the cupcake myself."

He kissed her, forced-kissed her, and to endure it, she had to respond. She just let him have his goodbye. When he was done, he stroked the side of her face and looked at her with love as if the kiss was proof that nothing had changed. Then a smile crossed his face as he stepped back, confident he could come for her again when it suited him.

She turned and shoved open the barn door, half expecting him to follow. He walked slowly, stalking her.

Outside, his men formed a loose circle—witnesses to the execution of their love. She stopped cold, looking back at Carmelo. The raw hurt in his eyes had hardened to something worse than hate. Something final and lethal.

Her fingers found the chain at her throat. The one she'd worn hidden for two years in Butts, close to her heart like a secret prayer. She yanked hard, the links biting into her neck before snapping free. The ring—that cheap gold band he'd slipped on her finger in Mama Stewart's, when they'd believed in forever—caught the late afternoon sun.

She held it up so he could see. So he could remember. Then she hurled it with all her strength toward the tree line, watching it disappear into tall grass and shadows.

"We're done!" The words tore from her throat. "*Capice?*"

He wiped his lips slowly, reminding her of his kiss. Then he winked at her.

She marched to the car, climbed in, and slammed the door. Through the window, she saw Matteo looking to his brother for orders. Carmelo just turned and walked back into the darkness of the barn. Alone.

The ride back was silent until she recognized the bend near Big Mama's road.

"Let me out here."

The car stopped. Matteo followed her out, desperation creasing his battered face. "Kathy! Why can't you forgive him?"

She gathered her things—purse, books, the ordinary pieces of a life he'd never be part of. "Let me ask you something, Matteo. If Debbie had run off with José, gotten pregnant, kept it secret—would you forgive her? Would you forgive me for helping her hide it?"

His head dropped. When he looked up, she saw the truth in his good eye.

"My father wins. You know that, right?" His voice was hollow. "Told Carmelo if he came down here and you wanted him, he was free. Could leave the marriage, the family, everything. But if you rejected him..." He spread his hands. "Then he belongs to the old man. Forever."

The weight of the news crushed what was left of her heart in her chest. Cosimo's final play—using her as the knife to cut his son's last thread of hope.

"There's no going back," Matteo continued softly. "But there's still time to go forward. You just have to forgive him."

Every cell in her body screamed to get back in that car. To run to the barn. To save him from what he'd become without her. But she was done letting her heart lead. Look where it had gotten them.

"It's over." Each word was a nail in a coffin. "Make sure he knows it. Don't come to Butts again. And I'll never go back to New York."

"Goodbye, Kathy," said Matteo, sadly. "I tried."

She turned and walked away, refusing to watch them leave. Only when the engine faded to nothing did she stop. Then, quietly, she turned back the way they'd come. She had another destination in mind.

CHAPTER 32

NO LONGER THE GOOD GIRL

"Ely? You hungry?" Lea called from the kitchen doorway, her voice warm and soft.

Though they weren't married yet, she'd been coming by an hour early each evening—after her shift at the Jensens' main house ended—to cook his supper and sit with him on the porch swing, planning their small wedding for spring.

"I'm good, Sugar," he said, unlacing his work boots with the same methodical care he brought to everything. Sugar—that's what he called her, sweet and necessary as she'd become to him the past year.

Lea smiled, wiping her hands on her apron. She was nothing like Kathy—shorter, rounder, with skin dark as fertile soil and a laugh that filled up empty spaces. Where Kathy had been lightning and dreams, Lea was steady rain and solid ground. Precisely what a man needed to build something lasting. A good woman.

"Let me know when you're ready," she said, already turning back to check on the meat in the stove.

The knock came just as Ely pulled off his second boot.

Lea's shoulders relaxed—probably one of the men from the construction site, needing Ely to settle some dispute or lend a tool. Everyone in Butts came to Ely for something. He had that way about him, steady as a heartbeat, reliable as sunrise. She hummed softly and returned to her cooking, content in the rhythm they'd built together.

Ely looked at the door, barefoot and bone-tired, ready to send whoever it was away so he and his Lea could watch the sun sink behind the pines before he drove her home or took her to his bedroom, whichever she preferred, was fine by him.

When he opened the door, his heart stopped beating.

Kathy stood there, trembling. The hem of her dress and her feet were dusty from the road, her eyes swollen from crying. "I'm sorry for coming here. I'm so very sorry. But I have nowhere else to go. I'm out of time, Ely."

Before he could speak, she dropped her bag and collapsed against him, her tears soaking through his shirt. "Help me, Ely. Please."

For a moment, muscle memory took over—his arms started to close around her. Then he heard Lea calling him from the kitchen, and reality crashed back. He gently but firmly set Kathy back, holding her at arm's length.

"Kathy, you can't—" He glanced over his shoulder, then stepped out onto the porch, pulling the door shut behind him. "Wait. Just wait." He collected her things. Took her hand and walked her around to the back of the house. He guided her to the old bench seat against the wall, keeping his voice low. "Just... wait, here. Don't move."

She nodded, wrapping her arms around herself like she might fall apart.

Ely slipped back inside, his mind racing as he entered the kitchen. Lea looked up from stirring the pot, her smile fading at his expression.

"What's wrong?" She asked.

"Big Mama," he said, the lie bitter on his tongue. "One of the Jensen boys just came by—she's taken poorly. Real bad. I need to run you home quick, then get over there."

Lea's face creased with concern. She knew how much Big Mama meant to him, to all of them. "Oh Lord. Let me just—"

"No time, Sugar. Come on." He grabbed her shawl from the hook, already moving toward the front door—away from where Kathy waited like a ghost at the back of the house. "I'll come back for the food later."

As he helped Lea into the truck, guilt twisted his stomach. But what else could he do? Two years of carefully built peace, and here was Kathy, bringing her storms to his door again.

"You sure you don't need me to come with you? Is Kathy there?" Lea asked as they pulled away.

"No, baby. Might be a long night. I'll see you tomorrow."

He drove the familiar route to Lea's family's place, every minute stretching like an hour, knowing Kathy sat on his porch—desperate, alone, and still able to undo everything he'd worked to build without her.

Half an Hour Later:

Ely drove back up the dirt road to his house, the truck's headlights cut through the gathering dusk. Kathy had stayed exactly where he'd left her, planted on the bench like she'd grown roots there. He pulled around to the back, where no passing neighbor could see, killed the engine, and sat there in the dark.

Through the windshield, he could see her lift her head at the sound of his return. Even from there, even in the fading light, he could see how broken she was. Not just tired or sad—broken in a way that scared him.

He sighed deeply, his hands still gripping the wheel. If he got out of this truck and went to her, as he had so many times before, he'd be risking everything he'd built with Lea. Sweet Lea, who called him her rock, who hummed while she cooked, who loved him simply and uncomplicated. The wife he'd always thought he wanted.

But sitting there in the truck, he finally admitted what he'd always known. He still loved Kathy Freeman. Had never stopped. Maybe never would. That kind of love didn't care about common sense or carefully built lives or sweet women who deserved better.

Their eyes met across the yard—hers pleading, his already surrendering. She looked away first, and in that small gesture, he saw her shame over needing him again.

"Fuck it," he muttered.

He climbed out and walked straight to her, each step feeling like fate. She stood when he approached, gathering her things with trembling hands.

"I'm sorry for coming here. I saw you leave with Lea." Her voice was small, broken. "I don't want to cause any trouble. If you could take me to get Big Mama's medicine before the drug store closes, and drop me home, I'd be fine."

"You aren't fine." He lifted her chin gently, making her meet his eyes. "Are you?"

"No." The word came out on a sob. "No, I'm not. I'm in big trouble, Ely. Bigger than any trouble I've ever been in. And I'm terrified."

He took her bag from her hands and led her inside. The house still smelled of Lea's cooking—collard greens with ham hocks, cornbread in the iron skillet, sweet tea cooling in the pitcher. The kitchen looked like a woman's love made visible—clean dish towels she'd embroidered, flowers from her mama's garden in a mason jar, everything in its place.

Kathy froze in the doorway, taking it all in. He watched her understand what this kitchen meant, what kind of woman had made it this way.

"Hungry?" he asked, though his voice came out rougher than intended.

"No, no, no, I shouldn't have come." She turned for the door, but he caught her hand gently, like he was afraid she might shatter. That small touch undid her. Kathy burst into tears and collapsed against him, and suddenly they were back to being eighteen when she'd cry about missing Carmelo and he'd hold her, pretending it didn't kill him to comfort her about another man.

Right there in Lea's carefully kept kitchen, between the covered pots and embroidered towels, she told him everything. Two years of sneaking around to see Carmelo. The lies she'd told Big Mama. The risks she'd taken. How hope kept her going even when she knew better.

By the time she got to the part about Carmelo coming to Butts, about him forcing her into that barn, they'd moved to the sofa. Ely was on his feet, pacing.

"He put his hands on you?" His voice was dangerous now.

"He was desperate. Said he'd die without me. Said I was killing him." She wiped her eyes. "Then he grabbed me, pushed me against the door."

Ely's fists clenched. The gentle man who'd never raised his hand to anyone was gone, replaced by someone she didn't recognize.

"Ely, stop." Her voice was weary. "I don't need this from you. Please. I came to you because you're not like them."

That stopped him cold. He studied her—really looked at her for the first time. Thinner than before, shadows under her eyes, hands protective over her stomach though nothing showed yet.

"What else?" He sat down beside her, his voice gentle again. "I know he hurt you, broke your heart. But I know you, Kathy. You aren't afraid of him. And no matter how much I want to kill him right now, he isn't going to hurt you physically. So there's something else. You said you were out of time. You came here to me. You need help, not protection. What aren't you telling me?"

She lowered her gaze to the floor, hands twisting in her lap. The silence stretched between them, heavy with what she couldn't say.

"You're pregnant, aren't you?"

She put her hands to her face and cried—not the tears from before, but deep, terrified sobs that came from her soul.

"Does he know?" Ely asked quietly. "Does anyone know?"

She shook her head, unable to speak.

He pulled her back into his arms and let her cry it all out—the fear, the shame, the desperation of a woman with no good choices left. When her sobs finally quieted, he held her a moment longer, breathing in the scent of her hair, knowing everything was about to change.

"It's okay, baby," he said finally. "I'll protect you."

"How?" Her voice was muffled against his chest.

"I'll marry you. Fast as we can manage it."

She pulled back to look at him, "Ely, I can't ask you to give up Lea—"

"Don't play with me, Kathy." His voice was rough. "You knew what I'd say when you climbed those porch steps. You know I love you. Only ever you."

"You knew I'd come to you," she said.

"I've been waiting," he admitted. "Maybe not for this, but... I could've married Lea some time ago. I've been waiting."

She nodded. "I'm out of time. I can't do it anymore—the lies, the shame. I'm scared for this baby, for my family. You warned me, and I didn't heed your warning. I chose this path because everyone else is choosing it. Debbie went to José. Willa went to Janey and Carmine. No one is walking in truth, and innocent babies are being born in the crossfire."

"I don't understand what happened to Willa. I saw what happened to Debbie. I'm not going to let it happen to you. If you're my wife, this baby is mine. And you're mine." The words were a vow.

She nodded slowly.

"I know what being a wife to you means. And I will be, Ely. I swear. I will be yours, only yours. If we do this, Carmelo Ricci does not exist."

The weight of what she was promising, what she was asking him to sacrifice, sat heavily between them. Kathy had never kissed a man other than Carmelo. Never let another man hold her the way Ely was holding her now. Her heart hammered with uncertainty, guilt, and desperate gratitude. But she was out of options, and Ely... Ely had always been her safe place.

She reached up slowly, touching at first his lips, then his jaw. He went still, barely breathing, as she drew him down. The kiss was nothing like the passion she'd known with Carmelo. This was quieter, sadder, tasting of tears and sacrifice and the death of dreams. But underneath, she felt Ely's years of patient love, his joy at finally having even this broken version of what he'd wanted.

When the kiss ended, something fundamental had shifted. She wasn't a dreamer anymore. She was a woman who understood exactly what this bargain would cost them both—Ely giving up a woman who loved him and truly, her giving up the last hope that somehow she and Carmelo could find their way.

She stood, wiping the last of her tears, and straightened her spine. The girl in the attic was gone. In her place stood a woman ready to do what she needed to, to bring her child into the world safely. She extended her hand to him. Maybe this was why Debbie and Willa did the same.

He stared at her hand, then up at her face.

"You don't have to do this, Kathy. Not now, it's too soon for you, and I understand that," Ely said.

She gave him a sad smile. "Always selfless, Ely. Always putting me first before even your own well-being. I don't have to do anything. I want to. I want to forget him. Really and truly forget. I want to start over, be her again. The girl you knew before all of this began. Can you make me forget? Do you want to try? Because I want you too, Ely."

She saw the desire bloom in his eyes, years of longing mixed with uncertainty about her surrender.

He took her hand.

She led him through his own house to the bedroom. And there, surrounded by more evidence of Lea's presence—her robe on a hook, her slippers by the bed—Kathy Freeman undressed for another man. She gave herself to Ely Brown, not with passion or joy, but with gratitude and determination and the kind of desperate affection that grows when two people save each other.

Behind that closed door, her new life began.

CHAPTER 33

HARLEM NEW YORK 1952

"Hey," Matteo called out as he stepped into the brownstone, closing the door against the evening chill. "José home?"

Debbie's client was still counting out bills when Junior spotted his father. The boy took off on wobbly legs, arms outstretched, squealing "Papa!" Matteo scooped him up in one smooth motion, tossing him gently in the air.

The client—Mrs. Washington from Harlem—kept her eyes down as she handed over the money, but Debbie caught the sideways glances she threw at Matteo. There was gossip amongst women who were once her childhood friends. People whispered about whose son Junior really was. Debbie walked her to the door, shoving the bills deep into her apron pocket and giving her client a kiss on the cheek goodbye.

She locked the door. "Junior! I told you about calling him Papa. We said he is Matteo."

Matteo grinned. "You did well, son."

Debbie shook her head and smiled, too. Then her smile faded. She nervously rubbed her hands together. "Thank you for coming so fast," she said once they were alone. The downstairs was her domain—

where she pressed hair and cooked meals, keeping their life respectable. Upstairs was where the bedrooms were; that was a different territory.

"Had some business to handle first." Matteo shifted Junior to his hip as the boy reached for his mama. "You said emergency. Everything okay?"

Debbie kissed her son's forehead, avoiding Matteo's searching gaze. "How's Carmelo?"

"Same. Angry. Spending all his time behind closed doors with Pa, planning God knows what." His jaw tightened. "They're freezing me out. My Vegas plans, everything. I think Carmelo's undermining me, but..." He shook his head. "Something's brewing. I can feel it."

She nodded, her stomach churning. "Yeah. Something is. I spoke to Big Mama."

"And?"

"There's a wedding tomorrow."

Matteo's eyes narrowed. "Whose wedding?"

"Stay calm, Matteo."

"Whose wedding, Debbie?" His voice had gone dangerously quiet.

She exhaled, the lie crumbling. "Okay. I didn't talk to Big Mama. I've known for a week." The words tumbled out faster now. "Auntie Brenda and Uncle Henry are already in Butts. Mom is sick with one of her headaches again, so Pa is staying here to keep an eye on things and take care of her. The wedding—it's Kathy's. She's marrying Ely."

Matteo went utterly still, Junior squirming in his rigid arms. His mouth opened, closed, and no sound came out.

"Kathy told the family she didn't want me there." Debbie's voice broke as tears spilled over. "She's getting married, and I can't even go. She doesn't answer my letters, she doesn't take my calls. Big Mama keeps asking me what I've done. And I can't tell anybody. I couldn't even tell you about the wedding. After everything I've done to her, I had to at least honor that one wish—"

Matteo pulled her against him, Junior sandwiched between them, the boy's small hands patting his mother's wet cheeks.

"Shh, it's okay." He pressed his lips to the top of her head. "I understand why you didn't tell me. I do."

"What about Melo?" she whispered against his chest. "Will you tell him?"

"No." His voice was firm. "I'm done standing between them. Done being caught in their war. You neither. My focus is on you and Junior now." He tightened his hold on them both. "I just pray Kathy knows what she's doing. For her sake. For that poor bastard Ely's sake."

"Why?"

"Because my brother..." Matteo's voice went hollow. "He's not going to stop, Debs. And she just signed that man's death warrant."

Travelers Rest Church of God, Butts, Mississippi - 1952

The little shotgun church sat proud despite its peeling white paint, its narrow frame packed tight with everyone who mattered in Butts' colored community.

Morning light streamed through the stained-glass windows. It caught dust motes that danced above the congregation like blessings. Someone had strung white sheets from the rafters and gathered wildflowers—black-eyed Susans and Queen Anne's lace—from the roadside ditches, transforming the humble space into something almost magical.

Big Mama sat front and center in her wheelchair, dressed in her best navy dress with the pearl buttons, her Bible clutched in her lap. An amputee who had lost both feet, and one leg was cut up to the knee, she was still a force of pride and strength for the community of Butt's. Behind her, the wooden pews groaned under the weight of sharecroppers in their Sunday clothes—men in their only suits that smelled of mothballs, women in dresses they'd pressed with irons heated on wood stoves.

Henry Freeman stood rigid in his good black suit, jaw set like granite, waiting for Kathy outside the sanctuary. At the same time, Brenda dabbed at her eyes with one of her embroidered handkerchiefs, sitting next to Big Mama and four of her sisters, minus Janey, who had traveled in for the wedding. The entire family arrived from different states a week ago, and Henry had covered their travel expenses and all necessary costs. Henry was so proud that he couldn't stop passing out cigars.

Today, Henry's eyes held something softer than his pride or stubborn ego. Today, he was Daddy again as he waited for Kathy.

She came out from a side door in all white, and she was more beautiful than he could have imagined.

"Hi, Daddy," she said.

Tears slipped from Henry's eyes. "My baby girl. all grown up."

"Yes, Daddy. And I'm getting married today," Kathy said in tears. He went to her and hugged her with pride. She held on to him and released her tears of relief and joy, tears of joy at having her father's love again, pure and unrestrained.

"I knew this day would come," Henry said. "I don't pray for much, Kathy, but I prayed every day since I sent you here for this day to come. For me to know that you will be loved and safe, baby. That's all I ever wanted. It's all any father ever wants."

"I am Daddy. I'm going to be happy because of you," she reached up and brushed away his tears. "Don't blame yourself, Daddy. Coming to Butts was good for me. I understand life now. I'm ready to live it with a man who is just as special as my Daddy."

Henry nodded, and more tears welled. Kathy had spent all night crying over the upcoming nuptials, while burning all of Carmelo's letters. She had her family back, and Carmelo had his. She told herself that this was what God had always wanted.

The organ began to play.

Sister Flora gave Kathy her freshly picked bouquet. She accepted it with pride. Henry took her arm with pride. The doors opened. Just as they did, a flash of a thought went through Kathy's mind. Carmelo was doing the same routine two years ago in a big Cathedral church with another woman. She closed her eyes and banished him from her thoughts. The door opened, and she looked into the eyes of her future husband, Ely.

Ely's family filled the right side—his mother weeping openly with joy, his father standing proud despite the arthritis that bent his spine. They'd picked cotton alongside the Freemans for generations, and now their families would be joined by more than just hardship.

Kathy walked down the aisle with her father and was handed over to Ely, who was grinning as well. She winked at him.

Reverend Daniels cleared his throat, his voice rolling out rich and deep: "Dearly beloved, we are gathered here today in the sight of God and these witnesses..."

Kathy stood in her auntie Izzy's altered wedding dress, the ivory silk yellowed with age but still beautiful. Every Elliot sister, except the oldest, Mae, Brenda, Betsie, and the other one, Everlene, who had disappeared into Oregon and a life of passing, was present. Her hands trembled slightly as she held the small bouquet of field flowers. Beside her, Ely looked like a man who'd won a prize he'd never dared dream of claiming, his face shining with something between joy and disbelief.

The reverend continued, but Kathy heard only the blood rushing in her ears, felt only the weight of the secret growing inside her uterus, and the terrible kindness of the man who was about to pledge his life to her, knowing precisely what burdens she carried.

* * *

"*CIAO*, WHERE HAVE YOU BEEN?" Carmelo asked as Matteo came inside and closed the door.

"Oh, had to stop by and see Debbie and Junior," Matteo said. "Junior is calling me Papa like I taught him. Pisses Debbie off. So I stayed the night with them. Decided to come home, get Nino, and take him to the park before I had to put in work. Where is he?"

"At the center," Carmelo said and dropped into the chair nearest the sofa.

Matteo froze.

"What? You and I agreed that he isn't going to be put in any institution! Who took him there? Why? When!"

"Calm down," Carmelo said. "It's only for a few hours. Pa and I agreed that it would do him good to be around others like him."

"Are you fucking out of your mind? *People like him*? Like what, Melo? Where is Pa?" Matteo turned to head to his office. "Fuck if I let him get away with this shit!"

"Gone. He left me to deliver the message," Carmelo said.

Matteo stopped. He looked back at the mocking smile on his brother's face and the fury in his brother's eyes. He didn't understand it. He paused. "Who are you angry at? Me? Is that what this is? You blame me for Kathy?"

"You let her run from me. Let her escape. Let her play with me for two days, and didn't give me a fighting chance to make things right with her. You did that, big brother."

"Me? You were shitting your drawers and drooling all over the place. I brought her back to you to save your life!"

"NO!" Carmelo stood up. "You brought her back to me to save your deal. To make the Marcellos happy. To get Vegas so you and Debbie can live happily ever after. You didn't give a shit about me losing Kathy!"

Matteo's eyes stretched wide. "What have you done?"

Carmelo's smile turned wicked. "I killed it. All that work and negotiating you were doing with Pa and the Marcellos. Investing in Vegas. You're not moving down there to run the investment. It's dead. If there is no me and Kathy, there is no you and Debbie."

Matteo charged at his brother. His fury exploded hotter than dynamite. He punched him first and then threw him into the door. Matteo grabbed him by the throat and started choking him. Carmelo didn't fight back. He just smiled as he choked, wanting to die. So enraged at the laughter Matteo could see in Carmelo's eyes, he drew his pocket knife and put it up against Carmelo's throat instead.

"You're fucking with my family! MY LIFE! For what? For that demon who killed our mother? You turned on me!"

Carmelo shrugged. "If I can't have Kathy, you can't have Debbie! That's the way life works. We are brothers. The same."

Matteo stepped back, and Carmelo dropped. His neck bleeding from the tiny cut the knife left. He choked for air.

In tears, Matteo shook his head. "I was going to spare you. Going to protect you. Even though nothing I do or have done for you, Melo, is ever good enough. So fuck ya. Kathy is getting married today."

Carmelo's head shot up. "Fucking liar! Fucking liar!"

"I'm not lying. Call your contacts. Call Bonano. She's marrying Ely."

"You're lying!" Carmelo kicked his feet and shouted.

"Already done. And let me tell you, I'm not losing Debbie. She's mine. She loves me, and only me. I'm the only man she ever let touch her. Wonder what Kathy is going to be doing for Ely tonight."

Carmelo launched himself up from the floor and charged Matteo, who ducked and swiped his blade across Carmelo's arm. Carmelo dropped in pain and gripped his bleeding arm.

Matteo wiped his brother's blood on his shirt. He folded his knife. "That shit that happened in Memphis? That's your one and only, little bro. I'll fucking carve you like a Christmas turkey if you ever come at me again with your fist, or with business." He then turned and stormed out.

Carmelo was left sitting on the floor in pain and agony, not from the wound to his neck or arm, but to the one in his heart. He dropped back on the floor, turned on his side, and folded inward. He lay there dying.

CHAPTER 34

THE DROWNING MAN. - 1978

Present. Kathy approached Carmelo on silent feet. Her hand hovered just above his shoulder. On the paper, her face surfaced with each savage stroke—captured perfectly.

She touched him.

Carmelo's pencil stopped mid-stroke. He froze, his breath caught in his chest. He couldn't bear to turn around—what if she disappeared again? After decades of phantom Kathys haunting his nights, how could he trust that this one was flesh and blood?

"Melo, I need you. I can't sleep without you." Her voice was barely a breath as she kissed the back of his head. The confession came from a place so deep in truth it hurt—the most valid words she'd ever spoken. "I'm trying, Melo, you have to meet me halfway. Do you want me to leave you alone?"

In one swift motion, he turned and wrapped his arms around her, crushing her to him. His face found refuge between her breasts as years of pain finally broke free. She cradled him like a child, feeling his shoulders tremble and heave beneath her hands.

"Don't go," Carmelo said, voice muffled against her. Raw with old terror. "I'm tired of dreaming. Don't go."

"Dreaming? Never." She held him tighter. She kissed the top of his head. "I'll never leave you again."

His fingers explored upward from her thighs, skimming over bare hips that told him everything about what she'd chosen not to wear beneath his shirt. He pulled her to him with practiced strength, positioning her on his lap while the barstool spun lazily beneath them, somehow holding steady despite their precarious balance. She could feel him fiddle with his pajama pants beneath her to release his cock and bring it up into her opening as she kissed his face. She gasped when he aimed and drove the head of his cock up into her, and he bit down on her bottom lip. Kathy shuddered and moved in slow rhythmic waves, trusting that he'd keep her balanced. Up and down she went. All for him until they both began to breathe in sync.

Making love was easier than talking. Because when they talked, they only said the same thing: *I'm sorry. Forgive me. I wish it hadn't happened. This time will be different. Give me one more chance. You're killing me.*

Over and over, they repeated the cycle. At least when he was in her, connected to her, their bodies and souls joining, she could erase the past and hold onto what felt real. Kathy shuddered through a premature climax, and her vibrating body became too much to hold. Carmelo stood, and the stool spun away. He was strong enough to balance her as she worked her pussy on him. He pinned her down on the drafting table, on top of the drawing. She lifted her leg and dropped it on his shoulder. He fucked her in rapid jerky strokes while squeezing her breasts and staring down at his disappearing cock as it tunneled deep. She closed her eyes and then opened them to the drawings he had wallpapered on the ceilings. Nude images of her, in different poses. She closed her eyes and breathed. Her head dropped over to the left as he fucked her harder and faster while rubbing her clitoris. She opened her eyes and saw the picture he drew of a fallen family, from Uncle Pete, Ely, to her father, to his, to Jose, and others. Tears welled in her eyes. She closed them again. Carmelo dropped on her and ravaged her, grunting through his climactic release.

Pinned beneath him, she dared to open her eyes again. This time, she saw an image of a man she didn't at first recognize but later did. A man from her neighborhood in Harlem named Joe Tems, who had gone missing so many years ago. Joe was sweet. Joe wanted to be helpful. Joe took her to dinner and told her about the Vietnam War and what could have happened to Ely during the war before Matteo was healed by the monks in Sicily. He returned to her first, and told her the truth of Ely to make amends to everyone for his sins, including José. Joe told her the actual truth. Joe asked her for help to start a business, and she said she would invest. He asked her for a date, and she declined. She just needed a friend, someone not under Carmelo's control. Joe disappeared. Kathy looked at the other drawings of men whom she had encountered in Harlem over the years, who had disappeared for befriending her, or even attempting something more.

Kathy's heartbeat slowed. Understanding dawned on her. But her body was in distress and responding to Carmelo against her internal conflict. She tried again to focus. Joe. Joe Tems. Why did he draw Joe Tems and these men? How did he know them, and what had he done to them?

This place wasn't a memorial—it was a tomb. Here, he had buried their past, their mistakes, their regrets, and their sins. She had stepped into the heart of darkness itself. This was where the Wolf made his den.

He squeezed her breast hard as his urgency burst, and she groaned through his lasting, powerful thrusts with her leg pinned at his shoulder, opening her wider for his plunging cock. Panting, he lifted and slipped out of her. He turned from her and put his hands to his face. His dick was still semi-erect. She sat up on the draft table that was sturdy enough for her weight. The incline of the table gave her leverage. She pulled down his shirt and covered herself. She watched him roam and pace.

"Melo, what's happening?"

"I don't want to talk to you," he wheezed.

"What is this place? Why did you create it?" she asked, feeling a cold sense of dread as she looked at the other dead men he drew that she didn't know.

"I said I don't want to talk," he said, looking back at her. Then he left. Kathy eased down from the table with his seed sticky between her thighs. She surveyed the room. She walked back through the past, focusing on the faces she had to recall. She put her hand to her mouth to see his crimes. Some of them out of rage, some out of jealousy, some out of business. But more than several because they got too close to her.

"What have you become?" she asked herself.

Finally, she understood. The federal indictment was a noose he couldn't slip away from. There would be no escaping justice. He'd reached the end of his road and was drowning.

Desperate Kathy went after him. She left the room, hurried down the dark staircase, following instinct more than sight. A refrigerator door closing guided her to the kitchen, where she found him—head tilted back, milk carton to his lips, drinking like it might save him. He drained it, then looked over and saw her there.

"Bad dream," he said. "Better now. Stay out of my room upstairs, its private."

"Bad dreams made you leave our bed? Or was it me you were leaving?" she asked.

A shrug was his only response. "Stay out of my room. I mean it."

"So you want my body but not my heart?" she asked.

He glared at her.

"This time you need to answer, Carmelo," she said.

"I have been fighting to win your heart back for decades, Kat," he mumbled.

"Going into that room won't do it," she countered.

"Needed to clear my head. That room helps," he said.

She hesitated. "All those drawings on the walls—how long have you been doing that?"

"Started... a long time ago," he mumbled.

"When did it start, Melo?"

"After the hospital. To help me remember your face when they sent you away. Matteo would come into my room and tear up the pictures so Mama wouldn't find them. So I hid them. And then after I shot Pa.

I drew him, wanted to remember the look on his face when the bullet hit him. Kept them." He looked away, ashamed.

"Like Janey kept barrettes from other women she helped," Kathy mumbled.

He frowned. He didn't understand the comparison. "I need to draw to calm myself, to make sure I remember."

"You put me on the ceiling?" she asked, crossing her arms to ward off the chill creeping over her skin. "Like some… thing…"

His gaze slipped over to her and then away. "I don't know why I did that. I'll take it down. Sorry."

"Do you have other rooms like that, Melo? Have you done that in other places? Other times?" she asked.

He refused to answer.

"Could the F.B.I. find rooms like that?" she asked, and her voice trembled.

He shrugged like a spoiled boy caught with his hand in the cookie jar.

Kathy let go of a deep sigh. She nodded. She walked over to him slowly, not getting too close. Gone was the comfort and lazy hugs. He only let her close now that the truth was revealed, when he wanted sex. But the intimacy between them, he ran from.

"Melo, are you feeling okay?" she asked.

"I'm not crazy, Kathy!" he snapped.

"I didn't say that," she spoke softly.

"I see it in your eyes," he said and started to walk away. "You're looking at me the way Maria did when—"

"When what?"

He kept walking.

"Stay! Damnit," she demanded.

He stopped.

"Stay, Melo, with me. Please," she said gently. "When did Maria look at you like this?"

He turned his gaze back to her.

"Did she find a room like that, too? In her house? With me in it? With all those memories?" Kathy asked.

He crossed his arms and stayed silent.

"She told me about what you did to Caesar and how you punished her over the lie about the twins," Kathy confessed.

"She told you?" He asked with a frown.

"We've been friends for years, ever since you broke Nicolas' heart. I know who you are, Melo. I just didn't know… about that room, and those men. Men from my life. Men who never harmed me or you. Melo? What have you done?"

Again, she was met with the stern gaze and nothing more.

"I'm not judging you. I've done things, Melo. I've done things without you, with you, to you, for you, over the years. You know me. I'm not innocent. I'm not judging you," she said.

He nodded. "You're right. I confess. Maria looked at me like that when I almost beat Caesar to death with my hammer. She looked at me like that when she found my room. She looked at me like that when I made her help us kill Pa. That's how she found out about Sandy. Before the accident… before you knew she knew about Sandy, she did. She said I was crazy, insane, obsessed, possessed by the devil. Maybe she is right. I can't tell anymore."

Kathy held back her emotion. It was hard. She wanted to stop peeling back the layers, but she knew she had to go on. She wiped at a tear that escaped and kept her spine straight. "She's a fucking liar. You're not crazy. No more crazy than me. You're a killer. Our fathers were killers. Matteo is a killer. I'm a killer, and so is my mother. My grandmother, Bessie, was a killer, probably better than all of us. Killers are what we are," she let go of a long sigh. "I wrote everything, Carmelo. Every moment, every heartache, every bit of our story I wrote in journals each time I had bad dreams about killing King Redmond and your father, I wrote it down to remember. It's the way we survived, okay?"

"I wanted to have everything with you, my first child, my first everything with you," he confessed. "I almost did. I proved to you that our marriage was legal. I gave you our only child. You took that from me, Kathy. So I did things, bad things, and took things from you."

Kathy nodded. "I know, Melo. I know."

"I'm sorry, Kathy. I told you, your love was poison. That you were killing me, but it was my fault too. That was the dream I had upstairs. The dream to remind me where it went wrong. The day I came to New Orleans was not long after I married Maria. And you said something was different about me. I should have told you then. Confessed it and been honest. Men died, many men, men you love and who loved you, because I was scared to be honest. I was so scared, Kathy. I was drowning in the East River, like my mother."

"I want to understand…" She took a step forward, and he took a step back. She nodded. "We talked about this many times over the years."

He nodded. "I know. I know. It's all in the past. I killed us. I buried us. I left our daughter behind. And I'm not sorry. Because, for once, I have you, Kathy. Just you. I was going to bring her, but I needed my time with you. I couldn't leave Nino behind. I had to do it this way. It was safest. And no one can take you away from me. I had to get Matteo out of prison. I had to give him and Debbie the life I took from them and the kids. I had to find a way to save my soul. My soul is you, Kathy. It's all I am now. Does that make me a monster? Does that make me my father?"

"It makes you human, Carmelo," she said. "Let me come closer."

He shook his head. "I'm tired. Go back to bed. I'll take you and Nino for a drive tomorrow. Make it up to you."

Kathy wiped her tears. She shuddered with repressed grief. "I won't touch you. Just let me come closer so you can be near me."

She walked toward him in the kitchen, and he watched her. She stopped a foot away from him.

"See. I'm here. I'm not running. I'm not arguing. I'm not pushing you away. We're not having sex. We're just here."

"I'm not sorry, Kathy. I'm not going to be sorry for any of it," he confessed.

"You live in fear, Melo. The boy inside of you is afraid. The wolf protects the boy. That room upstairs? It's your own personal torture chamber—a shrine to your regrets. And there are other shrines, aren't there? Other places you go to torture yourself. For Matteo, Ely, and the war. For Uncle Pete and Daddy. For Matteo killing José. For Mama Stewart dieing in that fire. For Sandy's brain injury. For stealing my business, for what you made me become and do to get it back, for everything we did to each other. But you forget—you tried to fix it all. God, how many times did you try? You are right for reuniting your brother with his first love. Look around you: Matteo's free, Sandy's thriving, we're together. What's left to atone for?"

Carmelo's defense crumbled. His head dropped, and tears began to fall. Kathy moved to him, gathering him into her arms as he broke apart completely. The sobs came from somewhere deep and ancient, his grip on her fierce and desperate. She held him steady, hands gentle on his back.

"I've got you, Melo. We're one person now, remember? Your mother drowned, but not you. Not on my watch. Never again."

She felt him cling to her with bruising strength as years of pain poured out. Her own eyes stayed dry—not from lack of emotion, but from understanding. This was his moment of release, his reckoning. She could feel it happening: the terrible weight lifting, forgiveness seeping into the cracks where guilt had once resided.

"I need to take care of you," she murmured. "Shower first, then bed." She laced her fingers through his, drawing him from the kitchen and up to their bedroom. Under the hot spray, she washed the grief from his skin. Afterward, they sank into bathwater tinted purple, then blue, then green, thanks to the dissolving beads. With her back pressed to his chest, she felt his voice rumble through her as he spoke of federal charges—conspiracy, racketeering, the case they'd built on murder by his hand and command. One agent called him a serial killer, and he had to explain to her what that meant. She kept her questions sparse and practical: What evidence? What deal? What options remained?

He told her about the Battaglia crime family in Italy—not Sicilian Mafia, but Camorra, the Neapolitan syndicate that controlled the southern region. Luciano had made the introduction years ago, bringing him to Don Tomosino Battaglia himself after Mama Stewart's death. Now, with all their investments entangled in the mob business, that connection could save them. Since his father's death, he'd cultivated the relationship carefully, deal by deal.

He broke every rule of Omertà that night, telling her about the Thorned Rose. The medallion of the Castellammarese—a silver and gold disc where rubies bloomed like drops of blood among twisted thorns. It tied him to Mama Stewart, and through her to the ghost of Don Emilio Cattano, the young Don. A Sicilian who'd died wearing it. One medallion, one man: Boss of all Bosses. The ultimate prize that could unite or destroy the Five Families. These were secrets men died to protect, but what did he care? The Mafia had been his means, never his end. Every brutal year in that life had one purpose—to become powerful enough to take her and keep her. He said their daughter may know where it is, but it's locked in that beautiful mind of hers.

"Wait, rubies? Silver and gold? Thorns," she repeated.

Carmelo frowned. "What?"

"Oh my God. I know where it is," Kathy said, sitting upright.

"Where?" he asked. "Kathy! Where?"

"I found it, in bed with Sandy when she was a baby. She was three, I think. It was after our fight. When you had taken her again without my permission, I grabbed her and her things and ran from you. She must have had it on her. I didn't know. I thought it belonged to my mom. I thought she got it out of her jewelry box. I put it up to give it back to Ma, but Ma… Carmelo. I buried it with Mama."

"You did?" he asked.

"All these years I've been looking for it, and Brenda has it? In her grave?" he said.

She nodded. "I put it on her, in her casket, before it closed. Let Sandy touch it. I thought it was something special between them. I put it under her dress lapel so her graver wouldn't discover it. Sandy was so excited to see me do it. She said it was a game. But I didn't understand what she meant. It's buried with Mama."

Carmelo laughed. "Are you fucking kidding me? I've been looking for it for damn near fifteen years, and you buried it with Brenda?"

"You never told me about it," Kathy said. "We never talk about things that are important. We're either fighting or having sex."

Carmelo laughed harder and harder. Kathy smiled and shrugged. He hugged her tight, and the water splashed out of the tub. He kissed the side of her face. "You're remarkable, Kathy."

"I'm your wife. You took me to court to prove it, remember," she teased.

He laughed some more.

"Let me understand this," Kathy said, counting on her fingers. "We rob my mother's grave, take a medallion that makes kings, dodge federal agents and assassins, then convince two crime bosses in Italy and Sicily to bow to Matteo? Simple."

"When you put it that way..." he said with a wry smile.

"It's the only way, right?" she smiled.

She shifted in the water, creating small waves as she moved to face him from across the tub. She propped her foot in his hands, toes wiggling.

"Be honest—these grey hairs of mine. I could dye them, but you always said not to. Debbie thinks I'm insane, says women our age shouldn't have this much silver hair. Do I look like an old woman to you?"

"Those grey hairs are battle scars, baby. Everyone of them earned in our war," he said, nipping at her big toe with his teeth. She shrieked with laughter, splashing water everywhere as she fought to reclaim her foot.

"Now tell me the beautiful part," she whispered. "The part where we win. Where does our story end?"

"At the beginning," he said mysteriously.

Her brow furrowed. "What?"

"Picture it—a ship leaving New York harbor, cutting through the Atlantic to Spain. We sail through the Strait of Gibraltar, that ancient gateway where two seas kiss. Then... home."

"Home?" she breathed like a woman releasing her last sigh after an orgasm. Her eyes closed, and she listened to him speak.

"Tangier. Morocco. Africa," he said in that husky, deep Italian voice of his.

Each word was a promise from her magnificent Carmelo, and she could see it. She felt herself transported back in time to the attic, where they huddled in the cold against his body warmth and waited for the ovens to warm them. She listened to his voice.

"Just like we dreamed when we were young," he said.

"You already arranged it?" she asked.

"Every detail. Paid in gold."

Her eyes opened. His eyes searched hers.

"Sandy comes too, of course," she said and moved through the water like silk, pressing her lips to his. "A Ricci and a Freeman, allies at last. Who would have believed it?"

His fingers traced her cheekbone with reverence. "Partners, baby. The way we were meant to be. No more lies, no more secrets between us."

"Good. Because I'm running this operation now," she giggled. "I would kiss the ring, but I have something better in mind.

Before he could ask, she submerged under the water and put his dick in his mouth. Carmelo laughed and reclined into marital bliss.

Book Two

Matteo and Debbie

CHAPTER 35

CALVARY CEMENTARY - QUEENS NEW YORK 1978

P**resent.** The cemetery stretched endlessly beyond the tinted windows. Junior broke the silence first: "This is insane. Who gets married in a fucking graveyard?"

Sandy watched Daphne's reflection in the glass as Matteo's driver steered them deeper into Calvary's sprawling grounds. The city skyline loomed in the distance, a jarring contrast to the sea of headstones.

"She killed herself," Daphne said. "His mother. The Church wouldn't give her sacred ground, so she's out here, in the forgotten section. That's where he wants to pledge himself to Mama—in front of the woman who couldn't watch him get married or meet his children. Us."

The strangeness of it all settled over them. Even Christopher looked up from his comic and stared at the graves.

"Daddy is going to make it special for Mama. That's what he said," Daphne smiled.

"Already calling him Daddy," Junior observed, his tone softer than usual.

Daphne's jaw tightened. "He's earned it."

"Whatever," Junior mumbled.

Daphne shot him the middle finger.

"Sandy." Junior's eyes found hers. "Why the security? I heard him barking orders about you specifically."

She wanted to tell them everything—about the diaries, about Carmelo being her father, about the danger closing in. Instead, she shrugged. "Probably just being careful."

"Those diaries revealing anything interesting?" Daphne probed.

Everything, Sandy thought. *They revealed everything.* But the words lodged in her throat. Not here. Not yet. The car rolled to a stop among weathered headstones and overgrown grass.

"Awesome!" Christopher declared, oblivious to the tension. "A spooky wedding!"

Junior held the door, his expression grim. "Let's go watch them make it official—again."

Sandy emerged from the limo and reached for Christopher's hand. Though he was only fourteen, he looked much younger—he'd inherited the petite build of his mother rather than the Ricci height, his thin frame making him appear barely ten.

Together they approached the priest, where Aunt Debbie stood radiant as a movie star. Her white Chanel suit was impeccable; the tailored jacket and pencil skirt highlighted a figure that defied her forty-eight years. Her platinum blonde hair, swept into Marilyn Monroe waves, caught the light like spun silk. Every step in her white heels spoke of refinement. She was so beautiful that Sandy couldn't look away from her. And neither could Matteo.

Beside her, Matteo was pure controlled power—six feet of hardened Sicilian muscle, his deep Mediterranean tan making his dark sunglasses seem even more impenetrable. The black suit couldn't disguise what fourteen years in the penitentiary had carved into him: the tattoos snaking up from his collar, wrapping around his neck, spreading across his hands like a roadmap of survival. But it was the two figures at the graveside that made Sandy's breath catch: Nicolas and Nina Ricci.

The twins were from the funeral, and she had suspicions about their shared past, thanks to the diary. The ones whose existence had sent her pregnant mother running from her father, Carmelo, straight into her father Ely's arms. Looking at them now, Sandy felt the crushing weight of three generations of deception at Matteo's mother's gravesite.

Nicolas Ricci stared at her. She could feel his eyes through his dark sunglasses. She tried not to notice.

"The sun's brutal, baby. Let's do this," Debbie murmured against Matteo's shoulder. But he was lost in communion with his mother's spirit; the obsidian rosary beads, sliding through his scarred fingers, soothed him. The prayer ended with a kiss to the cross—tender, final—before he buried it deep in his pocket alongside his other secrets.

She caught Father Angelo's furtive glances and read the disapproval in his rigid posture. A priest blessing a mobster's union to a Black woman violated everything except the one law that mattered in their world: Matteo Ricci's word.

The church bowed to the famiglia, just as everyone else did. Debbie threaded her arm through Matteo's, her white Chanel against his black suit, creating their own language of defiance. She led him from the grave with practiced ease, and Father Angelo, trapped between heaven and the Ricci family's earthly power, began the ceremony his conscience protested, but his survival demanded.

* * *

In one smooth motion, Matteo scooped under Debbie's legs to bring her up into his arms, cradling her against his chest as if they were newlyweds leaving a chapel instead of a cemetery. Daphne and Christopher fell into step behind them, their faces bright with genuine happiness for their mother. But Junior stayed where he was, watching his family walk away without him.

Sandy noticed Nicolas Ricci approach Junior before she turned away and paused. The two fell into an immediate, intense conversation. And Nicolas kept glancing Sandy's way.

"Sandy. Hey? Remember me?" Nina asked.

When she turned, Sandy found herself face-to-face with Nina's striking beauty. Ink-black hair poured like silk from a razor-sharp center part, creating a dramatic frame for her porcelain features. Her eyes were the most transparent green Sandy had ever seen, like sea glass, and her smile had the calculated perfection of someone who'd learned to weaponize charm.

The tailored blue suit she wore transformed her into something between a fashion model and a femme fatale. Both twins had dressed in dark colors—a choice that seemed deliberate, as if acknowledging the morbid setting of their uncle's wedding in a cemetery.

"I don't really remember. But I suppose I do, to some extent. Nice to see you again. Thank you for coming to my mother's funeral," Sandy said.

Nina nodded. "We all loved Aunt Kathy. Can't believe she and Pops are gone. Strange coincidence, huh?"

Sandy frowned. "It's not a coincidence. Your father was murdered and my Mama.. She had a car accident."

"But the timing, it's just weird. Even the feds think so. It's on the news. And Uncle Nino is gone too. Pretty odd, huh?"

"I'm more concerned about losing her than any strange coincidences," Sandy said in a flat tone.

"Of course, that's what I meant. Weird coincidence, same thing," she smiled. "Nicolas said he invited you to our house out in Staten Island. Looks like Uncle Matteo and Aunt Debbie will be moving in with the kiddos, so... uhm, will you come visit?"

Sandy glanced back over to Junior and Nicolas. It was Junior who walked away from the conversation, his face pinched with anger. He marched over to Sandy, grabbed her hand, and yanked her to walk with him. She glanced back at Nina, who stared at her with a sly smirk on her face. And Nicolas, of course, approached his sister, watching them leave.

"Stop it, Junior! Let my hand go!" she yanked her hand free.

He blinked at her. "Don't talk to them."

"Why not? What's the matter with you?"

"Because I said so, damnit. I have to protect you and Debbie. You both are too stupid to know how to protect yourself," he stormed ahead of her. Sandy glanced back at the twins. They stood together side by side, watching her as well. There was something odd about their interest. And it felt unwavering.

She turned back and joined the family at the limos and got inside the car with her cousin. They all drove away.

* * *

"HAVE YOUR PEOPLE LOCATED JANEY YET?" Debbie's fingers drummed against her thigh as they rode toward Staten Island, the children's limo trailing behind them. Her new wedding ring caught the light with each nervous tap.

Matteo's jaw tightened. "She showed up right after we collected Sandy. She's waiting at the house with Coffey."

Debbie twisted in her seat to face him. "And you're just telling me this now?"

His hand found her knee, steadying her hand. "Today was about us, bambina. About giving my mother the peace of seeing her son settled and safe. Introducing my kids and wife to her. Janey could wait."

Debbie softened.

She didn't stop him when his calloused hand began to run smoothly up and between her thighs. It soon disappeared under her skirt. Matteo leaned in and kissed her on the neck. She smiled when his fingers reached her panties and made it past the seat to touch the lips of her sex. Debbie's head dropped back as Matteo made sure the divider between them and the driver of the limo remained up.

"Come here," he said in her ear.

Debbie opened her eyes and let him put her on his lap. Matteo yanked her expensive Chanel skirt up to her waist so she was able to grind on his thick hardness trapped behind his zipper. She deep-throated her kiss with him. And Matteo worked to undo his belt and lower his zipper, and she lifted on her knees so he could push his pants all the way down, allowing them to drop to his ankles.

Debbie giggled when she was on him again, taking him all the way in. She removed his sunglasses from his face and licked his nose.

Then, she licked his lip, and she moved in ways she knew made him crazy. Matteo groaned.

"You like that, baby?"

He spanked her ass, bouncing on his dick, and she let go of an excited laugh. He hugged her and laughed, too. "We're married. We're married!"

She kissed him deeper and remembered the time when she thought her world would be nothing but suffering and pain. And he was the cause.

Harlem 1952

"Ma? Ma, what's wrong?" Debbie said. She entered the tenement with Junior on her hip.

Her mother took her grandson into her arms and kissed the toddler as he kicked and fussed to be put down to explore. Debbie closed the door. All she knew was that her mother called and said to come home immediately.

"Tell me," Debbie urged, setting the baby bag and her purse on the sofa.

"It's your father," Claire said. She looked weak. Since the family diagnosis for her illness, she had spent time in and out of the hospital under treatments that seemed to age and drain her. Her state terrified Debbie.

"What's wrong with Pa?" Debbie asked.

"He's been missing. After Bumpy Johnson's arrest, they've been taking men who worked under him off the streets. Jimmy said he saw cops put him in the back of a police car. Brother and his friends are looking, but we haven't found him yet."

"What? No. What are you talking about? Why didn't you call me? Tell me! Ma c'mon!" Debbie raced to the phone.

"With everyone down in Butts for the wedding, and you so upset you couldn't go, I just didn't want to upset anybody if he's fine. Who are you calling?"

"Quiet, Ma!" Debbie said.

"*Ciao?*"

"Gino? I'm looking for Matteo. Is he there? It's Debbie. It's an emergency."

"Hold on, Debbie," Gino said.

Debbie let go of the deep breath she was holding. She kept her hand to her heart as she waited. Her mother had found something of interest for Junior and was entertaining him while keeping a close eye on her and listening.

"Debs? What's wrong, *cara*?" Matteo said.

"It's daddy. He's missing Matteo. Ma said Jimmy saw cops force him into a car. Did you know Bumpy Johnson was arrested? Matteo? If the cops have my father, my uncle is not here to help. He's down in Mississippi. You've got to help us. Please," she said.

"Okay, *bambina*. Where are you?"

"I'm staying with Ma. Brother is out looking for him." Debbie started hyperventilating. "Daddy never stays away from Ma too long. Not with her being sick. I got a bad feeling, Matteo."

"Debs, calm down. I got it. I'll find him. Stay there. I'll call you there."

"Okay, okay," she sighed.

She hung up.

"Who is Matteo?" her mom asked.

"Huh?" Debbie turned and saw her mother standing staring at her with Junior in her arms.

"Matteo. Who did you call?" Claire asked.

"Oh, him. Yeah, he's, he's, uhm, a friend… of José," she breathed.

"Can he help us?" her Mom asked. Debbie melted. She went to her mother and hugged her and Junior.

"Yes, Ma. He can help. You know how those cops are. They got Daddy down in some cell, locked away. But we'll get him out. He'll be home soon. I promise."

Claire handed the baby off to Debbie.

"I need to lie down. Wake me when Brother comes back, or if there is news. Okay?"

"Can I fix you something to eat?" Debbie asked.

"Warm up some stew in the fridge for me," Claire said, and Debbie gave her a weak smile and nodded. She watched her mama walk stiffly to the room. The moment she disappeared she wanted to cry. She needed help. She needed someone to talk to. Debbie looked over at the phone. She picked it up. She had to tell Uncle Henry.

She dialed Big Mama's number and heaved Junior up on her hip.

"Hello?"

"Kat? Kathy?" Debbie asked.

The line went silent.

"Kathy, it's me. Please. I need help," Debbie burst into tears. Just hearing her cousin's voice broke something inside of her. She couldn't even get her thoughts together.

"Hello? Debbie? It's Aunt Brenda. What's wrong, baby?"

Debbie closed her eyes. Kathy must have passed the phone to her mother. "It's Pa. I mean, Daddy. He's missing. Brother is trying to find him. Ma said Bumpy Johnson was taken to jail, and they've been snatching Bumpy's men off the streets."

"Oh lord, okay, baby, okay. Let me get Henry. Where are you?" Brenda asked.

"Is Kathy there, Auntie? Can you tell her I'm sorry? I'm scared. I need her. Please?" Debbie sobbed.

"Yes, baby, she's with her husband. They just got married today, but she will call you back. I promise. Where are you? Home?"

"No. I'm at Ma's. I'm with her. Brother is out searching. I'm not leaving until we hear something."

"Okay. Stay by he phone. We will call back," said Brenda, and the line went dead. Debbie held on tight to Junior and prayed.

CHAPTER 36

WHERE IS UNCLE PETE?

Matteo entered the gym on a mission. He'd considered starting with his father, but his gut told him Cosimo would do the exact opposite when it came to saving Pete Freeman. Ever since Carmelo ran off with Kathy and brought shame to the Ricci name, any opportunity to strike at the Freemans was a wet dream for dear old dad.

Carmelo would be his only hope of finding Debbie's father. His rising popularity and authority in the family had surpassed Matteo's. Bumpy Johnson's arrest changed everything. Bumpy's hold over Harlem—stronger than King Redmond's ever was—had been the last thing keeping their family from moving in and seizing the streets. His father had to be behind this.

He walked past young men lifting weights and training to be the next contenders. Carmelo's laughter carried over the music, and Matteo looked up to find him on the balcony talking to one of the managers. Their eyes met. Carmelo's smile faded.

A moment passed before Carmelo nodded, clapped the manager on the back, and took the stairs two at a time. Matteo didn't wait—he headed straight for one of the offices where they could talk privately.

By the time Carmelo walked in, Matteo was already pacing, his agitation kept building.

"Why are you here? We said all there is to say." Carmelo said.

Matteo's eyes swept over his brother in disbelief. Just hours ago, he'd left Carmelo shattered on the floor, blood seeping from his arm, destroyed by news of Kathy's marriage. Yet here he stood—calm, collected, as if it were any other day. Matteo had braced himself for months of his brother's breakdown. Instead, it had lasted mere minutes.

"Did you know?"

Carmelo's brow arched. "Know what?"

"Don't play dumb. Bumpy's arrest." Matteo's voice hardened. "You knew."

Carmelo held his gaze, unblinking.

"What's the endgame here, Melo? Kill Vegas, help Pa seize Harlem, and then what? What's in it for you?"

Nothing. Just that steady, maddening stare.

"Debbie's father is missing." Matteo's fists clenched. "He's one of Bumpy's top nine—probably in some jail hole as we speak. Her family's falling apart. You had to know the Freemans would be targets once Bumpy fell. You knew they'd sweep up her father."

"Families come together in crisis," Carmelo's voice was eerily calm. "I'm sure the Freemans will too."

"Jesus Christ." Matteo's eyes went wide. "That's your play? Start a war in Harlem? Force Henry Freeman and his brother into a fight they can't win? All this to bring Kathy back?" His voice rose. "Are you fucking insane? Do you have any idea how badly this could explode?"

"It's under control. Father knows what I want. Henry and his brother will survive it. We'll give them a little piece of Harlem to manage. Father will give me the rest to take over. And yes, Kathy will come home where she belongs. And by the way, she's not married to anyone but me. I married her first. Legally!" Carmelo snipped.

"You've lost your goddamn mind." Matteo slammed his fist on the desk. "People will die for Harlem. They'll fight to the end. And Father? He'll fill every corner with drugs and chaos. He'll destroy everything."

Matteo's voice cracked. "Don't you get it? When he destroys Harlem, he destroys Kathy. He destroys Debbie. My son. How can you not see that, you fucking idiot!"

"What I see is the world against me and Kathy. It's always been that way: everything and everyone against us. Even Mama, to put a curse on me from her grave."

"Watch your fucking mouth about our mother!" Matteo aimed a finger at him.

"NO! It's true! She made me marry Maria! She made me! And the world took Kathy."

"Your dick took Kathy. You created those kids," Matteo shot back.

Carmelo began to breathe hard. "I'm not going to just roll over and let her go, no matter what, I will have her, and if that means I need Harlem to get to her, then I'll take Harlem too."

"Debbie's father is missing. Did you hear me? We got to find him! If he dies, and Kathy thinks you got her uncle killed, you'll never have her again."

Carmelo paused. The realization that his brother's madness was complete came when he shrugged and said, "That's a risk I'll have to take."

Stunned, Matteo couldn't speak as Carmelo walked out of the office and left him there.

Butts, Mississippi

Kathy laughed from her perch on Ely's lap, her arms wrapped around his neck. Her father was in full storytelling mode, sharing with the family tales of how inseparable she and Ely had been as babies. She'd never known their bond went back that far.

"Henry!"

Her mother's sharp voice cut through the warmth. Kathy had been kissing Ely's jaw when she caught sight of Brenda's face—pure distress that made every man on the porch go still. Earlier, she'd heard that same panic in Debbie's voice on the phone, just for a moment before Kathy had set the receiver down to fetch Brenda.

Kathy straightened.

"What's wrong, Brenda?" Henry asked.

"Pete. They got him." Brenda's voice shook. "That was Debbie. He's missing, and Bumpy's in jail."

Everyone gasped, then came stunned silence. Kathy rose to her feet just as her father did, but he was already charging into the house, nearly bowling her mother over in his haste. Brenda's hand flew to her mouth. The uncles and cousins rushed after Henry, with Ely close behind.

"What's happening, Mama?" Kathy asked.

"The worst possible thing, baby. Nothing good comes from Bumpy being in jail—nothing." Her mother's voice trembled. "Debbie was beside herself. Said Brother's been searching for Pete, but he's been missing for days."

Kathy pulled her mother into a hug. This was supposed to be a celebration—she'd worked so hard to make it perfect for her family, for Ely. Especially now, when she'd finally see a doctor this week about the little one growing inside her. Why now?

"Ma, I have something to tell you."

But Brenda had turned away, straining to hear Henry's booming voice demanding answers about his brother.

"Ma! I have something important to—"

"Later, baby." Brenda hurried inside.

Kathy bit her bottom lip hard. From inside came Big Mama's wail, calling on the Lord as the news reached her. Her oldest boy was missing.

Tears blurring her vision, Kathy shook her head and escaped down the steps. She needed distance from the suffocating fear. If they lost Uncle Pete, everything would shatter. Her father would never recover. And Debbie—sweet God, it would crush her to dust.

She stared up at the sky, now darkening as the moon started to surface. She touched her stomach and wondered what the world, her family, and even her marriage would be like when her child was born. Would he or she have Carmelo's eyes, his smile? Would people look at her precious child and see the truth?

She ached with doubt until Ely's arms encircled her from behind. She melted into him, eyes closed.

"You okay?" His voice was gentle against her ear.

"No." She turned in his arms. "Is Uncle Pete—?"

"Everyone in Harlem is searching. Your parents are catching the first train back."

She searched his face. "It's bad, isn't it?"

"We're going with them," he replied.

"What?" she gasped.

"My Ma and sister will stay with Big Mama. Your parents will need us; your father will need my help. Bumpy in jail is causing people to rumble about the Italians having something to do with it."

The accusation hit like a slap, but she fought to hide it. "We can't go."

His brow furrowed. "Why not?"

"Please, Ely. Something feels wrong about all this. If you get involved with Daddy's business—" She gripped his shirt. "We just got married. Let's stay here."

"Are you sure, Kat?"

She pressed against him. "Yes. We'll care for Big Mama and pray Daddy finds Uncle Pete. We'll pray for all of Harlem. But we must always stay out of New York."

"You're putting me first." Wonder colored his voice.

Tears spilled down her cheeks. "You're saving me and this baby. I meant my vows—you come first. Always."

"Our baby," he corrected softly. "It's ours, Kat."

She nodded through her tears. "Yes. Ours."

Morning

The door opened. Debbie jerked awake on the sofa as Brother entered with José, who went to her and immediately pulled her into his arms.

"Where is he?" Her voice came out raw. "Tell me you found him."

Brother made it three steps before his legs gave out. He dropped into a kitchen chair and broke—her unbreakable brother shattered right in front of her, sobbing like she'd never seen.

"No." The word punched out of her. "No, no, no." She whirled on José. "WHERE IS MY DADDY?"

Tears gathered in José's eyes. "Brother came for me. Debs, I'm so sorry—"

"NO!"

She fled to her parents' room. Her mother lay still on the bed, Junior curled against her side. Debbie closed the door and pressed her back to it, sliding to the floor. Both hands clamped over her mouth, trapping the scream that wanted to tear free.

* * *

THE POUNDING knock at the door caused Ely to shoot upright. Kathy woke and rubbed her eyes. She pulled the sheet to her chest to cover her nudity as Ely left the bed nude. He pulled on his pants and walked out of the room.

Six in the morning. Kathy stared at the clock, dread pooling in her stomach. Nothing good came this early. She fumbled for her robe, her father's voice already booming through the thin walls.

She eased the bedroom door open just as Henry's rage exploded: "My brother! Those motherfuckers are going to pay!"

The words hit like a physical blow. Uncle Pete. Gone.

"Everyone ready by ten! We catch the eleven o'clock to Harlem!"

Kathy emerged from the bedroom, legs barely holding her. Every step felt like walking toward disaster.

Henry turned. The sight of him with his eyes raw and red, face destroyed by grief, confirmed everything.

"Daddy—" Her voice cracked. Her body started to tremble. "Please, no. NO!"

He lunged forward, catching her as her knees buckled. The dam broke. All her life, Uncle Pete had been invincible, untouchable. This couldn't be real. She clawed at her father's shirt, wailing into his chest while his own tears soaked her hair. They clung to each other like survivors of a shipwreck, drowning in shared grief.

•

Brooklyn, NY

The glass rattled under Matteo's fists. He pounded until light flooded the diner, until Mama Stewart appeared with her shotgun and her face set in a scowl.

"Boy, what in God's name—"

"Please." His voice cracked. "It's about Debbie."

Something in his face made her lower the gun. She'd seen him like this before—when Debbie stayed out too long, when she didn't answer her door or the phone. Mama Stewart was the only one who didn't mock his anxiety. José rolled his eyes. Debbie raged. But Mama Stewart? She understood that love could make you crazy with worry.

"Get in here." She locked the door behind him, setting the shotgun aside. "Sit down before you fall down. I'll make coffee."

"Pete Freeman is dead."

The words hung in the air like a gunshot.

Mama Stewart's hand stilled on the coffee pot. Big Pete—who stopped by for plates to take home to Claire, who moved through Harlem like a force of nature, Bumpy Johnson's top enforcer. Gone.

"Lord, have mercy," she whispered. "That child. My poor Debbie."

"They found him this morning." Matteo's voice broke. "Floating in the Hudson. Beaten to death and dumped like garbage." His head dropped into his hands. "They're telling Debbie right now. Right this minute."

Mama Stewart moved to him, gathering him into her arms like the broken boy he was. His whole body shook—reliving every body pulled from those waters, every life the river claimed. She stroked his hair as he sobbed.

"I tried to stop it." The words tore out of him. "The cops had him, and I got the money together to pay the bribe. Sneak him out. I tried—God, I tried to get to him, before... before. But I couldn't. I failed Debbie. I failed her, and I promised her I wouldn't."

Mama Stewart held him tighter, her eyes closing against her own tears. "This is war, baby. This is war."

* * *

THE KITCHEN FELT TOO small for grief this size. Kathy watched her mother cradle the phone between her cheek and shoulder as she packed lunches of fried chicken and biscuits for the journey. She murmured comfort to a shattered Debbie and relayed details on their return. Kathy had already packed her things and Ely's for the trip. The Reverend and the Jensens were all there, fretting and worrying over Big Mama, who had collapsed into inconsolable grief as her father raged and was restrained several times by the men of Butts outside.

"Let me talk to her," Kathy said.

Brenda handed over the phone like it weighed a thousand pounds, kissing Kathy's forehead before retreating to get totes to bring the food for the family with them.

"Debs?" Kathy asked.

Sobbing. Raw, broken sobbing was all that answered.

Kathy closed her eyes and silently cried, but tried to speak coherently through it. "Debbie, I'm so... so sorry. I didn't know when you called earlier. I'm..."

"It's okay," Debbie said. "I'm sorry, Kat. I'm sorry for what I did. I just wanted to believe them when they said the marriage was nothing, that you and Carmelo were already married, and then he had babies with her, and I didn't know how to tell you—."

"Debs. I don't care. We'll never talk about it again. Uncle Pete..." Kathy broke. Debbie cried as well. They cried together for a stretch, taken in with grief. Kathy put her back to the wall and tried to catch her breath. "We're coming, Debs. All of us. Hold on, okay?"

"I can't. I need Matteo. I need—"

"I know."

"Mama's dying, Kat. She's giving up. And Daddy—" The scream that followed was primal. "THEY BEAT HIM TO DEATH! THEY THREW HIM IN THE RIVER LIKE TRASH!"

"Listen to me." Kathy's voice turned steel. "We're coming. And whoever did this—they're going to pay, damnit."

They said their goodbyes, and Kathy hung up the phone, then gripped the sink for strength. She closed her eyes and counted down the rising rage inside of her, not sure where it was surfacing from. She did her best not to submerge herself in it. But she wanted it. She could taste it, she wanted it so bad. This pain would push her family to the brink. Nothing would ever be the same.

* * *

"CARMELO?" Maria's voice was barely a whisper.

She pushed open the door to his office—what used to be the guest room before he'd transformed it into his center of operations. Ledgers sprawled across the desk, each line a thread in the web he was weaving by understanding his father's financial empire.

"What do you want?" He didn't bother looking up.

Her sigh carried the weight of their marriage.

Finally, his gaze lifted. Maria stood in the doorway like a 1950s housewife—pressed dress, perfect hair, their daughter on her hip. Nina's toothless smile melted something in his face, and Maria knew enough to seize the moment. She crossed the room and placed the baby in his arms.

Carmelo's hands—the same ones that had been such a powerful weapon of destruction in the ring—cradled Nina with infinite gentleness. He kissed her forehead, breathing in her fresh baby smell. She was a gem, his heart.

"Two men are here to see you." Maria kept her voice neutral. "And Matteo's called three times. He says it's urgent—"

"I said no calls." But his voice stayed soft as he lifted Nina over his head, delighting in her giggles of the baby and kicking feet. One more kiss, a tickle under her chin, then he handed her back. "Send the men in."

Maria took their daughter, her eye roll saying everything her mouth couldn't. The moment the door closed, Carmelo returned to his ledger, squinting then lifting a magnifying glass to inspect the numbers so cramped they made his head pound. His father's consigliere was worthless—couldn't even keep proper books.

He'd have him replaced soon.

"Boss?"

Carmelo recognized the voice before he saw them—Midas and Luigi the Fish, his father's top capos. Luigi still carried the stench of his fixer days, a mix of formaldehyde and river water that no amount of cologne could mask. These were his eyes on Harlem's streets, reporting to him first on every shift in power since Bumpy's arrest.

"Did you find him?" Carmelo asked.

The men exchanged a look that made his stomach drop.

"Did you look for Pete Freeman?" His voice sharpened. "Bumpy's enforcer? I told you—anyone named Freeman was untouchable. Did you find him?"

Luigi shifted his weight. "Boss, we looked, but your father... he gave an order."

"What order?" The words came out dangerously quiet.

"We had to check in, boss. He—" Luigi faltered. "Tell him, Midas."

Midas swallowed hard. "Don Ricci said any order from you has to go through him. When we checked in about Freeman, he overruled. Called the cops, holding him. Told them to... handle it."

Carmelo rose slowly, his hands flat on the desk. "He did what?"

"Word on the street is they pulled him from the Hudson this morning." Midas couldn't meet his eyes. "He's dead, boss."

"I gave you an order!" The lamp was in his hand before he realized it, hurled across the room to explode against the wall inches from Midas's head.

"GET OUT! NOW!"

They fled. Carmelo sank into his chair, the truth hitting him like cold water. He'd sent them to save Pete Freeman. Instead, he'd painted a target on the man's back. His father had used his own rescue attempt as a death sentence.

He'd just killed Kathy's uncle.

He got up and rushed out of the office into the parlor where the phone was. He should have the fucking phone in his office. He dialed Matteo's place in East Harlem, and his brother never answered. He shook all over with panic and braved the call to his father.

"Hi, need to speak to Pa," he told his mother-in-law.

"He just left, sweetie. Is there something you need—"

He slammed the phone down hard enough to crack it. Breathing hard, he felt a surge of panic rising in his chest.

"Melo? You okay?" Maria asked.

"Get away from me," he said, trying to catch his breath. Thankfully, she didn't listen. She came over to him and touched his forehead. Carmelo couldn't breathe; his face turned red as a beet.

"Calm down. Calm down," Maria said patiently. She took his hands. "Breathe, Melo. Breathe."

He closed his eyes and breathed out of his mouth and through his nose, the way Maria was doing in front of him. Finally, the seizures in his chest stopped. But they were replaced by insurmountable fear. He burst into tears. Maria gathered him into her arms and held him. He had no choice but to hold on to her. He had no one. He had killed Pete Freeman, and Kathy would never forgive him.

CHAPTER 37

AFTERMATH - HARLEM 1952

José maneuvered his car close to the curb; the streetlights cast long shadows across the dashboard. "What time should I come back?"

Debbie juggled her belongings while balancing Junior in her arms. His chubby fingers reached desperately toward José as he called him Pa-Pee because Papa was for Matteo. "You heading over to Sam's?"

"Yeah, he's making his famous pot roast. He sends all his love, Debs." The words came out thick, weighted with unspoken grief.

She nodded, biting the inside of her cheek to keep composure. Her eyes caught the chrome gleam of Matteo's motorcycle parked beneath the flickering neon of Mama Stewart's Diner. Drawing in a shaky breath, she said, "I'll call you. They've sedated Mama—she needs the rest. Brother's already gone to the streets, and Ms. Gladys brought the church to sit vigil, so... I can't stay there." She paused, gathering strength. "I need to prepare myself for tomorrow. And right now, I need Matteo. Pick me up first thing in the morning?"

"What about the train? When do they arrive."

"Not until the afternoon. We'll all gather at Uncle Henry's when the family arrives."

"I'll request the day off. Count on me," José promised.

Debbie leaned in and pressed a kiss of gratitude to his stubbled cheek. He made no effort to hide the tears that slid down his face. Pete had become like a second father to him after the wedding—their lavender marriage (a term that José taught her) had blossomed into a genuine family.

She stepped out of the car and hurried toward their door. Before her hand touched the knob, it swung open. Matteo pulled her inside. He wrapped them both in his arms. Junior, caught between his parents, squealed in mild protest.

Debbie's bags hit the floor as something broke inside her. The sobs tore from her throat, violent and unstoppable. Matteo half-carried her inside, prying Junior from her shaking arms.

"How's Mama?" he asked, shifting the baby to his hip.

"She isn't good. Matteo? Can't—can't breathe—," Debbie panted.

Matteo helped her to the sofa, placing Junior on her lap. The toddler immediately cried out, reaching for his father. Matteo scooped him up again and headed to the kitchen. He returned with cognac over ice instead of water. She accepted it gratefully, sipping slowly as she tried to steady her breathing.

Matteo dropped beside her, pulling her tight against his side. She turned, buried her face in the crook of his underarm, still shaking. Junior's babbling filled the silence, punctuated by Matteo's ridiculous fish faces and the baby's resulting shrieks of laughter. His steady presence, his unflinching care—it was slowly taming the wild grief clawing at her insides. But part of her wanted to keep crying, terrified that if she stopped, she'd lose her grip on her father completely. The contradiction was driving her mad.

"They tortured him." The words scraped out of Debbie's throat as she clawed her way back from despair.

"Debs, don't—" Matteo's voice cracked.

She buried her face in his chest, sobbing hard. Junior's tiny fingers tangled in her hair. He tried to soothe. Matteo crushed them both against him, as if he could shield them from the horror. And tears slipped down his face, as his own trauma from his mother's suicide surfaced.

An hour crawled by. Junior had escaped earlier, leaving a trail of toys, but now he stumbled back, climbing Matteo like a tree before collapsing against his father's chest and putting his thumb in his mouth.

"I should put him to bed," Debbie mumbled, swaying as she stood. The cognac hit hard. He'd poured enough.

Matteo caught her hand. Moving like a man in a dream, he locked up the place, killed the lights, and pulled her upstairs.

Junior's crib waited in their room for nights like these, when closeness mattered most. And Matteo never truly slept, always ready for his son's escape attempts from the crib in the middle of the night.

He stripped the boy down with practiced efficiency, changing him quickly.

"Didn't bathe him. Can't remember if he ate." Debbie's words came out broken. "Can't remember anything today."

His eyes found hers in the dark. "I've got him, Debs."

She leaned against the doorframe, watching. Her gangster. Her baby's father. More tender with their son than she'd ever dreamed possible. Better than she deserved. The thought ambushed her with memories of her father's gentle hands when she was a girl, of how she had migrated from Mississippi with him, riding upon his sturdy shoulders. He was a stern disciplinarian, but he'd only taken his belt to her twice in life. He was their rock. He broke his back and bent his knee before men lesser than him to give his family all he could. His patient teaching and silent love carved her into the woman she would become.

Matteo looked back to see Debbie shivering and on the verge of another emotional collapse. She wore a dress and no shoes. He pulled the blanket up over his son and went to her.

"Want to take a shower?" he asked softly, thumbs brushing the tears from her cheeks.

She nodded, unable to speak.

He pulled her to the bathroom and left the doors open. Matteo was always listening for Junior. His hands were careful and tender as he peeled away her clothes. He did his best not to make any of his actions sexual. Though even distressed Debbie undressed made his loins ache. He reached in and twisted the taps to turn on the water until steam billowed.

Matteo stripped and followed her in. The warm water pounded her shoulders while he soaped her back with firm strokes, then turned her to wash her front. His hands moved with purpose—cleaning, caring. He barely rinsed himself, urgent to get her warm and dry.

Within minutes, he guided them back to their bedroom, where Junior slept peacefully in his crib.

"Matteo?" She said in barely a whisper.

"What is it?" He tucked her into bed, skin against skin.

"Do you think—was it bad? The torture?" Her voice cracked.

"Your father was iron, Debs. Whatever they did, he didn't give them satisfaction. Hell, he probably put a couple in the ground before they finished him."

She shattered again. He wrapped himself around her, blankets sealing them in. She pressed into his chest, wrung out and hollow.

"When Mama's stronger, I'm telling her everything. About us. How you've saved us—me and Junior—over and over. With Magdalena. And now. You're my guardian angel, Matteo. God's gift."

His smile felt like broken glass. She didn't know the truth—the bodies he'd left cooling in their own blood, the screams he'd drawn out with his blade on those who survived. She knew only this version: lover, protector, father. Not the Butcher who stalked through nightmares, and took the aggression Cosimo sealed in him out on the guilty and deserving. He'd keep it that way.

"Debs, when the dust settles, I've got plans for us. Vegas, just as we talked about. We'll go without my father's blessing—I'm building my own connections now. We'll bring your mother, find her the best doctors money can buy. Get the hell out of New York while we can." His voice dropped lower. "What's coming... it won't be good, baby. Mama Stewart warned me it would be bloody. She said Harlem would strike back, and that's exactly what my father's counting on. It's how he'll convince the other families to unite—to wipe Harlem off the map. This is going to be war, Debs. I won't have you and Junior anywhere near it."

The room fell silent.

He glanced down to find her breathing steady against his chest, lost to exhausted sleep. Matteo released a long breath, his gaze fixed on the shadows dancing across the ceiling.

"It's going to be war," he whispered to the darkness.

* * *

MATTEO'S BREATHING came faster and sudden. The need for oxygen brought his consciousness out of the deep sleep he'd finally achieved before his mind could grapple with the intense seizing in his dick. The strikingly hot shots of pleasure in his pelvis that spread heat through his balls. His back arched up on the bed, and his jaw clenched through a deep guttural grunt.

Debbie nearly swallowed his dick. She suctioned her jaws harder, and her tongue did a loving glide over his stalk as her head bobbed beneath the sheet. He lifted the sheet to look down the line of his body. His hips moved and rolled involuntarily from the assault. And his woman gave him the dick-suck of his life.

"Damn it, Debs, stop," he said, but he wanted her to go further.

She let him go before he released. His hips buckled in response. She grinned and came up on him. Straddling him. He looked over to their son and saw he was still asleep. She was on him again. Her hand gripped the head of his cock and fed it into her pussy before he could stop her.

"Deb's please… I can't control it."

"No. I need it. I don't want to dream anymore. I need you," she said.

Debbie, José, and her son lived by Matteo's rules—unspoken laws he'd established to protect what mattered most. This particular one remained unbreakable: their intimate moments would never touch the same space where Junior slept. Usually, they could leave him with José for a few hours. But Matteo, bound by old-world sensibilities, insisted on absolute separation even when that wasn't possible. On those nights, he'd lead her to the bathroom across the hall or press her against the wall outside their bedroom door—anywhere but near their sleeping son. She understood his fierce need to preserve Junior's innocence, to shield him from every shadow of the adult world. Still, in her heart where he lived as her faithful husband, she sometimes yearned for the simple normalcy of sharing their bed without calculation or compromise.

Debbie rode his dick hard and fast. Matteo was powerless to stop her. The passion unleashed from her was wild. Her tongue licked over his chest, neck, and lips. Her pussy tightened and never released or compromised. He looked over and saw his son stir and panicked. He had to please his woman. Somehow, do it without her mounting cries of pleasure disturbing Junior. He flipped her and pinned her down. He kissed her to keep her cries of passion muffled. He fucked her slowly to settle the urgency in her and deliver the release she needed. And masterfully, he got her there, just as Junior sat up. Debbie climaxed with her hands pinned down and mouth gaping. He could not. Though he desperately wanted it. He wanted it badly. When his son stood in the crib and stared at their moving bodies, he quit.

"Damn it, Matteo!" she cursed.

"Don't swear around Junior Debs," he said and left her. He pulled on his pants to bury his angry cock and reached for Junior, who immediately began to cry for his attention.

"I'll make him a bottle," Matteo said and headed for the door.

"He's too old for bottles!" she shouted after him.

They were gone. She rolled her eyes and turned over in bed, less than satisfied. But soon her anger dissolved. She had to smile. Though her heart was shattered, her hope was still there. She had Matteo, and in his imperfect world, he was perfectly perfect for her and Junior.

* * *

THE TRAIN CUT through midnight darkness. Ely had fallen asleep against the window, his breath fogging the glass in small, rhythmic clouds. Kathy snapped her journal shut and stared at him. The guilt hit like a physical thing—sharp, relentless, piercing her heart. This man had destroyed another woman to be with her. He'd asked for nothing, given everything, and where had it gotten him? On a train racing toward Harlem and her father's bloody vendetta. His peaceful life in Butts might as well have been a dream now. She'd done this to him. Her salvation had become his cause.

Her fingers found his cheek, memorizing the planes of his face. She loved this man—God, how she loved him—more than she'd thought possible. But love and passion were different creatures, and that distinction would remain forever unspoken. Ely's sacrifice demanded her absolute loyalty, which made returning to Harlem feel like walking into a trap. Carmelo existed there like a lit match near gasoline. What if her resolve crumbled? What if he said her name just right, looked at her that certain way? She could never face him alone again. The child they shared inside of her whispered his name in her dreams. She needed backup—someone who could keep her anchored when the past came calling.

Across the narrow aisle, her mother slept peacefully against her father's thigh. He sat wakeful, lost in the black landscape streaming past the train window. Another soul too troubled for rest.

Something made him glance her way. Their eyes met, and he offered that subtle wink that had always meant "everything will be alright, baby girl, daddy has you." Her smile was almost bashful. She pressed her hand to her heart and nodded—I love you—a gesture they'd shared since she was small. He returned it without hesitation. The exchange loosened the tight insecurity and worry in her chest. Maybe she could do this—return to Harlem as Ely's wife, carrying her secret child, protected by these two good men and faith.

Maybe not.

CHAPTER 38

THE FAMILY THAT SLAYS TOGETHER STAYS TOGETHER

Three days blurred together like watercolors in the rain. In the eye of this storm, Kathy and Debbie held each other steady. The bakery's familiar rhythms provided sanctuary from two unbearable extremes: the suffocating grief that enveloped the family and friends of gentle giant Pete Freeman, and the men's hushed conferences that reeked of gunpowder and revenge.

"Kathy?" Debbie called from the kitchen doorway, still wearing her work apron. The evening's last customer had gone, and Kathy finished counting out wages for their helpers. Now they just had to wait for Brother to drive them home.

"Sit. You need to rest," Debbie insisted, bringing over a sandwich and a tall glass of water.

Kathy's stomach growled with hunger, but she'd grown accustomed to long days of labor. Hard work had become her constant companion. With Uncle Pete's death rocking the family to its core, it would remain so. She and Debbie would run Kathy's Sweets until Ely and her Daddy decided otherwise.

She walked over, ready to get off her feet.

The reunion between cousins had remained pleasant, comforting, and natural for one solid reason. They both ignored their shared history with the Ricci brothers and made small talk about Harlem gossip.

"So you and Ely are staying in my bedroom, huh?" Debbie asked.

Kathy chewed on the sandwich and nodded. "Yep, I can be close to Auntie. I know you got a lot on your hands with Junior. Plus, home is a nonstop traffic of Bumpy's men now under the control of Daddy. He brought back so many men from Butts. I figured they could take my room," Kathy reasoned.

Debbie studied her.

Kathy looked up. "What?"

"You haven't been home in so long. You avoiding the place?"

"No. I just told you," Kathy rolled her eyes.

"I know Auntie Brenda misses you. And I figured you would want to stay in your old room. You know."

"Well, I don't wanna," Kathy mumbled. "Your place is fine."

Debbie nodded. She took a deep breath and tried a different approach at conversation: "I heard Brother last night. He was talking to his crew and José at my house. They had come by." Debbie's gaze lifted. She waited for Kathy to look up, but Kathy ate her sandwich, keeping her eyes down. "They are planning to do something in Queens on the day of the funeral. I don't know what, but… I'm worried."

Kathy ate in silence, just chewing.

"I ah, Kat, my son. I…" Deb's voice faltered. "I have to think of him, his father." There was a pause. "I think I should tell Matteo that Harlem is retaliating if we are going to war. If my brother goes after the Italians, he could be the next target. Right?"

Kathy set down what was left of her sandwich. "Are you loyal to anyone other than Matteo, Debs?"

"How could you say that to me? My Daddy just died!" Debbie frowned.

"How could you think about going to the Ricci's when they killed him?" Kathy asked.

Debbie stared at her for a moment, then dropped her head in sadness. "Not the Riccis. Don Cosimo killed him. Matteo tried to stop it. Uncle Henry said he found out that Daddy…" Debbie paused on the emotion clogging her throat. "He said that Cosimo Ricci paid the cops to kill Daddy. He knows it for a fact."

Kathy looked away. When Kathy turned her gaze back to Debbie, she was on the verge of tears. "How could you keep it from me, Debs?"

Debbie bit down on her bottom lip. "It didn't happen the way you think."

"Then how! HOW DID IT HAPPEN!" Kathy shouted.

"God, Kat, you have no idea how bad it was after their mother's suicide, do you? I called you. I was going insane. Everyone across the city said Matteo was hurting people. And Carmelo—Jesus, he didn't just break down. Something in him died, like his soul got ripped out. He was begging me and José for help like some lost little boy. I told him… I told him—."

"What? What did you tell him?" Kathy asked.

Debbie sobbed.

"WHAT!" Kathy demanded.

"God help me, but I told him to be a man for once. To be the man. To do something! Then it all exploded. Carmelo went home, got the gun, and shot his father, and suddenly the mob went insane. I saw them bring Don Ricci in off the streets, bleeding. They took him into Mama Stewart's."

Kathy's eyes stretched, though pooling with tears. "Why Mama Stewart?"

Debbie wiped her tears away. "Turns out she's some nurse for the Mafia. She used to work to heal folks. It's where all this stuff with him and her begins, I guess."

"Oh?" Kathy said, hiding her discomfort. She didn't want to open a door to her heart again; she closed it the night she made her vow to Ely to be his.

"Carmelo, after the shooting, was beaten up by Ricci's men for shooting his father. They brought him and Nino into Mama Stewarts. I don't know what happened in that meeting, but he was different the next time I saw him, Kat. Very different. He came over to my place one night early in the morning. He came with Nino, begging me to hide Nino and watch over him while he went in search of Matteo before… the other families found him. For two weeks, Matteo was out there turning Queens into a slaughterhouse. He went after everyone—soldiers, associates, anyone who'd ever worked with the families or for his father. The killing, Kat... knives, throats slit, butchery, I still don't believe the stories they tell about him. The papers called him New York's Jack the Ripper, the Butcher, hunting mobsters instead of women. The families wanted his head, the cops looked the other way. All I wanted was to find him and save him.

Kathy frowned. "You sure it was Matteo?"

"That's just it. If you saw him today with Junior, you wouldn't believe a word of what I'm saying. If you saw how sweet and protective he is with me and Junior. He's not some madman with a knife, hurting people. He's not a butcher."

Kathy shook her head in disbelief. "You can never know who someone truly is, Debs. Look at what you did, after everything you saw me go through to love Carmelo. You kept Carmelo's marriage and kids a secret from me for two years. You're my sister. My blood. And all you are doing is sitting here trying to get me to feel sorry for them? Who are you?" Kathy's voice broke, and tears welled in her eyes.

"Please let me finish explaining," Debbie pleaded.

Kathy rolled her eyes. "No, this is stupid! I'm a married woman now, and I have a—I have more important things to focus on."

"Please!" Debbie grabbed her arm and made her sit. "Please."

Kathy sat back down.

"Cosimo had been shot, and mob was divided," Debbie hurried to explain. "Mama Stewart stepped in to help. She sat me and Carmelo down and told us what would happen if we didn't find Matteo soon. The other families would take him out for attacking "made men," and then finish off Carmelo. Last would be Nino. In a year or two, Don Cosimo, with no family, would be exiled. The Ricci empire divided and given to the other four families. Carmelo had a chance to fix things because Don Ricci didn't die. He told the families that his son was sick with grief, and the other one is going insane. He saved his sons by telling them this, and from every corner of the Ricci family, we looked for Matteo. If we didn't find him, it would all end. This is their way. Their tradition. Their rules, Kathy."

"How did you find him?" Kathy asked.

"Mama Stewart said that she felt we would find him at his mother's grave. So for days, she had men watching it all through the night. And one night he appeared. But when they tried to approach him, he ran away." Kathy wiped her tears. "That made Carmelo remember a place their mother took them as kids. A place in Queens. He said that when Cosimo was mad at her or beat her, she would take them to a shelter with a church from her country. And there was a house there that was abandoned that they played at as kids. So he and I went. And that is where he was—drunk, dirty, unconscious in rats and filth. José picked him up and put him in the car. José and I took care of him while Carmelo worked on his father."

"Worked on him?" Kathy asked.

"Carmelo never breathed a word about finding Matteo. When Carmelo finally went to his father, he made what he still calls 'the devil's deal'. Kathy, it was all because of that letter. His mother wrote it before she jumped off that bridge. She said Carmelo was born to shield the family, not Matteo, and her sacrifice would guarantee he did it. She knew about you Kathy, and me, and her mind snapped. She demanded Carmelo marry that Italian girl to protect them all. So Carmelo said he negotiated for his brothers like his life depended on it. He'd obey his father completely, box, do whatever if Cosimo kept Nino out of those horrible institutions and found Matteo before the other families did. Mama Stewart spelled it out for us—without this deal, Cosimo would gladly serve Matteo up to all those grieving families just to gain some respectability. His reputation was in the toilet, with all the fractures in his family. The very next day after that wedding, you know what Carmelo did? Threw some clothes in a bag and took off for New Orleans. God's truth, he did. All that time, Kathy —he was trying to get back to you."

"He came home to her, though. Made babies," Kathy said, the words bitter even as Debbie's story lined up with what Carmelo had told her.

"Twins. And listen to me—it was killing him. He'd drink himself sick every time he had to leave you. Matteo told me Carmelo slept on the floor rather than share her bed. He was saving every penny from those boxing matches, planning to take you away somewhere safe. Then she claimed he got drunk and attacked her. He came to Matteo sobbing like a child, swearing he never touched her, terrified he'd lose you forever. He was coming apart at the seams, Kathy—trying to protect his family while holding onto you with both hands. When those babies came, he panicked. Begged me to keep it from you. He had this wild plan even Matteo didn't know about. He was going to steal from his father's operation and disappear with you to Vegas, had some connection with a Jewish gangster out there who'd protect you both."

Kathy went completely still, unable to speak as the truth settled over her like a shroud. She slumped in her seat, finally understanding. Carmelo had tried to tell her—she could see that now—but Aunt Janey's poison had already taken root. She'd been too furious to consider that maybe, just maybe, none of it had been planned.

"Kathy, honey... I tried everything to stop you from marrying Ely. Phone calls, letters, telegrams. I needed you to understand what was really happening here, but you'd already made up your mind."

The tears came hard and fast. Kathy's head fell forward as the weight of her mistake crushed down on her. "It's too late. I'm married now, Debs."

Debbie crossed to Kathy's side of the booth and gathered her close. They held each other the way only women who've known real loss can—fierce and gentle at once. Tears came freely, apologies tumbling over each other until the words themselves became a kind of healing.

"He never stopped loving you," Debbie murmured.

"I know. But it doesn't matter anymore." Kathy's voice was surprisingly calm. "We've been nothing but heartbreak from day one. Ely tried to warn me. You tried. Some loves are just... poison, Debs. I've made my peace with it."

"You're wrong. Everything good in my life—Matteo, Junior—exists because of what you and Carmelo had. That day at Magdalena's, when

I almost destroyed my baby, Matteo pulled me back from the edge. That's when I realized we're all connected by something bigger than this prejudice. We can't let their world or ours dictate our happiness."

"Maybe that's true for you. But I've spent three years becoming someone else in Butts. The girl you remember? She's gone. I don't belong here now. All I have left is my ba—" She stopped abruptly.

Debbie tilted her head, waiting.

"The bakery," Kathy corrected quietly. "Just the bakery and old memories."

"Kat, don't do this—"

"Brother will be here any minute. We should finish closing."

Debbie sighed deeply but moved away, understanding the dismissal. Left alone, Kathy allowed herself one last moment of grief before locking it away. She'd made her choices, played her part in this mess. Changing the past was impossible, and Carmelo couldn't be her future—not when she had a child to think about. She swore to herself she'd never look back, though even as she made the vow, she recognized its fragility. After all, every promise she'd ever made with her heart had eventually crumbled.

CHAPTER 39

THE DAY OF THE DEAD

The bells of Abyssinian Baptist Church tolled across Harlem like a heartbeat gone slow. From 138th Street to Lenox Avenue, people pressed against police barricades, handkerchiefs dabbing at eyes, voices rising in spontaneous hymns. Pete Freeman was going home.

Debbie had dressed little Junior in a little suit her mother had sewn in her grief. She smoothed his collar again, needing something to do with her hands, needing to avoid the eyes that cut toward her from every direction.

The Abyssinian Baptist Church had never felt smaller. Every pew groaned with Harlem royalty—numbers runners, jazz musicians, politicians, and hustlers all pressed together in their grief. The stained glass windows cast colored shadows across faces twisted with loss and fury. Her father lay in his bronze casket at the altar, and Uncle Henry sat stone-faced in the front row, accepting condolences like a king receiving tribute. He'd stepped into Bumpy's shoes without hesitation, and everyone knew what that meant. Blood would answer blood.

Kathy had almost turned back twice on the church steps. The last time she'd been inside Abyssinian, she'd been seventeen and in love with a boy her family called an enemy. Now she was twenty, married to another man, carrying Carmelo Ricci's child beneath her black mourning dress. Ely guided her to a middle pew, his presence both shield and reminder of how thoroughly she'd destroyed her life. The organ swelled with "Precious Lord," and she gripped the pew in front of her, nauseated by more than pregnancy. Somewhere in this crowd were men who'd kill her, despite who her father was, if they knew whose baby grew inside her. Somewhere outside, even more men circled Queens, ready to strike first against the Riccis and ignite the never-ending war between Harlem and Queens. The war everyone whispered about had already begun; they didn't know she carried its future in her womb.

* * *

THE FUNERAL PASSED in a haze of hymns and tears, both Kathy and Debbie trapped in their private agonies. When Claire's tremors worsened, Debbie pressed Junior into Kathy's arms without a word. Her mother's illness couldn't handle this kind of stress—already Claire could barely hold herself upright, her body betraying her in waves of distress.

"I'm here, Mama," Debbie whispered, supporting her mother's shaking frame. "I've got you."

Kathy bounced Junior gently, grateful for the distraction of his fussing as she watched her own parents. Her father sat like a monument—back straight, eyes fixed on his brother's casket. Her mother's hand moved from his neck to the space between his shoulder blades, her lips moving in what Kathy knew were words of comfort. But Henry Freeman might as well have been carved from marble for all the response he gave.

The procession from church to cemetery felt like a small mercy. Settled in the back of the chauffeured car, Kathy finally let herself breathe. She'd survived the church service. Now just the graveside ceremony remained before she could retreat to the bakery—her only refuge from the chaos threatening to swallow her whole.

"You okay?" Ely's voice was gentle.

She glanced up at him, Junior warm and heavy against her chest. When Ely reached over to cradle the baby's tiny hand, she saw it again —that soft light in his eyes whenever he was near children. It was why she'd chosen him. In Butts, he'd built more than a school and recreation center; he'd created a world where forgotten children mattered. Every swimming hole cleared, every baseball diamond carved from nothing was proof of the father he'd be.

"I'm worried about Aunt Claire," she admitted. "And Debbie."

The image haunted her—Brother carrying Claire's limp body from the church while Debbie stumbled behind, José's arms the only thing keeping her upright.

"I'm sorry, Kat. For all of it."

She managed a small smile. "I know you are."

The procession rolled to a stop at Woodlawn Cemetery. Ely shifted Junior into his arms with practiced ease, then took her hand for the walk to the graveside tent. Her family had already gathered—Claire propped between Brother and Debbie, the others arranged in a protective circle. Above them, storm clouds gathered like an omen. Kathy shivered despite the heat. Whatever was coming for them had already begun.

* * *

IT STARTED WITH WHISPERS—URGENT, shocked, rippling through the mourners like a spreading fire. Kathy's head came up slowly, dread pooled in her stomach as she watched faces twist with disbelief and rage.

"What is it?" Kathy asked.

Ely craned his neck. His eyes searched the crowd. She watched his expression transform from confusion to fury. "It can't be. The fucking Riccis are here."

"What?" But even as the word left her lips, Kathy turned, searching. Through gaps in the crowd, she caught glimpses—sharp suits, watchful faces, the unmistakable lines of made men. Her attention flew to her father at the graveside. His lieutenant was already there, whispering urgently. Still, Henry Freeman continued his ritual—placing the lily on his brother's casket with the same measured grace, as if the enemy hadn't just walked into his brother's funeral. The men lowered the coffin into the grave on long straps, and after it went in, her father gave the first shovel of dirt.

Her heart forgot how to beat.

Across the space, Debbie's terrified gaze locked with hers. They both knew what this meant—Matteo and Carmelo, here, now, when wounds were still bleeding. The audacity of it stole her breath.

The Freeman family moved together. Brother guided his mother's unsteady steps as they emerged from the tent's shelter. Twenty yards away, the Ricci family waited in perfect symmetry. Don Cosimo stood at the apex, Carmelo and Matteo flanked him like twin threats, soldiers—one to his left and the other to his right. Kathy marveled at how much of a man Carmelo now looked next to his father and brother. Before, she only saw the boy she loved.

Without a word, Ely handed Junior to José, his hand tightening and going protective over Kathy. Each step forward felt like walking to her execution. Even through dark sunglasses, she felt Carmelo's stare. She fought not to look at him. She reminded herself that it was over. That they both had failed each other. She was married. That was that. Still, her eyes betrayed her, and she was drawn to him like a compass finding north.

Then Ely's arm settled around her shoulders, claiming her. Everything changed.

The spell she had over Carmelo broke, and he took note of Ely. Even under the cover of his dark sunglasses, Kathy saw his attention shift to her husband ever so slightly. The shift in Carmelo's stature was instantaneous—from focused intensity to something volcanic. Even behind sunglasses, his rage breathed through him. Out of protective instinct, she felt the need to shield Ely. She'd seen Carmelo dangerous before, but never had she feared him. Never had she seen his deadliness aimed at someone she'd sworn to protect.

Junior's shriek split the air. "Papa! Papa!" His little body fought José's hold, arms reaching desperately for Matteo.

Time stopped.

Don Cosimo's gaze swiveled to his son with lethal speculation. The look that passed between father and son could have frozen blood. Henry noticed—of course, he noticed—so did Claire and Brother. Debbie stood rigid, frozen. Henry's suspicion of Debbie passed, and his face remained stone as he stopped the family march to the Ricci's and faced off with the Don. José slipped away with a wailing Junior in his arms, pulling poor Debbie away with him.

Matteo might have been carved from ice for all the reaction he showed to his son's cries. But Kathy saw the pain in his eyes as he watched her go.

"Henry Freeman." Don Cosimo's voice boomed with self-appointed authority. "On behalf of the Five Families and Lucky Luciano himself, I offer our deepest sympathies. Pete Freeman was an old-school man—a man who understood honor. And Bumpy Johnson remains the soul of Harlem, even in his current circumstances. When men like them fall, the whole city bleeds."

Kathy saw her mother's touch on her father's sleeve—gentle as a butterfly, strong as steel.

"Your sympathies mean nothing to me or my dead brother," Henry said quietly, and somehow the soft tone was more terrifying than shouting. "But I'll take your message to Bumpy when I see him. As for Harlem bleeding..." Henry's smile was winter itself. "We've bled before. We survive. We rebuild. And we remember. Harlem's been teaching this mob lessons for decades, now. Not the other way around," he paused a beat. No one else dared speak. "Here's another one: our territory is baptized in Peter Freeman's blood. Any Italian who forgets where Harlem begins and ends will get a personal geography lesson. Written in their own blood. By my command."

Don Cosimo chuckled. "You're King now?"

Henry held the Don's glare.

Don Cosimo said something in Italian to all of his men, who chuckled, except for his sons. He glanced at Carmelo and leaned in and whispered in his son's ear.

To Kathy's shock and horror, Carmelo nodded. He turned his gaze to her father. “My father understands this is a time for accounting. However, he is a generous man. You are mourning. He will forgive the disrespect. When you are ready, Mr. Freeman, he will be too.”

Henry smirked, and the gold tooth in his mouth gleamed.

“Stay ready, son,” Henry Freeman said. He leaned a bit forward and held Carmelo’s gaze. “I’m coming for you, too.”

Carmelo gave a curt nod of respect and a sly smile in return.

The mob turned and left. Not before Carmelo shot Kathy one last look and another to Ely, before he turned and walked away. Feeling faint, Kathy closed her eyes and lowered her head. Henry and the family stayed in place and didn’t move or retreat. They didn’t even speak until the last car driving the Ricci’s out of the cemetery was unseen.

* * *

"LET'S LEAVE," Kathy said from the brownstone's stoop. She watched Ely pace the sidewalk. "Please, Ely. Let's go back to Butts."

He didn't seem to hear her over the chaos of his own thoughts. Back and forth he went, past the corner boys who'd abandoned their dice games to stand around and watch, past the old women who'd pulled their children inside. Through the open windows came the voices of men—her father's lieutenants crowding their parlor. Outside, more men loaded crates into Buick trunks, the metallic sounds unmistakable. She didn't want to know what those crates held.

"Ely!"

He jerked to a stop, focusing on her with visible effort. The hardness in his face melted. "Hey, it's okay. We're okay."

"No. We're not." She gripped her knees to stop them shaking. "You saw what happened at the cemetery. They declared war right there over Uncle Pete's grave. Daddy won't let this go. He'll turn every gun in Harlem against the Italians. My mother knows it. Big Mama knows it. Don't pretend you don't."

Ely's examination made her squirm. "He affected you."

"What?"

"Carmelo. Seeing him today—it upset you."

"I don't give a damn about Carmelo!" But even she heard the protest ring hollow. "That's done. I married you, didn't I?"

"We both know why, Kathy." No accusation, just quiet truth. "At least be honest."

"I've been nothing but honest, Ely. From the moment I chose you, I shut that door. Locked it. I don't care about his looks or his anger. This baby and I—we're yours. That's the only truth that matters." She stood, needing to move. "So let's go home to Butts. Let Harlem do what Harlem does."

"Abandon them? Now?" He gestured at the brownstone, at the neighborhood, at all of it. "Your father's drowning in grief. Your family is under siege. And you won't even sleep in your childhood bed —you're camping out all day at the bakery, hiding in bed with me at Debbie's parents'. The Freemans became my family when I married you. We don't run. We unite."

"At what cost?" The tears ambushed him. "You think I chose this? You think I don't know I caused it all?"

That stopped him cold. "What?"

Everything tumbled out in a rush. "That attic. The sneaking around, the lies. New Orleans, Chicago, North Carolina…"

"Stop it, Kathy!" he pleaded.

"No. If I'd listened to you, if I'd been the daughter they raised me to be, Uncle Pete would be at Daddy's side right now."

Ely crossed the space between them in a heartbeat, sinking to one knee on the step below her. His hands found hers, solid as anchors. "Look at me. Kathy. Look at me."

She linked her gaze to his.

"You didn't kill Uncle Pete. You didn't start this war. You loved a boy your family called an enemy—that's not a crime. You've already paid too high a price for being a good person. We're not looking backward anymore, not with our child coming. Understood?" Ely asked.

She nodded, not trusting him or herself.

"Tell your mother about the baby. She needs something good to hold onto. Let me stand with your father. Then, when the payback is done, we'll go home even if Harlem burns. You have my word."

"Why tell her? Why now?"

"Because our child is not a secret to be ashamed of. You saw what happened with Junior reaching for Matteo. The whole cemetery saw. Debbie had to leave in shame." His voice grew fierce. "That will never be us. You have nothing to be ashamed of. Do you hear me?"

"I hear you, Ely." The smile surprised her.

He stood. He kissed the ring he spent his entire savings on to put on her hand. He pulled her against him, and she let herself be held. When they separated, she scrubbed her face clean and straightened her spine. Hand in hand, they climbed the steps and crossed the threshold she'd been avoiding. The house of her childhood waited, transformed now into a council of war. But she was done running from it.

CHAPTER 40

REVENGE OR REPRIEVE?

Kathy opened her bedroom door and froze. The familiar scents—lavender sachets, old books, her mother's cooking she'd sneak from the fridge to eat on the bed while thumbing through magazines—rushed over her. Despite evidence of houseguests scattered about, the room's essence remained unchanged.

She could see it clearly: three years old, Daddy triumphant after escaping the tenements, tossing her onto this bed like she weighed nothing. His fingers found every ticklish spot while she begged for mercy through helpless giggles. Then both of them sat beside the bed, hands clasped, blessing their new home and praying that Mama would hurry with lunch. God, she'd been lucky.

The luck had turned double-edged.

Having parents who loved that hard meant knowing exactly what you'd lost when life took pieces away. She crossed to her dresser, muscle memory guiding her to the drawer with the false bottom. The hiding spot stood empty—those letters to Carmelo had made the journey to Butts with her—but the gesture alone summoned fresh pain.

"Kathy?"

"Yes, Ma?" She quickly wiped her face, turning with practiced brightness. "Hey!"

"Hey, yourself. Danny-boy said you wanted to talk?" Brenda closed the door softly.

The moment it clicked shut, Kathy flew into her mother's arms. They stood there, holding each other up, tears mingling on shoulders that had carried too much. Brenda pulled back first, studying her daughter with fierce pride.

"My baby girl. All grown up and married. So beautiful. I know I fought letting you go, didn't understand your father's decisions. But seeing you with Ely..." She touched Kathy's cheek. "Maybe it was all part of God's plan."

Kathy stepped back. "Is it God's plan, Ma? Or just the consequences of my choices?"

"Kathy—?"

"You heard Junior. You heard him call Matteo 'Papa.'"

"Children that age get confused—"

"He's not confused, Ma. That's his father."

Brenda aged ten years in an instant. "Even if—we never say it. You understand? Never. This family can't take another blow."

"Ma, I have to tell you something." The dam broke. "Everything that's happened—Debbie and Matteo, this war, Uncle Pete—it all started with me and Carmelo. I'm the match that lit this fire."

"Baby, that's not—"

"Please. Sit. Let me tell you all of it." Kathy retreated from reaching hands. "You're all I have left who might understand."

"I'm your mother. I'd die for you. Nothing you say changes that."

The story poured out—Janey, the arrangement, the baby, the brutal end with Carmelo. Brenda listened like a priest taking confession, wincing but never judging.

When it ended, Kathy felt emptied and clean. Silence settled after the last word. Her mother stared at the wall, reorganizing everything she thought she knew. At first, she couldn't look at Kathy. She kept shaking her head. Kathy felt the worst. Brenda closed her eyes at last and squeezed them tightly shut. She mouthed a prayer Kathy could not hear. When it was over, she stood slowly, as if it were painful to do. Kathy trembled with shame and grief. Her mother's rejection would be the nail in her coffin. She needed her mother above all else.

"Come here, baby. Mama's got you." Brenda said with open arms. Kathy collapsed against her, feeling twelve again. "All I know, all I focus on is my baby is having a baby. Another Elliot girl. Cause we are Elliot girls. Made from pain and strength. We take care of each other. Always."

"Yes, Mama," Kathy wept.

"We'll protect this child like we protect each other. With everything in us."

* * *

The Triangle Social Club blew at 3:47 AM. Windows blasted outward in a violent symphony of shattered glass, cascading everywhere. The blast turned night into day on Mulberry Street. Ely was already running, legs pumping hard against the pavement, when the concussive blast wave slammed into his back. He stumbled, his boots skidding, but sheer momentum and terror kept him upright. *Let the boys have hit their marks,* he prayed silently, the thought sharp and desperate amidst the chaos. If the plan held, Don Cosimo Ricci's jewel – the hallowed ground where the Don conducted his most crucial meetings with his mob ties – would be lit up like a Christmas tree and reduced to a smoldering skeleton by dawn.

But plans, especially bloody ones, have a way of turning into shit. The Riccis had been tipped off about Harlem's retaliation. While Slim's warning arrived too late to stop Ely's dynamite from tearing through the club, it gave the Riccis just enough time to arrive and spring their trap on Bumpy Johnson's men, who now answered to Henry Freeman.

Gunfire erupted, sudden and brutal, from three directions at once. The Harlem crew scattered like startled cats into the labyrinth of

Little Italy. Through the acrid haze of smoke and the leaping orange glare of the burning building, Ely caught a glimpse of Carmelo Ricci unfolding himself from the black bulk of a Cadillac. The flames illuminated his face, etching it with pure, cold fury. Across the chaos – the staccato gunfire, the shouts, the groan of collapsing timbers – their eyes locked.

"That's him! The tall one!" Carmelo's voice sliced through the din. "Nail him!"

Ely hit Hester Street at a dead sprint, lungs already raw and burning. Ricci's foot soldiers faltered behind him, swallowed by the chaos, but Carmelo came on, relentless and fast. Ely risked two frantic glances over his shoulder. Bullets whined past his ears, stitching the air where he'd just been – the chilling realization hit him like a physical blow: Carmelo wasn't just chasing; he was hunting to kill.

Ely ran into the mouth of a narrow alley off Hester, the sudden stench of decay thick in his throat as he slammed trash cans aside with his shoulder. He scrambled over a splintered wooden fence, the sharp *crack* of a bullet tearing through the space his head had been barely a heartbeat before. *How the hell could he shoot and run at the same time with such accuracy?* He dropped hard onto the cobbles of the next alley and was moving again before his knees fully registered the impact. Terror surged within. He could die. He could actually die after all these years of waiting and dreaming of Kathy as his wife; he'd die and lose the chance to love her before their life began.

He was a fucking idiot.

He should have listened to her.

He made a vow to God that if he got back to her, he'd never take such risks again.

The heavy, determined *pound* of Carmelo's footsteps was closing the distance. A bullet sparked viciously off the iron rungs of a fire escape just above him, showering sparks like angry fireflies. Another *thwacked* into a brick wall inches from his shoulder, spraying stinging sparks. Desperate, he cut left into the deeper gloom of a connecting alleyway and skidded to a halt on loose gravel. Solid brick walls, stained and unforgiving, rose on three sides. Overflowing trash cans blocked any possible crevice.

A dead end.

The cloying reek of rot filled his nostrils.

Nowhere to run.

"Turn around." Carmelo's voice was steady, unnervingly calm despite the chase, cutting through Ely's ragged gasps for air.

Ely turned slowly, hands raised palms-out, but muscles coiled. Carmelo stood silhouetted against the alley's entrance, pistol unwavering, aimed squarely at Ely's chest. Behind him, the hellish glow of the Triangle Social Club fire pulsed with the encroaching sirens, painting the narrow alley in shifting patterns of violent orange and deep, impenetrable shadow.

"I've been waiting for this all day." Carmelo's words fell flat as stones. "You've wanted my Kathy from the beginning."

"I knew Kathy when you were still in short pants," Ely said, voice controlled despite the gun aimed at his heart. "She was mine before you existed, and she's mine now."

Carmelo advanced, the Colt steady as a surgeon's hand. "Then I'll hold her hand at your funeral. It's my turn." Something wild danced behind his eyes—part madness, part savage joy. His finger slowly tightened on the trigger. Ely's muscles coiled, waiting for the blast.

"Melo! Stop!" Matteo's command cracked like a whip from the alley mouth.

Neither man flinched. Ely kept his eyes on death's messenger; Carmelo's aim never wavered from Ely's chest.

"Melo! Listen to me!" Matteo stepped into the narrow space with the Judas, better known as Slim, as his shadow. Ely registered Slim's presence. The tall man who'd chosen the Ricci side, playing butler, chauffeur, and spy while feeding scraps to Bumpy Johnson to maintain his precarious middle ground. *Never trusted him,* Ely thought bitterly.

Matteo pressed on, his voice low and urgent. "You shoot him, you lose Kathy forever. That ain't a guess, brother. It's a stone-cold fact. I'm losing Debbie right now. I can feel her slippin' through my fingers.

You pull that trigger, this war... this poison between us and our women... it never ends. You hear me? *Never.*"

Ely held his gaze. "That's right. Kathy will never forgive you. And she'll know it's you. She'll see it in your eyes."

Carmelo's jaw muscle jumped like a trapped animal. His finger caressed the trigger's curve. Then, with a speed that blurred, he reversed the pistol and slammed the steel butt into Ely's temple. The crack echoed in the alley. Ely folded like a puppet with cut strings, crumpling onto the filthy cobbles. Barely conscious, blood bloomed from his nose and split lip, hot and metallic on his tongue.

Carmelo crouched low beside him, the gun now dangling loosely in his grip. His voice dropped to a whisper thick with venom. "You know what she is to me?"

Ely spat crimson onto the stones. "I know what she *was*."

"Is." Carmelo's voice cracked like ice. "Always will be." He brought the gun up slowly, the barrel finding Ely's face again. "You think a piece of paper? Some fake vows she made to you to forget me, changes a*nything*? It doesn't. But Henry Freeman ain't wrong. This is war. My war. Harlem will burn because I can't have her. You tell Henry Freeman this: Harlem is Don Cosimo Riccis, it's mine." He leaned closer, the smell of cordite and fury sharp in Ely's nostrils. "So here's your mercy, Ely the fake husband. Take her. Take her back to Mississippi and make her forget me if you can. But you stay the *fuck* out of Harlem. Breathe her air here again? Touch her again in front of me?" He tapped the barrel against Ely's bloodied forehead. "I'll put you down right in front of her. Make her watch. Take her home with me, where she belongs."

Ely stared up, past the gun, into Carmelo's eyes. There was no lie there, only a terrible, absolute conviction. *Gospel truth.* Carmelo's bottom lip trembled, a visible battle against the urge to finish it. With a sound like a choked growl, he pushed himself upright. He turned, a dark shape against the distant firelight, and walked away without another word.

Matteo stepped into the void Carmelo left, his face grim. "Get

Kathy out of Harlem," he said, urgency tightening his voice. "Now. I can't hold him twice."

Slim merely tipped his hat, a ghost of a smile touching his lips as he glanced down at the broken man. Then he and Matteo moved off, shadows melting after Carmelo. Ely was left alone in the stinking grime, the taste of blood and defeat thick in his mouth, the cold cobbles leaching the last warmth from his bones.

CHAPTER 41

TWO YEARS LATER - 1954 BUTTS MS

"Hey!" answered Kathy, cradling the phone between her shoulder and ear as she worked diligently at the stove.

Debbie smiled at the sound of crying Sandra in the background. "What's wrong with my baby-girl?"

"Spoiled, what else. Ely will be home from the Mill soon. She knows it, so she's giving me the business before he gets here and gives her everything she wants."

Debbie laughed.

"Hold on," Kathy said.

Debbie listened as she soothed her baby girl with a treat from the kitchen and set her in a high chair. Debbie smiled and touched the swell of her own belly fondly. Another child is exactly what she wanted. She loved how excited and attentive Matteo became whenever he even thought of the new baby she carried.

"Hey. Sorry. I'm back," said Kathy.

"It's okay. I'm here. How's it been? You going back to teaching or not?" Debbie asked.

"Yes, Ely and I finally came to an agreement. He doesn't want me away from Sandra, but she will be fine with his mother. I start teaching again next week."

“I’m happy for you. I love how you, too, are always able to compromise,” Debbie said. “I swear, between Matteo and José, I’m always dealing with drama.”

Kathy smiled. “Both of them spoil you in their own ways.”

“True,” Debbie agreed.

“I need to finish dinner. Been waiting all week for this call. So is it happening? Are you really moving to Vegas?" Kathy asked, tasting the spoon she'd used to stir the gravy for her husband's favorite beef stew, before taking the cornbread skillet out of the oven.

"So much has happened in a week. I mean, Mama's back in the hospital. Matteo says they're doing nothing but experimenting on her and making her suffer. In Vegas, he can get her better care."

"I don't know if that’s true, Debbie. Do you remember Tommy Peterson?" Kathy asked.

"I think so," Debbie replied.

"Well, he just came back from Vegas. He said it's segregated there. You can't have mixed marriages, and they really hate blacks and Natives in the entire state of Nevada. So why does Matteo and..." Kathy refused to say Carmelo's name, so she caught herself. "Why does Matteo keep saying Vegas is where you can be free?"

"It's the Mafia, Kat. The rules are different for them there. Kind of how you said the Sicilians were different in New Orleans," Debbie explained. “He said there's a hospital he can put her in, and they will help her. I dunno. It's my Mama. I talked to Mama Stewart, and she said to keep her in Harlem. If anyone's gonna see after her, it should be our own people. What do you think? She’s hanging on for me and Junior. I know she’s tired of the fight.”

"I think Mama Stewart is right. I'm glad you still have her. Big Mama has been dead two years now, and I still cry and miss her advice,” Kathy said. “Can’t even go to her house.”

“Ely’s parents live there now? Huh?” Debbie asked.

“Yep, moved in four weeks ago. The house just sat for so long. The Jensens didn’t want to turn it over. They hurt so bad for Big Mama. But it’s ours now, and the land it sits on. They’re doing good,” Kathy said. “I just... the world isn’t the same with Big Mama and

Uncle Pete gone. I want to believe she is in heaven keeping him straight."

"Me too," Debbie said, then her voice dropped. "So much has happened. Harlem isn't the same, Kathy. You wouldn't recognize it. The Italians hit the Apollo theater last month when everyone was there to see Billy Holiday."

"What!" Kathy gasped.

"Yep, some young ones got burned, too. Minton's Playhouse was so badly damaged that it closed indefinitely. The Italians are squeezing every numbers runner, every policy bank. Bodies turn up in the Hudson every week, both Italian and black. But we're not hurting them as badly as they're hurting us."

"Jesus, Debs—"

"That's not even the worst of it. Remember Mrs. Washington, who ran the beauty shop on 132nd? They found her in her shop with her throat cut because she wouldn't pay for her products through the Riccis and had reported the extortion to Uncle Henry. And, oh, little Marcus—you remember him from the bakery? They grabbed him off the street, held him for three days to make his father flip on your daddy's movements in operations. The boy came back different, Kat. Won't speak, won't eat right."

Kathy's hand trembled as she stirred the stew. "How many have we lost?"

"Too many. The Italians hit the Savoy Ballroom during a Saturday night dance. Seventeen people are dead, including three teenagers who were just there to dance. Your father retaliated—took out two of their social clubs in Little Italy. Then they came back harder. It's like watching Harlem bleed out, one block at a time."

"The police?" Kathy asked.

Debbie's bitter laugh cut through the line. "The police? They're worse than ever. As soon as Bumpy went away, they started treating every Negro man like he was Al Capone. Can't walk down Lenox without getting shaken down. They arrested Brother four times this month—just for being Henry Freeman's nephew. Beat him so bad last time, he can't see out his left eye properly. Gonna have surgery."

Kathy closed her eyes. "Daddy must be careful—"

"Your daddy's holding on. Trust me. Brother says he has allies with the Nation of Islam and a man named Malcom. Additionally, Brother mentioned that there is a Jewish mobster named Meyer Lansky who used to conduct business with Bumpy. He is cool with Matteo but sneaky. Brother says he really hates Cosimo Ricci for what he did to Bumpy. He is funding Harlem's war behind the scenes. But I have bad news."

"What... tell me," Kathy braced herself.

"Carmelo is, he's at the front of it, Kathy."

"That can't be true," Kathy mumbled.

"It is. Matteo says he's the one behind the scenes trying to destroy Harlem. Matteo can't be sure, but he thinks he is going after your dad. So for now, Uncle Henry can't leave the house without six men around him. Sleeps in a different place every night. Your Mama's not telling you. The Nation of Islam is protecting him. And..." Debbie paused.

"What?"

"It's not enough, Kat. Carmelo has found him twice. He barely escaped. He's not the boy you knew anymore. They call him the Wolf of Harlem now because he's always on the prowl, not in Brooklyn."

"The Wolf," Kathy repeated.

"Yeah, he hunts your daddy's men like a predator. That shooting at Small's Paradise? That was him. Walked in during the late set, killed four of your father's best soldiers while they were listening to Bird play. Just stood there in his perfect suit, smoking a cigarette while they bled out on the dance floor. There were witnesses, Kathy."

Kathy's knees went weak. She gripped the counter. "That's not... he couldn't..."

"He beat Smokey Johnson to death with a hammer—you remember him, ran numbers for your daddy, switched to work with the Italians before the war. Carmelo caught him in an alley behind the Apollo. Apparently, he was stealing from them. Playing both sides against each other."

"Stop, Debbie. That's enough," Kathy pleaded.

“They found what was left of him from 125th to 135th—” Debbie continued.

"Stop. Please—."

"You need to know!" Debbie snapped. She paused. She took a breath. “Sorry. You need to hear this. He's systematically destroying everything your father built. The loan sharks, the numbers games, the protection rackets—he's either taking them over or burning them down. And he's got half the police in his father’s pocket now. He’s obsessed. Possessed. They say he owns more of Harlem than your daddy does because people are scared and turning to the Wolf for protection of their businesses. Paying him under the table, and not Uncle Henry.”

"So José is on board to go to Vegas?" Kathy asked, desperate to change the subject.

Debbie sighed. She relented.

"One hundred percent. I told you that he and Sam broke up when the judge moved to California. Vegas is closer to Sam. I think José is trying to follow him. I don't want to leave my Mama."

"I know Debs. I guess you should talk to her. Really tell her what's going on. When I told Ma what was happening with me and... you know who, she helped me. Got Daddy to let Ely take me out of Harlem and back to Mississippi. She has been with me every step of the way in protecting Sandy.”

"I hear you. I'm going to see Mama at the hospital today. Brother is taking me—if he can see to drive. He has decided he's in love and will get married. Tells me to go and he'll look after Mama."

There was a cool silence between them.

Kathy spoke next: “I wish I could change things, Deb. There’s nothing I can do to stop him. And the more I hear about who he is now, the more determined I am to stay away to keep her away. I have to think of Sandy. If he ever knew about her Debs, I don’t know how I could protect her from him, or save Ely. I can’t do anything.”

"I understand, Kat. I just needed to say it to you. To let you know what is left here. Bumpy served a purpose—peace with the Italians meant our people could breathe, prosper. Now? The Italians want everything, and they're willing to turn Harlem to ash to get it. Your father's lost thirty soldiers this year alone. Good men with families."

"And Mama? She lies when she calls me. Makes it seem like everything is okay. Is she okay?"

"She's sad. The churches are empty on Sundays because people are afraid to gather. Reverend had to close the soup kitchen, too. The Schomburg had to be under your father's protection. There is a Puerto Rican gangster who has ties with your dad, too, from East Harlem, so they are pushing back. There is resistance."

Kathy's gaze slipped over to her daughter, stumbling around on her chubby legs. Ely had arrived and took her out of the high chair, watching her proudly. She looked like Carmelo the most when she laughed. From the moment the nurse put her in her arms, she saw him in her, prayed her skin would darken, and her hair would uncurl. It did. Still, she had his face, his smile, his laugh.

"Maybe I should come to visit. Maybe I can help stop all of this if I talk to him—leave her here, but reach out and tell him to stop. What do you think?" Kathy mumbled.

"Don't say it. Don't even think it. You can never come back, Kathy. Never. Carmelo's got eyes everywhere. He knows about Sandra—knows she exists. Matteo overheard him ranting once in his room alone about you betraying him as if he were having an argument with you. Matteo thinks he's insane."

Kathy closed her eyes as her heart shriveled.

"You are right. There is nothing you can do. So stay in Mississippi. We'll pray. We'll get through this," Debbie sighed. "I have to go. Brother will be here soon, and I need to dress Junior."

"Leave Harlem, Debbie. You're pregnant, and you have Junior. Vegas may not be the paradise we thought, but if you and Matteo can finally be together, take that chance."

"You talk to Janey? I know she's there," Debbie said. "Maybe she can tell me if Matteo is for real, or just telling me lies to get me out of Harlem?"

"No. I'm never speaking to her again. Just go. Okay? I love you," Kathy said.

"Love you too. And Kat? We are Freeman's. Made from true grit like Big Mama say. We're going to survive this."

The line went dead, leaving Kathy staring at her daughter—Carmelo's daughter—playing innocently on the floor, unaware that the secret of her very existence was written in blood across Harlem's streets.

* * *

CARMELO RICCI RECLINED in his chair, rolling the cigar between his fingers before lighting it. The door opened after a single knock—a sound that meant one of three men had arrived: Matteo, Slim, or Don Cosimo Ricci. The shortest list in New York, one that would never include his father by choice.

Slim stepped inside, fedora tucked under his arm, moving with the easy grace of a man who'd survived too much to fear ordinary dangers. "Got a minute?"

"No." Smoke punctuated the refusal.

"Might want to reconsider."

"Not in the mood for games, Slim."

"Fair enough. I've been sitting on information, trying to find the right moment. Starting to realize there isn't one, and my neck's getting itchy from waiting."

"Stop talking in riddles."

"Okay. Fine. It's about Kathy Freeman," Slim said.

Two words that changed everything. Carmelo's entire body shifted—not dramatically, just a subtle realignment that spoke of barely leashed violence. He set the cigar in the crystal ashtray with exaggerated care. "We had an agreement about that name. You're never to speak it in front of me. And I don't crack your jaw."

Slim swallowed a smile. He didn't care how many bodies the Wolf dropped; he raised the Ricci boys. Where Mama Stewart was their surrogate mother after Lucia's death, Slim was the father they wished for from the start. It killed him to see the honest, kind boy disappear into the violent, maniacal chaos of Cosimo's bloodline.

"Every move you make is about her. This war, the deaths, the territories—it's all one long suicide note to Kathy Freeman. Before you finish writing it in Harlem's blood, you should know the truth."

The silence that followed had weight. Slim watched his boss's fingers drum once on the desk, inches from the hammer that had ended more than one difficult conversation.

"There's nothing about Kathy I don't know. I pay well for information. I know about her Sunday picnics after church, with her daughter and new husband. I know she'll be back in the classroom soon, teaching kids. See? I know her world."

"You know what Maria made sure you'd know."

"Maria?" Something shifted in Carmelo's expression. "What the fuc—"

"Your wife. Mother of your twins."

"I'm aware of who she is." Carmelo's smile held no warmth. "She paraded the twins in front of Carmine Bonanno. Made sure Kathy heard about it. Old news, Slim."

Slim's response was a slow, deliberate head shake.

"If you have something to say, say it."

"Caesar's been warming her bed. You know this. I've reported it."

"And I've told you repeatedly—I don't give a shit. She can fuck whoever keeps her quiet. I'm there for my children. Why are you wasting my time with this?"

"Because you're carrying the wrong guilt." Slim straightened. "You think you raped her. Think you're a monster because you saw as a kid what Cosimo did to her mother."

"Among other things," Carmelo rolled his eyes.

"No. No son. Not other things. This here is the moment you gave up and gave in to the worst part of your nature. Every body you've dropped, every black woman in Harlem you've taken to bed trying to replace Kathy—it all comes back to you believing you're the monster Maria said you were. The rapist."

"You applying for consigliere now?" Carmelo smirked.

"You applying for Don?" Slim countered.

Carmelo's smile faded. "Spit it out, Slim."

"This needs saying. Caesar and Maria—it's not new. Goes back before your marriage. Before the so-called rape. Before the convenient pregnancy to land your plane permanently here with your father." Slim paused, measuring his words. "Cosimo has been in her ear the whole time through her mother. Planting the seed to harvest. He wanted you back in the fold. That's why he pretended not to care about you traveling and boxing to be with Kathy. He'd always had control. That's why Caesar stopped traveling with you. He was putting in work with Maria. Setting you up."

CHAPTER 42

REWRITING HISTORY

The weight of his father's betrayal pressed down on Carmelo's chest like a tombstone. For six days, he'd vanished from the family, holed up in what he called his *safe house.* A place he'd bought and rebuilt with his own hands after losing Kathy. New Jersey was his exile, his purgatory. There, he sketched her face until his fingers cramped, punched the heavy bag until his knuckles split, and drank himself into a stupor to sleep without dreaming of her.

Pete Freeman's blood was on his hands. He could never be clean of his complicity in his death. Whether his father ordered the hit or not, it was his fault. He believed it.

Only Slim knew where to find him. Only Slim had seen him like this—raw, unguarded, a man stripped down to grief and rage.

Today was the seventh day. The day he'd face the devil.

Carmelo slipped into the bar through the back door, the key cold in his grip. The place was a front for his father's operations, a poor replacement for the club the Freemans had burned to the ground. He carried a hammer at his side, its weight familiar, its purpose clear. This time, he'd kill him, and he didn't give a fuck who came for him for doing it. He was ready to die. Join his mother in hell. He was ready.

But he hadn't expected a sit-down.

Voices, sharp and raised, cut through the dim hallway. His father's. The underbosses. Carmelo froze in the shadows, listening.

"—tired of pretending that mongrel lover is my son!" Don Cosimo's voice carried through the heavy wood. "Two years. For two years, I've watched him parade that Negro whore and her bastard through my territory. They're like roaches. You get rid of one of them and more come!"

Carmelo dropped against the wall. He gripped the hammer tighter, wishing it were a gun instead.

"The Vegas arrangement is perfect," Big Eli's oily voice responded. "Clean, distant, untraceable to you. Once he and the bitch arrive, they're no longer under Ricci's protection. Any two-bit gun can take the contract. And you will be the grieving father. Lanskey can take the fall for letting one of ours drop on his watch."

"I want it done within the week of their arrival. All three of them—him, the girl, and especially that bastard abomination he created. No loose ends, no mixed blood carrying the Ricci name."

"What about Carmelo? He and Matteo—," said Slick Mike.

"Carmelo will understand," Don Ricci waved off the rest of the comment from Mike. "He's already proven himself. Once Matteo's gone, he'll be my only son. The way it should have been from the beginning."

Carmelo's hand found the wall for support, his mind racing. His father had smiled at Sunday dinner, had toasted Matteo's Vegas plans, and had played the supportive patriarch. All while planning his execution. And Nino? What would he do to Nino?

He backed away silently, his footsteps carrying him through the bar and to his car without conscious thought. Only when he reached the Holland Tunnel did he allow himself to process what he'd heard. His father would murder Matteo for the crime of loving wrongly. He would slaughter an innocent child for carrying the wrong blood. And kill the baby Debbie carried.

By the time he reached his destination, his rage had crystallized into something colder, more useful.

* * *

MAMA STEWART'S Diner sat on the corner like a lighthouse in hostile waters. It remained neutral ground even in wartime. Carmelo chose a booth in the back, positioning himself where he could see every entrance. The dinner crowd of mixed couples had thinned, leaving only the die-hards nursing coffee and the weight of their troubles.

Mama Stewart herself moved between tables with practiced grace, her eyes missing nothing. When she poured Carmelo's coffee, her gaze lingered on his face, reading something in the set of his jaw that made her pause.

"You waiting on somebody?" she asked.

"Two somebodies. They'll be here soon."

She nodded, moving away but keeping him in her peripheral vision. She'd seen the Ricci boys enough to recognize when they were teetering on the edge. Her form of mothering was not to hover but to counsel and let the strongest one stand. Now with the war in Harlem, she was weakening. She just wanted to put her arms around him and nurse him back to the boy she'd first met with Kathy. Stop the killing of her people, and heal whatever was left of them all.

Her gaze swiveled to the small table near the kitchen where he first arrived with Kathy years ago. Teenagers, on their forbidden date. How happy the two of them were before it all turned to ash. Love, in her experience, often led to pain.

Slim arrived first, sliding into the booth with his characteristic ease. "Urgent message from you at this hour usually means bodies or money."

"Both, potentially." Carmelo's voice carried no inflection.

Caesar entered minutes later, his bulk filling the remaining space. A flash of something—possession, defiance, guilt—crossed his features when he met Carmelo's eyes, but it vanished quickly.

Carmelo lit a cigarillo with steady hands. He gave Caesar a nod. "I need to discuss a delicate matter. Family business."

Mama Stewart wiped down a nearby table.

"Here?" Caesar asked. Carmelo ignored the question.

"Your Don, dear old dad, has decided that Matteo's Vegas relocation requires... adjustment. So yes, we discuss it here."

"What kind of adjustment?" asked Slim.

"The kind that involves bullets and shallow graves. Three of them, maybe four if he learns that Debbie is pregnant again."

Slim's expression didn't change, but Caesar's coffee cup rattled against the saucer. "Don Cosimo wouldn't—kill his son and his grandchildren."

"Wouldn't he?" Carmelo's smile was winter-sharp. "A mixed-blood grandchild offends him. Apparently, two years was his limit for tolerance."

The silence that followed was heavy enough to drown in. Mama Stewart continued her cleaning, watching Carmelo's face remain marble-still while his eyes burned with something volcanic.

"What do you need from us?" Slim asked finally.

"Options. Leverage. Anyone in our books who might prove useful for an alternative solution to fucking kill my father!"

Caesar cleared his throat. "We can't kill him. We all know that."

"Then I'll kill him!" Carmelo said.

"No," said Slim. "We need a different kind of solution. The kind that gets Matteo out of Cosimo's reach."

"There's Donovan. The army recruiter from Fort Hamilton. He's into us for fifteen large. Gambling debts. I was supposed to pay a visit next week. Knee breaking is on the menu."

Carmelo's cigarette paused halfway to his lips. "Military recruitment. Interesting. Tell me more about Donovan."

As Caesar outlined the recruiter's debts and desperation, Mama Stewart observed how Carmelo absorbed information, calculating, reformulating. His control never wavered, even as he planned his brother's salvation through a forced exile.

"Slim, you'll accompany me to visit Mr. Donovan tonight. Caesar, you'll prepare documentation suggesting Matteo's patriotic interests. Letters and newspaper clippings about the Communist threat. Make it convincing in case we need to submit something."

"Boss," Slim ventured carefully, "Matteo won't go willingly. He's got Debbie, the kids—"

"He'll go if the alternative is death. His and theirs." Carmelo stubbed out his cigarette with precise violence. "Sometimes mercy comes in uniform."

Caesar shifted uncomfortably. "What do we tell him? The truth?"

"Never the truth. Only my version of it. That is the law," Carmelo said, and his gaze was laser sharp on Caesar. Slim and Caesar frowned. Not understanding. Carmelo rolled his eyes. "We'll set him up. An ambush, a dead rival, and witnesses placing him at the scene. We'll make him believe he has no choice." Carmelo's gaze found Caesar's again and held it. "After all, we're all excellent at keeping secrets in this family. Aren't we?"

The threat hung between them like a blade. Caesar nodded quickly, too quickly.

"Good. Slim, bring the car around. We have a recruiter to motivate."

As the men filed out, Mama Stewart approached the table. Carmelo met her eyes without flinching.

"That's a heavy burden you're carrying," she said quietly.

"Heavier than you know." He left a twenty on the table. "But some weights, we're born to bear."

She watched him leave, seeing not a man orchestrating salvation disguised as betrayal. It was the kind of terrible arithmetic she understood. The kind that might make him worthy of greater things.

* * *

PATRICK DONOVAN LIVED in a modest Bay Ridge apartment that reeked of desperation and cheap whiskey. When he answered the door at 11 PM to find Carmelo Ricci flanked by Slim, his face went from confused to terrified in the space of a heartbeat.

"Mr. Ricci, I—I have until next week. Your men said—"

"So, you know me?" Carmelo asked.

"Yes, sir, all of Brooklyn knows the Wolf," Patrick Donovan replied.

"Invite us in, Patrick." Carmelo's tone brooked no argument.

The apartment was exactly what fifteen thousand in gambling debt looked like—bare walls, minimal furniture, a kitchen table covered in past-due notices. Donovan backed against the wall, hands raised.

"Please, I can get the money. I just need—"

"Sit." Carmelo took the room's only comfortable chair, studying the recruiter like a specimen. "Tell me about your quotas."

"My... what?"

"Your recruitment quotas. The Army must be pushing hard with this situation in Indochina."

Donovan's confusion deepened. "Yes, sir. They want volunteers. Advisors especially. It's not a matter of war. Just need ground coverage. But what does that have to do with—"

"Everything." Carmelo said. "You said there will be no war?"

"I don't think so. There is no talk of war," he said.

"Good. Good." Carmelo looked at Slim and nodded. "You're going to have a visitor soon. A young man named Matteo Ricci. Strong, capable, exactly what Uncle Sam is looking for."

"Your brother? The Butcher?"

"My brother." The words carried weight. "You're going to give him your best pitch. Expedite his paperwork. Ensure he ships out for basic training within forty-eight hours. All paperwork on my end will be done."

"Mr. Ricci, I don't understand—"

Slim stepped forward, looming. "You don't need to understand. You need to comply."

"In exchange," Carmelo continued as if Slim hadn't spoken, "your debt disappears. Permanently. You'll also receive a bonus—let's say one thousand—for your exceptional patriotic service."

Donovan's face cycled through confusion, hope, and fear. "Just... recruit your brother?"

"Enthusiastically. Efficiently. Effectively. Quietly." Carmelo stood. "He may be reluctant. You'll overcome that reluctance with tales of duty, honor, and service. You'll process him so fast he won't have time for second thoughts."

"And if I don't?" Donovan asked.

Carmelo's smile was answer enough. "You're a smart man, Patrick. Smart men recognize opportunities for redemption when they're offered." He moved to the door, pausing. "Oh, and Patrick? If anyone asks, this was all Matteo's idea. His patriotic choice. You simply facilitated a young man's desire to serve his country."

"Yes, sir. Of course."

"Slim will provide you with the necessary background materials. Study them. Be convincing." Carmelo's eyes were chips of black ice. "My brother's life depends on your performance. Yours does too."

They left Donovan shaking in his kitchen. In the car, Slim glanced at his boss.

"You think it'll work?" Slim asked.

"It has to." Carmelo stared out at the Brooklyn streets. "The alternative is I shoot my father. And this time I don't miss."

"And when Matteo finds out it was really Cosimo that caused all this?"

"He'll be alive to hate me and dear dad. That's all that matters."

They drove back to Manhattan in silence; each lost in thoughts of the machinery they'd just set in motion. Somewhere in Harlem, Matteo Ricci was sleeping beside Debbie, unaware that his brother was rewriting his fate with invisible ink.

Carmelo's hands remained steady on the wheel, but Slim noticed the white-knuckle grip, the only sign of the storm raging beneath that icy control. Even wolves, it seemed, could love their pack.

CHAPTER 43

THE MOUSE TRAP

The Red Hook warehouse reeked of decades - stale motor oil, oxidized metal, and the faint tang of brine seeping through cracked concrete. Matteo checked his watch for the third time in seven minutes. 2:47 AM. Tommy Mangano was late again. The Mangano prince operated on his own arrogant timetable, even for meetings that could redraw New York's underworld map.

Their uneasy alliance balanced on a knife's edge. Tommy needed Matteo's inside knowledge to erode Ricci's control over Brooklyn's docks. Matteo needed Mangano's muscle to protect Debbie while she remained in Brooklyn until he could move them to Vegas. Something in his father's eyes alarmed him. He felt the need to be extra careful. Two traitors meeting in shadows, their families none the wiser.

The rusted door groaned. Tommy entered from the darkness, his crocodile smile gleaming. "Ricci. Was starting to think you'd developed common sense and run."

"Still here," Matteo countered, his right hand drifting toward his .38. Some instincts never faded.

They'd barely exchanged coded pleasantries when the lights died. In the sudden void, Tommy's Sicilian curse was cut short by the wet crunch of aluminum meeting bone. Matteo's gun cleared leather just as something solid and fast cracked against his temple. The last thing he registered before the blackness swallowed him was the rhythm - three sets of work boots moving in practiced synchronization.

Carmelo removed his mask first. Slim took off his mask, and then Caesar. They stood over two unconscious men. "Caesar? You know what to do."

"We will stash Magano until Matteo enlists in the army. Everyone will think he's dead. Matteo will find the body as we agreed. No one will trace it to us."

Carmelo looked over to Slim. "And?"

"I got it, Boss. I'll keep Harlem out of it. Spread the word that Magano is in debt to the Irish. That they got him. Have the families looking in that direction."

"It's important, Slim. None of this can be traced to Henry Freeman or Harlem. You got it?" Carmelo asked.

"Got it."

Carmelo pulled his mask back down. "Then it's showtime."

* * *

CONSCIOUSNESS RETURNED in waves of pain. Matteo's vision swam, focusing slowly on Tommy Mangano's corpse. The golden boy lay twisted at an unnatural angle, blood pooling beneath a head so mashed in he couldn't tell if it was really him—professional work—efficient, brutal.

Matteo's hands shook as he rushed outside and found a payphone, muscle memory dialing Caesar's number. "It's me. Red Hook warehouse. Come alone—no, bring Carmelo. And Slim. Something's happened."

He had no choice but to return to where he had left the dead man. He couldn't let anyone find him. Twenty minutes felt like twenty years. When the door opened, Carmelo entered first, taking in the scene with those calculating eyes Matteo had grown to hate. Slim secured the outsider while Caesar helped Matteo to his feet. Every time Matteo tried to stand on his own, he felt wobbly from the blow to his head and had to sit.

"Tommy Mangano," Matteo said unnecessarily. "We were... discussing territory."

"Without family sanction." Carmelo's voice held no judgment, just fact. "Who else knows about these meetings?"

"No one. We kept it—" Matteo stopped. "Wait. We left Rao's together. Tommy's crew saw us. Fuck. *Fuck. I'm fucked.* They'll pin it on me!"

Carmelo knelt beside the body, studying the wounds with clinical detachment. "Professional hit. Meant to send a message by letting you live." He stood, fixing Matteo with that penetrating stare. "You understand what this looks like?"

"Like I killed a made man, again. A Mangano captain's son." The full weight crashed down on Matteo. "They'll want blood. The whole family will—"

"Father will use this against us. He'll use it, Matteo. And Debbie? He'll come after her," Carmelo warned.

Matteo's legs gave out. Caesar caught him, easing him onto a crate. "I'll cut Pa's throat myself before I let that happen. No one threatens Debbie, Junior, my baby—"

"Unless..." Carmelo said.

"Unless what?" Desperation crept into Matteo's voice.

"Unless we cover this up. Get rid of the body. Pin it on Henry Freeman. Make it part of the war."

"No! No more of that shit! Carmelo, the war has to stop. Too many people are dying. Debbie's people are dying. You swore to me that you would force Pa and the families to barter a truce with Henry Freeman. Put an end to it."

"How the fuck do I do that with a fresh body on my hands!" Carmelo shouted back. "You fucked this up. You did it! Always working behind the family's back, now look! I won't let Pa kill you or the Maganos!"

Slim and Caesar exchanged a look over Carmelo's performance.

Matteo dropped his head in shame. "There has to be something else. Some way to fix this. Damn it. She's pregnant. She's all I got, and my kids. I got to protect them, Carmelo."

Carmelo exhaled. He put his hands to his head and paced before the corpse. He froze. "There's a recruiter in Bay Ridge. Owes us favors. You could be in uniform within forty-eight hours. Basic training by week's end. The Army doesn't care about Mafia politics."

"Army? You fucking insane?" Matteo's eyes stretched.

"If you are not a target, and out of the way, I can work things with Pa and the families," Carmelo said.

"You want me to run? Abandon my family?" Matteo asked in disbelief.

"I want you to live." For a moment, something human flickered across Carmelo's face. "All of you. Two years and you're back. Clean. I'll take care of Debbie and the family."

Matteo looked to Slim with pleading eyes. The one person he trusted completely. The older man's face was grave. "It's a good plan, kid. Maybe the only plan. Your brother's offering you a way out."

"This is convenient." Suspicion flared through Matteo's panic. "Too convenient. Did you—"

"Careful." Carmelo's voice turned lethal. "I'm trying to save your life. Question my methods later, when you're alive to do it. We are out of time."

The warehouse fell silent except for the distant sound of ships in the harbor. Finally, Matteo nodded. "What about Debbie? The baby is coming, Junior—"

"I said I'll protect them." Carmelo met his eyes. "I swear on our mother's grave. While you serve, they'll be untouchable. I'll force Father to the table, negotiate peace with Harlem. By the time you return, this war will be over."

"And if you're lying?" Matteo asked. "I give up my life and my kids, and you do nothing. I'll fucking kill you."

"Then I'm no worse off than you are now." Carmelo gestured to Tommy's cooling corpse. "Decide, brother. The Maganos won't wait for a compromise."

Matteo buried his face in his hands. When he looked up, tears tracked through the blood on his face. "I need to see them. Explain..."

"You have until sunrise. Caesar will drive you. Slim, we need to stage this scene. Make it clean." Carmelo said. "Matteo, you were never here. You spent the night at Debbie's. Anyone asks, you know nothing about Tommy Mangano's last movements."

"Carmelo..." Matteo's voice broke. "I don't think I can do it. I don't think I can leave them. Let's think of something else."

"There's nothing else. Trust me. You know I know how hard it is to let go."

Matteo studied Carmelo for a moment, feeling as if his brother was partly satisfied by his misery. But he pushed the thought from his mind when he saw Magano's mutilated corpse. He had no choice.

"Nothing will happen." The promise fell between them like a blood oath. "Now go. You have goodbyes to make."

* * *

THE MOTORCYCLE'S growl faded into the predawn hush that covered the empty street. Matteo killed the engine. He stared up at the darkened window where he knew Junior slept—his little soldier safe in his fortress, guarded by a mother who never left her post. Four hours until sunrise. Not enough time. He needed weeks, months, a year to watch his new baby take first steps, to hear childish laughter fill these walls a little longer.

The house exhaled silence as he entered. It was as heavy as his burden. He navigated the stairs by memory, fingertips brushing the banister like a blind man reading braille. Inside the moonlit room he found Junior sprawled across his bed, one foot dangling over the edge. His little soldier was always fighting sleep even in his dreams. Matteo's calloused hand enveloped the tiny foot, warm and perfect. A contented snore answered in response. He tugged the blanket up, tucking in the edges like armor against the night.

"Hey." Debbie's voice rasped with sleep from the corner chair. She rubbed her eyes, the moonlight catching her lovely auburn hair and soft features "He waited for you again."

"I told you Debs—"

"—to put him to bed." She shifted, the wicker creaking beneath her. "But he won't close his eyes until he smells your leather jacket, Matteo. You trained him. Don't change the rules now that business keeps you out late."

The lump in Matteo's throat threatened to choke him. He kept his face turned away, blinking hard until the burn behind his eyes subsided. Debbie's grunt as she rose—that particular seven-months-pregnant sound—preceded the shuffle of her slippers across the floor. Her arms encircled his waist from behind, her swollen belly pressed in against the small of his back.

"Mmm." Her sigh warmed his shoulder blade through the thin fabric. "You smell like outside."

He turned, gathering her into the shelter of his arms. Her face tilted up instinctively, lips parting before their mouths even met. She tasted of mint toothpaste and sleep, of home. "I love you so much," she murmured against his lips, the words vibrating through his chest.

"I saw Mama today." Her fingers rubbed over the buttons of his shirt. "Told her everything. She already knew—just waited for me to say it." A tremor ran through her. "I can't lose her, Matteo. I can't run to Vegas when—"

"Shhh." He cradled her jaw, thumbs brushing the apples of her cheeks. "We're not going anywhere."

Her breath hitched. "Really?"

"Let's take Junior to our bed." He kissed her forehead, her nose brushing his chin. "Just for tonight. We'll figure out the rest tomorrow."

Junior barely stirred as Matteo lifted him, the boy's arms looping around his neck with the unconscious trust of a child who knew his father would never drop him. Debbie's hand found his, their fingers interlacing as he guided her across the hall—her waddle more pronounced tonight, the weight of their daughter dragging at her steps.

Matteo performed the nightly ritual with extra care: peeling Debbie out of her housedress, coaxing her into the oversized nightgown she hated but needed, even donning the ridiculous striped pajama pants she'd bought him as a joke. When they finally settled—Junior sprawled half across his chest despite being far too big for it, Debbie curled into his side with a contented sigh—Matteo closed his eyes and committed every sensation to memory: the rhythm of their breathing, the heat of their bodies, the way Junior's hair smelled faintly of peanut butter from his bedtime snack.

This, he thought as Debbie's fingers found his in the darkness. This right here is what the saints promised. And for these stolen hours, he let himself believe it might last.

* * *

CARMELO HAD CALLED first thing in the morning. He told Matteo he had a full day with his family instead. But he'd have to do what they agreed tomorrow. And Matteo seized on the opportunity. Staying in to play and nurture Junior. Cooking and cleaning. Doing all of Debbie's bidding. Just being there as if it were the last day of his life. And it felt as if it was. When José came home from work, he sat them both down and told them the half-truth.

He done something

Something he couldn't undo.

He had to leave.

Join the army and go for two years.

There was no way to change any of it.

Debbie took it the worst. They had the worst fight he'd ever had with her. She screamed at him. Ran from him. Reduced Junior to tears with her rage and hysteria. It got so bad that José had to take Junior to Mama Stewart while Matteo did his best to calm her for the baby's sake, if not for their own.

After her body was exhausted, she was inconsolable. All she did was cry. And eventually he cried with her. He'd not shed a tear since his mother died. And this felt just as painful. A death to their dreams and their plans. He knew they would not come back from this. He just knew it.

They spent the remaining hours holding each other, memorizing touches, storing up love for the separation ahead. When Caesar arrived at dawn the following day, Matteo kissed his family one last time.

"I love you," he whispered against Debbie's lips. "More than my life. Remember that."

"Matteo—please, please, I can't do this without you."

But he was already walking away, because if he looked back, he'd never leave. Behind him, Junior's cries pierced the morning air. "Papa! Papa, come back!"

In the car, Matteo broke completely. Caesar drove in respectful silence, letting a good man grieve for the life he was about to lose. Somewhere in Brooklyn, Carmelo was orchestrating the cover-up that would sell this fiction.

By nightfall, Matteo Ricci would be another volunteer, eager to serve his country against the Communist threat. No one would question a young man's patriotic choice.

No one except the family he left behind.

CHAPTER 44

LIFE OF LIES CHANGES EVERYTHING

The Ricci dining room gleamed with old-world elegance—crystal, silver, and hypocrisy polished to a high shine. Maria had outdone herself. Don Cosimo held court at the head, flanked by his remaining lieutenants, while Carmelo sat at his right hand where Matteo should have been, and instead of his wife, Nino sat next to him.

"A toast," Maria suggested in Italian, raising her glass of sparkling cider. "To family."

"To family," the table echoed in kind, though the words rang hollow with one son conspicuously absent.

"Where is Matteo?" Don Cosimo finally asked, his tone deceptively casual. "He was supposed to discuss the Vegas timeline tonight."

Carmelo set down his fork with deliberate precision. "Matteo won't be going to Vegas, Father."

The table fell silent. Maria's hand froze halfway to her glass.

"Explain," said the Don.

"He enlisted. Left for Fort Dix this afternoon. Said he wanted to serve his country before settling down." Carmelo's delivery was flawless—a hint of surprise, a touch of pride, no trace of the puppet strings he'd pulled.

Don Cosimo's face cycled through confusion, rage, and something that might have been relief. "Enlisted? Without consulting me?"

"Apparently, the Communist threat motivated him. That, and perhaps a desire to prove himself worthy of the Ricci name since he's made some mistakes in the past." Carmelo met his father's eyes steadily. "He asked me to tell you he was sorry for not asking permission, but felt that you would understand."

"This is... unexpected." The Don's fingers drummed on the table.. "And the colored girl? His bastard?"

A more profound hush fell over the table. It was the first time at a family gathering that Cosimo had mentioned he knew of Debbie and Matteo's child. The first time, he acknowledged the truth. And it all but solidified Carmelo's deep-seething hatred for the man who contributed to his and his brothers' birth and destruction. He had to wonder what kind of man he and Matteo would have been if they'd been born to anyone else but the Demon at the head of the table.

"She will move to Harlem under my protection, as I have promised him." Carmelo's tone suggested this was non-negotiable. "Matteo serves honorably, and they stay safe. It's a matter of family honor now. Which I think he has restored. Wouldn't you agree, Father?"

Don Cosimo glared at Carmelo. Everyone waited. Maria's gaze remained lowered as she fed his daughter from her lap, while her mother tended to his son.

Cosimo shrugged. "As long as she understands her place is never at this table, everything is fine."

The meal continued in strained conversation. Nino sat silent and pale, understanding more than any man of his intellect would with the loss of his brother, along with his mother. When dessert was cleared, Don Cosimo and his entourage left, his wife in tow, leaving the younger generation to their own devices.

Maria supervised the twins' bedtime routine while Carmelo escorted the guests out and put Nino to bed. He waited in their living room, studying the family photos she'd arranged on the mantel. Happy fictions, all of them. When she returned, her face glowed with anticipation.

"They missed their papa tonight," she said, settling beside him on the sofa. "Your son asked if you'd read to them tomorrow."

"Did he?" Carmelo's voice held no inflection.

"I'm glad Matteo's gone." The words tumbled out in a rush. "I mean, I'll miss him, but now... now maybe we can be a real family. The twins need their father, and I—"

"You've been patient." His gaze dropped over to her, and he stared directly into her eyes. "Two years of patience. That's admirable, Maria."

She flushed, pleased by what she took as praise. "I knew you needed time. After everything... I understood."

"Did you?" he asked and moved her hair gently to tuck behind her ear so he could see her fully. "Tell me, Maria. What understanding is it you have now?"

"That you blamed yourself. For that night, we conceived our babies. For... forcing things." She reached for his knee. "But I forgave you long ago. You were drunk and upset—"

"Interesting." He didn't pull away from her touch, but didn't return it either. "That's very noble of you."

A flicker of uncertainty crossed her features. "Carmelo?"

"I have a proposition." He cut her off. "Tomorrow night. Dinner at my club. Just the two of us. We'll discuss our future properly. Make some... decisions about the future."

Her face lit up like Christmas morning. "Really? Oh, Carmelo, I've hoped—I mean, yes. Yes, of course."

"Good. Wear something nice. Red, perhaps. You look beautiful in red."

She launched herself at him, arms wrapping around his neck, lips seeking his. For a moment, he remained still as marble. Then his hands came up, cupping her face, returning the kiss with passion he'd never given her.

"Carmelo," she breathed against his mouth. "Stay tonight. Please. The kids would love to wake up with you here, and I—"

"All right. I'll stay."

She pulled back, shocked. "Really?"

"Why not?" His smile didn't reach his eyes. "As you said, we're a family."

She led him to the bedroom with eagerness she could barely suppress, hardly believing this sudden change. He was gentle, attentive, everything she'd dreamed of for two years. When she curled against him afterward, tears of joy on her cheeks, she whispered, "I love you. I've always loved you. I've done everything in my power to have you."

"I know," he said to the darkness.

She fell asleep smiling, unaware that her husband lay awake calculating exactly how tomorrow night would unfold. In his mind, he could see Caesar's face when he revealed what he knew.

But not yet. Let her have this night, this illusion of happiness. Tomorrow would bring truth, consequences, and the settling of all accounts.

* * *

THE RECRUITMENT OFFICE in Bay Ridge buzzed with nervous energy. Young men filled out papers, took physicals, swore oaths. Matteo stood among them in plain clothes, his leather jacket left in Caesar's car.

Patrick Donovan appeared at his elbow, clipboard in hand, smile too bright. "Mr. Ricci! So glad you decided to serve. Your paperwork's been expedited—you'll ship out to Fort Dix this evening."

"This evening?" Matteo asked.

"Special circumstances," Donovan continued smoothly. "You yourself mentioned your enthusiasm to begin training. The Army appreciates such dedication."

Matteo nodded once, then walked through the processing door without looking back. If he looked back, he could never see it through.

* * *

A KNOCK INTERRUPTED the rhythm of packing. Debbie paused, wearing Matteo's old button-down shirt that hung loose enough to hide her growing belly, and a pair of his pants with his belt tied around the waist. Not because she didn't have her own pants and shirt, but because they were his. She wanted his smell on her. She needed it.

Her eyes, swollen nearly shut from crying, lifted toward the door.

She opened it to find Carmelo waiting. The moment of silent staring stretched between them, heavy with everything unsaid. Then she turned and allowed him entry by default rather than by invitation.

"I came to give you this." He closed the door. He extended his hand with a thick envelope of cash.

She glanced at it, then away. "Leave it on the table. José will count it later."

He set it down. She looked up to see him surveying the empty room. Furniture gone, only boxes remaining. The home she and Matteo had built was a skeleton of a life being dismantled. The brownstone sold by Matteo to Carmelo was done fair and square. So the payment was delivered as promised.

"The Army will be good for him, Debbie—and Harlem's safer for you than Brooklyn. I'm here for whatever you need. Any time. Any help."

"You know what I think?" She didn't look up from her folding.

His eyebrow arched, waiting.

"I think you've been sick with jealousy since the day you learned he loved me." Her hands moved steadily, mechanically.

"Jealous? Of what exactly?"

"Of happiness. Of the life he built for me and his kids right here in your father's face. Jealous of his courage. Jealous because you can see that our love is real, solid, unbreakable. Something you couldn't have with Kathy." Now she met his eyes. "Matteo has true grit. That's what my Big Mama would call it. He didn't care what people thought, didn't care about defying your father. He was—is—the man you could never be."

Carmelo's smirk was razor-thin. "You don't know Matteo. He's killed so many men—"

"I know all of him. Good and bad. The difference is, I love his darkness too." She resumed packing. "Kathy can't even stomach the mention of you."

"All right, Debs—"

"Don't." Her voice cracked like a whip. "I'm not your 'Debs.' I'm his. And whatever lies you fed him to make him abandon us, I see through them. He loves you Melo. He still thinks you're that smart kid who is misunderstood. But I see through you, Wolf of Harlem. You'll never fool me."

"Are you finished?"

"No. Your people think Matteo is dumb. Just some muscle with a knife. I think your mother thought it, too. But he's smarter than all of you. Even with all your book smarts, he created the perfect love and didn't run or hide to do it," her voice choked on a sob. "Now he gave his life for it."

"I think you already covered that," Carmelo rolled his eyes.

"Go ahead. Roll your eyes. You know I'm right. Get out. Don't contact me or Junior again. Get out and stay gone. I don't ever want to see your face until my real husband comes home."

The Wolf's smile was cold as winter itself. "We're family now, Debs. I'll never be far away. Tell Kathy I said hello."

The door slammed with enough force to rattle the windows. Debbie stood frozen, feeling gutted, as if Carmelo had reached inside and torn something vital from her chest. Her hand found her belly as her knees gave way, dropping her into the nearest chair.

Her heart was shattered—that much would never heal. But as she sat there, breathing through the pain, something hardened inside her. This would be her last collapse. Her final tears. If Matteo could find the strength to walk away from everything he loved to keep them safe, then she could find the strength to build a life for her kids and him worth returning to.

And that life would have nothing to do with the Ricci name.

. . .

1978 Staten Island - Ricci Estate

Debbie hated how the past could ambush her. Standing there, it all rushed back—every wound, every regret, every irreversible choice. This day was supposed to be about new beginnings, but her mind kept circling back to old pain. Only José's death had cut deeper than the day Matteo walked into that recruitment office.

She pressed her fingertips to her eyes, catching the tears before they could fall. Through the estate's massive picture window, she had seen the spectacle arranged for Don Matteo Ricci's wedding reception. Matteo didn't want anyone there but family. So, the celebration was limited to top-ranking associates and their families. Outside pristine lawns, laughing guests, the facade of family unity was on display.

Her children moved through it all like actors in different plays. Junior stood rigid beside Sandy, watching the festivities as if calculating threats. Matteo's oldest son could do no wrong in Matteo's eyes. Countless times, Debbie would complain of Junior's rebellion, and Matteo would chuckle over the prison phone call and say to let him be. Cars, and any prizes Junior wanted, Matteo insisted Carmelo gave to him. Spoiling Junior made him even harder for her to raise alone. And even now, Junior blamed him for José's death and wouldn't let Matteo close.

But Junior was here. And he was playing his part. That was progress.

Being jaded wasn't his fault. He'd inherited his father's wariness and her wounds. Daphne and Christopher, floated through the crowd with eagerness, desperate to belong in this glittering new world their father had built.

Were the Ricci cousins genuinely welcoming, or simply well-trained in the politics of blood? Debbie suspected the latter.

"There you are." His voice wrapped around her like memory—deep, smooth, unchanged despite everything.

She looked back and time folded. Beneath the hardness sat the same beautiful roughneck who'd once feared nothing and no one. War had etched new lines, prison had stolen softness, but her Matteo remained. She'd spend their marriage rediscovering every tender place the world had tried to destroy.

His expression shifted. "Why are you looking at me like that? What's wrong?"

She crossed to him in three steps, burrowing into his embrace. This house—being here openly, wearing his ring—it awakened every sleeping grief. The memories crashed down: the empty years, the damaged man who'd finally come home to her.

"I spent so long hating your brother." The words spilled out raw. "Hating him with everything in me. Now he's gone and I just want to say thank you."

"Bella." He lifted her face, reading her tears. "Did someone say something? Who—"

"I need to thank him," she whimpered through fresh tears.

"For what, baby?"

"For whatever devil's bargain he made to bring you home. For pulling strings to get you out of prison. For trying to stitch our family back together." She fisted her hands in his shirt. "He sent you away, but he also brought you back. I want to thank him for this chance to remember what we were. What we could be with our children. I saw the Wolf and all the destruction he caused. This is Melo. I feel it. This is him trying to make it right for us."

His eyes went liquid. "I thanked him for both of us. You were always the only thing I needed, Debs. The only thing that mattered. He knew that. He hugged me in that prison and said he wanted me to be free."

Something broke free in her chest—not tears but laughter, bright and startling. She pressed closer, laughing against his neck, tasting happiness after so much sorrow.

"We're really going to be okay," he said, wonder in his voice.

"Yes."

"Come meet the other wives. Let them see who really runs this family," he said.

"Not yet." She caught his sleeve. "I need to tell you something first."

His brow furrowed. "Tell me what?"

She caught her bottom lip between her teeth. gathering courage. "Something happened this morning. I was sick, and when I'm queasy, you know I always smoke to calm my stomach."

"I didn't know that?" he frowned.

"Yes, you do!" she snapped.

"Sorry, sorry, babe, okay, tell me what's wrong?"

His expression sharpened with concern.

"Cigarette didn't help. I threw up more. And then Janey comes, and I got upset and threw up again." Color bloomed in her cheeks.

"You ill now?" His palm found her forehead, checking for fever.

She caught his wrist, moving his hand away. "Not ill. Pregnant."

"What?" He searched her face for the punchline. "Pregnant?"

Her smile was answer enough.

"Bella, you're forty-eight years old!" His laugh was pure shock mixed with amusement.

The joy fled from her face. She pushed against his chest. "I know what I know, Matteo. My body doesn't lie."

"Can women even make babies at forty-eight?"

"Apparently, this one can!" Her stance turned defensive.

He studied her, understanding dawning. "You're serious."

"Dead serious. I'm pregnant. I ain't seen my period since you been after me when you came back," she rolled her eyes.

"But how? Explain it to me," he insisted.

"Explain what? You idiot! Whenever we get back together, I get knocked up. It's how it works!"

"But Debs, we're older now. Is it even possible? Did you go to a doctor?" he asked.

"I don't need a damn doctor. I got common sense. You've been on me since you got out of prison. *Sex, Debs, I want it. Sex, Debs. Wake up, Debs. Suck it, Debs! Pussy! Pussy! Pussy!"*

He watched her pace and rant. His eyes traveled over her body—her beauty, her spirit. Could it be possible? Could God really be giving him another chance to be a father, a complete father, with his family intact? After all these years, at their age? He couldn't believe it.

"And?" she said, arms folded, glaring at him. "What you got to say to that?"

"Have you seen a doctor?" he said, trying to hide the humor in his voice. Debbie and her crazy ideas always made things fun with her. But he knew not to mock her. She'd punish him good if she felt he was making fun of her.

"Not yet, but I've done this dance before. Three times." Her voice gentled. "Every time you love me, we create life. It's our pattern."

"Debs..." He seemed lost for words. "This is unexpected. If you're right, then—"

"I am right! I am!"

He summoned the patience for her that he often used when he was unable to deny her wishes, even her most impossible wishes. "Then I'm the luckiest man breathing."

"You mean that?" Her smile lit her entire face.

He lifted her clean off her feet, spinning them both. "Another baby! God, woman, I love how you grow our children!"

She shrieked with laughter, legs dangling, arms wrapped around his neck. When her feet touched ground again, she straightened her expensive suit jacket and fixed her golden hair. She was radiant.

"Now, introduce me to those Mafia bitches. They need to meet the woman who is now in charge."

His hand connected with her bottom in playful possession before he took her hand properly. Leading her through his father's blood-bought mansion, he felt ready for whatever came next.

CHAPTER 45

DAUGHTER AND SON

Present. Having a good time?" A voice asked.

Sandy turned. Nicolas Ricci stood closer than comfort allowed, and his expensive cologne created an invisible barrier of temptation for her. He extended a drink like a peace offering.

It was his eyes that she could not look away from. Brown and deep, they had a dreamy appeal with dark lashes under his straight brow. She had very little experience in dating and even less in flirting.

After a heartbeat of indecision, she accepted the drink.

"Thank you," she said.

"*Prego*," he winked.

"*Prego*? What does that mean?" she asked.

"It means *you're welcome*," he replied.

"*Grazie*," she replied.

His left brow winged up. "You speak Italian?"

"No. I dunno, heard words before," she shrugged.

"You don't know if you speak my language?" Nicolas asked.

She blushed. "Growing up, I just knew it sometimes. Spoke it sometimes. It's a running joke. I was teasing. I knew what "Prego" means, and I am familiar with some other words. It just comes from nowhere, I guess."

"I doubt that. I think it comes from some place special," he replied.

She glanced away. "Do you live here?"

"We all do now. Family," he said. The word 'family' rolled off his tongue like ownership instead of belonging. The comment drew her gaze back to his.

She sampled the drink cautiously. "Why do you keep staring at me?"

"Do I stare?" he asked, as if shocked.

"You stared at the funeral for Mama. You stared across from the bakery. You stared at the weird wedding at the graveyard. You stare a lot," Sandy commented.

"You're beautiful. You look like Aunt Kathy at her age."

The comparison chilled her. The hurt over the loss of her mother was too raw for the compliment. "You never saw my mother at my age," she countered.

"Sorry, didn't mean to make it weird—I just—"

"It's okay," Sandy said.

He nodded, but didn't explain further.

His bakery visit surfaced in fragments thanks to that cultured voice, words wrapped in silk. But the actual conversation? Gone, like so many memories lately. She struggled to surface it to keep the conversation flowing. D.C. had been the same. Lucky for her, she lived in a dorm with roommates who had their own special needs.

"How's it going?" he asked when the silence went too long.

"How's what going?" she answered.

"Your research. The diaries." Impatience leaked through his charm. "Any new revelations?"

The pieces snapped together. He'd wanted information, needed intel from those pages. She'd just finished her mother's time in New Orleans and then the subsequent war of Harlem that eventually killed her uncle and sent the Penny Man into the military—pages filled with nothing but contradictions of the man who was her true father, Carmelo Ricci.

"Nothing," she said.

His disappointment softened his features. It was as if he stepped closer without moving. She just felt him reaching for her without words or touch as his inspection of her turned deliberate, possessive. "Let me show you around. Privately. I won't hurt you, Sandy."

"How about you fuck off instead." Junior appeared like a guardian angel, drinks in hand—when had she asked for one?

Nicolas kept his focus on Sandy. "I don't fuck off in my own house, cousin. You're free to leave."

Sandy watched them both, embarrassed.

"Nah, I'll stay and crack your fucking jaw," Junior's voice dropped low, deadly.

"Junior, stop!" Sandy gasped.

The party's attention shifted, men straightening like soldiers sensing conflict. Nicolas finally graced Junior with his attention, utterly unmoved.

"Take your best shot, hero," said Nicolas.

"Nicolas, thank you, but I should stay with my cousin."

The staring contest stretched until Nicolas offered a mocking bow, turned, and walked away as casually as he had appeared.

"What is wrong with you?" Sandy demanded.

Junior's jaw worked. "He murdered two of my friends. For the crime of knowing me. You're looking at a killer, Sandy."

"He's family."

"Fuck this." Junior hurled both drinks onto the manicured lawn. "I'm out."

Sandy caught his arm. "Wait. Please."

"They don't want us here," Junior hissed.

"You have every right to be here." She reminded him of the pride and confidence her mother had taught her over the countless years, when her differences made her feel like an 'other' among people.

"What are you talking about?" Junior frowned.

"Those diaries make it clear—your father adores you. The army and prison stole him and your birthright, not lack of love. Don't let them win. He is in danger too, and you're all he has. Stand and—"

Applause broke through the cousins' standoff. Sandy and Junior's heads turned in sync. Matteo and Debbie had made their grand entrance. He stood with his characteristic stillness, but Debbie bounced beside him, clutching flowers and radiating joy. Her grin could have lit the entire estate. If the Ricci family harbored reservations about their new matriarch, they buried them deep—even the wives raised their glasses in practiced celebration.

"God, look at her," Sandy breathed. "She's so pretty, so happy."

Junior couldn't look away as his father kissed his mother like a proud prince, then scooped her up as if she weighed nothing. The crowd parted respectfully while Don Matteo Ricci carried his bride deeper into their circle of his world, and Debbie clung to him, ready for the journey.

The contradiction of his parents—violence and tenderness, separation and devotion—had shaped Junior's whole life. Through his father's absence, his dramatic and troubled return, this inexplicable bond endured.

"See what they have?" Sandy's voice held hope.

"I need the truth." The words tumbled out of Junior, soft but raw.

"Truth about what?" she asked.

He forced himself to meet her eyes. "About José. Why did my father murder the man who raised me? Have you reached that part in the diaries?"

"Junior, no." Her shock was genuine. "They were best friends in everything I've read. Both of them were partners in protecting you and Auntie. Why would you think—"

The memory slammed into him. Rain streaming down windows. Five-year-old Daphne argued with her mother about going inside and wanting to see her Papa. His mother was angry and distressed, crying and shouting at them to be quiet, just be silent. Daphne's cries turned hysterical. Junior, ten and desperate for quiet, disobeyed.

His mother spun around: "Get back in the car!"

Debbie threw open her car door and got out. She caught Junior by his shirt, and he fought her. He knew where to go. He knew where his fathers were.

The sound came first. Glass exploding twenty stories up, crystalline glass fell with the rain. A shape, dark against the grey sky, arms and legs splayed like a broken marionette.

Poppy.

Time stretched as their beloved José fell. Junior's brain refused to process what his eyes saw—his surrogate father windmilling through space, tie whipping behind him like a banner.

The impact. Hard. Wet. Final. And blood... there was so much blood.

His mother's scream joined Daphne's from the car until Debbie, pregnant, fainted. Junior stood there shaking. His gaze lifted up. He didn't see his father's face. He saw his shape, his dark silhouette outlined by the light behind him. He stood there staring, then turned away.

"Junior? Junior!" Sandy's touch made him flinch. He walked away, swiping at his eyes.

"Junior, please—" Sandy reached for him, but he was gone fast.

She looked helplessly toward the party. Matteo had clocked his son's distress, fatherly concern cracking his public mask as everyone fawned over his wife. She saw him kiss Debbie and go after Junior. She felt a twinge of hope.

"Poor kid's a mess."

Nicolas stood behind her again, persistence personified. "Seriously, what is your problem?"

"Time-sensitive problem. I need your help. Now," said Nicolas.

"Too bad. Find someone else." She turned to leave.

"You're his daughter," Nicolas called after her.

Everything stopped. "What did you say?"

"You're his daughter," he said.

"I told you I wasn't having that conversation with you in the bakery. I know who my father was," she replied.

"It's the truth. It's what Aunt Kathy could never tell you. That's why they want you to read those diaries, my guess. So you can remember and tell us his secrets."

"That's insane—"

"You're Carmelo Ricci's daughter. The Wolf of Harlem's lost

princess." His smile held secrets. "I can prove it. Unlock what your mother sealed in your mind."

Sandy's world tilted. She scanned desperately for family but found only strangers.

Nicolas's hand appeared before her, steady and sure. "My father left something behind. Something that will make you remember—everything."

Logic screamed warnings. But the more she read about her parents, the more questions she had. Sandy took his hand and let him lead her away from safety, toward whatever truth waited in the shadows.

CHAPTER 46

THE PINK LADY CLUB AND BAR 1954

Maria Ricci savored the unfamiliar sensation of happiness. Five years, she'd been Mrs. Carmelo Ricci in name only, watching her husband mourn a love that had betrayed him for a Mississippi farmer. Five years of careful moves, calculated sacrifices, and swallowed pride while he treated her like furniture in his life. But something had shifted. Last night, he'd crossed the threshold of their bedroom with purpose. He'd made love to her—not performed a duty, not maintained appearances, but claimed her as his wife. It would be the only way for her complete destruction and punishment. To give her what her heart wants and then rip it away, like she'd done to him.

She'd earned this moment through methods he'd never need to know about. After all, what were a few necessary evils compared to a lifetime of being loved?

When the car glided to a stop, Slim's familiar face appeared at her window. He opened the door with practiced grace, offering his hand.

"You look beautiful, Maria."

"Thank you, Slim." Her pulse quickened. "He's here?"

"Waiting inside."

She draped her fur stole over one shoulder and moved toward the entrance, the red dress flowing around her legs. The restaurant transformed as she entered—lights dimmed to intimate shadows, tables cleared away, hundreds of candles creating pools of golden light. A jazz quartet played something soft and smoky just for them.

Carmelo sat at the lone table, white roses spilling from a crystal vase. When his dark eyes found hers, her heart performed the same treacherous flip it had when they were teenagers and he'd first noticed her existence.

Carmelo stood, smoothed down his tie, and let his gaze travel over his wife's attire and beauty as if impressed. Heat flooded Maria's cheeks. He was handsome, strikingly so. All the girls in their circle of friends had crushes on Matteo, and even though they thought Nino was attractive, they found him strange. She was the one who got close enough to snag the prince.

Her cheeks flushed when he stared, and her heart pounded in her chest, but she maintained her confidence. Last night's touch—finally, after five years—had revived the dream she thought lost after he learned she had a part in revealing the twins to that colored girl he had obsessed over.

"Ti stavo aspettando," he said in that deeply low and seductive voice.

"Well, thank you for waiting," she replied.

She crossed the open space and approached him without hesitation, arms circling his neck as her fur stole pooled forgotten on the floor. The kiss she gave him held five years of hunger. He responded with measured control before drawing out her chair with old-world courtesy.

One of Carmelo's soldiers emerged from the kitchen, bearing plates of pasta, and moved with silent efficiency. Carmelo uncorked the wine himself.

"Hi, Jimmie," Maria offered.

Jimmie's eyes stayed down as he retreated wordlessly to the kitchen. The deliberate snub made her shoulders tighten.

"Where are the kids?" Carmelo asked, noticing Jimmie's stiff behavior.

"With your father. He asked for them tonight. He spoils them so much, Carmelo." She forced brightness into her voice. "Ma says he's wonderful with them. And Nino is really excited when they visit your dad lately. They all adore him. I was thinking that I'm ready for Nino to come live with us. Give Ma a break. I know you would like that if I did more."

"You love him too." Carmelo's tone was neutral as he raised his wine.

"Nino? Of course—"

"No, my father. You love him too, just like the kids," Carmelo remarked.

The statement made her stomach tighten. Maria kept her smile steady while shifting in her chair, a movement Carmelo might interpret as mere discomfort. The truth about his father was far more sinister. Cosimo Ricci terrified her to her core. He had since he'd orchestrated her mother's marriage to him after Carmelo's mother's suicide. She'd watched him break her mother's spirit with calculated kindness and affection, then seen him turn violent when Carmelo and Matteo were away. She'd seen how his affection always came with invisible chains, and her mother walked a tightrope in search of that common ground that made her marriage bearable.

How many times had he mocked her mother's cooking, saying Lucia's was better? How many times had he ranted about anything being changed in his home from Lucia's vision? Now he lavished that same possessive attention on her twins, and it made her skin crawl, because she feared that too would come at a price.

The lie about that night—letting Carmelo believe he'd forced himself on her—had been her only shield against Cosimo's plans. Better to be the wife of a guilty son than whatever Cosimo might have made her become.

"I asked you a question, Maria. You and father are really close?"

Maria paused mid-bite, the exquisite pasta suddenly difficult to swallow. "Of course. He's my father, too, now. After everything that happened, he married my mother and helped bring us together. He's a good man, Carmelo. I know he was hard on you once, but seeing you two close now makes me happy."

Carmelo lowered the glass and studied her for a moment. "You think we're close?"

She smiled. "I mean closer. Yes. You're in his business, and with him all the time. You stopped boxing to help build the family. You do more than Matteo. Ma, says your father is often speaking about how smart you are."

He continued to stare. Having his attention focused solely on her made her head swoon. She glanced over to the band and smiled. "They are so good. I never really get to hear live music. I'm always with the kids or at home. We never… well, never used to go out and do this."

"Is that what you want? Nights out? Freedom to go hear jazz bands?" Carmelo asked.

"No, Carmelo," she gave a light chuckle. "I swear, men are so dense at times. I want you. I've only wanted you," she said softly.

"Even after what I've done. To you? How I have treated you?" Carmelo asked. His manner was cool, his stare unblinking. "Don't you deserve better, Maria, than any of this?"

"Stop. That night is buried and forgiven. I've dreamed of this. To sit with you like this. To build our family and be truly yours. If I hurt you by revealing it, I'm sorry. But look at what we have now. Two beautiful children who need their father. A wife who's waited five years for your love." Her voice dropped to an intimate softness. "They are your blood, they are you, Carmelo. And for us, you are our only real family. I've forgiven everything. Please, please do the same. Last night was our fresh start. Who knows? Maybe we'll be blessed with another baby. Imagine that joy."

"Dance with me," he said, already standing, already reaching for her. The empty restaurant, the watching shadows, the flickering candles. It all faded away. When his arms closed around her, the world contracted to just this—his heartbeat against hers, the whisper of the saxophonist floating through candlelight. They moved with the synchronicity of souls who'd always belonged together, despite the years of distance. Maria surrendered to the feeling, letting five years of longing culminate in this perfect moment. This was the marriage she'd envisioned, the love she'd killed for, the happiness that finally felt within reach.

Tears threatened to release behind her closed lids. She'd never wanted to steal his dreams of freedom or burden him with false guilt over a rape that existed only in her fiction. But his father's wishes had been explicit. She must get pregnant. Each month that no baby announcement was made, he took it out on her mother. Carmelo was never around, and neither was Matteo. It was just her and Nino to witness Cosimo's savagery.

Maria had to do something.

So she and her mother revealed that Carmelo would not sleep with her. Cosimo was infuriated. He came up with another plan, even more horrible. Seduce one of the capu's in the family. A man who could not be touched if the plot was uncovered by anyone without the Don's consent. Her choice. Cosimo didn't care as long as she conceived, and Carmelo believed without a doubt that the baby was his. It was the only way to secure at least one of his sons to the Ricci family.

Her mother's cold logic had prevailed. She would make him think he was a rapist like his father. Caesar wanted her, would protect her, could give her children to trap Carmelo. The plan had seemed monstrous until she'd discovered Caesar's unexpected gentleness, his desire to please, his willingness to be what Carmelo refused to be. And in truth, she did care deeply for him and his companionship.

For five years, she'd lived split in half—her body finding solace with Caesar while her heart remained imprisoned by Carmelo's indifference. The guilt ate at her like acid, even as she played the devoted wife to a man who could barely stand her presence.

But sins could be forgiven, wounds could heal. With that, Kathy Freeman finally out of their lives, perhaps she could build something real from the lies.

"I have a surprise for you," Carmelo murmured against her temple.

"A surprise?" Delight bubbled up through her voice.

"Can I give it to you now?" he asked.

The music continued as their swaying came to a stop. Maria

opened her eyes, searching his face, trying to read the depths of the mystery that lay within. "Yes. Give it to me now."

He lifted her hand to his lips and pressed the most tender kiss there. He winked at her, and she felt like she was floating. He then tugged her away from their romantic dinner. His fingers laced through hers as he led her on a meandering path through the empty restaurant. She followed eagerly, scanning for wrapped packages or hidden gifts.

Only when he turned toward the kitchen did a flicker of confusion cross her joy.

Carmelo moved like he always did—commanding space with his boxer's build, shoulders blocking her view as they passed through the doorway. His presence filled the frame so completely that she saw nothing beyond him.

Then he released her hand and stepped aside.

Maria's scream tore through the jazz music, through the candlelit romance, through every illusion of the evening.

Matteo Ricci Estate - 1978

Sandy had gone too far. She'd let him lead her away from the party, down into the belly of the Ricci's prominent estate. A basement so large that there were rooms and doors everywhere. He actually took her into an office with wood paneling for walls, dark leather chairs, and a stench of a hundred cigars smoked at once. To the back corner of the room was a locked door. Nicolas had the key.

"Come inside. I have something to show you," Nicolas said.

Sandy's feet refused to move. The basement door gaped before her like a mouth.

"It's in here." Nicolas's patience was wearing thin. "What you need to see."

"I've changed my mind." She turned to flee. "I'm going back upstairs."

"Do you remember anything about him?"

The question stopped her cold. She looked back, trying to read his face in the dim light. "I don't know your father."

"He's your father. Not mine." His smile was not as warm as it had been all the times before. "You can return to those diaries, swallow Aunt Kathy's lies. Or you can step through this door and see the truth. Maybe even remember it yourself."

The words hit like physical blows. Since her mother's death, she'd stopped taking the pills that kept her mind from becoming foggy with chaotic thoughts, stopped the dreams she could never remember when she woke up.

She had expected the headaches to return along with the confusion, but instead, it was replaced by raw grief and her mother's written secrets. But now, standing at this threshold, she felt dangerously empty. Incomplete.

Nicolas disappeared into the darkness beyond the door.

After a heartbeat's hesitation, Sandy followed.

The Pink Lady - 1954

Maria's scream died in her throat, replaced by a desperate hand pressed to her mouth. The kitchen's fluorescent lights turned the scene before her into a waking nightmare—too bright, too real, too impossible to deny.

Carmelo's men formed a semicircle of judgment. Slim had materialized from the back entrance, completing their ranks. They stood motionless as executioners, their eyes boring into her with collective condemnation.

At their center, Caesar slumped in a chair, wrists and ankles bound with wire that cut into swelling flesh—his face—God, his face. The handsome features she'd kissed in secret were now a geography of bruises and split skin. Blood ran in twin streams from his nose, mixing with saliva that dripped from his slack jaw. Each labored breath bubbled red.

The hammer lay discarded at his feet, its head caked with evidence of methodical violence.

"Look at me."

She obeyed without thinking, meeting Carmelo's gaze. The expression waiting for her transcended mere cruelty. This was the face of a man who'd discovered the exact depth of his own capacity for violence—and embraced it.

"Surprise," he said softly, making the word obscene.

Speech failed her entirely.

"Cat got your tongue? Or is that Caesar's job?" The casual vulgarity made her stomach heave. "Come now, Maria. You've been so poetic about our fresh start. Our new beginning. Surely you have something lovely to say now?"

"Wha-wha-why?" The stammer betrayed her disintegrating control.

"Why?" He stepped closer, and she saw Caesar's blood decorating his cuffs. Why hadn't she noticed the blood before? Her mind pondered. The answer was clear. When it came to Carmelo, she only saw what she wanted to see. Not the Wolf inside of him.

"You want to know why? Where were your questions when you let another man fill your womb? When you made me believe I was a monster? When you gave me another man's children to raise. Made me love a lie?"

"Please... Carmelo... we thought... it was to protect—"

"PROTECT?" His control shattered, the roar made Caesar flinch despite his injuries. "YOU CONSPIRED TO BREAK ME AND CALLED IT PROTECTION?"

"Is he dead?" Her voice came out small, childlike. "Did you kill him?"

The rage in Carmelo's eyes banked to something colder. "Not yet. That decision belongs to you."

He approached. She stepped back. "If he lives, you both become mine. And I'm not talking about what's between your legs, darling. That currency's worthless now. Your debt runs deeper."

"Last night you said—"

"I lied. You lied. We lie to each other. I treated you like the whore you've always been."

"How?" Tears carved tracks through her makeup. "How can you turn this way. We build a life together. Is it perfect? no. But we did. Our… my kids love you, Melo. You're the only father they know. I love you. I have done everything to be worthy of you, but you never gave me any hope. How can you be this? After everything? All for her?" Maria wiped her tears. "She's gone, Melo. She's never coming back."

"Choose," he said. "Caesar made his choice an hour ago, but I decided to have some fun with him. Now choose. His life is bound to mine, or his death is on your conscience. Decide." His tone turned almost businesslike. "If you choose life, I'll let you take him. Hospital, home, your bed—I don't give a shit. Just ensure you're both ready when I call."

She searched the room for sympathy, finding only stone faces. Slim cleaned the hammer with methodical care.

"What do you want from me?"

Carmelo's smile promised horrors. "You'll know when I collect."

He walked out, leaving silence. Slim pocketed the cleaned hammer, moving to follow.

"Slim! Please! Help us! You and Caesar are friends. You're like a father to Melo! Help him, please!" Maria begged.

Slim paused at the door. His shoulders did sag a bit. "Get him to Bellevue. Car accident—that's your story. The boys will help load him." His gaze shifted to Caesar's broken form. "Don't deviate from that story. I know Caesar won't."

"Is he going to kill me?" Maria asked.

"No." Slim's expression held grim certainty. "He needs you to help him kill his father. And you will, Maria. We all will."

She shook her head in horror. She watched as the men freed Caesar's limp body. Jimmie spoke only a few words to reassure her he'd get them to the hospital.

Outside, Slim slid into the passenger seat of the idling car. Neither he nor Carmelo spoke during the long drive back to New Jersey, the silence heavy with promises of what was to come.

CHAPTER 47

WELCOME TO THE JUNGLE - MATTEO & JOSÉ

Present. Matteo surveyed his kingdom from the edge of the tent, tasting victory and defeat in equal measure. Through endless nights in prison, he'd built this moment in his mind —returning triumphant, crowning Debbie and their children with the respect they deserved. Reality had exceeded even his grandest visions, yet something felt hollow at its core.

Under the tent's soft lights, Daphne and Christopher spun across the dance floor with their mother, her joy infectious enough to draw other wives and children into their orbit. The men maintained their typical distance—clustered around card tables and ashtrays, conducting business through cigar smoke and measured words.

His gaze tracked across the assembled faces. Capos who'd prospered financially under Carmelo. Street soldiers who'd bled for the Wolf. Dealers who still whispered his brother's name in reverence. They wore loyalty like armor. All except Caesar, whose dedication had cost him more than anyone knew through the decades of Matteo's absence. He was broken, conditioned to be nothing but loyal. Him and his wife Maria.

The crowd skewed heavily male—enforcers, earners, and associates outnumbering family three to one. Not a single face reflected the mixed heritage Matteo had tried to protect. No wonder Junior had vanished into the night. The boy understood what Matteo was only beginning to grasp: this was still the Wolf's pack, merely tolerating new leadership.

Caesar's hand landed on his shoulder from behind.

"Where is he?" Matteo asked without turning. "I searched and couldn't find him."

"Found him. He's in his mother's car smoking weed. We've got eyes on him."

"So he didn't leave?" Genuine surprise colored Matteo's voice.

"Nope. Still here."

Matteo located Debbie in the dancing crowd, watching her coax Christopher through how to do dance steps called the Robot, and she was wrong. The other younger children got in on the fun and mimicked the dance as well. "Keep them happy. Nobody ruins their night. Especially for my baby-boy. Clear?"

"Got it."

"Wait." Matteo scanned the crowd again. "Where's Sandy?"

"No idea. She's not with Junior."

"Find her! Christ." Matteo was already moving. "I'll be back."

He strode inside his home and ignored those who either wanted to kiss his ass with congratulations or talk business. He walked straight out the family door, past the parade of chauffeured cars lining the street. This stretch of coastline belonged to his top men exclusively—he could walk barefoot to the beach without concern. But Junior alone out here was different. Unacceptable.

The Mercedes sat where he'd expected, music drifting from barely cracked windows along with telltale smoke. A smile tugged at his mouth. Kid had balls, at least.

Junior shot upright at his approach, frantically rolling down windows to release the evidence. Debbie would raise hell about her car reeking after Matteo had just had it detailed.

By the time Matteo reached the driver's door, Junior was climbing out.

"Get back in. You're driving."

"What?" Junior's confusion was evident.

Matteo walked around the car and slid into the passenger seat. Junior hesitated before returning to the driver's seat, adjusting his seatbelt properly. "What about Ma? We can't just leave—"

"She doesn't need your protection anymore. I'm home. Nobody touches what's mine." Matteo reclined his seat. "Drive."

"Where?"

"To the beach," he replied, staring straight ahead.

"Why?"

Matteo's gaze cut over to him. "You asked me a question about the man you called Father. I said I would tell you what happened that night when you were ready."

Junior felt his hands shaking.

"You're ready," Matteo gaze moving back to the road ahead.

Junior studied his father's face, then nodded slowly. The engine turned over, and they pulled away from the curb into the night.

1961 - Brooklyn, the Gardens

The Carroll Gardens apartment had become a tomb for Matteo Ricci. Kicked out of Debbie's house for the final time, the Gardens was the best his brother would give him.

This was his hell. The lights were kept off. Darkness thick as tar soothed him. The rot and stench of half-eaten plates mixed in with his senses as he heard the scratch of rats in corners. All of it added to its suffocation. The silence of his loneliness was broken only by the sound of bottles rolling when he reached for one. His fingers found one at last. He drank to forget. The gag was that his drinking made him remember.

The apartment dissolved.

Jungle stench rose like his fevers whenever he entered his haunted dreams. It was a sweet decay instead of the apartment stench. Pebbling rain on elephant grass instead of windowpanes, but pounding through the triple canopy of the forest leaves, his mind had transported him back to.

Thump-thump-thump.

The Huey helicopter that had dropped them into the combat zone was pulling away, its rotor blades fading into the distance. They were alone now in the hot LZ—a landing zone under enemy control—with no quick escape, no door gunners for cover, no medevac if things went wrong. Just them and the terrible silence that meant Mr. Charlie, the enemy, Viet-cong, was out there, watching, waiting.

Then, the world tore open.

The first mortar landed and opened the earth. Then the world became violence—erupting mud, vegetation turned shrapnel, spider holes lids flipped open as the black-pajamed Vietnamese joined the fight from holes that shouldn't exist. Their muzzle flashes competed with the steady *thud-thud-thud* of American return fire.

He was down, sighting his rifle. Beside him, Ely Brown—Mississippi by way of Harlem—matching his rhythm shot for shot. When Ely had arrived in-country and been assigned to Matteo's unit, the coincidence had seemed impossible. Two men from the same New York streets, ending up in the same squad in this green hell. But after months of firefights and midnight conversations, they'd discovered the thread: the same recruiting office, the same over-eager sergeant, the same expedited papers. No coincidence at all. Someone had engineered this.

The enemy and envy of his brother had become salvation for Matteo and a lifeline. Together, he and Ely survived, determined to return to the women they loved. They laid down a suppressing fire that was a thing of brutal beauty.

"Tunnel rats comin' up for air, Sarge!" Ely yelled at Matteo, his voice cutting through the din, not a trace of fear in it. Only a fierce, focused joy. "Time for a little pest control!"

They worked in sync, a perfect, deadly dance. *Crack.*

Matteo's shot. A shadow fell.

Thud-thud-thud.

Ely's tracers walked a line across a spider hole, silencing it. They were winning. In that moment, drenched in sweat and rain and fear, they were Gods of war, holding back the chaos. He flashed a grin, teeth white in his grime-caked face. "Ain't nothin' but a th—"

The world dissolved into a single, soundless flash of pure, white light. It came from the ground itself, two feet from Ely's right boot—a buried Bouncing Betty.

The sound returned, a deafening *CRUMP* that was felt more than heard.

Matteo was thrown back, his ears ringing. He blinked through the haze of smoke and suspended dirt. Ely was on the ground. The bottom half of his legs were just... gone. The rest of him was tossed aside like a broken doll, his uniform smoking.

The firefight faded. The world shrank to the three yards of churned earth between them. Matteo was crawling fast, screaming, crying, but he couldn't hear his own voice. He reached Ely, his hands scrambling, pressing against the unthinkable ruin of his torso, trying to stem a tide that was everywhere. The blood was hot. So hot. It soaked through his sleeves and his vest, leaving a sticky, warm residue.

Ely's eyes were wide open, locked on his. Not afraid. Just... surprised. His mouth moved, forming a word Matteo would never hear but would forever see: *"Sandy...tell..."*

Then, the light behind those eyes just... went out. It didn't fade. It snapped off. A switch was thrown.

A final, single mortar round landed twenty yards away, its shrapnel whining overhead, but Matteo didn't flinch. He just knelt in the red mud, holding what was left of his best friend, the hot rain washing the blood down his arms in thin, pink rivers. Then they came. The Vietnamese soldiers had him, dragging him down into the hole... into the tunnel.... into hell.

A flash of light...

Matteo threw his arm up, shielding his eyes against an explosion that wasn't there. Electric light. Apartment light. Not jungle fire. He was on the floor of his Carroll Gardens apartment, screaming at ghosts.

His arm lowered slowly, vision swimming with tears he couldn't stop. His heart hammered against ribs that remembered other impacts. Ely's surprised face. The wet sounds from the tunnels where his squad died by degrees.

"Matteo." José's voice was carefully modulated. Standing clear of the grabbing range.

"Don't touch me!" The words ripped out, half-warning, half-plea.

"I'm done watching this." José's tone held finality. "Debbie, the kids —I'm taking them to California. Tonight. She'll die before she abandons you, so I'm choosing for her."

"No—she can't—they're fine—" Matteo tried to stand, knocking bottles aside, hands moving through garbage like he could find salvation in the debris. "Getting better. See? Cleaning up. Just need to get my head right—"

"She knows about the whores, Matteo. The drinking's one thing, but the women?" José's voice held grief now. "You're destroying her, and she won't save herself. Won't leave you. So I'm taking them. Sam has work for me in California. He loves your kids as if they were his own. We'll protect them."

"Nobody takes Debbie!" The rage mixed with panic, past bled into the present. "Those whores lied! Never touched them. Used them for a place to hide from Mr. Charlie. Never touch. Never. Debbie, my sweet Debbie. Only Debbie. But they're coming—can hear them digging in the walls—" He beat his fists against his temples, trying to separate *then* from *now*. "Debbie's fine. I'm home. I can fix this."

His fists hammered his skull, trying to beat sense into scrambled synapses. "Home now. Safe. Fix it. Fix everything. Tomorrow. Fix Debbie tomorrow. Baby coming."

He made it upright through pure will. José caught him, propped him against the wall, where he could pretend to be functional. And there were times when he was. Months could go by without a single trigger. He'd make the kids laugh, play cards with Jose, and coax Debbie into letting him into her bed. Then BAM, out of nowhere, he was on the ground, digging his way out of hell.

"Look at me." José's hands framed his face. "Really look. Your family loves who you were. Not this ghost. Not this violence waiting to happen. See yourself, *hermano*. Please."

Matteo's eyes focused, and with clarity came the breaking. Every defense crumbled. "I try." The words came out in a shredded voice between his sobs. "Jesus Christ, I try so hard, but it's all still happening. It never stopped happening!"

He collapsed into José, who held him as he shook through sobs. "Make it stop, José,! Whatever it takes, make it fucking stop!"

"Your brother. He's offered to help. To send you out for help," José tried to reason.

Matteo kept wailing in agony.

"Breathe, Matteo. Come on, breathe through it...brother," José said.

That word. Always that word. Matteo mind convulsed—Back in the earth. Buried alive with the dying. His squad was reduced to meat and moans. Captain Minh crouching beside him, professional interest in his eyes, cigarette glowing in the dark.

"You breathe now. Good American. Breathe for Minh."

The ropes held as Matteo thrashed, screaming himself raw—

He surfaced from hell on his hands and knees, apartment floor beneath him. Rain was slashing inside through the window. Shattered. When had he fallen to the ground? Sounds from the street caused him to look up. Something was wrong.

He crawled to the jagged opening of a shattered window. He staggered to a standing position.

Street scene from hell greeted him: José broken on pavement, rain pooling blood around him. Debbie's knees giving way, her scream ascending. And Junior—his boy, just a boy drowning in rain—staring up at the window with naked horror, finger pointing, mouth open in accusation that needed no words.

The past and present collided, leaving only the truth: *he'd brought the war home, and now everyone he loved was a casualty.*

* * *

THE BEACH STRETCHED empty except for two figures. Matteo had shed his shoes, sitting just beyond where the waves could reach—close enough to taste salt, far enough to stay dry. Junior, beside him, tears falling freely as the story ended.

Matteo had confessed it all. No euphemisms, no excuses. The bottle that became his closest friend after Vietnam was gone. The needles that promised to quiet screaming ghosts with heroin were gone. How many times had Debbie found him broken, cleaned him up, and believed his promises? How José had covered for him, carried him, forgiven him—until that night when forgiveness ran out.

The cruelest legacy wasn't his own suffering but the horror he'd gifted his children. Junior, his sweet baby boy, was watching his father become a monster in a window frame. That image carved into a boy's psyche, shaping every year since.

Matteo reached out tentatively, hand trembling. His son—this man who'd grown up without him—turned and collapsed against him, holding his chest. So many years of absence bridged by shared grief.

Part of him wanted to join Junior's tears, to mourn José properly at last. But prison had taken that from him, too. Fourteen years of concrete and regret had cried him empty. All those nights replaying José's fall, Junior's scream, Debbie's collapse—he'd grieved until grief became just another fact of existence.

"I'm sorry, son. I'm so sorry. I did it. It's all my fault," Matteo sighed.

Junior's response was silence, but his presence was answer enough. They sat holding each other while the tide pulled back, taking nothing with it but time.

CHAPTER 48

AFTER THE PAIN

Present. Sandy blinked in the darkness. Nicolas walked around the room with practiced memory, turning on lamps that cast pools of amber light. As her eyes adjusted, she realized she stood in some kind of private gallery. The walls were covered with sketches—beautiful, lifelike, all depicting the same subject at different ages.

A little brown girl.

She frowned. She stepped closer to the nearest drawing. Why had he dragged her down here to look at—? Her breath caught. *That dress.* A sailor's dress with a white collar and navy stripes. A dress her mom had made. She wore it in a picture sitting on her grandma Brenda's lap. It hung in the house in Harlem. She knew that dress.

"When he died, I finally got the key to this room from Uncle Matteo." Nicolas's voice came from behind her. "The one room in the whole house I could never enter. I expected to find money, guns, the medallion—hell, anything but this."

"What is this?" Sandy's voice came out smaller than intended.

"It's you," Nicolas said with exasperation.

She turned slowly, taking in the progression. The earliest sketches showed her at three or four—gap-toothed smile, pigtails, eyes that hadn't yet learned wariness—the drawings aged with her, documenting years she couldn't quite grasp. By the time she reached the far wall, the girl in the pictures was nine, maybe ten.

An easel stood apart from the others; this portrait was rendered in color. Sandy approached it with growing dread. The girl—herself—sat alone in a sterile room, staring at a window. But it was the helmet that made her knees weak. White plastic and metal, covering her head like a cage.

"That one caught my attention, too." Nicolas moved beside her. "That's after your accident. When everything went sideways."

"Why am I wearing a helmet?" The question emerged without thought.

"Seizures. Bad ones. The helmet was protection—it kept you from cracking your skull when you fell." He studied the painting. "My mother said they had to take you to specialists in Canada. Experimental treatments."

The word 'seizures' triggered something. A flash—*falling, can't breathe, Mom's face above her, scared—*

Sandy shivered. "I don't—"

"Everyone knows the story of the Ricci brothers and the Freeman girls. Everyone." Nicolas's tone carried bitter amusement. "You're his kid. He and Aunt Kathy went to war over you. I knew it the first time I saw you two together, the way you held his hand like it was the most natural thing in the world." His voice dropped. "What I didn't know until a few years ago is I'm not his son. Somehow missed that little detail growing up."

"I'm sorry, but these drawings don't prove anything." Sandy forced steadiness into her voice. "My mother and Carmelo were close, yes. But I knew my father. Ely Brown. This is just... art."

"Art." Nicolas laughed without humor. "Right. Let me show you something else."

He moved to a cabinet she hadn't noticed, producing a manila folder. "Hospital records. December 1960. Seven-year-old female, severe head trauma from vehicular accident. Patient name: Alessandra Ricci."

Sandy's hand trembled as she took the papers. The admission form bore her photo—bruised, bandaged, but unmistakably her. And the name. That name. She knew that name. Memories came. They poured in. She finally remembered Carmelo. The time she spent with him. How he'd teach her Italian songs. Play marbles with her, take her to get ice-cream, sit with her on his lap in a big chair watching baseball on a television while she combs her doll's hair. So many memories came at once, she felt like fainting. Each time one surfaced, so did his voice in her head: Alessandra is what he called her.

"My name is Cassandra," she said, clinging to the one truth she would confess.

"He wanted it changed." Nicolas shuffled through papers with practiced efficiency. "Here—name change petition. And this, a revised birth certificate listing him as your father. Both signed by your mother. You were to become Alessandra Ricci, not Cassandra Brown."

"These are forgeries—"

"Look at this one." He handed her another document with careful reverence.

She recognized it immediately from the diaries. A marriage certificate dated 1949—Kathy Freeman and Carmelo Ricci. This one was real. Her mother had written about that desperate day, the ceremony that bound them before everything fell apart.

Nicolas watched her face change. "Every document here is legally sound. I had attorneys verify them. The birth certificate revision, the name change—your mother's signature is authentic. They just were never filed with the state."

"Why wouldn't they file them?" She asked.

"Maybe he used them as leverage—sign these or lose your daughter forever. Maybe they were filed and later destroyed. But look —" He pointed to the medical records. "Every hospital bill, every specialist report lists you as Alessandra Ricci. For three years after your accident, that's who you were in every legal document except the ones locked in courthouse files."

"Coincidence? Here's another." He handed her a document. "Bank records. Trust fund established in 1965 for 'A.R.' Deposits made monthly by C. Ricci until his death."

"This doesn't—"

"Your medical bills from the accident? Paid by Ricci family accounts. Your specialists in Canada? Arranged by my father's—by Carmelo's personal physician." Each time he said the truth it landed like a blow. "Your mother tried to run with you. He brought her back to Harlem. The accident happened because he couldn't stay away from her, you, or that bakery."

Another flash—*car, Carmelo screaming, the world turning upside down—*

"Still think you're Ely Brown's daughter now? Because I have more." Nicolas pulled out a photograph. "This is you, me, and Nina at my father's place in New Jersey. He called it his safe house. He kept us all there with him. I remember this picture. He took it. When he treated us all the same, before you had that car accident, and everything changed. He blamed… me," Nicolas voice choked on emotion.

"He visited Canada so much after your accident, he found a place for Uncle Nino. A center he could stay in for half the year. He and Aunt Kathy nearly lived in Canada for two years. And these images?" He turned and pointed to sketches of her sleeping in a bed, with bandages. "He sat by your bed. Drew these for you." Nicolas gestured to the walls. "Who does that for a stranger?"

Sandy's legs gave out. She sank onto a dusty chair, the helmet in the painting seeming to press against her own skull. Memories flickered—*a man's voice, soft, reading stories, smell of expensive cologne mixed with paint—*

"There's one more thing." Nicolas produced a final document with the reverence of someone handling explosives. "His will. Filed a week before he died."

Sandy's eyes immediately found her name. Not Sandy Brown. *Alessandra Cassandra Brown Ricci, my beloved daughter.* Listed alongside Nicolas and his siblings as a beneficiary. They weren't equal shares. Sandy got 60 percent of his wealth. He and Nina had to divide the forty between them.

"He gave you the lion's share. Everything that should be mine, is now yours. Because you're not my sister, Sandy." Nicolas's voice carried years of resentment. "You're not even my cousin. I'm not a Ricci, and this Will tells the world that. Destroys my life and my grandfather's legacy that he wanted me to have!"

The room spun as her headache surfaced. She fought nausea that had nothing to do with the basement's musty air. "Why are you doing this?"

"Because I need you to accept it so we can fix it. Remember. Really remember." He knelt before her, desperation cracking his controlled facade. "He told you things. Showed you things. Before the accident scrambled your brain, you knew where he kept his secrets. Including the medallion."

"I don't know about any medallion—" She shook her head.

"Yes, you do. You can't access it. But it's in there, locked away with all the other memories your mother paid doctors to bury." He gripped her hands. "I need you to try for both our sakes. My life depends on it. Uncle Matteo is Don now. I barely have any standing at all. But if these men knew I was never a Ricci, I'm dead. My sister is dead. Remember being Alessandra Ricci. Remember your real father. Remember where he hid the one thing that could legitimize me."

"What the hell's happening here?"

The voice hit like a slap. Sandy jerked her gaze to the door where a mountain of a man stood surveying the scene. Nicolas rocketed to his feet, hands balling into fists.

"We're talking! Get out!"

"Watch your tone, son." The man's casual authority filled the room. "You forget who you're speaking to?"

"I said, don't call me that!" Nicolas walked away from her. He shouldered past the man violently as he left.

Sandy found herself alone with the stranger, tears still wet on her cheeks. He studied the portraits with an unreadable expression before focusing on her.

"Shouldn't have shown you this place. Some doors are better left closed."

"Who are you?" Her voice came out smaller than intended.

"Name's Caesar. Your uncle Matteo asked me to keep an eye on things." He gestured toward the exit. "Let's go. Party's still happening upstairs."

"Is it true?" She held up the crumpled documents, needing confirmation from someone, anyone. "Am I really Carmelo Ricci's daughter Alessandra?"

Caesar's look held years of buried secrets. "Truth's a luxury, men our life can't afford. He's in the ground. That's all the truth you need."

Sandy turned back to the gallery—her childhood preserved in charcoal and paint, her identity rewritten in legal documents. The ache for her mother became unbearable. Mama would have had answers, explanations, comfort. Instead, Sandy stood in a basement surrounded by proof of a life she couldn't fully remember, with only a mobster's dismissal for guidance.

* * *

"WHY ARE YOU ANGRY WITH ME?" Matteo asked, leaning against the doorframe.

He watched Debbie storm around their room, a whirlwind of silk and frustration, hurling stuff onto a chair and kicking off her heels with lethal precision. The house was finally quiet. The kids—including Junior—were settled. Sandy was safe and with them. Caesar had efficiently exiled Nicolas and Nina back to their own dramas. It was just them. A time for peace. And he desperately wanted his bride.

"Debs, talk to me. Why are you mad?" Matteo's voice was soft, a low rumble meant to soothe. He walked over to the bed and sat down with patience.

"How the hell do you disappear from your own reception?" she shot back, yanking an earring out of her lobe. "Leaving me to make small talk with your second cousin who breeds attack dogs. Abandoning me! Then you waltz back in with Junior, both of you smelling like a Grateful Dead concert. You said you don't do that anymore!"

Matteo closed his eyes and sighed, a small smile playing on his lips.

"I don't *fuck* with drugs, woman. I shared a single, celebratory joint with my son because we…" He paused. Bringing up José now, the ghost who'd forever be between them, felt like tempting fate. The ice he was on with her was still thin. "It was a father-son thing. A peace treaty. That's all."

"And that's even worse! You're supposed to be the responsible one now! You stop him from doing drugs, you don't join in!"

"Enough!" he yelled, the word cracking through the room.

Debbie froze, her eyes wide.

Matteo immediately winced, running a hand over his face. "Debbie, I'm sorry. I didn't mean to yell. Christ. It's just… sometimes, babe, you come at me with both barrels. All I need is a chance to explain."

She hugged her arms around herself, the fight slowly leaving her posture, replaced by a familiar, wounded pride and sexy pout.

He humbled himself, his voice dropping to a whisper. "I'm sorry. I'm very sorry. Forgive me. Please. I was wrong. No more weed. No more disappearing. I'm sorry. Okay?"

Debbie rolled her eyes, but the edge was gone. "I'm not being a bitch."

"Never in a million years said you were," he said, holding his hands up in surrender. "You're a lioness protecting your pups."

"And my King," she said. A faint smile touched her lips. "I was just embarrassed. And… left out. These people are only nice because you're their boss. They don't really like me and my children. I'm not stupid."

"I know, baby. I know," he said, his heart aching for her to be accepted and happy always. She had paid a heavy price for his mistakes. He only wanted to make life better.

"So you and Junior made up?" she asked, her voice softening. "Really?"

He nodded, with a genuine warmth spreading in his chest. "He's my boy again. I feel it."

"You sure?" She searched his eyes, looking for the truth she'd waited years to see.

“He’s my boy,” he repeated, his voice firm and full of promise. “And I’m not going to fuck it up this time.”

He smiled. "I'm the luckiest man in the world to have kids with you. All I ever wanted was for us to be a family. All I dreamed about in prison was a second chance with you, Debs. That I could be forgiven and given a chance. And now I’ve got one. The best one. Because you forgave me, and I got you."

She finally relented. "Of course you got me, stupid. You've always been mine. Now I’m going to get fat. And my feet are already swelling.”

The tension melted away as she walked her sexy ass over to him, each step a promise of a wild night. He grabbed her by the hips the moment she stepped between his parted legs, pulling her close. He buried his face in the soft warmth between her perfect breasts and inhaled her perfume—home, and hope, and everything he’d almost lost.

She rubbed his head, her fingers gentle in his hair, and kissed the top of his head. “We did it. We finally did it,” she whispered, her voice thick with emotion.

“I’m so happy,” Matteo murmured against her skin, holding her tighter, feeling his dick get harder.

“We still got Janey,” she sighed, the worry creeping back in. “I mean, she has to be somewhere in Harlem.”

“My men found her at the bakery having lunch,” he said, leaning back to look up at her. “They gave her the key to Kathy’s old place. She’s there. Got a man watching the door.”

Debbie stepped back, surprised. “You did? Why didn’t you tell me?”

“Because I was too busy getting married!” he said.

She laughed. He smiled.

“Willa’s plane lands in the morning. She’ll help us with Janey. We’re finally gonna get this family together, Debs. For real this time.”

Debbie bit down on her bottom lip, a gesture of submission that still drove him wild after all these years. “I hope so.”

His hands slid down to cup her glorious backside. “Do better than hope. Get undressed and sit on my face. Let me show you how sorry I am with my tongue."

She giggled, a real, unfiltered sound of joy as he gave her ass an appreciative squeeze. She nodded, a slow, seductive smile spreading across her face as she began to peel off the wedding suit. He stared, mesmerized by the reveal of her body, and wondered for the hundredth time if it was one of her wild premonitions or the God's-honest truth. Could she really be pregnant after all these years? The thought would absolutely blow his mind.

But if she wasn't? It didn't matter. He had her. He had the kids. He had everything José told him he would have if he just got his shit together.

And he finally, finally did.

CHAPTER 49

SOLDIER BOY - BUTTS MISSISSIPPI 1956

"Mama?" Sandy called out.

Kathy paused in her dusting and looked back at her daughter. The little girl had managed to climb up on Ely's wooden chair and was leaning precariously toward the window, her small hands pressed against the glass. Kathy had been so absorbed in her Saturday morning cleaning ritual that she hadn't noticed Sandy's adventure.

"Sandy, get down from that chair," she said firmly.

"Man!" Sandy exclaimed, pointing outside.

Kathy's brow furrowed. "Man?" She crossed the room, absently rubbing her hands on her faded apron, and peered out the window. A dark sedan had pulled up their dirt drive, and a man in a crisp military uniform was stepping out. Through the glass, she could see Ely approaching from around the side of the house, his stride purposeful.

Without hesitation, Kathy scooped Sandy into her arms and hurried to the screen door. Standing just inside, she could hear every word exchanged between the men.

"Ely Brown?" the white soldier inquired, his voice carrying the authority of rank.

"Yes, sir, and you are?" Ely responded cautiously.

"Name is Donovan. Sergeant Patrick Donovan. I'm out on scouts. Heard your name more than once in town. Good things, of course."

"What you looking for?" Ely's tone remained guarded.

"Men. To serve their country. Special forces. We're considering forming a troop for a special Negro unit. Talking about two years of your life and the kind of benefits where you can rebuild anywhere." The sergeant's gaze shifted to the screen door, and he tipped his hat slightly at Kathy. "That your family?"

Ely glanced back, his eyes meeting Kathy's for a brief moment before returning to Donovan. "Yes. And I got no plans to leave them."

"Mind if I ask what your plans are?" Sergeant Donovan pressed, undeterred.

Ely remained silent, his jaw set.

"How about a sign-on bonus?"

"A what?" Ely's confusion was evident.

"You heard me, son. Two thousand dollars. For enlisting."

"I ain't never heard of nobody getting that much money for anything with the military," Ely said, suspicion creeping into his voice.

"Like I said. Special recruits. This one moves fast. It's the kind of money that buys your loyalty and silence. You can never mention it was offered or you accepted, ever."

The sum was staggering. Ely had never imagined holding that much money at once. He didn't make that in a year of backbreaking work. It seemed impossible. His father's warnings about government tricks echoed in his mind.

"Tell you what, I'm here three days on recruitment. Here's my card. Give me a call. Staying at the Clover."

Ely accepted the card wordlessly and watched as the sergeant returned to his car. Only when the dust settled did he turn and head back to the house. Kathy had already retreated from the door, and Sandy's wails filled the small space. He knew why—the child always seemed to mirror her mother's emotions.

As soon as he crossed the threshold, Kathy confronted him.

"What did he want?" Her voice was sharp with fear.

"He's a recruiter, Kat," Ely said wearily.

"You swore to me. You swore when I told you what happened to Matteo. How he disappeared into that war, leaving Debbie behind, you swore you would never go into the military."

"Kat..."

"No! Ely, no! You hear me? No!"

She whirled away and marched into their bedroom. The door slammed with finality, and Sandy's cries intensified. Defeated, Ely sank onto their worn sofa. Two thousand dollars represented more than money—it was freedom from debt, security for his family, a chance at something better. It could pay off this land and give them the head start they desperately needed.

He closed his eyes and released a heavy sigh.

* * *

KATHY CAME TO BED LATE, as had become her habit. After the nightly ritual of tucking Sandy in and taking her own bath, she'd retreated to the living room, losing herself in the pages of her books and the scratch of a pen against journal paper. Ely had dozed off waiting for her, the empty space beside him a cold reminder of the distance growing between them.

The silent treatment had always been her most effective weapon. She wielded it skillfully, withdrawing affection and attention until he crumbled. But tonight, he had to stand firm. He had to make her understand that this opportunity could be their salvation—a real chance to build the life they'd only dared whisper about. The military had always called to him, ever since he was a boy watching the soldiers march through town.

When she finally eased under the covers, her movements careful not to wake him, she presented her back like a wall. He reached for her, his fingers grazing her nightgown, but she remained stone. He knew she was awake—her breathing too controlled, too aware.

"Two thousand dollars, Kathy," he began, his voice low in the darkness. "I enlist for two years. Just two years. Then I come home, and we're free."

"Don't sell me lies," she said, her voice sharp despite its quietness. "There is no freedom in this world. Everything has a price, Ely. Everything. There are whispers of war in the newspapers. Another war brewing."

"I won't do it without you," Ely insisted. "I'll never do anything that goes against our family. But I need your support."

Kathy turned onto her pillow, and even in the moonlight filtering through their thin curtains, he could see the tears glistening in her eyes. "Since our phone got cut off, once a week, I walk to that payphone on Main Street. I stuff it with every coin I can spare to listen to Debbie cry about how scared she is for Matteo. She tells me he no longer writes. Three months of silence, Ely. Three months. It's killing her, bit by bit. Two kids at home, and she's trapped in this terrible limbo. He left two years ago. Why isn't he home now?"

Ely found himself staring up at the ceiling, its familiar cracks and water stains offering no answers. The Mill had cut his hours. Everyone was so poor now in Butts; there were no more luxuries. Ely refused to let her father help or even say they needed it. Brenda snuck money to her in her letters that she used to help them manage. They were all just surviving. She was making pennies as a teacher. Life was hard. And she refused her father's offer to move back to Harlem. What choices did he have?

Kathy's hand found his chest, her touch gentle despite everything. He covered her hand with his own. "I never mention Carmelo to you," she said softly. "Out of respect for our marriage, mostly, but there's another reason."

He turned to look at her, waiting.

"He was a dreamer. Always had some plan that would set us free, some scheme that would change everything. And I chased those dreams with him, believed in every word. But what happens when dreams don't materialize? We begin to create a different reality, one that blinds us to the dangers of our actual circumstances. With you, this is real. Nothing is built on dreams and wishes. And I feel safe in that. Do you understand? I feel safe because you and I are real. What we have is solid. We survive because we know dreams don't come true unless you work hard, unless you build them with your own hands."

Ely gave her a sad smile that she probably couldn't see in the darkness. "I'm sorry he took away your ability to dream, Kat..."

"No... that's not what I'm saying," she stammered, frustrated.

"It's okay. I see it. I've always seen it. You lost something when you gave up on your dreams. He wasn't the only dreamer in that relationship. You were, too. I want you to dream again, Kathy. I want you to have hope. To believe in something—in me."

"I do," she said, but the sadness in her voice betrayed her.

"This dream of mine—to be in the military, to serve as a soldier—I've carried it since I was a kid, Kat. Then this man rolls up our drive and offers not just the opportunity but a reward for making the sacrifice. A sacrifice that could help me give you back your dreams. How can I resist that?"

She closed her eyes and nodded, surrendering inch by inch.

"A man wants to provide for his family," he continued. "You never belonged in Butts, Kathy. I know we're happy now. You're the head of the school. I know we're planning on having a baby. But I keep stopping us from taking that step because I want to give you more before we do."

"I don't need more, Ely. That's the whole point," she said gently, her fingers tracing patterns on his chest.

"The war in Harlem has cooled. Your father and the Italians have stopped the killing. Your father is in charge now, and he's tried to send for us twice. You won't go home. You need family, Kathy. You need more than what I can give you here, and I'm not going to sit back and watch you slip away, watch you disappear into yourself."

Kathy rolled to her back with a deep, shuddering sigh.

"I'm not saying you still think about Carmelo Ricci or that you fear Harlem because of him. But I do, Kathy. I still think about the warning he gave me in that alley. About how scared you've been to go home and see your parents."

"I don't trust him. I don't trust myself," she sighed.

"It's okay. I need you to trust me. I need to free my wife. We don't have to go back to Harlem. But we have to start somewhere fresh, for us. That's real freedom. To just be a family. And if we're going to settle somewhere, let's do it where we can build fresh. Two thousand dollars, Kathy? Who turns down that kind of money?"

Kathy closed her eyes, and the tears came silently, tracking down her temples into her hair. Ely drew her closer, enveloping her in his arms as she turned into his chest and wept. They both knew the truth that hung between them—his mind was made up. He was going to enlist. And she was going to have to find a way to live with it.

ONE YEAR EARLIER. The black Cadillac rolled to a stop in front of Kathy Sweets like a hearse arriving at a funeral. Carmelo Ricci sat in the back, a .45-carrying soldato at his left shoulder. Behind the wheel, Slim kept the engine running, another gunman riding shotgun beside him. Two more cars idled behind them, packed with enough firepower to turn this corner of Harlem into Normandy Beach. If Henry Freeman so much as twitched wrong, they'd paint the entire block red.

"Slim, you're with me." Carmelo's voice cut through the tension as his door swung open.

He stepped out into the bitter February frost that had seized New York by the throat. His charcoal fedora sat low over his eyes, cashmere coat whipping back in the wind like a cape. Two Nation of Islam officers flanked the bakery entrance—ramrod straight, bow ties crisp as their contempt, eyes full of righteous fury.

The Nation of Islam had run tight operations in their partnership with Henry Freeman. Carmelo understood it. The Nation had kept Henry Freeman breathing through two years of bloody warfare, and here stood the enemy at their gates.

Carmelo's gloved hands curled into fists. The standoff stretched taut as piano wire.

Slim stepped forward, breaking the spell. "Mr. Ricci here to see Mr. Freeman. He's expected."

One officer disappeared inside without a word. The other maintained his death stare, unblinking, as if he could will Carmelo out of existence through sheer force of hatred.

The door opened. The first officer reappeared, stepping aside just enough to allow passage. No words. The message was clear: *You're tolerated, not welcomed.*

Carmelo never entered enemy territory first—that was how men got their brains blown out. He nodded to Slim, who walked through the doorway, hands visible, allowing the Muslims to pat him down for iron. Only when Slim entered did Carmelo follow.

Inside, the bakery smelled of sugar and Kathy's tenderness. He had to take a moment to inhale. Henry Freeman commanded a corner booth like a general surveying a battlefield. To his left sat a man of equal bearing—tall, sharp-featured, with the kind of eyes that had seen men die and slept soundly after. This had to be Nicky Barnes, the man who'd stepped into Pete Freeman's blood-soaked shoes as Henry's right hand. Carmelo had heard whispers about Barnes—that he was clever and twice as ruthless.

Carmelo crossed the black-and-white checkered floor, each footstep deliberate, measured. He slid into the booth opposite the two men, the leather creaking under his weight.

Henry Freeman's stare could have frozen the East River. No greeting. No acknowledgment. Just pure, undiluted hatred radiating across the table like heat from a furnace.

The war had brought them to this moment—blood demanding blood, territory demanding respect, and somewhere in between, the possibility of money to be made. But first, they had to survive this conversation.

"Henry, you look well," Carmelo said with a sly smile.

Henry didn't speak.

Carmelo let his gaze sweep over Kathy's Sweets. "Been a long time since I've been here. Business good?"

"You said you came to be heard." Henry Freeman's voice cut through the diner's smoke like a straight razor. "Speak before I silence you."

"Thank you for seeing me." Carmelo smoothed his silk tie, a

gesture calculated to show ease where none existed. "This war between you and my father—"

"It's between us now, too, boy. Has been for some time." The words came out like bullets from a Tommy gun, each one meant to wound.

Carmelo absorbed the hit with a barely perceptible nod. "This war has grown expensive. Bodies stacking up like unpaid bills." He traced a gloved finger across the table's battle scars—knife marks, cigarette burns, the archaeology of violence. "My father and I, we've had words. The real money ain't in spilling blood on 125th Street. It's in the peace. Therefore,"—he paused for effect—"he's prepared to return Harlem to your... ownership."

Henry's eyes, cold as a February morning in Central Park, slid to Nicky Barnes before returning to rest on Carmelo like the barrel of a .38. "What's the vig on that generosity?"

"A modest request." Carmelo held up black gloved fingers. "Twenty percent of gross on all the white horse that rides at night through Harlem. And control of its distribution."

The laughter that erupted from Henry Freeman could've frozen the Hudson. His gold tooth caught the overhead light like a muzzle flash. Beside him, Nicky Barnes added his own dry chuckle.

"Twenty percent and the keys to my kingdom?" Henry's laughter died like a snitch in the East River. "Listen here, little Don Ricci. You ain't buying no partnership. You're trying to put a leash on a lion. My people see me taking orders from downtown, they'll feed me to the streets piece by piece. The Honorable Elijah Muhammad himself would see it as blasphemy. So let's discuss terms that don't require me to sit as low as your father's feet."

Carmelo's jaw tightened, but his voice remained silk over steel. "I'm all ears."

"Here's how it plays in Harlem." Henry leaned back, spreading his arms across the booth like a king on his throne. "Ten percent off one numbers bank—location of my choosing—for twelve months. Plus a one-time tribute for the blood your father spilled on my streets. Call it reparations. Everybody saves face. Your old man gets his taste without me looking like his house nigger."

“I think the tribute goes in reverse. You have taken out legitimate businesses of ours. You owe us that debt.”

“Fine,” Henry said. "The number?" The gold tooth made another appearance.

“Seventy large,” Carmelo replied.

The air between them was charged with enough electricity to light up the Apollo. Finally, Henry spoke. "Seventy it is. But here's the sweetener—my boys guarantee safe passage for your merchandise through Harlem to the East: no hijacks, no shakedowns, no mysterious fires. Your trucks roll through at any time of day, as if they have guardian angels. For this divine protection, we take five points on everything that moves. We ain't partners, little Don; we're your insurance policy. Hell, take it out of the seventy if it makes you sleep better."

Carmelo's fingers formed a church steeple, considering. "Counterproposal. Forty thousand cash, immediate. And our trucks roll through Harlem like ghosts—untouched, untaxed, unseen."

Henry's head tilted, appraising. "Now you're speaking my language, paesano."

"I ain't finished." Carmelo's voice dropped to a whisper that somehow filled the empty diner. "Matter of fact, forget the forty grand entirely. I want something worth more than money. I want my own killer cupcake: Kathy Sweets."

The temperature in the diner plummeted twenty degrees. Henry's mocking smile dried up, and his face turned to stone.

"What the fuck did you just say?" Each word dropped like a hammer on an anvil.

Carmelo's smile replaced his nervousness. "Simple transaction. I sell this deal to my father. You keep your money, pay your ten percent like a gentleman, let my trucks pass through untaxed, and the war ends tonight. In exchange, I get the deed to Kathy Sweets. The whole building. Basement to attic. Definitely the attic.

The crack of Henry's fist against the table sounded like a gunshot. The rage in his eyes burned hot enough to melt steel—the same volcanic fury Carmelo had glimpsed years ago when he and his brother had arrived to try to muscle in on Henry's territory.

Fear crawled up Carmelo's spine like a cold-fingered junkie, but he kept his face marble-smooth.

Nicky leaned into Henry's ear, whispering urgently. But Henry's eyes never left Carmelo's face, reading every micro-expression, measuring the price of violence if he were to kill him in that very moment. Slim took a step forward, prepared to defend Carmelo.

"It will run as it always has, by Harlem. Hire whoever you want. I can't cook or bake..." Carmelo pressed on, twisting the knife. "In the grand scheme, it's just brick and mortar, right? It can't be as fond of you as it is to me."

"You listen to me, you mick-wop piece of shit." Henry's voice had gone subterranean, dangerous as a gas leak. "My Kathy is not now, nor will she ever be, for sale."

"I'm aware she's a married woman. Happily, from what I hear. A mother. Good for her." Carmelo's gaze swept the diner like he was already measuring it for new fixtures. "I'm not asking for the woman. I'm asking for the monument to her to be put under my care."

He slid from the booth with practiced grace, adjusting his wool coat. Henry sat coiled tight as a switchblade spring, violence radiating from every pore. Carmelo pretended not to notice.

"You have twenty-four hours to consider my terms. If you're smart —and I know you are—my lawyers will pay you a visit tomorrow and you will save lives, including our own. Harlem goes back to being yours." He pulled on his gloves with deliberate care. "And Kathy Sweets... she's mine."

He turned and walked toward the door, each curse and threat bouncing off his back like bullets off a tank. In the reflection of the diner window, he caught a glimpse of Henry Freeman—a man capable of unspeakable violence, held back by the thinnest thread of restraint.

Carmelo smiled and stepped out into the Harlem winter.

CHAPTER 50

NEW YORK - RICCI CONSTRUCTION

The knock silenced the room instantly. Slim stood. He walked to the door of Carmelo's office. He checked the peephole before glancing back at Carmelo. At his boss's subtle nod, he opened the door.

The others stood in unison—not scrambling, but moving with the synchronized respect of men who understood hierarchy.

Leone "The Fox" Ferrara entered. Cosimo Ricci's second consigliere, since DeMarco's death, swept his gaze across the assembled soldiers, each look an apparent dismissal. They called him Fox for good reason—where others used force, Ferrara wielded strategy like a scalpel. Clever, cunning, and impossible to pin down, he solved problems with an elegant brutality that even Carmelo admired.

"Thanks for coming." Carmelo's tone suggested courtesy while his eyes promised consequences. He nodded to his men—a king dismissing his court. They filed out in practiced silence, Caesar last. Even Slim departed at Carmelo's gesture, though they both knew he'd position himself within earshot.

The Fox consulted his Patek Philippe with theatrical boredom. "I have court in three hours. Whatever this is, make it brief."

"Legal troubles?" Carmelo kept his voice neutral, fishing.

"Nothing concerning you. Especially after that deal you convinced your father to sign over Harlem for. I think you should leave all business matters in the future to me!"

The dismissal came with that signature sneer as Ferrara claimed the sofa—a calculated insult. By refusing the chair facing Carmelo's desk, the consigliere broadcast his contempt for the younger man's growing power. Old school arrogance, Carmelo noted. The kind that made men blind to shifting tides.

But Leone Ferrara was still the sharpest legal mind in La Cosa Nostra. Thanks to months of Slim and Caesar's intelligence work, Carmelo finally understood how to transform that asset from his father's weapon into his own.

The Fox made a show of settling in—unbuttoning his jacket, crossing his legs, radiating the confidence of a man who'd survived two decades in this life through intellect alone. "Well?"

Carmelo's hand found the drawer, extracting a folder with deliberate care. He placed it flat on his desk, palm pressed against it like a poker player protecting a winning hand. "I need your expertise. This document requires immediate filing and enforcement. No negotiations."

The Fox's mask slipped for an instant—curiosity overruled his smug defiance. His gaze tracked between Carmelo's face and the folder, running calculations. When Carmelo remained seated, it forced the mountain to come to Mohammed. Ferrara's nostrils flared.

The older man stood with exaggerated dignity, each step across the room a small surrender. The folder was slid toward him. He opened it. His reaction was instantaneous.

"*Dio santo...?*" The words escaped before he could stop them. His eyes snapped up, searching Carmelo's face. "Does Don Cosimo know this exists?"

Carmelo's smile was answer enough.

"This bears the seal of the New York Superior Court." Ferrara's voice climbed despite himself. "You said it needs filing? How is that possible when—"

"It was never filed."

"Impossible. Judge Foley's seal—"

"Never filed." Carmelo leaned back, savoring the moment. "Which is why I need you to ensure the courts recognize its validity. Today."

"A marriage certificate? To the Freeman girl?" The Fox's composure cracked entirely. "After you orchestrated peace between our families and cost us thousands in profit? Accepted scraps while that—"

"While I secured Las Vegas." Carmelo's voice cut like ice. "Lanskey already has territory in Harlem; it's worthless to us with Henry Freeman and him in alliance. I gave Papa Las Vegas, a vision in tribute to my brother. And now we have the casinos that generate more in a month than Harlem produced in a year. No war. No bloodshed. Just profits. So cut the bullshit. You have never produced anything close."

"This family was built on heroin, loan sharking, empire building, not roulette wheels." The Fox's carefully calm demeaning cracked, revealing depths of resentment. Here was the brilliant legal mind, reduced to a stuttering fool over being outmaneuvered by what he considered a kid.

"File it," said Carmelo.

"Bigamy is a felony. You have a wife and children. This document would delegitimize—"

"Obstacles for lesser lawyers. Not for the legendary Fox."

Ferrara drew back, reverting to the voice that had cowed judges. "And if I refuse? If I walk out and head to your father right now and show Cosimo his son's betrayal?"

"Then I show him yours." Carmelo opened another drawer, producing photographs, documents, and even copies of wired communications made by Ferrara. "Shipping manifests to Naples. Coded communications with Luciano. Bank accounts in Zurich feeding the old boss while my father pretends at kingship."

The consigliere aged a decade in seconds.

"Every family dinner, you sit at his right knowing Lucky Luciano still runs New York through you." Carmelo spread the evidence like a deck of tarot cards. "While I sit at his left, knowing the true hustle. How long do you think you'd survive that revelation? An hour? Less?"

"You don't understand the complexities—"

"I understand perfectly. You hedged your bets. Smart, until now." Carmelo gathered the photos with a gambler's efficiency. "New management, new rules. You work for me. First task: legitimize this marriage."

"Your wife—"

"Maria signs whatever you draft. Clean annulment, whatever legal fiction necessary." Carmelo returned the marriage certificate to its folder. "Forty-eight hours."

"The church! The church will not bend to this," Ferrara tried to reason.

"I will make my peace with God," Carmelo said. "Just as I plan to make peace with Kathy. I am the Wolf of Harlem, remember?"

"You're not listening. The legal complexity alone—"

"Forty-eight hours. Or I convene a special meeting to discuss your divided loyalties." Already, Carmelo was looking through him, business concluded. "We're done here."

Leone Ferrara—the Fox who'd outwitted FBI, IRS, and five ambitious prosecutors hunting down his father—shuffled out like a beaten dog. The moment of solitude returned, Carmelo retrieved a worn business card, fingers tracing numbers he knew by heart.

The prince had become king. Time to claim his queen.

* * *

"Sergeant Donovan speaking."

"Ricci. Tell me it's done."

"Mr. Brown enlisted this morning. Signed, sealed, delivered to the U.S. Army."

Relief flooded through Carmelo's system like morphine. His body sagged into the leather chair. "Departure date?"

"Two days. Fast-tracked as requested."

"The wife—was she present? Was she upset?" He fought to keep desperation from bleeding through.

"Lovely lady. Sweet little girl, too. She sat silently at his side, holding the child. Her eyes were down. She didn't say anything. Quite the looker, if you don't mind me saying."

"Can any of this be traced back to me?" Carmelo asked.

"Negative. He believes the bonus is standard. Paperwork's been expedited. He signed for two years, but the contract reads four, just like your brother. Your problem is solved."

"My brother. They cannot be stationed together. Arrange it."

"Mr. Ricci, I'm a recruiter, not a general. Once the recruit boards that bus, they're in God's hands. Or the Army's, which might be worse. Besides, with this situation in Asia, we'll all be shipping out soon."

"What? You said no wars. That the Cold War was just politics, not combat!" Carmelo sat upright.

"Do you read the paper? There is always wars to be fought. It is a risk every soldier takes when he enlists. I thought you understood that."

"My brother... he's not in a war, he's doing military stuff, advising," Carmelo reasoned.

Donovan remained silent.

Carmelo ground his teeth. Two years since discovering Kathy carried another man's child. Two years of meticulous planning while his soul rotted from the inside by pretending at civility with his father. It had pushed him into complete darkness. Kathy's marriage to that farm-boy meant the end of every dream he had planned to share with her. And the child should have been his. All hope was lost until he discovered the truth. That money and power, not good intentions, could get you anything you wanted in the world. It could bring her to him. And he'd take her in any way he could.

"Payments in your account." The line went dead.

Slim appeared in the doorway. "Fox stormed out like his ass was on fire."

"Good. Everything's aligning perfectly."

"That's what scares me." Slim's weathered face showed concern. "Getting what you want can be its own punishment."

"All I want is her back in Harlem, where I can reach her. Where she belongs, she's trapped in that shithole town because of me. I'm helping her."

Slim retreated, recognizing the futility of arguing with obsession. In the silence, Carmelo let himself imagine it—Kathy back in New York, close enough to touch. For the first time in two years, something resembling happiness flickered in his chest. Even if it was just the phantom pain of a limb he'd lost, it was better than the nothing he'd been living with.

Quebec - 1978

Kathy slept upstairs. Marco, his most trusted man, approached with the American newspaper he requested. It was several days old, but current enough. Carmelo set his coffee down and reached for it.

"Your newspaper, sir." The soldato placed it beside the cooling coffee.

"When does Ernesto land?" Carmelo kept his voice level, though urgency pressed beneath.

"Flight arrived forty minutes ago. He called from the tarmac—should be here within the hour."

"Bene." He opened the paper methodically, each section carefully separated.

Page three stopped him cold. Twin photographs—his own from federal booking, Kathy's from happier days. The headline alone made his blood freeze:

> NEWARK, N.J. — Federal authorities confirmed yesterday that Carmelo "The Wolf" Ricci, the reputed organized crime figure found dead in a car bombing last month, had been secretly married to Harlem bakery owner Kathy Freeman Brown for 30 years.
>
> Kathy Brown, 48, was discovered dead in a burnt vehicle off Interstate 287 near Exit 14. New Jersey State Police initially attributed the incident to weather-related conditions following recent storms in the area.
>
> Court documents obtained by the FBI reveal the couple first wed in a civil ceremony in 1949. The marriage was reaffirmed by New York State courts in 1956 and recognized by the Catholic Church in

1963. Sources indicate the pair underwent another religious ceremony just two weeks before Ricci's death.

"We are investigating all connections between these deaths," said Special Agent Michael Torres of the FBI's Organized Crime Task Force. "The timing raises questions we intend to answer."

Ricci, a former light-heavyweight boxer turned businessman, had long been suspected of running criminal operations throughout Harlem and Queens. Freeman Brown operated the popular Kathy's Bakery on 125th Street.

The FBI declined to comment on whether Freeman Brown's death is being investigated as a homicide.

"Why is my picture in the paper?"

Carmelo was startled, coffee sloshing. Kathy stood behind him, hair wild from their night of fighting and reconciliation. Her silk kimono—the kind he loved to unwrap from her—hung loose at the shoulders. She rubbed sleep from her eyes, waiting.

Old habits die hard. The King of Lies had sworn honesty, but the words came anyway: "Nothing important. More federal harassment."

"Let me see."

He folded the paper with reluctance and handed it over. She read it while he studied her face. Carmelo watched for the moment she'd understand. When she finished, her expression remained neutral.

"Our marriage was never secret from the government. You made that certain years ago. They are using this to bait your enemies into providing more information on us."

The comment was loaded with accusations he had hoped not to hear from her since they reconciled. But he understood why. That date: 1956, it was when he turned her world inside out. The moment she saw the date, Ely Brown's ghost walked into the room. He'll probably be in every room they shared for the rest of the day. Carmelo looked away, unable to meet her eyes. Some sins were too heavy for confession.

Shame burned through him. Ely Brown—recruited, deployed, destroyed. The price of his obsession was paid in another man's blood.

She closed the space between them. Her fingers found his jaw, gentle but insistent. She forced his gaze upward. "Some wounds aren't supposed to heal. Some scars are permanent. That is life, Melo. I understand that now. Do you?"

He couldn't speak.

"Our love kept us alive while everything around us fell into ashes. I forgave you for Ely, Melo. Because I've done things I wish to be forgiven for, too. You need to forgive yourself."

"I'm trying." His voice cracked. "But this plan means we do it again. We set everything on fire, and I don't—"

"What?" she asked.

"I don't want Sandy to know the truth about me, this way. I want her to know me in a different way. I'm terrified it'll be too much for her to trust me or even love me," he said.

"It will be. And you know that, it's why you brought me here and boxed us all in. You're not scared that it is too much for us. You're scared that we'll escape."

She knelt before him. "I'm not running, Melo. We'll help Sandy understand her parents aren't perfect. But we won't lie anymore about what we are and what we've done. Not anymore."

He pulled her onto his lap, and she guided his head to her breast, holding him like a broken bird. They stayed that way as morning light strengthened, sharing silence and touch. Eventually, he fed her from his plate while she spoke of Sandy, of next year's plans, of anything except the man whose shadow would always live between them.

* * *

Marco DelSilva emerged from the villa's entrance. At six-foot-three, he moved with the agility of an experienced enforcer. Each step deliberate, measured, dangerous. His tailored black suit couldn't disguise the coiled power in his broad shoulders, nor the weapon holstered beneath his jacket.

Marco's dark hair, slicked back from his forehead, gleamed like coal in the light. But it was his eyes that made men step back—eyes the color of bitter espresso, piercing and unforgiving, that seemed to catalog every weakness, every tell, every possible threat. Women found those same eyes irresistible, though few were brave enough to hold his gaze for long.

The limo's engine ticked as it cooled. Marco nodded to one of his men, who immediately opened the rear door. Consigliere Ernesto Rossi emerged slowly, his movements betraying the exhaustion of the back-and-forth flights between Quebec and New York. Where Marco was all sharp angles and lethal elegance, Ernesto was soft around the edges—a man who wielded words and strategy rather than bullets.

Their eyes met. Marco's full lips curved into something that wasn't quite a smile—more an acknowledgment between men who understood the weight of secrets.

"*Bentornato, Consigliere,*" Marco said, his voice a low rumble. His accent turned the simple greeting into something almost friendly, though his tone remained professionally distant.

Ernesto's Adam's apple bobbed as he swallowed. "How is he?"

"Unpredictable." Marco's jaw tightened almost imperceptibly. "But things have... stabilized with him and the Queen. He's with her now." He tilted his head toward the villa, where somewhere behind those ancient walls, their Don played out his elaborate seduction of the woman he worshipped and would destroy his empire for.

Ernesto followed his gaze, taking in the three-story fortress. The consigliere's fingers twitched, a nervous habit Marco had noticed intensifying over recent months.

"And Matteo?" Marco asked, crossing his arms over his chest. The movement made his jacket pull tight across his shoulders, revealing the outline of muscle earned through violence rather than any gym. "Is he surviving without his brother?"

"Caesar and Slim guard him well." Ernesto tugged at his collar. "But he refuses my counsel. He's obsessed with finding that medallion, convinced Carmelo lives." A bead of sweat traced down his temple despite the mild weather. "It's time to move forward with the plan."

Marco studied him with those unnerving eyes, reading the fear that radiated from the older man like heat from pavement. He'd seen Ernesto face down rival families without flinching, but their Don—even in his supposed death—inspired a different kind of terror. It was because of the hammer.

He respected The Wolf's methods of discipline or execution. The hammer was an instrument of justice. But lesser men in their world feared Don Carmelo Ricci's temper. Marco didn't abide by fear.

"Then you'd better go in and face him," Marco said softly. The words were gentle, but something in his tone made them sound like a judge pronouncing a sentence. "He doesn't appreciate delays."

Ernesto's laugh was hollow. "Madonna, help me." He straightened his tie with trembling fingers, squaring his shoulders as if preparing for battle. Which, Marco reflected, wasn't far from the truth.

As the consigliere trudged toward the villa's entrance—each step heavy with dread—Marco called after him. "Ernesto."

The older man turned.

"Breathe," Marco advised, a hint of dark amusement in his voice. "He can smell fear. Makes him... creative."

Ernesto's face paled further before he disappeared into the shadows of the doorway.

Marco shook his head, a genuine smile finally breaking across his features—transforming his face from merely handsome to devastatingly attractive. But the smile never reached his eyes. Those remained cold, watchful, already calculating the moves required to keep their volatile Don's empire intact.

He turned and strode toward the guard posts, his long legs eating up the distance. There was work to be done, and Marco DelSilva never failed in his duty to the Ricci family.

Never.

CHAPTER 51

WAR AND PEACE

Present. “Morning!"

Sandy rolled over to see a grinning Aunt Debbie standing at her bedside. She wore a white satin robe, her blonde hair disheveled and frizzy.

"Hi! Morning!" Sandy forced cheer into her voice. Her stomach churned with yesterday's revelations, and she'd cried herself to sleep thinking of her mother and father, remembering fragments of the past with them both.

Aunt Debbie must have sensed her distress because she sat on the bed and touched her knee gently. "What's the matter?"

"Nothing," Sandy lied.

"Matteo told me that Nicolas took you to the basement of this house." Debbie's expression grew serious. "Do you know who this house used to belong to?"

"Carmelo Ricci?"

Debbie nodded. "Yes. This was his kingdom. And Nicolas was his prince until now. Nicolas has an agenda; he’s not to be trusted, Sandy. He had no right to take you down there and show you what he did."

"You've seen those sketches? The drawings of me?" Sandy's voice came out smaller than she intended.

"No, sweetie. I didn't know Melo—Carmelo—could even draw. Kathy never mentioned that he had that talent. Apparently, it was something he did in private, and Nicolas was wrong to violate the privacy, whether Carmelo is dead or alive. I'm sorry he showed them to you."

Sandy pulled her knees up to her chest. "You wanted me to read the diaries. I stopped at my daddy being tricked into going to war. But before that, I read about New Orleans. They seemed so happy—Mama and Carmelo. Too happy." She paused, gathering courage. "Is that where I was... made? When they were happy and together?"

Debbie shrugged. "I suppose the diary will tell you the exact truth. But yes, it was around that time that your mother and father made you out of love. Your mama was so happy in New Orleans. The happiest I think I've ever known her to be."

"I don't want to read them anymore." The words tumbled out. "I can't, Auntie. All they do is confuse me, and then I have these dreams—"

"What dreams?" Debbie asked.

"I don't remember. When I wake up, they're gone. Just confusion left behind." Sandy's frustration mounted. "Tell me the truth. Be honest with me. Nicolas said I had an accident that he was responsible for. He said before the accident, I knew Carmelo Ricci was my father, but Mom erased it. Said Mama told me lies about who my Daddy was before she sent me away to keep me from him. Are they enemies or not? I don't understand."

"They aren't enemies. But for a time they were," Debbie said.

"Then what happened? Damn it!" said Sandy. "I know I'm different. That I'm forgetful, and sometimes I block things. But I haven't been taking my medicine—not since Mama died. And guess what? I'm fine!"

"You listen to me!" Debbie grabbed her arm firmly. "That medicine stops your seizures. Yes, it affected your memory. Made you forgetful at times. And yes, it was bad at first—you had to relearn who we all were. So your mother gave you a world without the pain and the shame she carried. Her and Carmelo loved you enough to give you what they never had. The ability to live free of our legacies. Those diaries help you reach her and learn the truth, but that medicine keeps you whole! You hear me? You take your medicine, or the seizures will come back."

Sandy flinched at the intensity of the words and the grip on her arm. "Yes, ma'am."

Debbie's grip relaxed, her voice softening. "The truth is, Ely was your father, too. He was there the day your mom gave birth. He pulled you out of her. He was there when you took your first steps, taught you how to talk. He loved you, and he went to war to give you a future he couldn't afford. Your mother mourned him for so long, I didn't think she'd ever get past it. She blamed herself for his death. It nearly destroyed her when she found out the truth."

"That Carmelo sent him to war to bring her home? I read it, Auntie, and she did blame herself in the diaries. She wanted to die," Sandy said.

"That's the past." Debbie's eyes glistened with unshed tears. "She did her best to give you a normal life, but Carmelo Ricci wouldn't let her go. And eventually, she realized she didn't want to let go of him either. It's this thing between them and us. I'd call it crazy if my thing with Matteo weren't even crazier than your mom's story." She managed a watery smile. "Do you remember anything about the time you spent with Carmelo as a little girl? Anything about a medallion you used to play with? It had red rubies on it."

Sandy's eyes widened. "I... yes, I remember. I saw it in the drawings too, in that room. I would hide it from him. I was little, and I remember him going to the safe and giving it to me. He talked to me... taught me... Italian? And we would play a game. I dream about it, and other things too. Him, his voice, but sometimes he doesn't have a face."

Debbie leaned forward. "Where? Where did you hide it? Can you remember?"

"I don't know. I was just a kid. I only remember the game."

"You have to remember, baby. It's important," Debbie said.

Sandy closed her eyes, trying to grasp the wispy memories. "I don't know. I'd play with it, and then he would look for it. We were at a house. A big house. It was scary when I lost him, but he would find me, and he would find it. Then…"

"This house?" Debbie asked.

"I was a kid," Sandy said helplessly. "I don't know. But it could be."

Debbie nodded slowly. "Okay. It's okay."

"Did I do something wrong?" Sandy asked.

"No, sweetie." Debbie pulled her into a warm hug. "It's time for all this to end." She pulled back, brushing Sandy's hair from her face. "I need you to get dressed. You have a visitor."

"Who?"

"Willa. She's arriving soon, and we will meet her at the airport. And guess who else? Aunt Janey is in town. She's at the house waiting for you. Coffey is here, too. We're all going over to see them."

"Really? Really?" Sandy's face lit up for the first time. "I haven't seen Coffey or Janey and Willa in so long!"

"I know." Debbie stood, smoothing her robe. "Go to Daphne's room and pick something to wear. Matteo had clothes bought for her by the women in this family, and her room decorated. She has a lot there. Take whatever you want. Tell her I said it. Let's see what the day brings."

"Auntie?"

"Yes?" Debbie said at the door.

"I'm happy for you. I really do like the Penny Man for you. I'm glad you're a family again," Sandy said.

"We're all family. That's the secret. No matter what happens or who tries to hurt us, or how much we hurt each other, we survive because we're family," Debbie winked. "Now let me go give the Penny Man some sugar so we can get this day started."

Sandy laughed and smiled. The door closed. Sandy dropped back on her pillows, and her head turned toward the window. She thought of the game she played with the man with no face. She was beginning to remember. If she took her medicine, would the memories stop? She had to wonder.

* * *

"THE FEDS DON'T THINK I'm dead?" Carmelo's voice cut through the tension.

Ernesto's gaze slipped to Kathy, who stared back unflinchingly. Her presence at the table—a violation of every tradition—made him hesitate.

Carmelo's jaw tightened with restraint. "Look at me, not her. I told you—she sits in on all meetings going forward. This affects her and our daughter."

Ernesto exhaled slowly. The consigliere had counseled generations of powerful men, but Carmelo defied every rule. From his obsessive control of Harlem to this insane anonymity escape scheme, nothing followed tradition. How could he advise a Don who shared his crown with a woman—a Black woman, no less?

"Speak." The single word carried lethal weight.

Ernesto flinched. "There's one Fed who won't let it go. He's investigating Ms. Kathy, particularly her past alliance with Nicky Barnes and then Frank Lucas. His theory? When the Black Council fell, you two disappeared together, taking a lot of the trafficking money with you. He's using the media to spread it. Soon they'll squeeze the families for information."

"And Matteo?" Carmelo asked.

"He married Debbie. At your mother's grave."

Kathy's lips curved into a knowing smile. "Good for them."

"He's also demanding his son be accepted into the family. That's... problematic. The kid—"

"Junior." Kathy's correction was sharp. "His name is Junior."

"Of course. Forgive me." Ernesto swallowed. "Junior and Nicolas have history. His ties to Frank Lucas complicate things. Matteo's moving too fast—transferring property, accounts. I can't intervene quickly enough. And your son Nicolas is on the warpath, secretly conspiring to take down his uncle. I think he's making moves to kill him. To take over. The kid lost it when he saw you left him scraps in the Will. He's spending too much time cozying up to your enemies. And the feds are watching everything."

Carmelo's fingers drummed once on the table. "It's Matteo's family —his choice. Nicolas is my problem. I think I know how to solve it."

"Don Battaglia won't accept these fractures. Mancini's worse—they see you as Americans playing at being Mafioso. That medallion represents tradition, but if Matteo shows up with his half-Black son to the families, they will all implode to keep Junior out." Ernesto spread his hands helplessly.

"Interesting." Kathy's voice could have frozen blood. "That medallion was protected by a Black woman for decades. Your precious traditions exist because she preserved them."

Ernesto bowed his head, chastened. "Much respect to Mama Stewart. I'm only conveying reality. The families prefer Nicolas. Unless you rise from the dead—"

"Giovanni Battaglia." Kathy turned to Carmelo, her mind already three moves ahead. "His son. How old?"

"Twenty-three, maybe twenty-four. Fresh from college."

"And half-Irish, you said." Her eyes gleamed with calculation. "His Sicilian father broke tradition for love. Left Sicily and started his Mafia empire with the Camorra. Perhaps Giovanni will understand Junior's position."

Ernesto watched them communicate without words—a look, a gesture, perfect synchronization.

"We go to Italy," Kathy continued, her strategy crystallizing. "The entire family. Naples."

"What?" Ernesto sputtered.

"She's right." Carmelo's approval energized her further. "Matteo, Debbie, all the children—including Sandy. We take Nicolas and Nina to get them away from the conspirators. To deal with my… son. A family reunion beyond the Fed's reach."

"Getting you two out of Quebec, I can manage. Convincing Matteo—"

"I know where the medallion is." Kathy's bombshell silenced the room.

Ernesto's eyes bulged. "Where?"

"Our daughter played a hiding game with it years ago. Somehow, she brought it from Jersey to Harlem." Kathy's fingers intertwined with Carmelo's—united, unbreakable. "Right before my Mama died, I found it in bed with her. She thought it was her treasure." Kathy looked over to Carmelo. "She wanted her Papa to come to our house and find it. To stay with us."

Carmelo blinked.

"I remember now. What she said. She said Papa was coming and he would stay with the treasure. That's what she meant, that's why she brought it back instead of hiding it in your place. So you could find her."

Carmelo smiled.

Kathy sighed. "I thought it was Mama's. Daddy, before he died, started buying her expensive jewelry she refused to wear. It was different, really pretty. I placed it in her casket."

"*Madonna!*" Ernesto crossed himself. "You're certain?"

"Positive."

Carmelo took control seamlessly. "You'll inform Matteo. Get someone from the family to agree to dig up Brenda Freeman. That will convince him to arrange the Naples trip as a family vacation; the Feds won't question. While Matteo retrieves his crown, we'll have already laid groundwork with Giovanni."

"Giovanni's young, impulsive. Your wife's race—"

"If the Battaglias and Mancinis refuse us," Kathy interrupted sweetly, "I'll simply bake them a cake and we'll help ourselves to what's left."

Carmelo's laughter filled the room. Ernesto paled, understanding the threat beneath her honeyed words. Now facing two killers, united by a single cause. *La famiglia.*

"It's perfect," Kathy said, her hand tightening on Carmelo's. "Together. And best of all, we get to say goodbye to our kids, and to the past. We get to start over."

"Together," Carmelo confirmed.

EPILOGUE

Present Day. Debbie sat on the exam table. Her legs moved back and forth like a kid in a candy store. She watched Matteo pace the floor. *He is such a worrywart, she thought.* First, they'd had to wrangle Janey and her five-alarm tantrum about Willa coming to Harlem to collect her. Matteo and Janey at war was something to behold. The family sat and watched as Matteo put his foot down in a way that even Janey hesitated. Debbie and Willa thanked God for Sandy. She stepped between the two of them and became the peacemaker. The one who could handle her Aunt Janey better than them all. It was one of many times Debbie saw the quiet strength of Kathy in her niece.

Thanks to Sandy, Janey had agreed to sign the papers to have her sister exhumed. Tonight, the whole family would witness Brenda's grave being opened and the medallion retrieved. Then off to Italy—every last one of them, including Janey, Willa, and Coffey.

Everything was falling into place. Except for one tiny detail growing in her belly that nobody believed existed. Her miracle baby. God's gift to her for being faithful to Matteo after all these years.

Debbie loved babies. She loved the way they smelled. How their bodies drew up when you picked them up. The way her babies suckled her breast. Most of all, she loved the way Matteo was with his babies when allowed access to them. There was nothing better to behold.

"Would you sit down?" she said, rolling her eyes. "You're making me dizzy."

"Leave me alone. I got thoughts," he grumbled, still pacing.

"We don't need this doctor to tell us I'm pregnant. I already know! I ain't no fool."

Matteo stopped mid-stride, pain flickering in his eyes. "You think I don't want you to be pregnant? You think I don't want a hundred babies with you, Debs? But we gotta be realistic here. Even if you are —and that's a big, big, big, if—you're..."

"Old. Say it. I'm old," she seethed.

"I wasn't gonna say old, *bambina*. I was gonna say... mature."

"Oh, that's much better," Debbie frowned.

"The doctor said pregnancies at this stage—"

"The doctor can kiss my *mature* ass. My body is made for this. It's made for you." She grabbed his hand, pulled him close. "We're the same soul, Matteo. This baby won't hurt me. You just gotta have faith."

Matteo sighed, taking a step closer just as the door swung open. The doctor walked in with the poker face of a man who'd delivered both good news and bad for thirty years.

Matteo's heart tried to escape through his throat. Debbie crossed her arms, ready for battle.

The doctor cleared his throat. "Well, Debbie. Turns out you know your body better than medical science. You're pregnant."

"What?" Matteo's voice cracked like a teenager's.

"Ha! I told you! I TOLD you!" Debbie bounced off the table and put her hands on her hips. "Mature, my ass! Telling me I can't make babies!"

"But... how? I mean, when? I mean how—?" Matteo stammered.

"Oh, for crying out loud, Matteo. You were there. Asking him how. You want me to tell him how many times you—"

"Stop! Debs! Cut the shit! For Christ's sake, woman. This is not normal. Is it doctor?" Matteo snapped.

Debbie rolled her eyes.

The doctor chuckled. "It happens. More than you know. And it's normal for Debbie. She's fertile."

"See. I'm fertile," Debbie said and tossed her chin up. "Not some old bitty that can't make a baby!"

"Jesus," Matteo sighed. "How long before the baby comes?"

"Debbie is about two months along, we estimate. We'll know more with blood work, but she's strong, healthy, and definitely pregnant."

Matteo stared at Debbie like she'd just pulled a rabbit from a hat. She glared back, daring him to doubt her again.

Then his face cracked. A laugh bubbled up from somewhere deep. "This isn't happening. This can't be happening."

"Thank you, Doctor. We're good now. I've done this before," Debbie announced, picking up her purse. "Let's go, Matteo."

"Hold on there," the doctor interjected. "As I explained, Debbie, at your age, there are precautions—"

"I never took precautions before."

"Pills. He means pills, not precautions," Matteo translated. "She'll take them. Doc, give me everything—instructions, pills, phone numbers, backup phone numbers. We gotta fly to... uh, we're traveling soon. That okay?"

"Should be fine, but—" the doctor stammered.

"Perfect. Thank you." Matteo pumped the doctor's hand while the man tried to lecture Debbie, who responded with Olympic-level eye rolling.

The moment the door closed behind the doctor, Debbie rounded on Matteo. "You never believe me when it counts!"

Instead of answering, he swept her up in his arms, spinning her around. He kissed her face—forehead, cheeks, nose—until she dissolved into giggles.

"Okay, okay! You're forgiven!" Debbie squealed.

He set her down gently, then dropped to his knees. Pressing his face against her belly, he whispered something she couldn't hear, then kissed the spot where their miracle was growing.

"See?" Debbie's voice went soft, fingers threading through his hair. "I told you we're a family again."

"If it's a boy..." Matteo looked up at her, eyes shining. "I want to name him Jose."

Debbie's hand stilled. "What?"

He stood, cradling her face in his hands. "Jose. He's up there with Ma, watching over us. He always believed in us, Debs. Even when we didn't believe in ourselves. This baby... it's his faith paying off too. Because Junior has forgiven me. My son has forgiven me."

Tears spilled down Debbie's cheeks. She pulled him close, holding on tight. Matteo breathed deep—relief, gratitude, and something that felt dangerously close to redemption.

After all the bad he'd done, maybe God was finally giving him a chance to do something good.

Cefalù - Sicily 1978

Kathy woke to the sun kissing her face. It was a gentle, persistent warmth; the light was soft and golden. It's painted the inside of her eyelids yellow. She stirred, turning into the pillow with a contented murmur, only to feel the cool, empty space beside her. The surprise of it made her open her eyes.

Carmelo was a silhouette against the blazing blue sky, flinging open the final set of French doors. Light, pure and unfiltered, came pouring into the room, not just through windows but from all sides, as if the very walls of the Sicilian villa were designed to drink in the morning.

"Stop," she groaned, her voice husky with sleep. She shielded her eyes, a smile playing on her lips. "What time is it? Come back to bed."

Carmelo turned from the doorway. He looked good in his linen pants and shirt, freshly shaved. His posture was all taut wire and purpose. "I told you Giovanni would be here today. We need to get up. Get dressed. He's agreed to meet for breakfast."

The words were a bucket of cold water. He didn't come back to bed. He just walked out.

Debbie sighed; the last vestiges of her dreamlike bliss evaporated. She stretched, the sheet slipping from her bare skin, and looked around the sun-drenched room. Four days. Four perfect days of isolation, of rediscovering each other without the shadow of names like Battaglia or the Wolf. Then the call came yesterday. His mood had shifted, hardened. Even when he'd made love to her last night, it was different—possessive, intense, as if marking his territory before a war.

Seeking solace, she looked out through the wide-open doors. The world outside was a masterpiece. With the windows thrown open, the villa breathed in the essence of Sicily: the salt-kissed air, the intoxicating perfume of jasmine clinging to ancient stone, the distant, comforting scent of frying olive oil and dark espresso from the village below.

She slipped from the bed and pulled on his shirt left discarded on a chair. The fine cotton smelled of him, of sandalwood and sun, and she wrapped herself in it before walking to the balcony.

The view stole her breath every time. The first and forever dominant feature was La Rocca, a mighty fortress-like rock that guarded the town. In the morning haze, it looked like something from one of Carmelo's medieval fantasy books—a wild, ancient place where dragons might still nest. Below it, the emerald fields were dotted with scruffy sheep, and further down, the medieval town of Cefalù cascaded toward the sea in a breathtaking jumble of sun-bleached stone. It was a tangled labyrinth of secrets and stories, with narrow cobblestone alleyways and endless arches draped with lines of white laundry fluttering like surrender flags.

The sounds of the waking village floated up to her: the distant, rhythmic crash of waves, the profound, echoing bells of the Duomo marking the hour, the melodic rise and fall of rapid Sicilian from workers already tending the land, the cheerful putt-putt of a single Vespa in a hidden alley.

This. This was the paradise he had whispered about all those years ago in the attic. A place of isolated freedom and breathtaking beauty. A place to get lost in, together. After all their battles, they had finally made it.

Last night felt like a dream now—the Mediterranean spread before them like black silk, stars scattered across the sky like diamonds. They'd made love on the balcony with an abandon that belonged to their youth, but with a tenderness earned through decades of war. In his arms, she'd remembered what victory tasted like.

Don Battaglia's son would arrive soon. As much as she wanted paradise, they had serious business to tend to before their family arrived and learned the truth of their resurrection.

"Cara?" Carmelo's voice pulled her back. "You need to get dressed. Please! For the hundredth time. Get dressed."

She didn't move from the window. After a long moment, she eventually turned. When he saw the tears tracking down her cheeks, his entire demeanor transformed.

"Kathy?"

"Do you realize," she said slowly, "that for the first time since we were teenagers, we're just two people in love? Not Henry Freeman's girl and Cosimo Ricci's boy. Not the scandal. Just... us. No one cares, here. No one."

He approached. "People always care when it comes to us. That's been the problem from the start."

"Not here. Not in this moment. Not until that medallion arrives in Italy with us and the Ricci brothers inherit the earth. Not until you start negotiating for everyone's lives."

"Touché. Now get dressed. I want him to meet you face to face. Give him something worth caring about." His hands slid up her silk robe, settling at her waist. "Let him see what twenty years of fighting for the perfect woman looks like."

"You want to parade your aging trophy around to a kid who is playing at Mafia games behind his father's back?" she laughed.

The words had barely left her mouth before he spun her, pressing her back against the wall. His hands captured her face, forcing her to meet his eyes—dark, intense, absolutely certain.

"You're not a trophy. You're bigger than the fucking prize I've ever fought for in the boxing ring." His thumb traced her lower lip. "You're the reason I became more than my father's name. You're why there's still a Ricci empire to inherit. You're my soul."

"I thought the Wolf worked alone," she teased.

"The Wolf found his mate." He lifted her easily, her legs wrapping around him. "And she taught him that some victories are worth sharing."

Their mouths met in a clash of greed. Both were unable to stop sharing in the love that felt so honest and pure between them now. She tasted possession in his kiss, but also partnership. When he carried her to bed, when her hands found his skin, when he pressed her down into goose-feather softness—it was both claiming and surrender.

They moved together with the synchronicity of lovers who'd memorized each other's rhythms through years of separation and reunion. And there, in their temporary Eden, they wrote their victory in each other's skin, until the approaching storm of Giovanni Ricci became nothing more than a distant thunderclap in their perfect sky.

* * *

THE KNOCK CAME SOONER than expected. Carmelo had to take a call from Stefano before he hopped back in the shower to prepare for his meeting. That left her to meander through the villa.

She turned and looked over at Marco. He nodded in respect and approached the door.

"Wait." The command in her voice surprised them both. "Let me answer it. I'd like to greet this Giovanni Battaglia first."

Kathy walked with her spine straight and chin up toward the door . Lethal grace she'd perfected over decades—a walk that had stopped conversations in New Orleans speakeasies and Harlem back-door meetings alike. The Elliot blood ran thick in her veins, her father's ruthless cunning matched only by her mother's legendary skill with both seasoning and poison. Her turquoise summer dress flowed like the Mediterranean itself, the front split revealing her slender legs that ended in pointed heels sharp enough to draw blood. At forty-eight, she'd traded youth's raw beauty for something far more dangerous: the striking elegance of a woman who'd survived every game the underworld could play. The silver threading through her dark hair caught the light like moonlight on obsidian, framing features that had launched a thousand vendettas by her Don.

She opened the door and felt the world shift.

The man standing there could have stepped from Michelangelo's fever dreams—all sharp Mediterranean angles carved by gods who understood both beauty and cruelty. He was taller than most Sicilians she'd known, easily, with the build of a gladiator wrapped in modern elegance. Dark hair and lashes ringed cunningly deceptive eyes; he couldn't be more than twenty-three or four, the same age as her daughter. His white linen shirt, rolled to the elbows, revealed forearms corded with the kind of strength that came from more than just gymnasium visits.

"Ciao," she said, letting the word roll off her tongue like aged bourbon.

"Ciao, bel—" His voice, velvet poured over broken glass, caught mid-word. Then he paused, letting his gaze sweep over her. She could read the calculations spinning behind that beautiful face: *Black. American. Here. Wife?*

The confusion lasted barely a heartbeat before his training kicked in, but Kathy had been reading men since before this boy had taken his first breath. She'd seen that look before—in Manhattan boardrooms, in Little Italy restaurants, in a hundred places where her presence upset careful equations about power and place.

"Is this the Ricci place?" He recovered smoothly, but she heard the slight adjustment in his tone, the recalibration of a young man raised on stories of Sicilian and Italian purity encountering something outside his world.

"It is for now." She leaned against the doorframe with deliberate ease, studying him with the same intensity he'd shown her. Let him look. Let him wonder how Henry Freeman's daughter had become Carmelo Ricci's queen. "And you must be Giovanni Battaglia?"

The visitor smirked at her coy manner.

"Please, come in."

Something dangerous flickered across his face—pride wounded, perhaps. "Grazie, for the warm greeting, but I am not Giovanni."

Marco's hand moved subtly toward the weapon under his arm. Kathy's pulse quickened with the thrill of the unexpected, though her face remained a mask of polite interest. She stopped her step and turned to face him. "Oh? Then who are you?"

His gaze swept over the accommodations they had acquired in the village with approval, then landed on her again. She saw him make a decision—to play this game on equal footing, tradition be damned. The hunger in his eyes sharpened into something more calculating. Here was a boy raised to inherit an empire, finding something he'd never factored into his equations for power.

"Lorenzo Battaglia." He paused, letting the name settle between them like a declaration of war. "I'm his other half. The better half. And you must be...?"

"Donna Katherine Freeman Ricci." She used her full name deliberately, adding the label of Donna to her Don. Something Ernesto coached her on before the visit. She watched him again process the information he had presumed. "I'm Don Ricci's better half."

His perfectly sculpted features arranged themselves into an expression of intrigued recognition. This young wolf had done his homework, but clearly, the briefings hadn't included her. "Ah? I've heard of you." The lie came smooth as silk, but she heard the curiosity bleeding through. A Black American woman who'd claimed a Don. In his uncle's rigid world, she was an impossibility made flesh.

"Now I'm confused. Who invited you, Lorenzo? This party is for Giovanni only."

The bark of laughter that escaped him was genuine—dark chocolate laced with arsenic. He walked deeper into the villa, passing her, with the confidence of a young god who'd never met a rule he couldn't break, but she noticed how his eyes kept returning to her, trying to solve the puzzle she represented.

"I'm the man he needs to speak to." Each word dripped with the arrogance of youth convinced of its own immortality. "Trust me. I run things."

"Do you?" She let amusement color her voice. This boy, trying to steal his cousin's thunder, had no idea he'd just walked into a game where the rules had been written by survivors, not inheritors.

"We shall see," she purred, moving past him with deliberate grace, letting him catch a whisper of her perfume—jasmine and lavendere, her mother's formula.

"Come with me," Kathy said, leading him toward the veranda where breakfast waited like a beautifully laid trap. He followed, and she could feel his eyes on her, trying to reconcile everything he'd been taught about the old ways with the reality of her American existence.

Marco followed them both, his attention sharp as a blade. He knew, as she did, that Lorenzo Battaglia had just complicated everything. This wasn't just Giovanni's ambitious cousin—this was a young man who'd walked in expecting to find the usual players and discovered instead that the game itself had changed.

As they stepped onto the sun-drenched, white limestone veranda, Kathy allowed herself a small, private smile. Carmelo had prepared for Giovanni—steady, traditional Giovanni who played by the rules. But Lorenzo? Lorenzo was hunger made flesh, ambition without wisdom, beauty without restraint. A wild card. Possibly the only card in the deck they needed.

THE
LETHAL
Crumbs
The Power of
the Don Shall
Not Be Forgotten.
SIENNA MYNX

AFTERWORD

Another Love Letter to My Readers

The Killer Cupcake is the third book in *The Poison Cherry Series,* and if you've journeyed this far with me, you know we don't do simple love stories. We do *soul-deep reckonings.* The kind that forces you to look at what love costs—and what forgiveness demands—when trauma has carved its mark on everyone you touch.

It's 1978, and I brought you back to Kathy and Carmelo not to give you easy answers, but to show you what happens when two people must face the wreckage they've made of each other. Because sometimes the hardest person to forgive isn't your enemy—it's the one who still holds your heart after they've shattered it.

Writing this book meant delving into the darkest corners of obsession. It meant exploring how grief transforms us (looking at you, Matteo), how legacy can be both blessing and curse (Janey's hidden trauma and the Elliot Sisters), and how sometimes becoming a team means accepting that your scars will always show. This isn't just a mafia romance—it's a story about Black women who refuse to be anyone's footnote, who wield power in kitchens and bedrooms, who love fiercely even when that love burns.

I've learned so much since this series began. About my craft, yes, but more importantly about *us*—the readers who demand our stories be told with the complexity we deserve. You've taught me that we don't need our heroines softened or our men sanitized. We need them *real*.

So let's talk:

- **What gutted you most?** (Kathy and Carmelo's betrayals? Learning the truth about how Matteo and Ely ended up in one of the worst wars in our history? José's death and how it changed everything? Or the fact that book four will take us to the Battaglias?)
- **The Elliot Sisters? Should we fear or love to hate Janey?** (Because power in the wrong hands is still power, and Janey's backstory reveals how deep those roots go. Her treatment of Willa and Kathy, what are your thoughts?)
- **Carmelo's obsession after losing Kathy—do you now see how the Wolf came to be? Should he be forgiven? Or has his transgressions damn him in your eyes?** Kathy lost people close to her because of Carmelo's interference. Now, mind you, where you find her in 1978 is nearly 15 years after those people died. But still, how do you love a man who caused that level of betrayal and pain?
- **Matteo and Debbie after José. What are your thoughts, and do you think Matteo can have it all—Junior and his family? Or is this destined to fail?** I know the American Mafia is deeply entrenched with racism. The story of Matteo knighting his son Junior is so complicated that I want to make it realistic. Which is why I created the medallion. I will suggest you suspend reality for the fantasy I am creating, where Junior can and should rise to power. It's my world and my story, and I can make Kings out of anyone I choose. Do you agree?
- **What questions about this world still haunt you?** (Because Book Four - the final story - is coming, and your voices shape where we go next).

Thank you for staying with me through every plot twist, every betrayal, every hard-won moment of grace. Thank you for believing that our stories deserve all the historical depth, all the cultural richness, all the unapologetic passion we can pour into them. This series exists because *you* exist—readers who invest in my imagination. Thank you! Thank you! Feel free to Google some of the events and people in the book. You might be surprised by what you find!

With profound gratitude, **Sienna**

P.S. Ready to go deeper? Join me on [Sienna's blog/Socials/YouTube] where we're discussing the real history behind the Elliot Sisters, Carmelo's journey through obsession, and yes—early hints about what's brewing for Book Four... 💋

SOCIAL MEDIA

Please follow me on my social media accounts. Look for exciting announcements to come for more books in this series and original works from me!

Instagram: Sienna_Mynx
Threads: Sienna_Mynx
Tiktok: Author Sienna Mynx
Facebook: Sienna Mynx Fan Hub
Discord: the_poison_cherry
BlueSky: DEI_Author
YouTube: TheDEIAuthor

My advice to all of you is to stay away from X - Twitter! Yuck! 😬

Made in the USA
Middletown, DE
21 September 2025

17908103R00262